GALUSHA THE MAGNIFICENT

GALUSHA THE MAGNIFICENT

A NOVEL

BY

JOSEPH C. LINCOLN

AUTHOR OF

("THE RISE OF ROSCOE PAINE," "CAP'N WARREN'S WARDS,"
"MR. PRATT," ETC.

GROSSET & DUNLAP

PUBLISHERS   NEW YORK

By arrangement with D. Appleton-Century Co.

TO
JAMES A. FAIRLEY

GALUSHA THE MAGNIFICENT

CHAPTER I

MR. HORATIO PULCIFER was on his way home. It was half-past five of a foggy, gray afternoon in early October; it had rained the previous day and a part of the day before that and it looked extremely likely to rain again at any moment. The road between Wellmouth Centre, the village in which Mr. Pulcifer had been spending the afternoon, and East Wellmouth, the community which he honored with his residence, was wet and sloppy; there were little puddles in the hollows of the macadam and the ruts and depressions in the sand on either side were miniature lakes. The groves of pitch pines and the bare, brown fields and knolls dimly seen through the fog looked moist and forsaken and dismal. There were no houses in sight; along the East Wellmouth road there are few dwellings, for no one but a misanthrope or a hermit would select that particular section as a place in which to live. Night was coming on and, to accent the loneliness, from somewhere in the dusky dimness a great foghorn groaned at intervals.

It was a sad and deserted outlook, that from the seat of Mr. Pulcifer's "flivver" as it bounced and squeaked and rattled and splashed its way along. But Mr. Pulcifer himself was not sad, at least his appearance certainly was not. Swinging jauntily, if a trifle ponderously, with the roll of the little car, his clutch upon the steering wheel expressed serene confidence and his manner self-satisfaction quite as serene. His plaid cap was tilted carelessly down toward

his right ear, the tilt being balanced by the upward cock of
his cigar toward his left ear. The light-colored topcoat with
the soiled collar was open sufficiently at the throat to show
its wearer's chins and a tasty section of tie and cameo scarf-
pin below them. And from the corner of Mr. Pulcifer's
mouth opposite that occupied by the cigar came the words
and some of the tune of a song which had been the hit of a
"Follies" show two seasons before. No, there was nothing
dismal or gloomy in Mr. Horatio Pulcifer's appearance as
he piloted his automobile toward home at the close of that
October afternoon.

And his outward seeming did not belie his feelings. He
had spent a pleasant day. At South Wellmouth, his first port
of call, he had strengthened his political fences by dropping
in upon and chatting with several acquaintances who prided
themselves upon being "in the know" concerning local political opinion and drift. Mr. "Raish" Pulcifer—no one in
Ostable county ever referred to him as Horatio—had already held the positions of town clerk, selectman, constable
and postmaster. Now, owing to an unfortunate shift in the
party vote, the public was, temporarily, deprived of his services. However, it was rumored that he might be persuaded
to accept the nomination for state representative if it were
offered to him. His acquaintances at South Wellmouth had
that day assured him there was "a good, fair fightin' chance"
that it might be.

Then, after leaving South Wellmouth, he had dined at the
Rogers' House in Wellmouth Centre, "matching" a friend
for the dinners and "sticking" the said friend for them and
for the cigars afterward. Following this he had joined
other friends in a little game in Elmer Rogers' back room
and had emerged from that room three dollars and seventy-
two cents ahead. No wonder he sang as he drove homeward. No wonder he looked quite care free. And, as a
matter of fact, care free he was, that is, as care free as one
is permitted to be in this care-ridden world. Down underneath his bright exterior there were a few cankers which
might have gnawed had he permitted himself to think of

them, but he did not so permit. Mr. Pulcifer's motto had always been: "Let the other feller do the worryin'." And, generally speaking, in a deal with Raish that, sooner or later, was what the other fellow did.

The fog and dusk thickened, Mr. Pulcifer sang, and the flivver wheezed and rattled and splashed onward. At a particularly dark spot, where the main road joined a cross country byroad, Raish drew up and climbed out to light the car lamps, which were of the old-fashioned type requiring a gas tank and matches. He had lighted one and was bending forward with the match ready to light the other when a voice at his elbow said:

"I beg your pardon, but—but will you kindly tell me where I am?"

It was not a loud, aggressive voice; on the contrary, it was hesitating and almost timid, but when one is supposedly alone at twilight on the East Wellmouth road any sort of voice sounding unexpectedly just above one's head is startling. Mr. Pulcifer's match went out, he started violently erect, bumping his head against the open door of the lamp compartment, and swung a red and agitated face toward his shoulder.

"I—beg your pardon," said the voice. "I'm afraid I startled you. I'm extremely sorry. Really I am."

"What the h—ll?" observed Raish, enthusiastically.

"I'm very sorry, very—yes, indeed," said the voice once more. Mr. Pulcifer, rubbing his bumped head and puffing from surprise and the exertion of stooping, stared wide-eyed at the speaker.

The latter was no one he knew, so much was sure, to begin with. The first impression Raish gained was of an overcoat and a derby hat. Then he caught the glitter of spectacles beneath the hat brim. Next his attention centered upon a large and bright yellow suitcase which the stranger was carrying. That suitcase settled it. Mr. Pulcifer's keen mind had diagnosed the situation.

"No," he said, quickly, "I don't want nothin'—nothin'; d'you get me?"

"But—but—pardon me, I——"

"Nothin'. Nothin' at all. I've got all I want."

The stranger seemed to find this statement puzzling.

"Excuse me," he faltered, after a moment's hesitation, during which Raish scratched another match. "I—— You see—I fear—I'm sure you don't understand."

Mr. Pulcifer bent and lighted the second lamp. Then he straightened once more and turned toward his questioner.

"*I* understand, young feller," he said, "but you don't seem to. I don't want to buy nothin'. I've got all I want. That's plain enough, ain't it?"

"But—but—— All you want? Really, I——"

"All I want of whatever 'tis you've got in that bag. I never buy nothin' of peddlers. So you're just wastin' your time hangin' around. Trot along now, I'm on my way."

He stepped to the side of the car, preparatory to climbing to the driver's seat, but the person with the suitcase followed him.

"Pardon me," faltered that person, "but I'm not—ah—a peddler. I'm afraid I—that is, I appear to be lost. I merely wish to ask the way to—ah—to Mr. Hall's residence—Mr. Hall of Wellmouth."

Raish turned and looked, not at the suitcase this time, but at the face under the hat brim. It was a mild, distinctly inoffensive face—an intellectual face, although that is not the term Mr. Pulcifer would have used in describing it. It was not the face of a peddler, the ordinary kind of peddler, certainly—and the mild brown eyes, eyes a trifle nearsighted, behind the round, gold-rimmed spectacles, were not those of a sharp trader seeking a victim. Also Raish saw that he had made a mistake in addressing this individual as "young feller." He was of middle age, and the hair, worn a little longer than usual, above his ears was sprinkled with gray.

"Mr. Hall, of—ah—of Wellmouth," repeated the stranger, seemingly embarrassed by the Pulcifer stare. "I—I wish to find his house. Can you tell me how to find it?"

Raish took the cigar, which even the bump against the

lamp door had failed to dislodge, from the corner of his mouth, snapped the ash from its end, and then asked a question of his own.

"Hall?" he repeated. "Hall? Why, he don't live in Wellmouth. East Wellmouth's where he lives."

"Dear me! Are you sure?"

"Sure? Course I'm sure. Know him well."

"Oh, dear me! Why, the man at the station told me——"

"What station? The Wellmouth depot, do you mean?"

"No, the—ah—the South Wellmouth station. You see, I got off the train at South Wellmouth by mistake. It was the first Wellmouth called, you know, and I—I suppose I caught the name and—ah—rushed out of the car. I thought —it seemed to be a—a sort of lonely spot, you know——"

"Haw, haw! South Wellmouth depot? It's worse'n lonesome, it's God-forsaken."

"Yes—yes, it looked so. I should scarcely conceive of the Almighty's wishing to remain there long."

"Eh?"

"Oh, it's not material. Pardon me. I inquired of the young man in charge of the—ah—station."

"Nelse Howard? Yes, sure."

"You know him, then?"

Mr. Pulcifer laughed. "Say," he observed, patronizingly, "there's mighty few folks in this neighborhood I don't know. You bet that's right!"

"The young man—the station man—was very kind and obliging, very kind indeed. He informed me that there was no direct conveyance from the South Wellmouth station to Wellmouth—ah—Centre, but he prevailed upon the driver of the station—ah—vehicle——"

"Eh? You mean Lem Lovett's express team?"

"I believe the driver's name was Lovett—yes. He prevailed upon him to take me in his wagon as far as a crossroads where I was to be left. From there I was to follow another road—ah—on foot, you know—until I reached a second crossroad which would, he said, bring me directly into Wellmouth Middle—ah—Centre, I should say. He told me that Mr. Hall lived there."

"Well, he told you wrong. Hall lives up to East Wellmouth. But what I can't get a-hold of is how you come to fetch up way off here. The Centre's three mile or more astern of us; I've just come from there."

"Oh, dear me! I must have lost my way. I was quite sure of it. It seemed to me I had been walking a very long time."

Mr. Pulcifer laughed. "Haw, haw!" he guffawed, "I should say you had! I tell you what you done, Mister; you walked right past that crossroad Nelse told you to turn in at. *That* would have fetched you to the Centre. Instead of doin' it you kept on as you was goin' and here you be 'way out in the fag-end of nothin'. The Centre's three mile astern and East Wellmouth's about two and a ha'f ahead. Haw, haw! that's a good one, ain't it!"

His companion's laugh was not enthusiastic. It was as near a groan as a laugh could well be. He put the yellow suitcase down in the mud and looked wearily up and down the fog-draped road. There was little of it to be seen, but that little was not promising.

"Dear me!" he exclaimed. "Dear me!" And then added, under his breath: "Oh, dear!"

Mr. Pulcifer regarded him intently. A new idea was beginning to dawn beneath the plaid cap.

"Say, Mister," he said, suddenly, "you're in a bad scrape, ain't you?"

"I beg your pardon? What? Yes, I am—I fear I am. Is it—is it a *very* long walk back to Wellmouth?"

"To the Centre? Three good long Cape Cod miles."

"And is the—ah—the road good?"

"'Bout as you see it most of the way. Macadam ain't so bad, but if you step off it you're liable to go under for the third time."

"Dear me! Dear me!"

"Dear me's right, I cal'late. But what do you want to

go to the Centre for? Hall don't live there. He lives on ahead here—at East Wellmouth."

"Yes—that's true, that's true. So you said. But the South Wellmouth station man——"

"Oh, never mind Nelse Howard. He's a smart Aleck and talks too much, anyhow. He made a mistake, that's all. Now I tell you, Mister, I'm goin' to East Wellmouth myself. Course I don't make a business of carryin' passengers and this trip is goin' to be some out of my way. Gasoline and ile are pretty expensive these days, too, but—— Eh? What say?"

The pale face beneath the derby hat for the first time showed a ray of hope. The eyes behind the spectacles were eager.

"I—I didn't say anything, I believe," was the hurried answer, "but I should like to say that—that if you *could* find it possible to take me with you in your car—if you *could* do me so great a favor, I should be only too happy to pay for the privilege. Pay—ah—almost anything. I am—I have not been well and I fatigue easily. If you could——"

Mr. Pulcifer's hand descended squarely upon the shoulder of the dark overcoat.

"Don't say nothin' more," he ordered, heartily. "I'm only too glad to do a feller a favor any time, if it's a possible thing. That's me, that is. I shouldn't think of chargin' you a cent, but of course this cruise is a little mite off my track and it's late and—er—well, suppose we call it three dollars? That's fair, ain't it?"

"Oh, yes, quite, quite. It's very reasonable. Very generous of you. I'm extremely grateful, really."

This prompt and enthusiastic acceptance of his offer was a bit disconcerting. Raish was rather sorry that he had not said five. However, to do him justice, the transaction was more or less what he would have called "chicken-feed stuff." Mr. Pulcifer was East Wellmouth's leading broker in real estate, in cranberry bog property, its leading promoter of deals of all kinds, its smartest trader. Ordinarily he did not stoop to the carrying of passengers for profit. But this particular passenger had been delivered into his hand and gasoline *was* expensive.

"Jump right in, Mister," he said, blithely. "All aboard! Jump right in."

His fare did not jump in, exactly. He climbed in rather slowly and painfully. Raish, stowing the suitcase between his feet, noticed that his shoes and trouser legs above them were spattered and daubed with yellow mud.

"You *have* had some rough travelin', ain't you, Mister?" he observed. "Oh—er—what did you say your name was? Mine's Pulcifer."

"Oh, yes—yes. Ah—how do you do, Mr. Pulcifer? My name is Bangs."

"Bangs, eh? That's a good Cape name, or used to be. You any relation to Sylvanus Bangs, over to Harniss?"

"No—no, not that I am aware. Ours is a Boston branch of the family."

"Boston, eh? Um-hm. I see. Yes, yes. What's your first name?"

"Mine? Oh, my name is Galusha."

"Eh? Ga—— *What* did you say 'twas?"

"Galusha. It *is* an odd name."

"Yes, I'd say 'twas. Don't cal'late as I ever heard tell of it afore. Ga—— Ga——"

"Galusha."

"Galushy, eh? I see. Strange what names folks 'll christen onto children, ain't it? There's lots of queer things in the world; did you ever stop to think about that, Mister —Mister Bangs?"

Mr. Bangs, who was leaning back against the upholstered seat as if he found the position decidedly comforting, smiled faintly.

"We have all thought that, I'm sure," he said. "'There are more things in heaven and earth, Horatio, than are dreamt of in your philosophy.'"

Mr. Pulcifer was not easily startled, but his jerk of surprise sent the car perilously near the side of the road.

"How in the devil did you know my name?" he demanded.

"Your name? Why, you told me. It is Pulcifer, isn't it?"

"No, no. My first name—Horatio. I never told you that, I'll swear."

Mr. Bangs smiled and the smile made his face look younger.

"Now that's rather odd, isn't it?" he observed. "Quite a coincidence."

"A what?"

"Oh, nothing, nothing. I didn't know your name, Mr.—ah—Pulcifer. My using it was an accident. I was quoting—ah—from *Hamlet*, you know."

Mr. Pulcifer did not know, but he thought it not worth while advertising the fact. Plainly this passenger of his was a queer bird, as queer within as in dress and appearance. He turned his head slightly and looked him over. It was growing too dark to see plainly, but one or two points were obvious. For instance, the yellow leather suitcase was brand new and the overcoat was old. It was shiny about the cuffs. The derby hat—and in October, in Wellmouth, derby hats are seldom worn—the derby hat was new and of a peculiar shade of brown; it was a little too small for its wearer's head and, even as Raish looked, a gust of wind lifted it and would have sent it whirling from the car had not Mr. Bangs saved it by a sudden grab. Raish chuckled.

"Come pretty nigh losin' somethin' overboard that time, didn't you?" he observed.

Mr. Bangs pulled the brown derby as far down upon his head as it would go.

"I—I'm afraid I made a mistake in buying this hat," he confided. "I told the man I didn't think it fitted me as it should, but he said that was because I wasn't used to it. I doubt if I ever become used to it. And it really doesn't fit any better to-day than it did yesterday."

"New one, ain't it?" inquired Raish.

"Yes, quite new. My other blew out of the car window. I bought this one at a small shop near the station in Boston.

I'm afraid it wasn't a very good shop, but I was in a great hurry."

"Where was you comin' from when your other one blew away?"

"From the mountains."

"White Mountains?"

"Yes."

Raish said that he wanted to know and waited for his passenger to say something more. This the passenger did not do. Mr. Pulcifer whistled a bar or two of his "Follies" song and then asked another question.

"You any relation to Josh?" he asked.

"I beg your pardon?"

"Eh? Oh, that's all right. I just asked you if you was a relation of Josh's—of Hall's, I mean, the folks you're goin' to see."

"Oh, no, no. We are not related. Merely friends."

"I see. I thought there wan't any Bangses in that family. His wife was a Cahoon, wan't she?"

"I—I *beg* your pardon?"

"I asked you if she wan't a Cahoon; Cahoon was her name afore she married Hall, wan't it?"

"Oh, I don't know, I'm sure. . . . Now, really, that's very funny, very."

"What's funny?"

"Why, you see, I——" Mr. Bangs had an odd little way of pausing in the middle of a sentence and then, so to speak, catching the train of his thought with a jerk and hurrying on again. "I understood you to ask if she was a—a cocoon. I could scarcely believe my ears. It *was* funny, wasn't it?"

Raish Pulcifer thought it was and said so between roars. His conviction that his passenger was a queer bird was strengthening every minute.

"What's your line of business, Mr. Bangs?" was his next question.

"I am not a business man. I am connected with the Archæological Department of the National Institute at Washington."

If he had said he was connected with the interior department of a Brontosaurus the statements would have conveyed an equal amount of understanding to the Pulcifer mind. However, it was a fixed principle with Raish never to admit a lack of knowledge of any subject whatsoever. So he said:

"From Washin'ton, eh? I see. Yes, yes. Cal'latin' to stay here on the Cape long, Mr. Bangs?"

"Why, I don't know, I'm sure. I have not been—ah—well of late. The doctors advise rest and—ah—outdoor air and all that. I tried several places, but I didn't care for them. The Halls invited me to visit them and so I—well, I came."

"Never been here to the Cape afore, then?"

"No."

"Well, sir, you've come to the right place when you came to Wellmouth. I was born right here in East Wellmouth and I've lived here for fifty-two year and if anybody should ask me what I thought of the place I'd tell 'em——"

He proceeded to tell what he would tell 'em. It was a favorite topic with him, especially in the summer and with visitors from the city. Usually the discourse ended with a suggestion that if the listener should ever think of investing a little money in real estate "that'll be wuth gold dollars to you—yes, sir, gold dollars——" he, Horatio G. Pulcifer, would be willing to point out and exhibit just the particular bit of real estate to invest in. He did not reach the climax this time, however. A gentle nasal sound at his shoulder caused Raish to turn his head. Mr. Bangs had fallen asleep. Awakened by a vigorous nudge, he apologized profusely.

"Really," he declared, with much embarrassment, "I—I am quite ashamed of myself. I—you see—I have, as I say, been somewhat unwell of late, and the fatigue of walking—I *do* hope you will excuse me. I was very much interested in what you were saying. What—ah—what was it?"

Before Raish could have repeated his real estate sermon,

even had he so desired, the car came to the top of a hill, emerged from the clumps of pines shutting in the road on both sides, and began to descend a long slope. And through the fog and blackness at the foot of the slope there shone dimly first one and then several lights. Mr. Bangs leaned forward and peered around the edge of the wet windshield.

"Is that it?" he asked, in much the same tone that Mrs. Noah may have used when her husband announced that the lookout had sighted Ararat.

Raish Pulcifer nodded. "Yes, sir," he declared, proudly. "Yes, sir, that's East Wellmouth."

The fog in the valley was thicker even than that upon the hill and East Wellmouth was almost invisible. Mr. Bangs made out a few houses, a crossroads, a small store, and that was about all. From off to the right a tremendous bellow sounded. The fog seemed to quiver with it.

"*What* is that?" asked Mr. Bangs, nervously. "I've heard it ever since I left the train, I believe. Some sort of a—ah—steam whistle, isn't it?"

"Foghorn over to the light," replied Raish, briskly. "Well, sir, here you be."

The car rolled up to the side of the road and stopped.

"Here you be, Mr. Bangs," repeated Mr. Pulcifer. "Here's where Hall lives, right here."

Mr. Bangs seemed somewhat astonished. "Right here?" he asked. "Dear me, is it possible!"

"Possible as anything ever you knew in your life. Why not? Ain't sorry, are you?"

"Oh, no—no, indeed, I'm very glad. I was—ah—a trifle surprised, that is all. You said—I think you spoke of Mr. Hall's cottage as being—ah—off the track and so I—well I scarcely expected to reach his house so easily."

Raish had forgotten his "off the track" statement, which was purely a commercial fiction invented on the spur of the moment to justify the high price he was charging for transportation. He was somewhat taken aback, but before he could think of a good excuse his companion spoke again.

He was leaning forward, peering out at the house before which the car had stopped. It was a small, gray-shingled dwelling, sitting back from the road in the shadow of two ancient "silver-leafs," and Mr. Bangs seemed to find its appearance surprising.

"Are you—are you *sure* this is the Hall cottage?" he stammered.

"Am I sure? Me? Well, I ought to be. I've lived in East Wellmouth all my life and Josh Hall's lived in this house ever since I can remember."

This should have been reassuring, but it did not appear to be. Mr. Pulcifer's passenger drew a startled breath.

"What—*what* is his Christian name?" he asked. "The —the Mr. Hall who lives here?"

"His name is—— Why? What's the matter?"

"I'm afraid there has been a mistake. Is this Mr. Hall an entomologist?"

"Eh? He ain't nothin' in particular. Don't go to meetin' much, Josh don't. His wife's a Spiritu'list."

"But—but, I mean—— Dear me, dear me!" Mr. Bangs was fumbling in the inside pocket of his coat. "If I—— Would you mind holding this for me?" he begged. "I have a photograph here and—— Oh, thank you very much."

He handed Pulcifer a small pocket electric lamp. Raish held it and into its inch of light Mr. Bangs thrust a handful of cards and papers taken from a big and worn pocketbook. One of the handful was a postcard with a photograph upon its back. It was a photograph of a pretty, old-fashioned colonial house with a wide porch covered with climbing roses. Beneath was written: "This is our cottage. Don't you think it attractive?"

"Mrs. Hall sent me that—ah—last June—I think it was in June," explained Mr. Bangs, hurriedly. "But you *see*," he added, waving an agitated hand toward the gray-shingled dwelling beneath the silver-leafs, "that *can't* be the house, not if"—with a wave of the photograph in the other hand—"if *this* is."

Mr. Pulcifer took the postcard and stared at it. His brows drew together in a frown.

"Say," he said, turning toward his passenger, "is this the house you've been tryin' to find? This is a picture of the old Parker place over to Wellmouth Centre. I thought you told me you wanted to be took to Joshua Hall's house in East Wellmouth."

"Joshua? Oh, no, I'm sure I never could have said Joshua. That isn't his name."

"Then when I said 'Josh Hall' why didn't you say so?"

"Oh, good gracious! Did you say 'Josh?' Oh, dear, that explains it; I thought you said 'George.' My friend's name is George Hall. He is an entomologist at the New York Museum of Natural History. I——"

"Say," broke in Raish, again, "is he a tall, bald-headed man with whiskers; red whiskers?"

"Yes—yes, he is."

"Humph! Goes gallopin' round the fields chasin' bugs and grasshoppers like a young one?"

"Why—why, entomology is his profession, so naturally he——"

"Humph! So *that's* the feller! Tut, tut, tut! Well, if you'd only said you meant him 'twould have been all right. I forgot there was a Hall livin' in the Parker place. If you'd said you meant 'Old Bughouse' I'd have understood."

"Bughouse?"

"Oh, that's what the Wellmouth post-office gang call him. Kind of a joke 'tis. And say, this is kind of a joke, too, my luggin' you 'way over here, ain't it, eh? Haw, haw!"

Mr. Bangs' attempt at a laugh was feeble.

"But what shall I do now?" he asked, anxiously.

"Well, that's the question, ain't it? Hum . . . hum . . . let's see. Sorry I can't take you back to the Centre myself. Any other night I'd be glad to, but there's a beans and brown-bread supper and sociable up to the meetin' house this evenin' and I promised the old woman—Mrs. Pulcifer, I mean—that I'd be on hand. I'm a little late as 'tis. Hum . . . let's see . . . Why, I tell you. See that store over on the corner there? That's Erastus Beebe's store and Ras is a good friend of mine. He's got an extry horse and team and he lets 'em out sometimes. You step into the store and ask Ras to hitch up and drive you back to the Centre. Tell him I sent you. Say you're a friend of Raish Pulcifer's and that I said treat you right. Don't forget: 'Raish says treat me right.' You say that to Ras and you'll be *treated* right. Yes, *sir!* If Ras ain't in the store he'll be in his house right back of it. Might as well get out here, Mr. Bangs, because there's a hill just ahead and I kind of like to get a runnin' start for it. Shall I help you with the suit-case? No, well, all right . . . Sorry you made the mistake, but we're all liable to make 'em some time or another. Eh? Haw, haw!"

Poor Mr. Bangs clambered from the automobile almost as wearily and stiffly as he had climbed into it. The engine of the Pulcifer car had not stopped running so Raish was not obliged to get out and crank. He took a fresh grip on the steering wheel and looked down upon his late passenger.

"Well, good-night, Mr. Bangs," he said.

"Good-night—ah—good-night, Mr. Pulcifer. I'm very much obliged to you, I am indeed. I'm sorry my mistake made you so much trouble."

"Oh, that's all right, that's all right. Don't say a word . . . Well—er—good-night."

"Good-night, sir . . . good-night."

But still the little car did not start. It's owner's next remark was explanatory of the delay.

"Course I *hope* you and I'll meet again, Mr. Bangs," said Raish. "May see you in Wellmouth, you know. Still, such things are—er—kind of uncertain and—er—sendin' bills is a nuisance, so perhaps 'twould be better—er—easier for both of us—if we settled that little matter of ours right now. Eh?"

"I beg your pardon. Little matter? I'm afraid I don't quite——"

"Oh, that little matter of the three dollars for fetchin' you over. Course it don't amount to nothin', but I kind of like to get them little things off my mind, don't you? Eh?"

Mr. Bangs was very much "fussed." He hurriedly dragged forth the big pocketbook.

"I beg your pardon—really I *beg* your pardon," he stammered over and over again. "I quite forgot. It was inexcusable of me. I'm *so* sorry."

Evidently he felt that he had committed a crime. Mr. Pulcifer took the three one dollar bills and waved the apologies aside with them.

"Don't say a word, Mr. Bangs," he called, cheerily, as the car began to move. "Anybody's liable to forget. Do it myself sometimes. Well, so long. Hope to see you again one of these days. Good-night."

The flivver moved rapidly away, gaining speed as it rushed for the hill. Galusha Bangs watched its tail-light soar and dwindle until it disappeared over the crest. Then, with a weary sigh, he picked up the heavy suitcase, plodded across the road and on until he reached the step and platform of Erastus Beebe's "General and Variety Store." There was a kerosene lamp burning dimly upon the counter within, but the door was locked. He pounded on the door and shook it, but no one answered. Then, remembering Mr. Pulcifer's instructions, he entered the yard behind the store, found the door of Mr. Beebe's house and knocked upon that. There was not even a light in the house. The Beebes had gone—as most of East Wellmouth had gone— to the baked beans and brown-bread supper and sociable at the church. Galusha Bangs was not aware of this, of course. What he was aware of—painfully, distressingly aware—was the fact that he was alone and supperless, very, very weak and tired, and almost discouraged.

However, there was no use in standing in the wet grass of the Beebe yard and giving way to his discouragement. Galusha Bangs was a plucky little soul, although just now a weak and long-suffering one. He waded and slopped back to the store platform, where he put down his suitcase and started on a short tour of exploration. Through the fog and darkness he could dimly perceive a signpost standing at

the corner of the crossroad where the store was located.
He tramped over to look at it.

There were two signs affixed to the post. By the aid of
the pocket flashlight he read them. That at the top read
thus: "To THE LIGHTHOUSE—1½ MILES." There was an
arrow pointing along the crossroad and off to the right.
Galusha paid little attention to this sign; it was the other
nailed beneath it which caught and held his attention. It
was a rather gaudy sign of red, white, and blue, and it read
thus: "THE RESTABIT INN AT GOULD'S BLUFFS—1 MILE."
And the arrow pointed in the same direction as the other.

Mr. Bangs uttered his favorite exclamation.

"Dear me! Why, dear me!"

He read the sign again. There was no mistake, his first
reading had been correct.

He trotted back to the platform of Mr. Beebe's store.
Then, once more dragging forth the big pocketbook, he
fumbled in its various compartments. After spilling a good
many scraps of paper upon the platform and stopping to
pick them up again, he at length found what he was looking
for. It was an advertisement torn from the Summer Resort
advertising pages of a magazine. Holding it so that the
feeble light from Mr. Beebe's lamp fell upon it, Galusha
read, as follows:

> THE RESTABIT INN at Beautiful Gould's Bluffs, East
> Wellmouth, Mass. Rest, sea air, and pleasant people:
> Good food and plenty of it. Reasonable prices. NO
> FRILLS.

He had chanced upon the advertisement in a tattered,
back number magazine which a fellow passenger had left
beside him in a car seat a month before. He had not quite
understood the "NO FRILLS" portion. Apparently it must
be important because the advertiser had put it in capital
letters, but Mr. Bangs was uncertain as to just what it
meant. But there was no uncertainty about the remainder
of the "ad."

Rest! His weary muscles and aching joints seemed to relax at the very whisper of the word. Food! Well, he needed food, it would be welcome, of course—but rest! Oh, rest!!

And food and rest, not to mention reasonable prices and pleasant people and no frills, were all but a mile away at the Restabit Inn at Gould's Bluffs—beautiful Gould's Bluffs. No wonder they called them beautiful.

He returned the pocketbook to his inside pocket and the flashlight to an outside one, turned up his coat collar, pulled the brown derby down as tightly upon his brow as he could, picked up the heavy suitcase and started forth to tramp the mile which separated his tired self from food and rest—especially rest.

The first hundred yards of that mile cut him off entirely from the world. It was dark now, pitch dark, and the fog was so thick as to be almost a rain. His coat and hat and suitcase dripped with it. The drops ran down his nose. He felt as if there were almost as much water in the air as there was beneath him on the ground—not quite as much, for his feet were wetter than his body, but enough.

And it was so still. No sound of voices, no dogs barking, no murmur of the wind in trees. There did not seem to be any trees. Occasionally he swept a circle of his immediate surroundings with the little flashlight, but all its feeble radiance showed was fog and puddles and wet weeds and ruts and grass—and more fog.

Still! Oh, yes, deadly still for a long minute's interval, and then out of the nowhere ahead, with a suddenness which each time caused his weakened nerves to vibrate like fiddle strings, would burst the bellow of the great foghorn.

Silence, the splash and "sugg" of Galusha's sodden shoes moving up and down, up and down—and then:

"OW—ooo—ooo—ooo—OOO!!"

Once a minute the foghorn blew and once a minute Galusha Bangs jumped as if he were hearing it for the first time.

The signboard had said "I MILE." One hundred miles.

one thousand miles; that was what it should have said to be truthful. Galusha plodded on and on, stopping to put down the suitcase, then lifting it and pounding on again. He had had no luncheon; he had had no dinner. He was weak from illness. He was wet and chilled. And—yes, it was beginning to rain.

He put down the suitcase once more.

"Oh, my soul!" he exclaimed, and not far away, close at hand, the word "soul" was repeated.

"Oh, dear!" cried Galusha, startled.

"Dear!" repeated the echo, for it was an echo.

Galusha, brandishing the tiny flashlight, moved toward the sound. Something bulky, huge, loomed in the blackness, a building. The flashlight's circle, growing dimmer now for the battery was almost exhausted, disclosed steps and a broad piazza. Mr. Bangs climbed the steps, crossed the piazza, the boards of which creaked beneath him. There were doors, but they were shut tight; there were windows, but they were shuttered. Down the length of the long piazza tramped Galusha, his heart sinking. Every window was shuttered, every door was boarded up. Evidently this place, whatever it was, was closed. It was uninhabited.

He came back to the front door again. Over it was a sign, he had not looked as high before. Now he raised the dimming flashlight and read:

"THE RESTABIT INN. Open June 15 to September 15."

September 15!!! Why, September was past and gone. This was the 3rd of October. The Restabit Inn was closed for the season.

Slowly, Galusha, tugging the suitcase, stumbled to the edge of the piazza. There he collapsed, rather than sat down, upon the upper step. Above him, upon the piazza roof, the rain descended heavily. The flashlight dimmed and went out altogether.

"OW—ooo—ooo—ooo—OOO!!" whooped the foghorn.

Later, just how much later he never knew exactly, Mr. Bangs awoke from his faint or collapse or doze, whichever it may have been, to hear some one calling his name.

"Loosh! Loosh! Loosh!"

This was odd, very odd. "Loosh" was what he had been called at college. That is, some of the fellows had called him that, those he liked best. The others had even more offensive nicknames. He disliked "Loosh" very much, but he answered to it—then.

"Loosh! Loosh! Loosh, where are you?"

Queer that any one should be calling him "Loosh"—any one down here in . . . Eh? Where was he? He couldn't remember much except that he was very tired—except——

"Loosh! Looshy! Come Looshy!"

He staggered to his feet and, leaving the suitcase where it was, stumbled away in the direction of the voice. The rain, pouring down upon him, served to bring him back a little nearer to reality. Wasn't that a light over there, that bright yellow spot in the fog?

It was a light, a lighted doorway, with a human figure standing in it. The figure of a woman, a woman in a dark dress and a white apron. It must be she who was calling him. Yes, she was calling him again.

"Loosh! Loosh! Looshy! Oh, my sakes alive! Why don't you come?"

Mr. Bangs bumped into something. It was a gate in a picket fence and the gate swung open. He staggered up the path on the other side of that gate, the path which led to the doorway where the woman was standing.

"Yes, madam," said Galusha, politely but shakily lifting the brown derby, "here I am."

The woman started violently, but she did not run nor scream.

"My heavens and earth!" she exclaimed. Then, peering forward, she stared at the dripping apparition which had appeared to her from the fog and rain.

"Here I am, madam," repeated Mr. Bangs.

The woman nodded. She was middle-aged, with a pleasant face and a figure of the sort which used to be called "comfortable." Her manner of looking and speaking were quick and businesslike.

"Yes," she said, promptly, "I can see you are there, so you needn't tell me again. *Why* are you there and who are you?"

Galusha's head was spinning dizzily, but he tried to make matters clear.

"My name is—is—— Dear me, how extraordinary! I seem to have forgotten it. Oh, yes, it is Bangs—that is it, Bangs. I heard you calling me, so——"

"Heard *me* calling *you?*"

"Yes. I—I came down to the hotel—the rest—Rest—that hotel over there. It was closed. I sat down upon the porch, for I have been ill recently and I—ah—tire easily. So, as I say——"

The woman interrupted him. She had been looking keenly at his face as he spoke.

"Come in. Come into the house," she commanded, briskly.

Mr. Bangs took a step toward her. Then he hesitated.

"I—I am very wet, I'm afraid," he said. "Really, I am not sure that——"

"Rubbish! It's because you are wet—wet as a drowned rat—that I'm askin' you to come in. Come now—quick."

Her tone was not unkind, but it was arbitrary.

Galusha made no further protest. She held the door open and he preceded her into a room, then into another, this last evidently a sitting room. He was to know it well later; just now he was conscious of little except that it was a room—and light—and warm—and dry.

"Sit down!" ordered his hostess.

Galusha found himself standing beside a couch, an old-fashioned sofa. It tempted him—oh, how it tempted him! —but he remembered the condition of his garments.

"I am very wet indeed," he faltered. "I'm afraid I may spoil your—your couch."

"Sit *down!*"

Galusha sat. The room was doing a whirling dervish dance about him, but he still felt it his duty to explain.

"I fear you must think this—ah—very queer," he stammered. "I realize that I must seem—ah—perhaps insane, to you. But I have, as I say, been ill and I have walked several miles, owing to—ah—mistakes in locality, and not having eaten for some time, since breakfast, in fact, I——"

"Not since *breakfast?* Didn't you have any dinner, for mercy sakes?"

"No, madam. Nor luncheon. Oh, it is quite all right, no one's fault but my own. Then, when I found the—the hotel closed, I—I sat down to rest and—and when I heard you call my name——"

"Wait a minute. What *is* your name?"

"My name is Bangs, Galusha Bangs. It seems ridiculous now, as I tell it, but I certainly thought I heard you or some one call me by the name my relatives and friends used to use. Of course——"

"Wait. What was that name?"

Even now, dizzy and faint as he was, Mr. Bangs squirmed upon the sofa.

"It was—well, it was Loosh—or—ah—Looshy," he admitted, guiltily.

His hostess' face broke into smiles. Her "comfortable" shoulders shook.

"Well, if that doesn't beat everything!" she exclaimed. "I was callin' my cat; his name is Lucy—Lucy Larcom; sometimes we call him 'Luce' for short. . . . Eh? Heavens and earth! Don't do *that!*"

But Galusha had already done it. The dervish dance in his head had culminated in one grand merry-go-round blotting out consciousness altogether, and he had sunk down upon the sofa.

The woman sprang from her chair, bent over him, felt his pulse, and loosened his collar.

"Primmie," she called. "Primmie, come here this minute, I want you!"

There was the sound of scurrying feet, heavy feet, from the adjoining room, the door opened and a large, raw-boned female, of an age which might have been almost anything within the range of the late teens or early twenties, clumped in.   She had a saucer in one hand and a dish-cloth in the other.

"Yes'm," she said, "here I be."   Then, seeing the prone figure upon the sofa, she exclaimed fervently, "Oh, my Lord of Isrul! Who's that?"

"Now don't stand there swearin' and askin' questions, but do as I tell you.   You go to the——"

"But—but what *ails* him? Is he drunk?"

"Drunk?   What put such a notion as that in your head? Of course he isn't drunk."

"He ain't—he ain't dead?"

"Don't be so silly.   He's fainted away, that's all.   He's tired out and half sick and half starved, I guess.   Here, where are you goin'?"

"I'm a-goin' to fetch some water.   They always heave water on fainted folks."

"Well, this one's had all the water he needs already. The poor thing is soaked through.   You go to the pantry and in the blue soup tureen, the one we don't use, you'll find a bottle of that cherry rum Cap'n Hallet gave me three years ago.   Bring it right here and bring a tumbler and spoon with it.   After that you see if you can get Doctor Powers on the telephone and ask him to come right down here as quick as he can.   *Hurry!* Primmie Cash, if you stop to ask one more question I—I don't know what I'll do to you.   Go *along!*"

Miss Cash went along, noisily along.   Her mistress bent over the wet, pitiful little figure upon the sofa.

And thus, working by devious ways, did Fate bring about the meeting of Galusha Cabot Bangs, of the National Institute, Washington, D. C., and Miss Martha Phipps, of East Wellmouth, which, it may be said in passing, was something of an achievement, even for Fate.

CHAPTER II

AND in order to make clear the truth of the statement just made, namely, that Fate had achieved something when it brought Galusha Bangs to the door of Martha Phipps' home that rainy night in October—in order to emphasize the truth of that statement it may be well, without waiting further, to explain just who Galusha Cabot Bangs was, and who and what his family was, and how, although the Bangses were all very well in their way, the Cabots—his mother's family—were "the banking Cabots of Boston," and were, therefore, very great people indeed.

"The banking Cabots" must not be confused with any other branch of the Cabots, of which there are many in Boston. All Boston Cabots are "nice people," many are distinguished in some way or other, and all are distinctly worth while. But "the banking Cabots" have been deep in finance from the very beginning, from the earliest of colonial times. The salary of the Reverend Cotton Mather was paid to him by a Cabot, and another Cabot banked whatever portion of it he saved for a rainy day. In the Revolution a certain Galusha Cabot, progenitor of the line of Galusha Cabots, assisted the struggling patriots of Beacon Hill to pay their troops in the Continental army. During the Civil War his grandson, the Honorable Galusha Hancock Cabot, one of Boston's most famous bankers and financiers, was of great assistance to his state and nation in the sale of bonds and the floating of loans. His youngest daughter, Dorothy Hancock Cabot, married—well, she should, of course, have married a financier or a banker or, at the very least, a

24

millionaire stockbroker. But she did not, she married John Capen Bangs, a thoroughly estimable man, a scholar, author of two or three scholarly books which few read and almost nobody bought, and librarian of the Acropolis, a library that Bostonians and the book world know and revere.

The engagement came as a shock to the majority of "banking Cabots." John Bangs was all right, but he was not in the least "financial." He was respected and admired, but he was not the husband for Galusha Hancock Cabot's daughter. She should have married a Kidder or a Higginson or some one high in the world of gold and securities. But she did not, she fell in love with John Bangs and she married him, and they were happy together for a time—a time all too brief.

In the second year of their marriage a baby boy was born. His mother named him, her admiring husband being quite convinced that whatever she did was sure to be exactly the right thing. So, in order to keep up the family tradition and honors—"He has a perfect Cabot head. You see it, don't you, John dear"—she named him Galusha Cabot Bangs. And then, but three years afterward, she died.

John Capen Bangs remained in Boston until his son was nine. Then his health began to fail. Years of pawing and poring over old volumes amid the dust and close air of book-lined rooms brought on a cough, a cough which made physicians who heard it look grave. It was before the days of Adirondack Mountain sanitariums. They told John Bangs to go South, to Florida. He went there, leaving his son at school in Boston, but the warm air and sunshine did not help the cough. Then they sent him to Colorado, where the boy Galusha joined him. For five years he and the boy lived in Colorado. Then John Capen Bangs died.

Dorothy Hancock Cabot had a sister, an older sister, Clarissa Peabody Cabot. Clarissa did not marry a librarian as her sister did, nor did she marry a financier, as was expected of her. This was not her fault exactly; if the right financier had happened along and asked, it is quite probable that he would have been accepted. He did not happen along; in fact, no one happened along until Clarissa was in her thirties and somewhat anxious. Then came Joshua Bute of Chicago, and when wooed she accepted and married him. More than that, she went with him to Chicago, where stood the great establishment which turned out "Bute's Banner Brand Butterine" and "Bute's Banner Brand Leaf Lard" and "Bute's Banner Brand Back-Home Sausage" and "Bute's Banner Brand Better Baked Beans." Also there was a magnificent mansion on the Avenue.

Aunt Clarissa had family and culture and a Boston manner. Uncle Joshua had a kind heart, a hemispherical waistcoat and a tremendous deal of money. Later on the kind heart stopped beating and Aunt Clarissa was left with the money, the mansion and—but of course the "manner" had been all her own all the time.

So when John Bangs died, Aunt Clarissa Bute sent for the son, talked with the latter, and liked him. She wrote to her relative, Augustus Adams Cabot, of Cabot, Bancroft and Cabot, in Boston, who, although still a young man, was already known as a financier, and looked out for her various investments, saying that she found young Galusha "a nice boy, though rather odd, like his father," and that she thought of taking his rearing and education into her own hands. "I have no children of my own, Augustus. What do you think of the idea?" Augustus thought it a good one; at least he wrote that he did. So Aunt Clarissa took charge of Galusha Bangs.

The boy was fourteen then, a dreamy, shy youngster, who wore spectacles and preferred curling up in a corner with a book to playing baseball. It was early spring when he came to live with Aunt Clarissa and before the summer began he had already astonished his relative more than once. On one occasion a visitor, admiring the Bute library, asked how many volumes it contained. Aunt Clarissa replied that she did not know. "I have added from time to time such books as I desired and have discarded others. I really have no idea how many there are." Then Galusha, from the recess by the window, looked up over the top of

the huge first volume of *Ancient Nineveh and Its Remains*
which he was reading and observed: "There were five thousand six hundred and seventeen yesterday, Auntie."

Aunt Clarissa started so violently that her eyeglasses fell
from her aquiline nose to the end of their chain.

"Good heavens, child! I didn't know you were there.
What did you say?"

"I said there were five thousand six hundred and seventeen books on the shelves here yesterday."

"How do you know?"

"I counted them."

"*Counted* them? Mercy! What for?"

Galusha's spectacles gleamed. "For fun," he said.

On another occasion his aunt found him still poring over
Ancient Nineveh and Its Remains; it was the fifth volume
now, however.

"Do you *like* to read that?" she asked.

"Yes, Auntie. I've read four already and, counting this
one, there are five more to read."

Now Aunt Clarissa had never read *Ancient Nineveh* herself. Her bookseller had assured her that it was a very remarkable set, quite rare and complete. "We seldom pick
one up nowadays, Mrs. Bute. You should buy it." So
Aunt Clarissa bought it, but she had never thought of reading it.

She looked down over her nephew's shoulder at the broad
page with its diagram of an ancient temple and its draw-
ings of human-headed bulls in bas-relief.

"Why do you find it so interesting?" she asked.

Galusha looked up at her. His eyes were alight with
excitement.

"They dig those things up over there," he said, pointing
to one of the bulls. "It's all sand and rocks—and everything, but they send an expedition and the people in it
figure out where the city or the temple or whatever it is
ought to be, and then they dig and—and find it. And you
can't tell *what* you'll find, exactly. And sometimes you
don't find much of anything"

"After all the digging and work?"

"Yes, but that's where the fun comes in. Then you figure all over again and keep on trying and trying. And when you *do* find 'em there are sculptures like this—oh, yards and yards of 'em—and all sort of queer, funny old inscriptions to be studied out. Gee, it must be great! Don't you think so, Auntie?"

Aunt Clarissa's reply was noncommittal. That evening she wrote a letter to Augustus Cabot in Boston. "He is a good boy," she wrote, referring to Galusha, "but queer—oh, dreadfully queer. It's his father's queerness cropping out, of course, but it shouldn't be permitted to develop. I have set my heart on his becoming a financier like the other Galushas in our line. Of course he will always be a Bangs —more's the pity—but his middle name is Cabot and his first *is* Galusha. I think he had best continue his schooling in or near Boston where you can influence him, Augustus. I wish him well grounded in mathematics and—oh, you understand, the financial branches. Select a school, the right sort of school, for him, to oblige me, will you, Gus?"

Augustus Cabot chose a school, a select, aristocratic and expensive school near the "Hub of the Universe." Thither, in the fall, went Galusha and there he remained until he was eighteen, when he entered Harvard. At college, as at school, he plugged away at his studies, and he managed to win sufficiently high marks in mathematics. But his mathematical genius was of a queer twist. In the practical dollars and cents sort of figuring he was almost worthless. Money did not interest him at all. What interested him was to estimate how many bricks there were in "Mem" and how many more there might have been if it had been built a story higher.

"This room," he said to a classmate, referring to his study in old Thayer, "was built in ——" naming the year. "Now allowing that a different fellow lived in it each year, which is fair enough because they almost always change, that means that at least so many fellows," giving the number, "have occupied this room since the beginning. That is, provided there was but one fellow living in the room at a time. Now we know that, for part of the time, this was a double room, so——"

"Oh, for the love of Mike, Loosh!" exclaimed the classmate, "cut it out. What do you waste your time doing crazy stunts like that for?"

"But it's fun. Say, if they had all cut their initials around on the door frames and the—ah—mop boards it would be great stuff to puzzle 'em out and make a list of 'em, wouldn't it? I wish they had."

"Well, I don't. It would make the old rat hole look like blazes and it is bad enough as it is. Come on down and watch the practice."

One of young Bangs' peculiar enjoyments, developed during his senior year, was to visit every old cemetery in or about the city and examine and copy the ancient epitaphs and inscriptions. Pleasant spring afternoons, when normal-minded Harvard men were busy with baseball or track or tennis, or the hundred and one activities which help to keep young America employed in a great university, Galusha might have been, and was, seen hopping about some grass-grown graveyard, like a bespectacled ghoul, making tracings of winged death's-heads or lugubrious tombstone poetry. When they guyed him he merely grinned, blushed, and was silent. To the few—the very few—in whom he confided he made explanations which were as curious as their cause.

"It's great fun," he declared. "It keeps you guessing, that's it. Now, for instance, here's one of those skull jiggers with wings on it. See? I traced this over at Copp's Hill last spring, a year ago. But there are dozens of 'em all about, in all the old graveyards. Nobody ever saw a skull with wings; it's a—a—ah—convention, of course. But who made the first one? And why did it become a convention? And—and—why do some of 'em have wings like this, and some of 'em crossbones like a pirate's flag, and some of 'em no wings or bones, and why——"

"Oh, good Lord! I don't know. Forget it. You make a noise like a hearse, Loosh."

'Of course you don't know. *I* don't know. I don't suppose anybody knows, exactly. But isn't it great fun to study 'em up, and see the different kinds, and think about the old chaps who carved 'em, and wonder about 'em and——"

"No, I'll be hanged if it is! It's crazy nonsense. You've got pigeons in your loft, Loosh. Come on out and give the birds an airing."

This was the general opinion of the class of 19—, that old "Loosh had pigeons in his loft." However, it was agreed that they were harmless fowl and that Galusha himself was a good old scout, in spite of his aviary.

He graduated with high honors in the mathematical branches and in languages. Then the no less firm because feminine hand of Aunt Clarissa grasped him, so to speak, by the collar and guided him to the portals of the banking house of Cabot, Bancroft and Cabot, where "Cousin Gussie" took him in charge with the instructions to make a financier of him.

"Cousin Gussie," junior member of the firm, then in his early thirties, thrust his hands into the pockets of his smart tweed trousers, tilted from heels to toes of his stylish and very shiny shoes and whistled beneath his trim mustache. He had met Galusha often before, but that fact did not make him more optimistic, rather the contrary.

"So you want to be a banker, do you, Loosh?" he asked. Galusha regarded him sadly through the spectacles.

"Auntie wants me to be one," he said.

The experiment lasted a trifle over six months. At the end of that time the junior partner of Cabot, Bancroft and Cabot had another interview with his firm's most recent addition to its list of employees.

"You're simply no good at the job, that's the plain truth," said the banker, with the candor of exasperation. "You've cost us a thousand dollars more than your salary already by mistakes and forgetfulness and all the rest of it. You'll never make your salt at this game in a million years. Don't you know it, yourself?"

Galusha nodded.

"Yes," he said, simply.

"Eh? Oh, you do! Well, that's something."

"I knew it when I came here."

"Knew you would be no good at the job?"

"At this job, yes."

"Then for heaven's sake why did you take it?"

"I told you. Aunt Clarissa wanted me to."

"Well, you can't stay here, that's all. I'm sorry."

"So am I, for Auntie's sake and yours. I realize I have made you a lot of—ah—trouble."

"Oh, that's all right, that's all right. Hang it all, I feel like a beast to chuck you out this way, but I have partners, you know. What will you do now?"

"I don't know."

Cousin Gussie reflected. "I think perhaps you'd better go back to Aunt Clarissa," he said. "Possibly she will tell you what to do. Don't you think she will?"

"Yes."

"Humph! You seem to be mighty sure of it. How do you know she will?"

For the first time a gleam, a very slight and almost pathetic gleam, of humor shone behind Galusha's spectacles.

"Because she always does," he said. And thus ended his connection with the banking profession.

Aunt Clarissa was disgusted and disappointed, of course. She expressed her feelings without reservation. However, she laid most of the blame upon heredity.

"You got it from that impractical librarian," she declared. "Why did Dorothy marry him? She might have known what the result would be."

Galusha was more downcast even than his relative.

"I'm awfully sorry, Aunt Clarissa," he said. "I realize I am a dreadful disappointment to you. I tried, I honestly did, but——"

And here he coughed, coughed lengthily and in a manner which caused his aunt to look alarmed and anxious. She had heard John Capen Bangs cough like that. That very afternoon the Bute family physician saw, questioned and

examined Galusha. The following day an eminent spe-
cialist did the same things. And both doctors looked gravely
at each other and at their patient.

Within a week Galusha was on his way to an Arizona
ranch, a place where he was to find sunshine and dry climate.
He was to be out of doors as much as possible, he was to
ride and walk much, he was to do all sorts of distasteful
things, but he promised faithfully to do them, for his aunt's
sake. As a matter of fact, he took little interest in the matter for his own. His was a sensitive spirit, although a quiet,
shy and "queer" one, and to find that he was "no good" at
any particular employment, even though he had felt fairly
certain of that fact beforehand, hurt more than he acknowledged to others. Galusha went to Arizona because his
aunt, to whose kindness and generosity he owed so much,
wished him to do so. For himself he did not care where
he went or what became of him.

But his feelings changed a few months later, when health
began to return and the cough to diminish in frequency and
violence. And then came to the ranch where he lodged and
boarded an expedition from an eastern museum. It was an
expedition sent to explore the near-by cañon for trace of the
ancient "cliff dwellers," to find and, if need be, excavate
the villages of this strange people and to do research work
among them. The expedition was in charge of an eminent
scientist. Galusha met and talked with the scientist and
liked him at once, a liking which was to grow into adoration
as the acquaintanceship between the two warmed into friendship. The young man was invited to accompany the expedition upon one of its exploring trips. He accepted and,
although he did not then realize it, upon that trip he discovered, not only an ancient cliff village, but the life work
of Galusha Cabot Bangs.

For Galusha was wild with enthusiasm. Scrambling
amid the rocks, wading or tumbling into the frigid waters
of mountain streams, sleeping anywhere or not sleeping, all
these hardships were of no consequence whatever compared
with the thrill which came with the first glimpse of, high

up under the bulging brow of an overhanging cliff, a rude
wall and a cluster of half ruined dwellings sticking to the
side of the precipice as barn swallows' nests are plastered
beneath eaves. Then the climb and the glorious burrowing
into the homes of these long dead folk, the hallelujahs when
a bit of broken pottery was found, and the delightfully
arduous labor of painstakingly uncovering and cleaning a
bit of rude carving. The average man would have tired of
it in two days, a week of it would have bored him to distraction. But the longer it lasted and the harder the labor,
the brighter Galusha's eyes sparkled behind his spectacles.
Years before, when his aunt had asked him concerning his
interest in the books about ancient Nineveh, he had described
to her the work of the explorers and had cried: "Gee, it
must be great!" Well, now he was, in a very humble way,
helping to do something of the sort himself, and—gee, it
was great!

Such enthusiasm as his and such marked aptitude, amounting almost to genius, could not help but make an impression. The distinguished savant at the head of the expedition
returned the young man's liking. Before returning East,
he said:

"Bangs, next fall I am planning an expedition to Ecuador.
I'd like to have you go with me. Oh, this isn't offered merely
for your sake, it is quite as much for mine. You're worth
at least three of the average young fellows who have trained
for this sort of thing. There will be a salary for you, of
course, but it won't be large. On the other hand, there will
be no personal expense and some experience. Will you go?"

Would he *go?* Why——

"Yes, I know. But there is your health to be considered.
I can't afford to have a sick man along. You stay here for
the present and put in your time getting absolutely fit."

"But—but I *am* fit."

"Um—yes; well, then, get fitter."

Galusha went to Ecuador. Aunt Clarissa protested,
scolded, declared him insane—and capitulated only when
she found that he was going anyhow. He returned from

the expedition higher than ever in favor with his chief. He was offered a position in the archæological department of the museum. He accepted first and then told Aunt Clarissa.

That was the real beginning. After that the years rolled placidly along. He went to Egypt, under his beloved chief, and there found exactly what he had dreamed. The desert, the pyramids, the sculptures, the ancient writings, the buried tombs and temples—all those Galusha saw and took, figuratively speaking, for his own. On his return he settled down to the study of Egyptology, its writings, its history, its every detail. He made another trip to the beloved land and distinguished himself and his museum by his discoveries. His chief died and Galusha was offered the post left vacant. He accepted. Later—some years later—he was called to the National Institute at Washington.

When he was thirty-seven his Aunt Clarissa died. She left all her property to her nephew. But she left it in trust, in trust with Cousin Gussie. There was a letter to the latter in the envelope with the will. "He is to have only the income, the income, understand—until he is forty-five," Aunt Clarissa had written. "Heaven knows, I am afraid even *that* is too young for a child such as he is in everything except pyramids."

Cousin Gussie, now the dignified and highly respected senior partner of Cabot, Bancroft and Cabot, took charge of the Bute—now the Bangs—property. There was not as much of it as most people had supposed; since Uncle Joshua passed on certain investments had gone wrong, but there was income enough to furnish any mortal of ordinary tastes with the means of gratifying them and still have a substantial residue left. Galusha understood this, in a vague sort of way, but he did not care. Outside of his beloved profession he had no tastes and no desires. Life for him was, as Cousin Gussie unfeelingly put it, "one damned mummy after the other." In fact, after the arrival of the first installment of income, he traveled posthaste to the office of his Boston relative and entered a protest.

"You—you mustn't send any more, really you mustn't," he declared, anxiously. "I don't know what to do with it."

"*Do* with it? Do with the money, you mean?"

"Yes—yes, that's it."

"But don't you need it to live on?"

"Oh, dear me, no!"

"What *do* you live on?"

"Why, my salary."

"How much is your salary, if you don't mind telling us?"

Galusha did not in the least mind. The figure he named seemed a small one to his banking relative, used to big sums.

"Humph!" grunted the latter; "well, that isn't so tremendous. They don't overpay you mummy-dusters, do they? And you really don't want me to send you any more?"

"No, not if you're sure you don't mind."

"Oh, I don't mind. Then you want me to keep it and reinvest it for you; is that it?"

"I—I think so. Yes, reinvest it or—ah—something."

"But you may need some of it occasionally. If you do you will notify me, of course."

"Oh, yes; yes, indeed. Thank you very much. It's quite a weight off my mind, really it is."

Cabot could not help laughing. Then a thought struck him.

"Did you bring back the check I sent you?" he asked. Galusha looked somewhat confused.

"Why, why, no, I didn't," he admitted. "I had intended to, but you see—— Dear me, dear me, I hope you will feel that I did right. You see, our paleontological department had been hoping to fit out an expedition to the Wyoming fossil fields, but it was lamentably short of funds, appropriations—ah—and so on. Hambridge and I were talking of the matter. A very adequate man indeed, Hambridge. Possibly you've read some of his writings. He wrote *Lesser Reptilian Life in the Jurassic*. Are you acquainted with that?"

Cousin Gussie shook his head. "Never have been introduced," he observed, with a chuckle. Galusha noted the chuckle and smiled.

"I imagine not," he observed. "I fear it isn't what is called a—ah—best seller. Well—ah—— Dear me, where was I? Oh, yes! Hambridge, poor fellow, was very much upset at the prospect of abandoning his expedition and I, knowing from experience what such a disappointment means, sympathized with him. Your check was at that moment lying on my desk. So—so—— It was rather on the spur of the moment, I confess—I——"

The banker interrupted.

"Are you trying to tell me," he demanded, "that you handed that check over to that other—that other——?"

He seemed rather at a loss for the word.

Galusha nodded.

"To finance Hambridge's expedition? Yes," he said.

"*All* of it?"

"Yes—ah—yes."

"Well, by George!"

"Perhaps it was impulsive on my part. But, you see, Hambridge *did* need the money. And of course I didn't. The only thing that troubles me is the fact that, after all, it was money Aunt Clarissa left to me and I should prefer to do what she would have liked with it. I fear she might not have liked this."

Cabot nodded, grimly. He had known Aunt Clarissa very, very well.

"You bet she wouldn't," he declared.

"Yes. So don't send me any more, will you? Ah—not unless I ask for it."

"No, I won't." Then he added, "And not then unless I know *why* you ask for it, you can bet on that."

Galusha was as grateful as if he had been granted a great favor. As they walked through the outer office together he endeavored to express his feelings.

"Thank you, thank you very much, Cousin Gussie," he said, earnestly. His relative glanced about at the desks where rows of overjoyed clerks were trying to suppress delighted grins and pretend not to have heard.

"You're welcome, Loosh," he said, as they parted at the door, "but don't you ever dare call me 'Cousin Gussie' again in public as long as you live."

Galusha Bangs returned to his beloved work at the National Institute and his income was reinvested for him by the senior partner of Cabot, Bancroft and Cabot. Occasionally Galusha requested that a portion of it be sent him, usually for donation to this department or that or to assist in fitting out an expedition of his own, but, generally speaking, he was quite content with his modest salary. He unwrapped his mummies and deciphered his moldering papyri, living far more in ancient Egypt than in modern Washington. The Great War and its demands upon the youth of the world left the Institute short-handed and he labored harder than ever, doing the work of two assistants as well as his own. It was the only thing he could do for his country, the only thing that country would permit him to do, but he tried to do that well. Then the Hindenburg line was broken, the armistice was signed and the civilized world rejoiced.

But Galusha Bangs did not rejoice, for his health had broken, like the enemy's resistance, and the doctors told him that he was to go away at once.

"You must leave all this," commanded the doctor; "forget it. You must get away, get out of doors and stay out."

For a moment Galusha was downcast. Then he brightened.

"There is an expedition from the New York museum about to start for Syria," he said. "I am quite sure I would be permitted to accompany it. I'll write at once and——"

"Here, here! Wait! You'll do nothing of the sort. I said forget that sort of thing. You can't go wandering off to dig in the desert; you might as well stay in this place and dig here. Get away from it all. Go where there are people."

"But, Doctor Raymond, there are people in Syria, a great

many of them, and most interesting people. I have——"

"No. You are to forget Syria and Egypt and your work altogether. Keep out of doors, meet people, exercise —play golf, perhaps. The main trouble with you just now is nerve weariness and lack of strength. Eat, sleep, rest, build up. Eat regular meals at regular times. Go to bed at a regular hour. I would suggest your going to some resort, either in the mountains or at the seashore. Enjoy yourself."

"But, doctor, I *don't* enjoy myself at such places. I am quite wretched. Really I am."

"Look here, you must do precisely as I tell you. Your lungs are quite all right at present, but, as you know, they have a tendency to become all wrong with very little provocation. I tell you to go away at once, at once. And *stay* away, for a year at least. If you don't, my friend, you are going to die. Is that plain?"

It was plain, certainly. Galusha took off his spectacles and rubbed them, absently.

"Dear me! . . . Dear me!—ah—— Oh, dear!" he observed.

A resort? Galusha knew precious little about resorts; they were places he had hitherto tried to avoid. He asked his stenographer to name a resort where one would be likely to meet—ah—a good many people and find—ah—air and— ah—that sort of thing. The stenographer suggested Atlantic City. She had no idea why he asked the question.

Galusha went to Atlantic City. Atlantic City in August! Two days of crowds and noise were sufficient. A crumpled, perspiring wreck, he boarded the train bound for the mountains. The White Mountains were his destination. He had never visited them, but he knew them by reputation.

The White Mountains were not so bad. The crowds at the hotels were not pleasant, but one could get away into the woods and walk, and there was an occasional old cemetery to be visited. But as the fall season drew on the crowds grew greater. People persisted in talking to Galusha when he did not care to be talked to. They asked questions. And one had to dress—or most *did* dress—for dinner. He tired of the mountains; there were too many people there, they made him feel "queerer" than ever.

On his way from Atlantic City to the mountains he happened upon the discarded magazine with the advertisement of the Restabit Inn in it. Just why he had torn out that "ad" and kept it he was himself, perhaps, not quite sure. The "rest" and "sea air" and "pleasant people" were exactly what the doctor had prescribed for him, but that was not the whole reason for the advertisement's retention. An association of ideas was the real reason. Just before he found the magazine he had received Mrs. Hall's postcard with its renewal of the invitation to visit the Hall cottage at Wellmouth. And the Restabit Inn was at East Wellmouth.

His determination to accept the Hall invitation and make the visit was as sudden as it was belated. The postcard came in August, but it was not until October that Galusha made up his mind. His decision was brought to a focus by the help of Mrs. Worth Buckley. Mrs. Buckley's help had not been solicited, but was volunteered, and, as a matter of fact, its effect was the reverse of that which the lady intended. Nevertheless, had it not been for Mrs. Buckley it is doubtful if Galusha would have started for Wellmouth.

She came upon him first one brilliant afternoon when he was sitting upon a rock, resting his weary legs—they wearied so easily nowadays—and looking off at the mountain-side ablaze with autumn coloring. She was large and commanding, and she spoke with a manner, a very decided manner. She asked him if—he would pardon her for asking, wouldn't he?—but had she, by any chance, the honor of addressing Doctor Bangs, the Egyptologist. Oh, really? How very wonderful! She was quite certain that it was he. She had heard him deliver a series of lectures—oh, the most *wonderful* things, they were, really—at the museum some years before. She had been introduced to him at that time, but he had forgotten her, of course. Quite natural that he should. "You meet so many people, Doctor Bangs—or should I say 'Professor'?"

He hoped she would say neither. He had an odd prejudice of his own against titles, and to be called "Mister" Bangs was the short road to his favor. He tried to tell this woman so, but it was of no use. In a little while he found it quite as useless to attempt telling her anything. The simplest way, apparently, was silently and patiently to endure while she talked—and talked—and talked.

Memories of her monologues, if they could have been taken in shorthand from Galusha's mind, would have been merely a succession of "I" and "I" and "I" and "Oh, do you really think so, Doctor Bangs?" and "Oh, Professor!" and "wonderful" and "amazing" and "quite thrilling" and much more of the same.

She followed him when he went to walk; that is, apparently she did, for he was continually encountering her. She came and sat next him on the hotel veranda. She bowed and smiled to him when she swept into the dining room at meal times. Worst of all, she told others, many others, who he was, and he was aware of being stared at, a knowledge which made him acutely self-conscious and correspondingly miserable. There was a Mr. Worth Buckley trotting in her wake, but he was mild and inoffensive. His wife, however—Galusha exclaimed, "Oh, dear me!" inwardly or aloud whenever he thought of her.

And she *would* talk of Egypt. She and her husband had visited Cairo once upon a time, so she felt herself as familiar with the whole Nile basin as with the goldfish tank in the hotel lounge. To Galusha Egypt was an enchanted land, a sort of paradise to which fortunate explorers might eventually be permitted to go if they were very, very good. To have this sacrilegious female patting the Sphinx on the head was more than he could stand.

So he determined to stand it no longer; he ran away. One evening Mrs. Buckley informed him that she and a little group—"a really select group, Professor Bangs"—of the hotel inmates were to picnic somewhere or other the following day. "And you are to come with us, Doctor, and tell us about those wonderful temples you and I were discussing yesterday. I have told the others something of what you told me and they are quite *wild* to hear you."

Galusha was quite wild also. He went to his room and, pawing amid the chaos of his bureau drawer for a clean collar, chanced upon the postcard from Mrs. Hall. The postcard reminded him of the advertisement of the Restabit Inn, which was in his pocketbook. Then the idea came to him. He would go to the Hall cottage and make a visit of a day or two. If he liked the Cape and Wellmouth he would take lodgings at the Restabit Inn and stay as long as he wished. The suspicion that the inn might be closed did not occur to him. The season was at its height in the mountains, and Atlantic City, so they had told him there, ran at full blast all the year. So much he knew, and the rest he did not think about.

He spent most of that night packing his trunk and his suitcase. He left word for the former to be sent to him by express and the latter he took with him. He tiptoed downstairs, ate a hasty breakfast, and took the earliest train for Boston. The following afternoon he started upon his Cape Cod pilgrimage, a pilgrimage which was to end in a fainting fit upon the sofa in Miss Martha Phipps' sitting room.

CHAPTER III

THE fainting fit did not last long. When Galusha again became interested in the affairs of this world it was to become aware that a glass containing something not unpleasantly fragrant was held directly beneath his nose and that some one was commanding him to drink.

So he drank, and the fragrant liquid in the tumbler descended to his stomach and thence, apparently, to his fingers and toes; at all events those chilled members began to tingle agreeably. Mr. Bangs attempted to sit up.

"No, no, you stay right where you are," said the voice, the same voice which had urged him to drink.

"But really I—I am quite well now. And your sofa——"

"Never mind the sofa. You aren't the first soakin' wet mortal that has been on it. No, you mind me and stay still. . . . Primmie!"

"Yes'm. Here I be."

"Did you get the doctor on the 'phone?"

"Yes'm. He said he'd be right down soon's ever he could. He was kind of fussy 'long at fust; said he hadn't had no supper and was wet through, and all such talk's that. But I headed *him* off, my savin' soul, yes! Says I, 'There's a man here that's more'n wet through; he ain't had a thing but rum since I don't know when.'"

"Heavens and earth! *What* did you tell him that for?"

"Why, it's so, ain't it, Miss Marthy? You said yourself he was starved."

"But what did you tell him about the rum for? Never mind, never mind. Don't stop to argue about it. You go out and make some tea, hot tea, and toast some bread. And hurry, Primmie—*hurry!*"

"Yes'm, but——"

"*Hurry!* . . . And Primmie Cash, if you scorch that toast-bread I'll scrape off the burned part and make you eat it, I declare I will. Now you lie right still, Mr.—er—Bangs, did you say your name was?"

"Yes, but really, madam——"

"My name is Phipps, Martha Phipps."

"Really, Mrs. Phipps——"

"Miss, not Mrs."

"I beg your pardon. Really, Miss Phipps, I cannot permit you to take so much trouble. I must go on, back to the village—or—or somewhere. I—— Dear me!"

"What is it?"

"Nothing, nothing, my head is rather confused—dizzy. I shall be all right again, shortly. I am ashamed of myself."

"You needn't be. Anybody that has walked 'way down here, a night like this, on an empty stomach——" She paused, laughed, and exclaimed, "Of course, I don't mean you walked on your stomach, exactly, Mr. Bangs."

Galusha smiled, feebly. "There were times when I began to think I should be forced to," he said.

"I don't doubt it. There, there! now don't try to talk any more till you've had something to eat. Doctor Powers will be here pretty soon; it isn't very far—in an automobile. I'm afraid he's liable to have a queer notion of what's the matter with you. The idea of that Primmie tellin' him you hadn't had anything but rum for she didn't know how long! My, my! Well, 'twas the truth, but it bears out what my father used to say, that a little truth was like a little learnin', an awfully dangerous thing. . . . There, there! don't talk. I'll talk for both of us. I have a faculty that way—father used to say *that,* too," she added, with a broad smile.

When Doctor Powers did arrive, which was about fifteen minutes later, he found the patient he had come to see drinking hot tea and eating buttered toast. He was sitting in a big rocker with his steaming shoes propped against the stove. Miss Phipps introduced the pair and explained matters to the extent of her knowledge. Galusha added the lacking details.

The doctor felt the Bangs' pulse and took the Bangs' temperature. The owner of the pulse and temperature made feeble protests, declaring himself to be "perfectly all right, really" and that he must be going back to the village. He couldn't think of putting every one to so much trouble.

"And where will you go when you get back to the village?" asked Doctor Powers.

"Why, to the—ah—hotel. I presume there is a hotel."

"No, there isn't. The Inn across the road here is the only hotel in East Wellmouth, and that is closed for the season."

"Dear me, doctor! Dear me! Well, perhaps I may be able to hire a—ah—car or wagon or something to take me to Wellmouth. I have friends in Wellmouth; I intended visiting them. Do you know Professor Hall—ah—George Hall, of New York?"

"Yes, I know him well. He and his family are patients of mine. But the Halls are not in Wellmouth now."

"They are not?"

"No, they went back to New York two weeks or more ago. Their cottage is closed."

"Dear me! . . . Oh, dear! . . . Why, but—but there *is* a hotel at Wellmouth?"

"Yes, a kind of hotel, but you mustn't think of going there to-night." Then, with a motion of his hand, he indicated to Miss Phipps that he wished to speak with her alone. She led the way to the kitchen and he followed.

"Martha," he said, when the door closed, "to be absolutely honest with you, that man in there shouldn't go out again to-night. He has been half sick for some time, I judge from what he has told me, and he is weak and worn out from his tramp and wetting."

Miss Phipps shook her head impatiently.

"The idea of Raish Pulcifer's cartin' him 'way over here and then leavin' him in the middle of the road," she said.

"It's just like Raish, but that doesn't help it any; nothin' that's like Raish helps anything—much," she added.

The doctor laughed.

"I'm beginning to believe you're right, Martha," he agreed.

"I'm pretty sure I am. I think I know Raish Pulcifer by this time; I almost wish I didn't. Father used to say that if ignorance was bliss the home for feeble-minded folks ought to be a paradise. But I don't know; sometimes I wish I wasn't so wise about some things; I might be happier."

Her pleasant, comely face had clouded over. Doctor Powers thought he understood why.

"Haven't heard anything hopeful about the Wellmouth Development Company, have you?" he asked.

"Not a word. I've almost given up expectin' to. How about you?"

"Oh, I've heard nothing new. Well, I've got only ten shares, so the loss, if it is a loss, won't break me. But Cap'n Jethro went in rather heavily, so they say."

"I believe he did."

"Yes. Well, it may be all right, after all. Raish says all we need is time."

"Um-hm. And that's all the Lord needed when He made the world. He made it in six days. Sometimes when I'm out of sorts I wonder if one more week wouldn't have given us a better job. . . . But there, that's irreverent, isn't it, and off the track besides? Now about this little Bangs man. What ought to be done with him?"

"Well, as I say, he shouldn't go out to-night. Of course he'll have to."

"Why will he have to?"

"Because he needs to go to bed and sleep. I thought perhaps I could get him down to the light and Cap'n Jethro and Lulie could give him a room."

"There's a room here. Two or three of 'em, as far as that goes. He isn't very big; he won't need more than one."

"But, Martha, I didn't know how you would feel about taking a strange man into your house, at night, and——"

Miss Phipps interrupted him.

"Heavens and earth, doctor!" she exclaimed, "what *do* you think I am? I'm forty-one years old next August and I weigh—— Well, I won't tell you what I weigh, but I blush every time I see the scales. If you think I'm afraid of a little, meek creature like the one in the sittin' room you never made a bigger mistake. And there's Primmie to help me, in case I need help, which I shan't. Besides he doesn't look as if he would run off with the spoons, now does he?"

Doctor Powers laughed heartily. "Why, no, he doesn't," he admitted. "I think you'll find him a quiet little chap."

"Yes. And he isn't able to half look after himself when he's well, to say nothin' of when he's sick. Anybody—any woman, anyhow—could tell that just by lookin' at him. And I've brought up a father, so I've had experience. He'll stay right here in the spare bedroom to-night—yes, and to-morrow night, too, if you think he'd better. Now don't talk any more rubbish, but go in and tell him so."

Her hand was on the latch of the sitting room door when the doctor asked one more question.

"Say, Martha," he asked, "this is not my business, but as a friend of yours I—— Tell me: Cap'n Jim—your father, I mean—didn't put more money than he could spare in that Development scheme, did he? I mean you, yourself, aren't—er—likely to be embarrassed in case—in case——"

Miss Phipps interrupted hastily, almost too hastily, so Doctor Powers thought.

"No, no, of course not," she said.

"Truly, Martha? I'm only asking as a friend, you know."

"Why, of course. There now, doctor, don't you worry about me. You know what father and I were to each other; is it likely he would leave me in trouble of any kind? Now come in and see if Primmie has talked this little sick man of ours into another faintin' fit."

Primmie had not, but the "little sick man" came, apparently, very near to fainting when told that he was to occupy the Phipps' spare bedroom overnight. Oh, he could not possibly do such a thing, really he couldn't think of it! "Dear me, Miss Phipps, I——"

Miss Phipps paid absolutely no heed to his protests. Neither did the doctor, who was giving her directions concerning some tablets. "One to be taken now and another in the morning. Perhaps he had better stay in bed until I come, Martha. I'll be down after breakfast."

"All right, doctor. Do you think he's had enough to eat?"

"Enough for to-night, yes. Now, Mr. Bangs," turning to the still protesting Galusha, "you and I will go upstairs and see that you get to bed."

"But, really, doctor, I——"

"What's troublin' me, doctor," broke in Miss Phipps, "is what on earth to give him to sleep in. There may be a nightshirt of father's around in one of the trunks somewhere, but I doubt it, for I gave away almost everything of that kind when he died. I suppose he might use one of Primmie's nightgowns, or mine, but either one would swallow him whole, I'm afraid."

Doctor Powers, catching a glimpse of the expression on his patient's face, was obliged to wait an instant before venturing to reply. Galusha himself took advantage of the interval.

"Why—why——" he cried, "I—— Dear me, dear me, I must have forgotten it entirely. My suitcase! I—ah—it must be on the veranda of that hotel. I left it there."

"What hotel? The Restabit Inn?"

"Yes. I——"

He got no further. His hostess began issuing orders. A few minutes later, Primmie, adequately if not beautifully attired in a man's oilskin "slicker," sou'wester, and rubber boots, clumped forth in search of the suitcase. She returned dripping but grinning with the missing property. Its owner regarded it with profound thankfulness. He could at least retire for the night robed as a man and a brother.

"Everything in there you need, Mr. Bangs?" asked Doctor Powers, briskly.

"Oh, yes, quite, quite—ah—thank you. But really——"

"Then you and I will go aloft, as old Cap'n Jim would have said. Cap'n Jim Phipps was Miss Martha's father, Mr. Bangs, and there may have been finer men, but I never met any of 'em. All ready? Good! Here, here, don't hurry! Take it easy. Those stairs are steep."

They were steep, and narrow as well. Galusha went first but before he reached the top he was extremely thankful that the sturdy physician was behind to steady him. Miss Martha called to say that she had left a lighted lamp in the bedroom. Beyond the fact that the room itself was of good size Galusha noticed little concerning it, little except the bed, which was large and patchwork-quilted and tremendously inviting.

Doctor Powers briskly helped him to undress. The soaked shoes and stockings made the physician shake his head.

"Your feet are as cold as ice, I suppose, eh?" he inquired.

"Why, a trifle chilled, but nothing—really nothing."

Miss Martha called up the stairs.

"Doctor," she called, "here's a hot-water bag. I thought probably 'twould feel comfortable."

Doctor Powers accepted the bag and returned to the room, shaking his head.

"That woman's got more sense than a—than a barn full of owls," he declared, solemnly. "There, Mr. Bangs, that'll warm up your underpinning. Anything more you want? All right, are you?"

"Oh, yes, quite, quite. But really, doctor, I shouldn't permit this. I feel like a tresspasser, like—a—a——"

"You feel like going to sleep, that's what I want you to feel like. Lucky the rain has driven off the fog or the fog-horn would keep you awake. It sounds like the crack of doom down here. Perhaps you noticed it?"

"Yes, I did—ah—at least that."

"I shouldn't wonder. Anybody but a graven image would notice the Gould's Bluffs foghorn. Matches right there by the lamp, in case you want 'em. If you feel mean in the night sing out; Martha'll hear you and come in. I'll be on hand in the morning. Good-night, Mr. Bangs."

He blew out the lamp and departed, closing the door behind him. The rain poured upon the roof overhead and splashed against the panes of the two little windows beneath the eaves. Galusha Bangs, warm and dry for the first time in hours, sank comfortably to sleep.

He woke early, at least he felt sure it was early until he looked at his watch. Then he discovered it was almost nine o'clock. He had had a wonderful night's rest and he felt quite himself, quite well again, he——

Whew! That shoulder *was* a trifle stiff. Yes, and there was a little more lameness in his ankles and knees than he could have wished. Perhaps, after all, he would not get up immediately. He would lie there a little longer and perhaps have the hotel people send up his breakfast, and—— Then he remembered that he was not at the hotel; he was occupying a room in the house of a total stranger. No doubt they were waiting breakfast for him. Dear me, dear me!

He climbed stiffly out of bed and began to dress. This statement is not quite correct; he prepared to begin to dress. Just as he reached the important point where it was time to put something on he made a startling discovery: His clothes were gone!

It was true, they were gone, every last item of them with the unimportant exceptions of crumpled collar and tie. Galusha looked helplessly about the room and shivered.

"Oh, dear me!" he cried, aloud. "Oh, dear!"

A voice outside his chamber door made answer.

"Be you awake, Mr. Bangs?" asked Primmie. "Here's your things. Doctor Powers he come up and got 'em last night after you'd fell asleep and me and Miss Martha we hung 'em alongside the kitchen stove. They're dried out fine. Miss Martha says you ain't to get up, though, till the doctor comes. I'll leave your things right here on the 'oor. . . . Or shall I put 'em inside?"

"Oh, no, no! Don't, don't! I mean put them on the floor—ah—outside. Thank you, thank you."

"Miss Martha said if you was awake to ask you if you felt better."

"Oh, yes—yes, much better, thank you. Thank you—yes."

He waited in some trepidation, until he heard Primmie clump downstairs. Then he opened the door a crack and retrieved his "things." They were not only dry, but clean, and the majority of the wrinkles had been pressed from his trousers and coat. The mud had even been brushed from his shoes. Not that Galusha noticed all this just then. He was busy dressing, having a nervous dread that the unconventional Primmie might find she had forgotten something and come back to bring it.

When he came downstairs there was no one in the sitting room and he had an opportunity to look about. It was a pleasant apartment, that sitting room, especially on a morning like this, with the sunshine streaming in through the eastern windows, windows full of potted plants set upon wire frames, with hanging baskets of trailing vines and a canary in a cage about them. There were more plants in the western windows also, for the sitting room occupied the whole width of the house at that point. The pictures upon the wall were almost all of the sea, paintings of schooners, and one of the *"Barkentine Hawkeye,* of Boston. Captain James Phipps, leaving Surinam, August 12, 1872." The only variations from the sea pictures were a "crayon-enlarged" portrait of a sturdy man with an abundance of unruly gray hair and a chin beard, and a chromo labeled "Sunset at Niagara Falls." The portrait bore sufficient resemblance to Miss Martha Phipps to warrant Galusha's guess that it was intended to portray her father, the "Cap'n Jim" of whom the doctor had spoken. The chromo of

"Sunset at Niagara Falls" was remarkable chiefly for its lack of resemblance either to Niagara or a sunset.

He was inspecting this work of art when Miss Phipps entered the room. She was surprised to see him.

"Mercy on us!" she exclaimed. "*What* in the world are you doin' downstairs here?"

Galusha blushed guiltily and hastened to explain that he was feeling quite himself, really, and so had, of course, risen and—ah—dressed.

"But I do hope, Miss Phipps," he added, "that I haven't kept you waiting breakfast. I'm afraid I have."

She laughed at the idea. "Indeed you haven't," she declared. "If you don't mind my sayin' so, Mr. Bangs, the angel Gabriel couldn't keep me waitin' breakfast till half past nine on a Saturday mornin'. Primmie and I were up at half-past six sharp. That is, I got up then and Primmie was helped up about five minutes afterward. But what I want to know," she went on, "is why you got up at all. Didn't the doctor say you were to stay abed until he came?"

"Why—why, yes, I believe he did, but you see—you see——"

"Never mind. The main thing is that you *are* up and must be pretty nearly starved. Sit right down, Mr. Bangs. Your breakfast will be ready in two shakes."

"But Miss Phipps, I wish you wouldn't trouble about my breakfast. I feel——"

"I know how you feel; that is, I know how *I* should feel if I hadn't eaten a thing but toast-bread since yesterday mornin'. Sit down, Mr. Bangs."

She hastened from the room. Galusha, the guilty feeling even more pronounced, sat down as requested. Five minutes afterward she returned to tell him that breakfast was ready. He followed her to the dining room, another comfortable, sunshiny apartment, where Primmie, grinning broadly, served him with oatmeal and boiled eggs and hot biscuits and coffee. He was eating when Doctor Powers' runabout drove up.

The doctor, after scolding his patient for disobeying

orders, gave the said patient a pretty thorough examination.

"You are in better shape than you deserve to be," he said, "but you are not out of the woods yet. What you need is to gain strength, and that means a few days' rest and quiet and good food. If your friends, the Halls, were at their cottage at the Centre I'd take you there, Mr. Bangs, but they're not. I would take you over to my house, but my wife's sister and her children are with us and I haven't any place to put you."

Galusha, who had been fidgeting in his chair, interrupted.

"Now, Doctor Powers," he begged, "please don't think of such a thing. I am quite well enough to travel."

"Excuse me, but you are not."

"But you said yourself you would take me to Wellmouth if the Halls were there."

"I did, but they're not there."

"I know, but there is a hotel there, Mr.—ah—Pulcifer said so."

The doctor and Miss Phipps looked at each other.

"He said there was a hotel there," went on Galusha. "Now if you would be so kind as to—ah—take me to that hotel——"

Dr. Powers rubbed his chin.

"I should like to have you under my eye for a day or two," he said.

"Yes—yes, of course. Well, couldn't you motor over and see me occasionally? It is not so very far, is it? . . . As to the additional expense, of course I should expect to reimburse you for that."

Still the physician looked doubtful.

"It isn't the expense, exactly, Mr. Bangs," he said.

"I promise you I will not attempt to travel until you give your permission. I realize that I am still—ah—a trifle weak—weak in the knees," he added, with his slight smile. "I know you must consider me to have been weak in the head to begin with, otherwise I shouldn't have gotten into this scrape."

The doctor laughed, but he still looked doubtful.

"The fact is, Mr. Bangs," he began—and stopped. "The fact is—the fact——"

Martha Phipps finished the sentence for him.

"The fact is," she said, briskly, "that Doctor Powers knows, just as I or any other sane person in Ostable County knows, that Elmer Rogers' hotel at the Centre isn't fit to furnish board and lodgin' for a healthy pig, to say nothin' of a half sick man. You think he hadn't ought to go there, don't you, doctor?"

"Well, Martha, to be honest with you—yes. Although I shouldn't want Elmer to know I said it."

"Well, you needn't worry; he shan't know as far as I am concerned. Now of course there's just one sensible thing for Mr. Bangs here to do, and you know what that is, doctor, as well as I do. Now don't you?"

Powers smiled. "Perhaps," he admitted, "but I'd rather you said it, Martha."

"All right, I'm goin' to say it. Mr. Bangs," turning to the nervous Galusha, "the thing for you to do is to stay right here in this house, stay right here till you're well enough to go somewhere else."

Galusha rose from his chair. "Oh, really," he cried, in great agitation, "I can't do that. I can't, really, Miss Phipps."

"Of course I realize you won't be as comfortable here as you would be in a hotel, in a *good* hotel—you'd be more comfortable in a pigsty than you would at Elmer's. But——"

"Miss Phipps—Miss Phipps, please! I *am* comfortable. You have made me very comfortable. I think I never slept better in my life than I did last night. Or ate a better breakfast than this one. But I cannot permit you to go to this trouble."

"It isn't any trouble."

"Excuse me, I feel that it is. No, doctor, I must go— if not to the Wellmouth hotel, then somewhere else."

Doctor Powers whistled. Miss Martha looked at Galusha.

Galusha, whose knees were trembling, sat down in the chair again. Suddenly the lady spoke.

"If this was a hotel you would be willin' to stay here, wouldn't you, Mr. Bangs?" she asked.

"Why, yes, certainly. But, you see, it—ah—isn't one."

"No, but we might make it one for three or four days. Doctor, what does Elmer Rogers charge his inmates—his boarders, I mean—a day?"

"Why, from three to five dollars, I believe."

"Tut, tut, tut! The robber! Well, I presume likely he'd rob Mr. Bangs here as hard as he'd rob anybody. Mr. Bangs, I take it that what troubles you mostly is that you don't want to visit a person you've never met until last night. You've never met Elmer Rogers at all, but you would be perfectly willin' to visit him if you could pay for the privilege."

"Why—why, yes, of course, Miss Phipps. You have been very kind, so kind that I don't know how to express my gratitude, but I can't accept any more of your hospitality. To board at a hotel is quite a different thing."

"Certainly it is. I appreciate how you feel. I should probably feel just the same way. This house of mine isn't a hotel and doesn't pretend to be, but if you think you can be comfortable here for the next few days and it will make you feel happier to pay—say, three dollars a day for the privilege, why—well, I'm satisfied if you are."

Galusha gazed at her in amazement. The doctor slapped his knee.

"Splendid!" he exclaimed. "Martha, as usual you've said and done just the right thing. Now, Mr. Bangs, I'll see you again to-morrow morning. Take the tablets as directed. You may go out for an hour or so by and by if the weather is good, but *don't* walk much or get in the least tired. Good-morning."

He was at the door before his patient realized what he was about.

"But, doctor," cried Galusha, "I—I—really I—— Oh, dear!"

The door closed. He turned to Miss Phipps in bewildered consternation. She smiled at him reassuringly.

"So *that's* all settled," she said. "Now sit right down again, Mr. Bangs, and finish your breakfast. . . . Primmie, bring Mr. Bangs some hot coffee. *Hot* coffee I said, remember."

Later, perhaps ten minutes later, Galusha ventured another statement.

"Miss Phipps," he said, "I—I—— Well, since you insist upon doing this for me, for a person whom you never met until yesterday, I think the very least I can do is to tell you who—or—ah—what I am. Of course if the Halls were here they would vouch for me, but as they are not, I—— Well, in a case of this kind it is—ah—customary, isn't it, to give references?"

"References? As to your bein' able to pay the three dollars a day, do you mean?"

"Why, no, perhaps that sort of reference may not be necessary. I shall be glad to pay each day's board in advance."

"Then what sort of references did you mean, references about your character?"

"Why—why, yes, something of the sort."

Her eyes twinkled.

"Mr. Bangs," she asked, "do you really think I ought to have 'em?"

Galusha smiled. "For all you know to the contrary," he said, "I may be a desperate ruffian."

"You don't look desperate. Do you feel that way?"

"Not now, but I did last—ah—evening."

"When you were camped out on that Inn piazza in a pourin' rain, you mean? I don't blame you for feelin' desperate then. . . . Well, Mr. Bangs, suppose we don't worry about the references on either side of this bargain of ours. I'll take you on trust for the next two or three days, if you'll take me. And no questions asked, as they say in the advertisements for stolen property. Will that suit you?"

"Perfectly, except that I think you are taking all the risk. I, certainly, am not taking any."

"Hum, don't be too sure. You haven't tried much of Primmie's cookin' yet. . . . Oh, by the way, what *is* your business, Mr. Bangs?"

"I am an archæologist."

"Yes—oh—yes. . . . A—a what, did you say?"

"An archæologist. I specialize principally in Egyptology."

"Oh. . . . Oh, yes."

"Yes."

"Yes. . . . Well, I must run out to the kitchen now. Make yourself right at home, Mr. Bangs."

CHAPTER IV

GALUSHA CABOT BANGS' first day in East Wellmouth was spent for the most part indoors. He was willing that it should be; the stiffness and lameness in various parts of his body, together with the shakiness at the knees which he experienced when he tried to walk, warned him that a trip abroad would not be a judicious undertaking. The doctor having granted him permission, however, he did go out into the yard for a brief period.

Gould's Bluffs and their surroundings were more attractive on this pleasant October afternoon than on the previous evening. The Phipps house was a story and a half cottage, of the regulation Cape Cod type, with a long "L" and sheds connecting it with a barn and chicken yards. The house was spotlessly white, with blinds conventionally green, as most New England houses are. There was a white fence shutting it off from the road, the winding, narrow road which even yet held puddles and pools of mud in its hollows, souvenirs of the downpour of the night before. Across the road, perhaps a hundred yards away, was the long, brown—and now of course bleak—broadside of the Restabit Inn, its veranda looking lonesome and forsaken even in the brilliant light of day. Behind it and beyond it were rolling hills, brown and bare, except for the scattered clumps of beach-plum and bayberry bushes. There were no trees, except a grove of scrub pine perhaps a mile away. Between the higher hills and over the tops of the lower ones Galusha caught glimpses of the sea. In the opposite direction lay a little cluster of roofs, with a church spire rising above them. He judged this to be East Wellmouth village.

The road, leading from the village, wound in and out between the hills, past the Restabit Inn and the Phipps homestead until it ended at another clump of buildings; a house, with ells and extensions, several other buildings and sheds, and a sturdy white and black lighthouse. He was leaning upon the fence rail peering through his spectacles when Primmie came up behind him.

"That's a lighthouse you're lookin' at, Mr. Bangs," she observed, with the air of one imparting valuable information.

Galusha started; he had not heard her coming.

"Eh? Oh! Yes, so I—ah—surmised" he said.

"Hey? What did you do?"

"I say I thought it was a lighthouse."

"'Tis. Ever see one afore, have you?"

Galusha admitted that he had seen a lighthouse before.

"Kind of interestin' things, ain't they? You know I never realized till I come down here to live what interestin' things lighthouses was. There's so much *to* 'em, you know, ain't there?"

"Why—ah—is there?"

"I should say there was. I don't mean the tower part, though that's interestin' of itself, with them round and round steps—— What is it Miss Martha said folks called 'em? Oh, yes, spinal stairs, that's it. I never see any spinal stairs till I come here. They don't have 'em up to North Mashpaug. That's where I used to live, up to North Mashpaug. Ever been to North Mashpaug, Mr. Bangs?"

"No."

"Well, a good many folks ain't, far's that goes. Where *I* lived was way off in the woods, anyhow. My family was Indian, way back. Not all Indian, but some, you know; the rest was white, though Pa he used to cal'late there might be a little Portygee strung along in somewhere. It's kind of funny to be all mixed up that way, ain't it? . . . Hello, there's Cap'n Jethro! See him? See him?"

Bangs saw the figure of a man emerge from the door of the white house by the light and stand upon the platform. There was nothing particularly exciting about the man's appearance, but Primmie seemed to be excited.

"See him, Mr. Bangs?" she repeated.

"Yes, I see him. Who is he?"

"Don't you know? No, course you don't; why should you? He's Cap'n Jethro Hallett, keeps the lighthouse, he does—him and Lulie and Zach."

"Oh, he is the light keeper, is he? What has he got his head tied up for?"

"Hey? *Head* tied up?"

"Why, yes. Isn't there something gray—a—ah—scarf or something tied about his head? I think I see it flutter in the wind."

"That? That ain't no scarf, them's his whiskers. He wears 'em long and they blow consider'ble. Say, what do you think?" Primmie leaned forward and whispered mysteriously. "He sees his wife."

Galusha turned to look at her. Her expression was a combination of awe and excitement.

"I—I beg your pardon," he stammered, "but really I—— What did you say he did?"

"I said he sees his wife. Anyhow, he thinks he does. She comes to him nights and stands alongside of his bed and they talk. Ain't that awful?"

Galusha took off his spectacles and rubbed them.

"Ain't it awful, Mr. Bangs?" repeated Primmie.

Galusha's faint smile twitched the corners of his lips. "We—ll," he observed, "I—really I can't say. I never met the lady."

"What difference does that make? If a dead woman come and stood alongside of *my* bed 'twouldn't make no difference to me whether I'd *met* her or not. Meetin' of her then would be enough. My Lord of Isrul!"

"Oh—oh, I beg your pardon. Do I understand you to say that this—ah—gentleman's wife is dead?"

"Um-hm. Been dead seven year, so Miss Martha says.

That's what I mean when I say it's awful. Wouldn't you think 'twas awful if a woman that had been dead seven year come and stood alongside of you?"

Galusha smiled again. "Yes," he admitted, "I am inclined to think I—ah—should."

"You bet you would! So'd anybody but Jethro Hallet. He likes it. Yes, sir! And he goes to every medium place from here to Boston, seems so, so's to have more talks with them that's over the river."

"Eh? Over the—— Oh, yes, I comprehend. Dead, you mean. Then this Mr. Hallet is a Spiritualist, I take it."

"Um-hm. Rankest kind of a one. Course everybody believes in Spiritulism *some,* can't help it. Miss Martha says she don't much and Zach Bloomer he says he cal'lates his doubts keep so close astern of his beliefs that it's hard to tell which'll round the stake boat first. But there ain't no doubt about Cap'n Jethro's believin', he's rank."

"I see. Well, is he—is he rational in other ways? It seems odd to have a—ah—an insane man in charge of——"

"Insane? My savin' soul, what put that idea in your head? He ain't crazy, Jethro Hallet ain't. He's smart. Wuth consider'ble money, so they say, and hangs on to it, too. Used to be cap'n of a four-masted schooner, till he hurt his back and had to stay ashore. His back's got to hurtin' him worse lately and Zach and Miss Martha they cal'late that's why Lulie give up her teachin' school up to Ostable and come down here to live along with him. I heard 'em talkin' about it t'other day and that's what they cal'late. Miss Martha she thinks a sight of Lulie."

"And—ah—this Miss Lulie is the light keeper's daughter?" Bangs was not especially interested in the Hallett family, but he found Primmie amusing.

"Uh-hm. All the child he's got. Some diff'rent from our tribe; there was thirteen young ones in our family. Pa used to say he didn't care long's we didn't get so thick he'd step on ary one of us. He didn't care about a good many things, Pa didn't. Ma had to do the carin' and most of the work, too. Yes, Lulie's Jethro's daughter and he just bows down and worships her."

"I see. I see. And is—ah—Miss Hallett as spookily inclined as her parent?"

"Hey?"

"Is she a Spiritualist, too?"

"No, no. Course she don't say much on her pa's account, but Zach says she don't take no stock in it. Lulie has to be pretty careful, 'cause ever since Cap'n Jethro found out about Nelse he—— Hey? Yes'm, I'm a-comin'."

Miss Phipps had called to her from the kitchen door. Galusha stood by the fence a while longer. Then he went in to supper. Before he went to his room that night he asked his landlady a question.

"That—ah—maid of yours has a peculiar name, hasn't she?" he observed. "Primmie. I think I never heard it before."

Miss Martha laughed.

"I should say it was peculiar!" she exclaimed. "Her Christian name is Primrose, if you can call such a name Christian. I almost died when I heard it first. She's a queer blossom, Primmie is, a little too much tar in her upper riggin', as father used to say, but faithful and willin' as a person could be. I put up with her tongue and her—queerness on that account. Some friends of mine over at Falmouth sent her to me; they knew I needed somebody in the house after father died. Her name is Primrose Annabel Cash and she comes from a nest of such sort of folks in the Mashpaug woods. She provokes me sometimes, but I have a good deal of fun with her on the whole. You ought to see her and Zacheus Bloomer together and hear 'em talk; *then* you would think it was funny."

"Is this Mr.—ah—Bloomer queer also?"

"Why, yes, I presume likely he is. Not foolish, you understand, or even a little bit soft like Primmie. He's shrewd enough, Zach is, but he's peculiar, that's about it. Has a queer way of talkin' and walkin'—yes, and thinkin'. He's put in the most of his life in out-of-the-way places.

boat-fishin' all alone off on the cod banks, or attendin' to lobster pots way down in the South Channel, or aboard lightships two miles from nowhere. That's enough to make any man queer, bein' off by himself so. Why, this place of assistant light keeper here at Gould's Bluffs is the most sociable job Zach Bloomer has had for ten years, I shouldn't wonder. And Gould's Bluffs isn't Washington Street, exactly," she added, with a smile.

"Have you lived here long, Miss Phipps?" inquired Galusha.

"Pretty nearly all my life, and that's long enough, goodness knows. Father bought this place in 1893, I think it was. He was goin' coastin' voyages then. Mother died in 1900 and he gave up goin' to sea that year. He and I lived here together until two years ago next August; then he died. I have been here since, with Primmie to help. I suppose likely I shall stay here now until I die—or dry up with old age and blow away, or somethin'. That is, I shall stay provided I—I can."

There was a change in her tone as she spoke the last words. Galusha, glancing up, saw that she was gazing out of the window. He waited for her to go on, but she did not. He looked out of the window also, but there was nothing to be seen, nothing except the fields and hills, cold and bleak in the gathering dusk. After an interval she stirred and rose from her chair.

"Ah, well," she said, with a shrug, and a return to her usual brisk manner, "there isn't a bit of use in makin' to-day to-morrow, is there, Mr. Bangs? And to-day's been nice and pleasant, and they can't take it from us."

Galusha looked very much surprised. "Why, dear me, dear me!" he exclaimed. "That's extremely odd, now really."

"What?"

"Why, your—ah—remark about making to-day to-morrow. Almost precisely the same thing was said to me at one time by another person. It is quite extraordinary."

"Oh, not so very, I guess. A million folks must have

thought it and said it since Adam. Who said it to you, Mr. Bangs?"

"A—ah—person in Abyssinia. He had stolen my—ah— shirt and I warned him that he should be punished on the following day. He laughed and I asked him what there was to laugh at. Then he made the remark about to-mor- row's being afar off and that to-day the sun shone, or words to that effect. It seems strange that you should say it. Quite a coincidence, Miss Phipps, don't you think so?"

"Why—why, I suppose you might call it that. But *what* did you say this man had stolen?"

"My—ah—shirt. I had another, of course; in fact I was wearing it, but the one he took was the only whole one remaining in my kit. I was quite provoked."

"I should think you might have been. What sort of creature was he, for goodness sakes?"

"Oh, he was an Arab camel driver. A very good man, too."

"Yes, he must have been. Did you get your shirt back?"

"No—ah—no. The fact is, he had put it on and—as he was rather—well, soiled, so to speak, I let him keep it. And he really was a very good man, I mean a good camel driver."

Miss Martha regarded her guest thoughtfully.

"Where did you say this was, Mr. Bangs?"

"In the Abyssinian desert. We were there at the time."

"Abyssinia? Abyssinia? That's in Africa, isn't it?"

"Yes, northern Africa."

"Mercy me, that's a long way off."

"Oh, not so very, when one becomes accustomed to the journey. The first time I found it rather tiring, but not afterward."

"Not afterward. You mean you've been there more than once?"

"Yes—ah—yes. Three times."

"But why in the world do you go to such an outlandish place as that three times?"

"Oh, on research work, connected with my—ah—profes-

sion. There are some very interesting remains in that section."

"What did you say your business—your profession was,
Mr. Bangs?"

"I am an archæologist, Miss Phipps."

"Oh!"

He went to his room soon afterwards. Martha went
into the dining room. A suspicious rustle as she turned
the door knob caused her to frown. Primmie was seated
close to the wall on the opposite side of the room in-
dustriously peeling apples. Her mistress regarded her intently, a regard which caused its object to squirm in her
chair.

"It's—it's a kind of nice night, ain't it, Miss Martha?"
she observed.

Miss Martha did not answer. "Primmie Cash," she said,
severely, "you've been listenin' again. Don't deny it."

"Now—now Miss Martha, I didn't mean to, really,
but——"

"Do you want to go back to the Mashpaug poorhouse
again?"

"No'm. You know I don't, Miss Martha. I didn't
mean to do it, but I heard him talkin' and it was *so* interestin'. That about the camel stealin' his shirt—my soul!
And——"

"If you listen again I *will* send you back; I mean it."

"I won't, ma'am. I won't. Now——"

"Be still. Where is our dictionary? It isn't in the closet
with the other books where it ought to be. Do you know
where it is?"

"No'm. . . . Yes'm, come to think of it, I do. Lulie
Hallet borrowed it the other day. Her and Zach Bloomer
was havin' a lot of talk about how to spell somethin' and
Lulie she got our dictionary so's to settle it—and Zach. I'll
fetch it back to-morrow mornin'. . . . But what do you
want the dictionary for, Miss Martha?"

Martha shook her head, with the air of one annoyed by
a puzzle the answer to which should be familiar.

"I'm goin' to find out what an archæologist is," she declared. "I ought to know, but I declare I don't."

"An arky-what? Oh, that's what that little Mr. Bangs said he was, didn't he? You know what *I* think he is, Miss Martha?"

"No, I don't. You go to bed, Primmie."

"*I* think he's an undertaker."

"Undertaker! Good heavens and earth, what put that in your head?"

"Everything. Look at them clothes he wears, black tail-coat and white shirt and stand-up collar and all. Just exactly same as Emulous Dodd wears when he's runnin' a funeral. Yes, and more'n that—more'n that, Miss Martha. Didn't you hear what he said just now about 'remains'?"

"*What?*"

"Didn't you ask him what he went traipsin' off to that —that camel place for? And didn't he say there was some interestin' remains there. Uh-hm! that's what he said— 'remains.' If he ain't an undertaker what——"

Martha burst out laughing. "Primmie," she said, "go to bed. And don't forget to get that dictionary to-morrow mornin'."

The next day was Sunday and the weather still fine. Galusha Bangs was by this time feeling very much stronger. Miss Phipps commented upon his appearance at breakfast time.

"I declare," she exclaimed, "you look as if you'd really had a good night's rest, Mr. Bangs. Now you'll have another biscuit and another egg, won't you?"

Galusha, who had already eaten one egg and two biscuits, was obliged to decline. His hostess seemed to think his appetite still asleep.

After breakfast he went out for a walk. There was a brisk, cool wind blowing and Miss Martha cautioned him against catching cold. She insisted upon his wrapping a scarf of her own, muffler fashion, about his neck beneath his coat collar and lent him a pair of mittens—they were

Primmie's property—to put on in case his hands were cold.
He had one kid glove in his pocket, but only one.

"Dear me!" he said. "I can't think what became of the
other. I'm quite certain I had two to begin with."

Martha laughed. "I'm certain of that myself," she said.
"I never heard of anybody's buying gloves one at a time."

Her guest smiled. "It might be well for me to buy them
that way," he observed. "My brain doesn't seem equal to
the strain of taking care of more than one."

Primmie and her mistress watched him from the window
as he meandered out of the yard. Primmie made the first
remark.

"There now, Miss Martha," she said, "*don't* he look like
an undertaker? Them black clothes and that standin' collar
and—and—the kind of still way he walks—and talks.
Wouldn't you expect him to be sayin': 'The friends of the
diseased will now have a chanct to——' "

"Oh, be still, Primmie, for mercy sakes!"

"Yes'm. What thin little legs he's got, ain't he?"

Miss Phipps did not reply to her housemaid's criticism
of the Bangs limbs. Instead, she made an observation of
her own.

"Where in the world did he get that ugly, brown, stiff
hat?" she demanded. "It doesn't look like anything that
ever grew on land or sea."

Primmie hitched up her apron strings, a habit she had.

" 'Twould have been a better job," she observed, "if that
camel thing he was tellin' you about had stole that hat instead of his other shirt. Don't you think so, Miss Martha?"

Meanwhile Galusha, ignorant of the comments concerning
his appearance, was strolling blithely along the road. His
first idea had been to visit the lighthouse, his next to walk
to the village. He had gone but a short distance, however,
when another road branching off to the right suggested
itself as a compromise. He took the branch road.

It wound in and out among the little hills which he had
noticed from the windows and from the yard of the Phipps'
house. It led past a little pond, hidden between two of

those hills. Then it led to the top of another hill, the highest so far, and from that point Galusha paused to look about him.

From the hilltop the view was much the same, but more extensive. The ocean filled the whole eastern horizon, a shimmering, moving expanse of blue and white, with lateral stretches of light and dark green. To the south were higher hills, thickly wooded. Between his own hill and those others was a small grove of pines and, partially hidden by it, a weather-beaten building with a steeple, its upper half broken off. The building, Galusha guessed, was an abandoned church. Now an old church in the country suggested, naturally, an old churchyard. Toward the building with half a steeple Mr. Bangs started forthwith.

There *was* a churchyard, an ancient, grass-grown burying ground, with slate gravestones and weather-worn tombs. There were a few new stones, gleaming white and conspicuous, but only a few. Galusha's trained eye, trained by his unusual pastime of college days, saw at once that the oldest stones must date from early colonial times. Very likely there might be some odd variations of the conventional carvings, almost certainly some quaint and interesting inscriptions. It would, of course, be but tame sport for one of the world's leading Egyptologists, but to Galusha Cabot Bangs research was research, and while some varieties were better than others, none was bad. A moment later he was on his knees before the nearest gravestone. It was an old stone and the inscription and carving were interesting. Time paused there and then for Galusha.

What brought him from the dead past to the living present was the fact that his hat blew off. The particular stone which he was examining at the moment was on the top of a little knoll and, as Galusha clambered up and stooped, the breeze, which had increased in force until it was a young gale, caught the brown derby beneath its brim and sent it flying. He scrambled after it, but it dodged his clutch and rolled and bounded on. He bounded also, but the hat gained. It caught for an instant on the weather side of a tombstone, but just as he was about to pick it up, a fresh gust sent it sailing over the obstacle. It was dashed against the side of the old church and then carried around the end of the building and out of sight. Its owner plunged after it and, a moment later, found himself at the foot of a grass-covered bank, a good deal disheveled and very much surprised. Also, close at hand some one screamed, in a feminine voice, and another voice, this one masculine, uttered an emphatically masculine exclamation.

Galusha sat up. The old church was placed upon a side-hill, its rear toward the cemetery which he had just been exploring, and its front door on a level at least six feet lower. He, in his wild dash after the brown derby, had not noticed this and, rushing around the corner, had been precipitated down the bank. He was not hurt, but he was rumpled and astonished. No more astonished, however, than were the young couple who had been sitting upon the church steps and were now standing, staring down at him.

Galusha spoke first.

"Oh, dear!" he observed. "Dear me!" Then he added, by way of making the situation quite clear, "I must have fallen, I think."

Neither of the pair upon the church steps seemed to have recovered sufficiently to speak, so Mr. Bangs went on.

"I—I came after my hat," he explained. "You see—— Oh, there it is!"

The brown derby was stuck fast in the bare branches of an ancient lilac bush which some worshiper of former time had planted by the church door. Galusha rose and limped over to rescue his truant property.

"It blew off," he began, but the masculine half of the pair who had witnessed his flight from the top to the bottom of the bank, came forward. He was a dark-haired young man, with a sunburned, pleasant face.

"Say, that was a tumble!" he declared. "I hope you didn't hurt yourself. No bones broken, or anything like that?"

Galusha shook his head. "No-o," he replied, somewhat

doubtfully. "No, I think not. But, dear me, what a foolish thing for me to do!"

The young man spoke again.

"Sure you're not hurt?" he asked. "Let me brush you off; you picked up a little mud on the way down."

Galusha looked at the knees of his trousers.

"So I did, so I did," he said. "I don't remember striking at all on the way, but I could scarcely have accumulated all that at the bottom. Thank you, thank you! . . . Why, dear me, your face is quite familiar! Haven't we met before?"

The young fellow smiled. "I guess we have," he said. "I put you aboard Lovetts' express wagon Friday afternoon and started you for Wellmouth Centre. I didn't expect to see you over here in East Wellmouth."

Galusha adjusted his spectacles—fortunately they were not broken—and looked at the speaker.

"Why, of course!" he cried. "You are the young man who was so kind to me when I got off at the wrong station. You are the station man at—ah—at South Wellmouth, isn't it?"

"That's right."

"Dear me! Dear me! Well, I don't wonder you were surprised to have me—ah—alight at your feet just now. We-ll," with his quiet smile, "I seem to have a habit of making unexpected appearances. I surprised Miss Phipps on Friday evening almost as greatly."

"Miss Phipps? Martha Phipps, Cap'n Jim's daughter; lives over here by the light, do you mean?"

"Why—why, yes her name is Martha, I believe."

"But how in the world did you get——"

His companion interrupted him. "Why, Nelson," she cried, "he must be the one—the man who is staying at Martha's. Don't you know I told you Primmie said there was some one there who was sick?"

Galusha looked at her. She was young, not more than nineteen or twenty, slender, brown-haired and pretty. The young man spoke again.

"But Lulie," he said, "he isn't sick. You aren't sick, are you?" addressing Galusha.

"My health has not been good of late," replied the latter, "and after my long walk on Friday evening I was rather done up. But I'm not ill at present, although," with a return of his faint smile, "I probably shall be if I continue to —ah—fly, as I did just now."

The young woman broke into an irresistible trill of laughter. The South Wellmouth station agent joined her. Galusha smiled in a fatherly fashion upon them both.

"I had quite a series of adventures after leaving you," he went on. "Quite a series—yes."

He told briefly of his losing his way, of his meeting with Raish Pulcifer, of his tramp in the rain, and of his collapse in the Phipps' sitting room.

"So that is—ah—my Odyssey," he concluded. "You see, we—ah—I beg your pardon, but I don't know that I learned your name when we met the other day. Mine is Bangs."

"Pleased to meet you, Mr. Bangs. My name is Howard —Nelson Howard. And this is——"

He paused. The young woman was regarding him in a troubled way.

"Nelson," she said, "don't you think, perhaps, we had better not——"

They were both embarrassed. Galusha noticed the embarrassment.

"Dear me! Dear me!" he said, hastily. "Please don't trouble. Ah—good-morning. I must go—really—yes."

He was on his way toward the bank, but the young woman called his name.

"Mr. Bangs," she said.

He turned. "Did you—did you wish to speak to me?" he asked.

"Why—why, yes, I—— Mr. Bangs, I—I want to ask a favor of you. I know, Nelson, but what is the use, after all? We've done nothing to be ashamed of. Mr. Bangs, my name is Hallett. My father is the keeper of the lighthouse."

Galusha bowed. He had guessed her identity. Primmie had spoken of Lulie Hallett in their conversation by the fence the day before.

"I am Lulie Hallett," she went on, "and—and Mr. Howard and I are—are——"

"We're engaged to be married," broke in Howard. "The fact is, Mr. Bangs, I came over on my bicycle this morning to meet Lulie here where—where no one would see us. You see—well, Cap'n Jethro—her father, you know—is prejudiced against me and—and so to save her trouble and—and unpleasantness we—well, we——"

He was red and confused and stammering. Galusha was almost as much embarrassed.

"Oh—oh, all right—ah—dear me, yes, of course," he said, hastily. "I am very sorry I—I interrupted. I beg your pardon. Ah—good-morning."

"But, Mr. Bangs," Lulie pleaded, earnestly, "you won't misunderstand this, will you? We meet in this way on my father's account. He is—you see, he is not very well, and rather prejudiced and—and stubborn, I'm afraid. Please don't think that—that——"

"Of course he won't," declared Howard. "Mr. Bangs won't think anything that he shouldn't."

"Oh, no—no," stammered Galusha, nervously. "I am—I am *so* sorry I interrupted. I *beg* your pardon."

"And Mr. Bangs," said Lulie, again, "I wonder if you will be kind enough not to tell any one you saw us? This is a small place, East Wellmouth, and people do talk—oh, dreadfully. If it got to father's ears he—— *Please* don't speak of it, will you, Mr. Bangs?"

"Oh, no; no, indeed, Miss Hallett. You may depend upon me."

"I shall tell Martha Phipps myself the next time I see her. She is my best friend, except——" with a becoming blush— "Nelson, and father, of course—and she understands. I never have any secrets from her."

Galusha began to climb the bank. As his head rose above its upper edge he stopped.

"Ah—dear me, there's some one coming in this direction," he said.

Howard started forward. "Coming? Coming here?" he cried. He sprang up the bank beside Mr. Bangs and peered over its top.

"Oh, confound it!" he exclaimed. "Lulie, it's your father."

"Father? Coming here? Why, he started for church. He never comes to the cemetery on Sunday *morning*."

"I can't help it, he's coming now. And there's some one with him, or coming after him. It looks like—— Yes, it's Raish Pulcifer."

Miss Hallett was very much distressed. "Oh, dear, dear, dear!" she cried. "If father finds us there will be another dreadful time. And I wouldn't have Raish Pulcifer see and hear it, of all people in the world. Oh, *what* made father come? Nelson, can't we run away before he gets here? Into the pines, or somewhere?"

"No chance, Lulie. He would see us sure. If he should stop at the other end of the cemetery it might give us a chance, but he probably won't. He'll come to your mother's grave and that is close by here. Oh, hang the luck!"

Galusha looked at the young people; he was almost as distressed as they were. He liked young Howard; the latter had been very kind to him on the fateful Friday afternoon when he had alighted at South Wellmouth. He liked Lulie, also—had fancied her at first sight. He wished he might help them. And then he had an idea.

"I wouldn't—ah—interfere in your affairs for the world, Miss Hallett," he faltered, "but if I might—ah—offer a suggestion, suppose I—ah—meet your father and talk with him for a few moments. Then you might—so to speak—ah—go, you know."

"Yes, of course, of course. Oh, *will* you, Mr. Bangs? Thank you so much."

Galusha climbed the bank. There was no one in sight, but he heard masculine voices from the hollow beyond the farther end of the cemetery. He hastened to that end and, stooping, began to examine the inscription upon a tomb.

The voices drew nearer as the men climbed the hill. The breeze now was stronger than ever and was blowing more from the west. The conversation, borne by the gusts, came to Galusha's ears clearly and distinctly. One of the speakers seemed to be explaining, urging, the other peremptorily refusing to listen.

"But, Cap'n Jeth," urged the first voice, and Mr. Bangs recognized it as belonging to his obliging guide and pilot of the fateful Friday evening, Mr. Horatio Pulcifer. "But, Cap'n Jeth," said Mr. Pulcifer, "don't fly off the handle for nothin'. I ain't tryin' to put nothin' over on you. I'm just——"

"I don't want to hear you," broke in the second voice, gruffly. "This is the Lord's Day and I don't want to talk business with you or nobody else—especially with you."

For some reason this seemed to irritate Mr. Pulcifer. His tone had lost a little of its urbanity when he answered.

"Oh, especially with me, eh?" he repeated. "Well, what's the 'especially with me' for? If you think I'm any more to blame than the rest, you're mistaken. I tell you when you and me and Cap'n Jim and all hands of us got the Wellmouth Development Company goin' it looked like a cinch. How was I to know?"

"I tell you, Raish, I don't want to talk about it."

"And I tell you, Jeth Hallett, I *do* want to. You've hove in that 'especially with me' and I don't like it. Look here, what are you pickin' on me for? How was I to—— No, now you wait a minute, Cap'n Jeth, and answer me. I've chased you 'way over here and you can give me five minutes even if 'tis Sunday. Come, Cap'n, come, just answer me and then I won't bother you any more."

There was silence for a brief interval. Galusha, crouching behind the tomb and wondering if the time had come for him to show himself, waited anxiously. But Captain Hallett's answer, when at last he did reply, sounded no nearer. Apparently the men were now standing still.

"Well," grunted the light keeper, "I'll listen to you for

the five minutes, Raish, but no more. I hadn't ought to do that. This is Sabbath day and I make it a p'int never——"

"I know," hastily, "I know. Well, I tell you, Cap'n Jeth, all's I wanted to say was this: What are we goin' to do with this Development stock of ours?"

"Do with it? Why, nothin' at present. *Can't* do anything with it, can we? All we can do is wait. It may be one year or three, but some day somebody will have to come to us. There ain't a better place for a cold storage fish house on this coast and the Wellmouth Development Company owns that place."

"Yes, that's so, that's so. But some of us can afford to wait and some can't. Now I've got more of the Development Company stock than anybody else. I've got five hundred shares, Cap'n Jeth; five hundred shares at twenty dollars a share. A poor man like me can't afford to have ten thousand dollars tied up as long's this is liable to be. Can he now? Eh? Can he, Cap'n?"

"Humph! Well, I've got eight thousand tied up there myself."

"Ye-es, but it don't make so much difference to you. You can afford to wait. You've got a gov'ment job."

"Ye-es, and from what I hear you may be havin' a state job pretty soon yourself, Raish. Well, never mind that. What is it you're drivin' at, anyhow?"

"Why, I tell you, Jeth. Course you know and I know that this is a perfectly sure investment to anybody that'll wait. I can't afford to wait, that's what's the matter. It kind of run acrost my mind that maybe you'd like to have my holdin's, my five hundred shares. I'll sell 'em to you reasonable."

"Humph! I want to know! What do you call reasonable?"

"I'll sell 'em to you for—for—well, say nineteen dollars a share."

"Humph! Don't bother me any more, Raish."

"Well, say eighteen dollars a share. Lord sakes, that's reasonable enough, ain't it?"

"Cruise along towards home, Raish. I've talked all the business I want to on Sunday. Good-by."

"Look here, Jethro, I—I'm hard up, I'm desp'rate, pretty nigh. I'll let you have my five hundred shares of Wellmouth Development Company for just half what I paid for it— ten dollars a share. If you wasn't my friend, I wouldn't—— What are you laughin' at?"

Galusha Bangs, hiding behind the tomb, understanding nothing of this conversation, yet feeling like an eavesdropper, wished this provoking pair would stop talking and go away. He heard the light keeper laugh sardonically.

"Ho, ho, ho," chuckled Hallett. "You're a slick article, ain't you, Raish? Why, you wooden-headed swab, did you cal'late you was the only one that had heard about the directors' meetin' over to the Denboro Trust Company yesterday? *I* knew the Trust Company folks had decided not to go ahead with the fish storage business just as well as you did, and I heard it just as soon, too. *I* know they've decided to put the twelve hundred shares of Wellmouth Development stock into profit and loss, or to just hang on and see if it ever does come to anything. But you cal'lated I didn't know it and that maybe you could unload your five hundred shares on to me at cut rates, eh? Raish, you're slick—but you ain't bright, not very."

He chuckled again. Mr. Pulcifer whistled, apparently expressing resignation.

"*All* right, Cap'n," he observed, cheerfully, "just as you say. No harm in tryin', was there? Never catch a fish without heavin' over a hook, as the feller said. Maybe somebody else that ain't heard will buy that stock, you can't tell."

"Maybe so, but—— See here, Raish, don't you go tryin' anything like this on—on——"

"I know who you mean. No danger. There ain't money enough there to buy anything, if what I hear's true."

"What's that?"

"Oh, nothin', nothin'. Just talk, I guess. Well, Jeth, I

won't keep you any longer. Goin' to hang on to *your* four hundred Development stock, I presume likely?"

"Yes. I shall sell that at a profit. Not a big profit, but *a* profit."

"Sho! Is that so? Who told you?"

"It was," the gruff voice became solemn, "it was revealed to me."

"Revealed to you? Oh, from up yonder, up aloft, eh?"

"Raish," sharply, "don't you dare be sacrilegious in my presence."

"No, no, not for nothin', Cap'n. So you had a message from the sperit world about that stock, eh?"

"Yes. It bade me be of good cheer and hold for a small profit. When that profit comes, no matter how small it may be, I'll sell and sell quick, but not sooner. . . . But there, I've profaned the Lord's day long enough. I came over here this mornin' to visit Julia's grave. There was a scoffer in our pulpit, that young whippersnapper from Wapatomac had exchanged with our minister and I didn't care to hear him."

"Oh, I see. So you come over to your wife's grave, eh?"

"Yes. What are you lookin' like that for?"

"Oh, nothin'. I thought maybe you was chasin' after Lulie. I see her meanderin' over this way a little while ago."

"Lulie?"

"Um-hm. Looked like her."

"Was there—was there anybody else?"

"We-ll, I wouldn't swear to that, Cap'n Jeth. I didn't *see* nobody, but—— Godfreys mighty! What's that thing?"

The thing was the brown derby. Galusha, crouching behind the tomb, had been holding it fast to his head with one hand. Now, startled by Pulcifer's statement that he had seen Miss Hallett, he let go his hold. And a playful gust lifted the hat from his head, whirled it like an aërial teetotum and sent it rolling and tumbling to the feet of the pair by the cemetery gate.

Jethro Hallett jumped aside.

"Good Lord! What is it?" he shouted.

"It's a—a hat, ain't it?" cried Raish.

From around the tomb hastened Mr. Bangs.

"Will you gentlemen be good enough to—to stop that hat for me?" he asked, anxiously.

The light keeper and his companion started at the apparition in speechless astonishment.

"It's—it's my hat," explained Galusha. "If you will be kind enough to pick it up before—— Oh, *dear* me! There it *goes*! Stop it, stop it!"

Another gust had set the hat rolling again. Captain Jethro made a grab at it but his attempt only lifted it higher into the air, where the wind caught it underneath and sent it soaring.

"Oh, dear!" piped the exasperated Galusha, and ran after it.

"Who in tunket *is* he?" demanded Jethro.

Mr. Pulcifer gazed at the thin little figure hopping after the hat. The light of recognition dawned in his face.

"*I* know who he is!" he exclaimed. "I fetched him over t'other night in my car. But what in blazes is he doin' here *now?* . . . Hi, look out, Mister! Don't let it blow that way. If you do you'll—— Head it *off!*"

The hat was following an air line due east. Galusha was following a terrestrial route in the same direction. Now Raish followed Galusha and after him rolled Captain Jethro Hallett. As they say in hunting stories, the chase was on.

It was not a long chase, of course. It ended unexpectedly —unexpectedly for Galusha, that is—at a point where a spur of the pine grove jutted out upon the crest of a little hill beyond the eastern border of the cemetery. The hat rolled, bounced, dipped and soared up the hill and just clear of the branches of the endmost pine. Then it disappeared from sight. Its owner breathlessly panted after it. He reached the crest of the little hill and stopped short— stopped for the very good reason that he could go no further.

The hill was but half a hill. Its other half, the half invisible from the churchyard, was a sheer sand and clay bluff dropping at a dizzy angle down to the beach a hundred and thirty feet below. This beach was the shore of a pretty little harbor, fed by a stream which flowed into it from the southwest. On the opposite side of the stream was another stretch of beach, more sand bluffs, pines and scrub oaks. To the east the little harbor opened a clear channel between lines of creaming breakers to the deep blue and green of the ocean.

Galusha Bangs saw most of this in detail upon subsequent visits. Just now he looked first for his hat. He saw it. Below, upon the sand of the beach, a round object bounced and rolled. As he gazed a gust whirled along the shore and pitched the brown object into the sparkling waters of the little harbor. It splashed, floated and then sailed jauntily out upon the tide. The brown derby had started on its last voyage.

Galusha gazed down at his lost headgear. He rubbed his chin thoughtfully. Then he turned and looked back toward the hollow by the front door of the old church. From the knoll where he stood he could see every inch of that hollow and it was untenanted. There was no sign of either human being or of a bicycle belonging to a human being.

Mr. Bangs sighed thankfully. The sacrifice of the brown derby had not been in vain.

CHAPTER V

AN hour or so later when Martha Phipps, looking out of her dining room window, saw her boarder enter the front gate, his personal appearance caused her to utter a startled exclamation. Primmie came running from the kitchen.

"What's the matter, Miss Martha?" she demanded. "Eh! My savin' soul!"

Mr. Bangs' head was enveloped in the scarf which his hostess had lent him when he set forth upon his walk. It—the scarf—was tied under his chin and the fringed ends flapped in the wind. His round face, surrounded by the yarn folds, looked like that of the small boy in the pictures advertising somebody-or-other's toothache cure.

"My savin' soul!" cried Primmie, again. She was rushing to the door, but her mistress intervened.

"Primmie," she ordered, briskly, "stay where you are!" She opened the door herself.

"Come right in, Mr. Bangs," she said. "No, don't stop to tell me about it, but come right in and sit down."

Galusha looked up at her. His face was speckled with greenish brown spots, giving it the appearance of a mammoth bird's egg. Primmie saw the spots and squealed.

"Lord of Isrul!" she cried, "he's all broke out with it, whatever 'tis! Shall I—shall I 'phone for the doctor, Miss Martha?"

"Be still, Primmie. Come in, Mr. Bangs."

"Why, yes, thank you. I—ah—*was* coming in," began Galusha, mildly. "I——"

79

"You mustn't talk. Sit right down here on the lounge. Primmie, get that rum bottle. Don't talk, Mr. Bangs."

"But, really, Miss Phipps, I——"

"Don't *talk*. . . . There, drink that."

Galusha obediently drank the rum. Martha tenderly untied the scarf.

"Tell me if it hurts," she said. Her patient looked at her in surprise.

"Why, no, it—ah—it is very nice," he said. "I—ah—quite like the taste, really."

"Heavens and earth, I don't mean the rum. I hope that won't *hurt* anybody, to say the least. I mean—— Why, there isn't anything the matter with it!"

"Matter with it? I don't quite——"

"Matter with your head."

Galusha raised a hand in bewildered fashion and felt of his cranium.

"Why—ah—no, there is nothing the matter with my head, so far as I am aware," he replied. "Does it look as if it were—ah—softening or something?"

Miss Martha ignored the pleasantry. "What have you got it tied up for?" she demanded.

"Tied up?" Galusha's smile broadened. "Oh, I see!" he observed. "Well, I lost my hat. It blew off into the—ah —sea. It was rather too cold to be about bareheaded, so I used the scarf you so kindly lent me."

Martha gazed at him for an instant and then burst into a hearty laugh.

"Mercy on me!" she cried. *"What* an idiot I am! When I saw you come into the yard with your head bandaged—at least I thought it was bandaged—and your face—— But what *is* the matter with your face?"

"My face? Why, nothing."

"Nonsense! It's a sight to see. You look the way Erastus Beebe's boy did when the cannon-cracker went off too soon. Primmie, hand me that little lookin'-glass."

Primmie snatched the small mirror from the wall.

"See, Mr. Bangs," she cried, holding the mirror an inch

from his nose. "Look at yourself. You're all broke out with a crash—rash, I mean. Ain't he, Miss Martha?"

Galusha regarded his reflection in the mirror with astonishment.

"Why, I—I seem to be—ah—polka-dotted," he said. "I never saw anything so—— Dear me, dear me!"

He drew his fingers down his cheek. The speckles promptly became streaks. He smiled in relief.

"I see, I see," he said. "It is the lichen."

This explanation was not as satisfying as he evidently meant it to be. Martha looked more puzzled than ever. Primmie looked frightened.

"*What* did he say 'twas?" she whispered. "'Tain't catchin', is it, Miss Martha?"

"It is the lichen from the tombstones," went on Galusha. "Most of them were covered with it. In order to read the inscriptions I was obliged to scrape it off with my pocketknife, and the particles must have blown in my face and—ah—adhered. Perhaps—ah—some soap and water might improve my personal appearance, Miss Phipps. If you will excuse me I think I will try the experiment.'

He rose briskly from the sofa. Primmie stared at him open-mouthed.

"Ain't there *nothin'* the matter with you, Mr. Bangs?" she asked. "Is the way your face is tittered up just dirt?"

"Just dirt, that's all. It came from the old tombstones in the cemetery."

Primmie's mouth was open to ask another question, but Miss Phipps closed it.

"Stop, Primmie," she said. Then, turning to Galusha who was on his way to the stairs, she asked:

"Excuse me, Mr. Bangs, but have you been spendin' this lovely forenoon in the graveyard?"

"Eh? Oh, yes, yes. In the old cemetery over—ah—yonder."

"Humph! . . . Well, I hope you had a nice time."

"Oh, I did, I did, thank you. I enjoyed myself very much indeed."

"Yes, I should think you must have. . . . Well, come down right away because dinner's ready when you are."

Galusha hastened up the stairs. His hostess gazed after him and slowly shook her head.

"Miss Martha, Miss Martha."

Martha turned, to find Primmie excitedly gesticulating.

"Didn't I tell you? Didn't I tell you?" whispered Primmie.

"Didn't you tell me what? Stop wigglin'."

"Yes'm. Didn't I tell you 'undertaker'?"

"What?"

"Undertaker. Him, the Bangs one. Yesterday 'twas remains, to-day it's graveyards. My savin' soul, I——"

"Hush, hush! Have you thought to get that dictionary from Lulie yet?"

"Oh, now, ma'am, I snum if I didn't forget it. I'll go right over this minute."

"No, you won't. I'll go myself after dinner."

That Sunday dinner was a bountiful repast and Galusha ate more than he had eaten in three meals at his mountain hotel. He was a trifle tired from his morning's stroll and so decided to remain indoors until the following day. After the table was cleared Miss Phipps, leaving Primmie to wash the dishes, went over to the light keeper's house.

"I'll be back soon, Mr. Bangs," she said. "If you get lonesome go out into the kitchen and Primmie'll talk to you. Goodness gracious!" she added, laughing, "that's a dreadful choice I'm leavin' you—lonesomeness or Primmie. Well, I won't leave you to either long."

During the meal he had told them of his chance discovery of the old church and graveyard and of the loss of the brown derby. Primmie plainly regarded the catastrophe to the hat as a serious matter.

"Well, now, if that ain't too bad!" she exclaimed. "Blowed right out to sea, and 'most brand-new, too. My savin' soul, Miss Martha, folks ought to be careful what they say, hadn't they? . . . Eh, hadn't they?"

"Oh, I guess so, Primmie. I don't know what you're

talkin' about. Can't I help you to a little more of the chicken pie, Mr. Bangs? Just a little *bit* more?"

Galusha had scarcely time to decline the third helping of chicken pie when Primmie plunged again into the conversation.

"Why, I mean folks ought to be careful what they say about—about things. Now you and me hadn't no notion Mr. Bangs was goin' to lose his hat when we was talkin' about it this mornin', had we?"

Miss Phipps was much embarrassed.

"Have a—a—— Oh, do have a little potato or cranberry sauce or somethin', Mr. Bangs," she stammered. "A—a spoonful, that's all. Primmie, be *still.*"

"Yes'm. But you know you and me *was* talkin' about that hat when Mr. Bangs started out walkin'. Don't you know we was, Miss Martha?"

This was the final straw. Martha, looking about in desperation, trying to look anywhere but into her guest's face, caught one transitory glimpse of that face. There was a twinkle in Galusha's eye.

"I never liked that hat myself," he observed, dryly.

Again their glances met and this time he smiled. Martha gave it up.

"Oh, dear!" she exclaimed, with a laugh. "You know what they say about children and—other folks, Mr. Bangs. Primmie, if you say another word while we're at this table I'll—I don't know what I'll do to you. *Stop!* You've said plenty and plenty more, as father used to say. Truly, Mr. Bangs, it wasn't as bad as it sounds. I honestly *didn't* think the hat was becomin', that's all."

"Neither did I, Miss Phipps. I didn't think so when I bought it."

"You didn't? Then for mercy sakes why did you buy it?"

"Well, the man said it was just the hat for me and—ah— I didn't wish to argue, that's all. Besides, I thought perhaps he knew best; selling hats was his—ah—profession, you see."

"Yes, *sellin'* 'em was. Do you always let folks like that pick out what they want to sell you?"

"No-o, not always. Often I do. It saves—ah—conversation, don't you think?"

He said nothing concerning his meeting with Miss Hallett and the South Wellmouth station agent, but he did mention encountering Captain Jethro and Mr. Pulcifer. Martha seemed much interested.

"Humph!" she exclaimed. "I wonder what possessed Cap'n Jeth to go over to the cemetery in the mornin'. He almost always goes there Sunday afternoons—his wife's buried there—but he generally goes to church in the mornin'."

Galusha remembered having heard the light keeper refer to the exchange of preachers. Miss Phipps nodded.

"Oh, yes," she said, "that explains it, of course. He's down on the Wapatomac minister because he preaches against spiritualism. But what was Raish Pulcifer doin' in that cemetery? He didn't have anybody's grave to go to, and he wouldn't go to it if he had. There's precious little chance of doin' business with a person after he's buried."

"But I think it was business which brought Mr. Pulcifer there," said Galusha. "He and—ah—Captain Hallett, is it? Yes—ah—thank you. He and the captain seemed to be having a lengthy argument about—about—well, I'm not exactly certain what it was about. You see, I was examining a—ah—tomb"—here Primmie shivered—"and paid little attention. It seemed to be something about some—ah—stock they both owned. Mr. Pulcifer wished to sell and Captain Hallett did not care to buy."

Martha's interest increased. "Stock?" she repeated. "What sort of stock was it, Mr. Bangs?"

"I didn't catch the name. And yet, as I remember, I did catch some portion of it. Ah—let me see—— Could there be such a thing as a—ah—'ornamenting' stock? A Wellmouth ornamenting or decorating stock, you know?"

Miss Phipps leaned forward. "Was it Wellmouth Development Company stock?" she asked.

"Eh? Oh, yes—yes, I'm quite certain that was it. Yes, I think it was, really."

"And Raish wanted Cap'n Jeth to buy some of it?"

"That was what I gathered, Miss Phipps. As I say, I was more interested at the time in my—ah—pet tomb."

Primmie shivered again. Miss Martha looked very serious. She was preoccupied during the rest of the dinner and, immediately afterward, went, as has been told, over to the Hallett house, leaving her guest the alternative of loneliness or Primmie.

At first he chose the loneliness. As a matter of fact, his morning's exercise had fatigued him somewhat and he went up to his room with the intention of taking a nap. But, before lying down, he seated himself in the rocker by the window and looked out over the prospect of hills and hollows, the little village, the pine groves, the shimmering, tumbling sea, and the blue sky with its swiftly moving white clouds, the latter like bunches of cotton fluff. The landscape was bare enough, perhaps, but somehow it appealed to him. It seemed characteristically plain and substantial and essential, like—well, like the old Cape Cod captains of bygone days who had spent the dry land portion of their lives there and had loved to call it home. It was American, as they were, American in the old-fashioned meaning of the word, bluff, honest, rugged, real. Galusha Bangs had traveled much, he loved the out of the way, the unusual. It surprised him therefore to find how strongly this commonplace, 'longshore spot appealed to his imagination. He liked it and wondered why.

Of course the liking might come from the contrast between the rest and freedom he was now experiencing and the fevered chase led him at the mountain hotel where Mrs. Worth Buckley and her lion-hunting sisters had their habitat. Thought of the pestilential Buckley female set him to contrasting her affectations with the kind-hearted and wholehearted simplicity of his present hostess, Miss Martha Phipps. It was something of a contrast. Mrs. Buckley was rich and sophisticated and—in her own opinion—cul-

tured to the highest degree. Now Miss Phipps was, in all
probability, not rich and she would not claim wide culture.
As to her sophistication—well, Galusha gave little thought
to that, in most worldly matters he himself was unsophisticated. However, he was sure that he liked Miss Phipps and
that he loathed Mrs. Buckley. And he liked East Wellmouth, bareness and bleakness and lonesomeness and all.
He rather wished he were going to stay there for a long
time—weeks perhaps, months it might be; that is, of course,
provided he could occupy his present quarters and eat at
the Phipps' table. If he could do that why—why . . .
humph!

Instead of lying down he sat by that window for more
than half an hour thinking. He came out of his reverie
slowly, gradually becoming conscious of a high-pitched conversation carried on downstairs. He had left his chamber
door open and fragments of this conversation came up the
staircase. It was Primmie's voice which he heard most frequently and whatever words he caught were hers. There
was a masculine grumble at intervals but this was not un-
derstandable on the second floor.

"Now I know better. . . . My savin' soul, how you do
talk, Zach Bloomer! . . . And I says to her, says I, 'Miss
Martha,' I says. . . . My Lord of Isrul! . . ."

These were some of the "Primmieisms" which came up
the staircase. Galusha rose to close his door but before he
could accomplish this feat his own name was called.

"Mr. Bangs!" screamed Primmie. "Mr. Bangs, be you
layin' down? You ain't asleep, be you, Mr. Bangs?"

If he had been as sound asleep as Rip Van Winkle that
whoop would have aroused him. He hastened to assure the
whooper that he was awake and afoot.

"Um-hm," said Primmie, "I'm glad of that. If you'd
been layin' down I wouldn't have woke you up for nothin'.
But I want to ask you somethin', Mr. Bangs. Had you
just as soon answer me somethin' if I ask it of you, had
you, Mr. Bangs?"

"Yes, Primmie."

"Just as soon's not, had you?"

"Yes, quite as soon."

"All right. Then I—I . . . Let me see now, what was it I was goin' to ask? Zach Bloomer, stop your makin' faces, you put it all out of my head. It's all right, Mr. Bangs, I'll think of it in a minute. Oh, you're comin' down, be you?"

Galusha was coming down. It seemed to be the advisable thing to do. Miss Cash was doing her "thinking" at the top of her lungs and the process was trying to one with uneasy nerves. He entered the sitting room. Primmie was there, of course, and with her was a little, thin man, with a face sunburned to a bright, "boiled-lobster" red, and a bald head which looked amazingly white by contrast, a yellowish wisp of mutsache, and an expression of intense solemnity, amounting almost to gloom. He was dressed in the blue uniform of the lighthouse service and a blue cap lay on the table beside him.

"Mr. Bangs," announced Primmie, "this is Mr. Zach Bloomer. Zach, make you acquainted with Mr. Bangs, the one I was tellin' you about. Mr.—Mr.—— Oh, my savin' soul, what *is* your first name, Mr. Bangs?"

"Galusha, Primmie. How do you do, Mr. Bloomer?"

The little man rose upon a pair of emphatically bowed legs and shook hands. "I'm pretty smart," he observed, in a husky voice. Then he sat down again. Galusha, after waiting a moment, sat down also. Primmie seemed to be wrestling with a mental problem, but characteristically she could not wrestle in silence.

"What was it I wanted to ask you, Mr. Bangs?" she said. "I snum I can't think! Zach, what was it I wanted to ask Mr. Bangs?"

Mr. Bloomer paid not the slightest attention to the question. His sad blue eye was fixed upon vacancy.

"Galushy—Galushy," he said, huskily. "Huh!"

Galusha was, naturally, rather startled.

"Eh? I—ah—beg your pardon," he observed.

"I was thinkin' about names," explained Mr. Bloomer.

"Queer things, names are, ain't they? Zacheus and Galushy.
. . . Godfreys!"

He paused a moment and then added:

> " 'Zacheus he
> Did climb a tree
> His Lord to see.'

Well, if he wan't any taller'n I be he showed good jedgment.
. . . Zacheus and Galushy and Primrose! . . . Godfreys!"

Primmie was shocked. "Why, Zach Bloomer!" she exclaimed. "The idea of your talkin' so about a person's name
you never met but just now in your lifetime."

Zacheus regarded the owner of the name.

"No offense meant and none given, Mr. Bangs," he observed. "Eh? That's right, ain't it?"

"Certainly, certainly, Mr. Bloomer. I'm not in the least
offended."

"Um-hm. Didn't cal'late you would be. Can't help our
names, can we? If my folks had asked me aforehand I'd
a-been named plain John. As 'tis, my name's like my legs,
growed that way and it's too late to change."

Galusha smiled.

"You're a philosopher, I see, Mr. Bloomer," he said.

"He's assistant keeper over to the lighthouse," explained
Primmie. As before, Zach paid no heed.

"I don't know as I'd go so far as to call myself that,"
he said. "When I went to school the teacher told us one
time about an old critter who lived in a—in a tub, seem's
if 'twas. *He* was one of them philosophers, wan't he?"

"Yes. Diogenes."

"That's the cuss. Well, I ain't never lived in a tub, but
I've spent consider'ble time *on* one; I was aboard a light-
ship for five or six year. Ever lived aboard a lightship, Mr.
Bangs?"

"No."

"Humph! . . . Don't feel disapp'inted on that account,
do you?"

"Why—ah—no, I don't know that I do."

"Ain't no occasion. 'Bout the same as bein' in jail, 'tis—only a jail don't keep heavin' up and down. First week or so you talk. By the second week the talk's all run out of you, like molasses out of a hogshead. Then you set and think."

"I see. And so much thinking tends to bring out—ah—philosophy, I suppose."

"Huh! Maybe so. So much settin' wears out overalls, I know that."

Primmie interrupted.

"I've got it!" she cried, enthusiastically. "*I* know now!"

Galusha started nervously. Primmie's explosiveness was disturbing. It did not disturb Mr. Bloomer, however.

"Posy here'd be a good hand aboard a lightship," he observed. "Her talk'd *never* run out."

Primmie sniffed disgust. "I wish you wouldn't keep callin' me 'Posy' and such names, Zach Bloomer," she snapped. "Yesterday he called me 'Old Bouquet,' Mr. Bangs. My name's Primrose and he knows it."

The phlegmatic Zacheus, whose left leg had been crossed above his right, now reversed the crossing.

"A-ll right—er Pansy Blossom," he drawled. "What is it you're trying to tell us you know? Heave it overboard."

"Hey? . . . Oh, I mean I've remembered what 'twas I wanted to ask you, Mr. Bangs. Me and Zach was talkin' about Miss Martha. I said it seemed to me she had somethin' on her mind, was sort of worried and troubled about somethin', and Zach——"

For the first time the assistant light keeper seemed a trifle less composed.

"There, there, Primmie," he began. "I wouldn't——"

"Be still, Zach Bloomer. You know you want to find out just as much as I do. Well, Zach, he cal'lated maybe 'twas money matters, cal'lated maybe she was in debt or somethin'."

Mr. Bloomer's discomfiture was so intense as to cause him actually to uncross his legs.

"Godfreys, Prim!" he exclaimed. "Give you a shingle and a pocket-handkercher and you'll brag to all hands you've got a full-rigged ship. I never said Martha was in debt. I did say she acted worried to me and I was afraid it might be account of some money business. She was over to the light just now askin' for Cap'n Jeth, and he's the one her dad, Cap'n Jim Phipps, used to talk such things with. They went into a good many trades together, them too. . . . But there, 'tain't any of your affairs, is it, Mr. Bangs—and 'tain't any of Primmie's and my business, so we'd better shut up. Don't say nothin' to Martha about it, Mr. Bangs, if you'd just as soon. But course you wouldn't anyhow."

This was a tremendously long speech for Mr. Bloomer. He sighed at its end, as if from exhaustion; then he crossed his legs again. Galusha hastened to assure him that he would keep silent. Primmie, however, had more to say.

"Why, Zach Bloomer," she declared, "you know that wan't only part of what you and me was sayin'. That wan't what I wanted to ask Mr. Bangs. *You* said if 'twas money matters or business Miss Martha went to see Cap'n Jeth about you cal'lated the cap'n would be cruisin' up to Boston to see a medium pretty soon."

"The old man's Speritu'list," exclaimed Zach. "Always goes to one of them Speritu'list mediums for sailin' orders."

"Now you let me tell it, Zach. Well, then *I* said I wondered if you wan't a kind of medium, Mr. Bangs. And Zach, he——"

Galusha interrupted this time.

"*I*—a medium!" he gasped. "Well, really, I—ah—oh, dear! Dear me!"

"*Ain't* you a kind of medium, Mr. Bangs?"

"Certainly not."

"Well, I thought undertakin' was your trade till Miss Martha put her foot down on the notion and shut me right up. You *ain't* an undertaker, be you?"

"An undertaker? . . . Dear me, Primmie, you—ah—well, you surprise me. Just why did you think me an undertaker, may I ask?"

"Why, you see, 'cause—'cause—well, you was talkin' yesterday about interestin' remains and—and all this forenoon you was over in the cemetery and said you had such a good time there and . . . and I couldn't see why anybody, unless he was an undertaker, or—or a medium maybe, would call bein' around with dead folks havin' a good time . . . Quit your laughin', Zach Bloomer; you didn't know what Mr. Bangs' trade was any more'n I did."

Mr. Bloomer cleared his throat. "Mr. Bangs," he observed sadly, "didn't I tell you she'd make a ship out of a shingle? If you'd puffed smoke, and whistled once in a while, she'd have cal'lated you must be a tugboat."

Galusha smiled.

"I am an archæologist," he said. "I think I told you that, Primmie."

Primmie looked blank. "Yes," she admitted, "you did, but——"

Zacheus finished the sentence.

"But you didn't tell *too* much when you told it," he said. "What kind of an ark did you say?"

And then Galusha explained. The fact that any one in creation should not know what an archæologist was seemed unbelievable, but a fact it evidently was. So he explained and the explanation, under questioning, became lengthy. Primmie's exclamations, "My savin' soul" and "My Lord of Isrul" became more and more frequent. Mr. Bloomer interjected a remark here and there. At length a sound outside caused him to look out of the window.

"Here comes the old man and Martha," he said. "Cal'late I'd better be gettin' back aboard. Can't leave Lulie to tend light all the time. Much obliged to you, Mr. Bangs. You've cruised around more'n I give you credit for. Um-hm. Any time you want to know about a lightship or—or lobsterin' or anything, I'd be pleased to tell you. Good-day, sir. So long—er—Sweet William. See you later."

The "Sweet William" was addressed to Primmie, of course. The bow-legged little man, rolling from side to side like the lightship of which he talked so much, walked out of the room. A moment later Martha Phipps and Captain Jethro Hallett entered it.

Both Miss Phipps and the light keeper seemed preoccupied. The former's round, wholesome face was clouded over and the captain was tugging at his thick beard and drawing his bushy eyebrows together in a frown. He was a burly, broad-shouldered man, with a thin-lipped mouth, and a sharp gray eye. He looked like one hard to drive and equally hard to turn, the sort from which fanatics are made.

Primmie scuttled away to the dining room. Galusha rose.

"Good-afternoon, Captain Hallett," he said.

Jethro regarded him from beneath the heavy brows.

"You know Mr. Bangs, Cap'n Jeth," said Martha. "You met this mornin', didn't you?"

The light keeper nodded.

"We run afoul of each other over to the graveyard," he grunted. "Well, Martha, I don't know what more there is to say about—about that thing. I've told you all I know, I cal'late."

"But I want to talk a little more about it, Cap'n Jeth. If Mr. Bangs will excuse us we'll go out into the dinin' room. Primmie's up in her room by this time. You will excuse us, won't you, Mr. Bangs? There was a little business matter the cap'n and I were talkin' about."

Galusha hastened to say that he himself had been on the point of going to his own room—really he was.

Miss Martha asked if he was sure.

"You needn't go on our account," she protested. "We can talk in the dinin' room just as well as not, can't we Cap'n Jeth?"

The captain bowed his head. "We ain't cal'latin' to talk very long anyhow," he said, solemnly. "This is the Lord's day, Mr. Bangs."

Galusha hastily admitted that he was aware of the fact. He hurried into the hall and up the stairs. As he reached the upper landing he heard the ponderous boom of the light keeper's voice saying, "Martha, I tell you again there's no use frettin' yourself. We've to wait on the Lord. Then that wait will be provided for; it's been so revealed to me."

Miss Phipps sighed heavily. "Maybe so, Jethro," she said, "but what will some of us live on while we're waitin'? *That* hasn't been revealed to you, has it?"

For the rest of that afternoon Galusha sat by his bedroom window, thinking. His thoughts were along the line of those interrupted by Primmie's summons. When, at supper time, he again descended the stairs, his mind was made up. He was going to make a suggestion, a suggestion which seemed to him somewhat delicate. In one sense of the term it was a business proposition, in another—well, he was not precisely certain that it might not be considered presuming and perhaps intrusive. Galusha Cabot Bangs was not a presuming person and he was troubled.

After the supper dishes were washed and Primmie sent to bed—"sent" is the exact word, for Miss Cash, having had a taste of Egypt and the Orient, was eagerly hoping for more—Miss Phipps and Galusha were together in the sitting room. Doctor Powers had paid a brief visit. He found his patient so much improved that he announced him well enough to travel if he wished.

"If it is really necessary for you to go to-morrow, Mr. Bangs," he said, "I think you're strong enough to risk it."

"Thank you, Doctor," said Galusha. Then he added, with his little smile, "I couldn't go before to-morrow. You see, I—ah—haven't any hat."

In the sitting room, after supper, Galusha was idly turning the pages of *Camp, Battlefield and Hospital*, a worn book of Civil War sketches, printed immediately after that war, which he had found upon the shelf of the closet in his room, along with another volume labeled *Friendship's Garland, a Nosegay of Verse*. Of the two, although a peace-loving individual, he preferred the camp and battlefield to the *Nosegay;* the latter's fragrance was a trifle too sweet.

Suddenly Martha, who had been sitting quiet in the rocker, spoke.

"Mr. Bangs," she said, "I saw Lulie Hallett when I was over at the light this afternoon. We had a good talk together before Cap'n Jethro came back. She told me about your bein' so kind to her and Nelson over by the old church this mornin': She was real grateful to you and she says she shall thank you herself when she sees you. She asked me to do it for her now."

Galusha was confused. "Oh, it was nothing, really," he hastened to explain. "I—ah—— Well, I intruded upon them somewhat suddenly. I see she told you of that."

Miss Phipps was smiling to herself. She looked a little guilty.

"Well," she admitted, "Lulie did say that you kind of—er—flew over the bank. She said no one was ever quite so surprised as she was at that minute."

Mr. Bangs thoughtfully shook his head.

"Except myself, perhaps," he observed.

Martha's smile became a laugh. "Probably that's so," she admitted. "But, Mr. Bangs, Lulie is awfully anxious that you shouldn't think there was anything wrong about her meetin' Nelson Howard in that way. There isn't. She's a splendid girl and he's a fine young man. I think the world of Lulie and I like Nelson, too."

She paused a moment and then went on.

"It's Cap'n Jethro that makes all the trouble," she said. "There's no reason in the world—that is, no sensible reason—why Lulie and Nelson shouldn't be engaged to be married. Of course he isn't doin' very well in a business way just now, but that's partly from choice on Lulie's account. Nelse was a telegraph operator up in Brockton before the war. When the war came he went right into the Navy and started in at the Radio School studyin' to be a wireless operator. Then he was taken down with the 'flu' and had to give up study. Soon as he got well he went into the transport service. Lulie, you see, was teachin' school at Ostable, but her father's health isn't what it used to be and then, besides, I think she was a little worried about his spiritualism. Jethro isn't crazy about it, exactly, but he isn't on an even keel on that subject, there's no doubt about that. So Lulie gave up teachin' and came here to live with him. When Nelson was mustered out he took the station agent's job at South Wellmouth so as to be near her. I think he doesn't feel right to have her here alone with her father."

"But—ah—she isn't alone, is she? I gathered that Mr.—ah—Bloomer——"

"Zach Bloomer? Yes, he's there, but Zach isn't lively company, especially for a girl like Lulie. If Jethro was taken—well, with a fit or somethin', Zach would probably sit down and cross those bow legs of his and moralize for an hour or so before he got ready to help pick the old man up. Nelson knows that and so he refused two real good offers he had and took the position at the South Wellmouth depot. But he's studyin' at his wireless all the time and some day—but I'm afraid that day will be a long way off. Cap'n Jeth is as set as the side of a stone wharf and you'd have to take him to pieces to move him. That was another of father's sayin's," she added, "that about the stone wharf."

"Why, why is the—ah—why is Captain Hallet so opposed to young Howard?" asked Galusha.

"Spiritualism. Foolishness, that's all. Before his wife died he was as sensible and shrewd a man as you'd care to see. He and father were old chums and father used to ask his advice about investments and all such things. They went into lots of deals together and generally made 'em pay, though Jethro usually made the most because he took more chances. He must be worth twenty or thirty thousand dollars, Cap'n Jeth Hallett is."

She spoke as if these were enormous sums. Galusha, to whom all sums—sums of money, that is—were more or less alike, nodded gravely.

"His wife's death broke Jethro dreadfully," continued Martha. "For six months or so he hardly spoke to anybody except Lulie. Then some Spiritualist or other—I think it was Ophelia Beebe or some rattlehead like her—got him to go to see a medium who was boardin' here at the Restabit Inn. He got—or thinks he got—a communica-

tion direct from Julia—his wife. After that he kept goin'
to the Spiritualist camp meetin's and to Boston and to
mediums from Dan to Beersheba, so to speak. A while ago
one medium creature—and I wish she had been struck dumb
before she could say it—told him that he must beware of a
dark man who was tryin' to work evil upon his daughter.
As luck would have it, Nelson Howard was home on leave
and callin' on Lulie when her father got back from seein'
that very medium. You can imagine what happened. And
Jethro has been growin' more rabid on the subject ever
since."

She stopped. Her guest said nothing. He was thinking
that if he were to make the suggestion—the proposition
which he had determined upon before he came down to
supper, he must make it soon. And he did not know how
to begin.

Martha went on talking. She apparently did not notice
his silence. It was more as if she were thinking aloud.

"If it wasn't for Lulie's bein' here," she said, slowly, "I
don't know what I should do sometimes, I get so lonesome.
When father lived it was all so different. He was bright
and cheerful and he and I were just as if we were the same
age, as you might say. He never was cross and he didn't
fret and if he worried he didn't let me know it. He just
loved this place. It was near the salt water, and he loved
that, and he had his garden and his hens and he was interested in town affairs and all. We didn't have much money,
but we had enough, seemed so. Before he died he told me
he hoped he'd left me well enough off to get along. 'The
only thing that troubles me, Martha,' he said, 'is that some
of the things I've put money into shouldn't turn out as I
hoped. I've tried to be careful, but you can't always tell.
If you want advice,' he said, 'go to Jethro Hallett. Jeth's
a shrewd business man.' Ah, well, he didn't know that the
spirits were goin' to run Cap'n Jeth. About the last words
he said to me, father, I mean, was, 'Martha, hang on to
the old place if you can. I hate to think of your sellin' it.'
Of course I told him I never should sell it."

"Well—ah—well——" Galusha felt that he ought to say something, "you don't intend selling it, do you, Miss Phipps?"

Martha did not answer immediately. And when she did speak it was not a reply.

"You must think we're a queer lot down here by the Bluffs, Mr. Bangs," she said. "Primmie—you've seen what she is—and Zach Bloomer and Cap'n Jethro with his 'spirit revelations.' As I say, if it wasn't for Lulie I don't know what I should do. Get to be cracked myself, I presume likely. . . . But there," she added, brightening, "do let's change the subject, for mercy sakes! Mr. Bangs, what do you suppose I did when I was over at the light this afternoon? Besides talkin' with Lulie, I mean."

"Why—why, I don't know, I'm sure."

"I don't believe you could guess, either. I looked up 'archæologist' in the dictionary."

Mr. Bangs blinked surprise behind the spectacles.

"In the—in the dictionary?" he repeated. "Oh—ah—dear me! Really!"

"Yes. I'm afraid you'll think I am awfully ignorant, but to save my soul I couldn't think what an archæologist did, what sort of a business it was, I mean. Of course, I knew I *ought* to know, and that I did know once, but it seemed to be perfectly certain that I didn't know *then*. So I looked it up. It fits in with what you told Primmie and me about travelin'—that camel driver creature and all—and yet—and yet, you know, I was surprised."

"Surprised? Really? Yes, of course, but—but why?"

"Well, because somehow you don't look like that kind of man. I mean the kind of man who travels in all sorts of wild places and does dangerous things, you know, and——"

Galusha's desire to protest overcame his politeness. He broke in hurriedly.

"Oh, but I'm not, you know," he cried. "I'm not really. Dear me, no!"

"But you said you had been to—to Africa, was it?—three or four times."

"Oh, but those were my Abyssinian trips. Abyssinia isn't wild, or dangerous, any more than Egypt."

"Oh, isn't it?"

"No, not in the least, really. Oh, dear me, no!"

"Not with darky camel drivers stealin' your—er—underclothes and goodness knows what? It sounds a little wild to *me*."

"Oh, but it isn't, I assure you. And Egypt—ah—Egypt is a wonderful country. On my most recent trip I. . . . May I tell you?"

He began to tell her without waiting for permission. For the next hour Martha Phipps journeyed afar, under an African sun, over desert sands, beside a river she had read of in her geography when a girl, under palm trees, amid pyramids and temples and the buried cities of a buried people. And before her skipped, figuratively speaking, the diminutive figure of Galusha Bangs, guiding, pointing, declaiming, describing, the incarnation of enthusiastic energy, as different as anything could be from the mild, dreamy little person who had sat opposite her at the supper table so short a time before.

The wooden clock on the mantel—it had wooden works and Martha wound it each night before she went to bed—banged its gong ten times. Mr. Bangs descended from Egypt as if he had fallen from a palm tree, alighting upon reality and Cape Cod with startled suddenness.

"Oh, dear me!" he cried. "What was that? Goodness me, it *can't* be ten o'clock, can it? Oh, I must have talked you almost to death, Miss Phipps. I must have bored you to distraction, I must really. Oh, I'm *so* sorry!"

Miss Martha also seemed to be coming out of a dream, or trance. She stirred in her chair.

"You haven't bored me, Mr. Bangs," she said.

"Oh, but I must have, really. I should know better. You see. . . . Well, it's quite extraordinary my talking to you in this way, isn't it? I don't do it often—ah—except to other members of my profession. Why, up there in the mountains—at the place where I spent the past month or two, I scarcely talked of—ah—my work at all. And I was constantly being asked to do so. There was a dreadful—ah —that is, there was a woman who. . . . But I promise you I won't go on in this way again, Miss Phipps, really I won't."

Martha drew a long breath and shook her head.

"I hope you won't promise any such thing," she declared. "I feel as if I had been readin' the most interestin' story-book that ever was. . . . My, my!" she added, with a sigh. "What a curious thing life is, isn't it? There's nothin' new in that thought, of course, but it comes to us all every little while, I suppose. Just think of the difference there has been in our two lives, for instance. Here are you, Mr. Bangs, you've been everywhere, pretty nearly, and yet you're —well, you're not so very big or strong-lookin'. The average person would say I was the one best fitted to trot around the world, and all my life—or nearly all—I've been keepin' house in this little corner of East Wellmouth. That's curious, isn't it? Of course I can't see myself doin' the things you do—ridin' a camel, for instance."

"Oh, but it is quite easy, quite," Galusha hastened to assure her. "You could do it very well, I'm sure, Miss Phipps."

"Maybe so, but I'm afraid I'm a little bit doubtful. I should want my camel on wheels, with a railin' around his hump. But *you* must feel lost enough down in this tame place, Mr. Bangs. The wildest thing around here is a wood-chuck."

She laughed. Galusha smiled, but he answered promptly.

"I like it here, Miss Phipps," he said, earnestly. "I do, really. I like it very much indeed. In fact—in fact—Miss Phipps, would you mind answering a question or two? . . . Oh, they're not personal questions, personal to you, I mean. Really they are not. May I ask them?"

She was puzzled and looked so.

"Why, of course," she said.

"Well . . . well, they're foolish questions, I suppose, for

I think I know the answers already. But, you see, I want my conscience to be quite clear before making a decision. . . . That is, the decision is already made, but you see. . . . oh, no, you don't see, of course, do you?"

"Why not ask your questions, Mr. Bangs?" she suggested.

"Yes—ah—thank you; yes, I will. The first one is about —ah—rest. This is a good spot for one to—ah—rest in, isn't it?"

She laughed. "Are you jokin', Mr. Bangs?" she asked. "Rest! I should say the average person would find it easier to rest here than to do anything else. But you are jokin', of course?"

"No; no, indeed, I am quite serious. Second, the air about here is—ah—good and—and fresh?"

"*Good!* Well, considerin' that most of it is blown over three or four thousand miles of salt water before it gets here it ought to be fairly good, I should say. As to its bein' fresh—well, if you were here when a February no'theaster was blowin' I'm afraid you might find it a little *too* fresh."

"That is satisfactory, that is very satisfactory indeed. Now what was the third thing the doctor said I must have? Oh, yes, people. And I know there are people here because I have met them. And very nice people, indeed. . . . Oh, this is *very* satisfactory, Miss Phipps. Now my conscience is quite clear concerning my promise to the doctor and I can go on to my proposal to you."

"Your—your *what?*"

"My proposal—the—ah—proposition I want to make you, Miss Phipps. And I *do* hope you will consider it favorably. You see, I like East Wellmouth *very* much. My doctor told me I must go where I could find fresh air, rest, and people. They are all here in East Wellmouth. And he said I must have exercise, and behold my daily walks to that most interesting old cemetery of yours. Now, you have been *very* kind to me already, Miss Phipps; could you be still more kind? Would you—ah—could you let me continue our present arrangement indefinitely—for a few months, let

us say? Might I be permitted to board here with you until
—well, until spring, perhaps?"

Martha Phipps leaned back in her chair. She regarded
him keenly.

"Mr. Bangs," she said, slowly, "has some one been tellin'
you that I needed money and are you makin' me this offer
out of—well, out of charity?"

Galusha jumped violently. He turned quite pale.

"Oh, dear, dear, dear!" he cried, in a great agitation.
"Oh, dear me, dear me! No, *indeed,* Miss Phipps! I am
very sorry you should so misunderstand me. I—I—— Of
course I know nothing of your money affairs, nor should I
presume to—to—— Oh, I—I—— Oh, dear!"

His distress was so keen that she was obliged to recognize it.

"All right, all right, Mr. Bangs," she said. "It wasn't
charity, I can see that. But what was it? Do I understand you to say that you like—actually like this lonesome
place well enough to want to stay here all *winter?*"

"Yes—ah—yes. And it doesn't seem lonesome to me."

"Doesn't it? Well, wait a little while. . . . And you
really mean you want to keep on boardin' here—with me,
with us?"

"Yes, if—if you will be so very kind as to permit me to
do so. If you will be so good."

"Good! To what? My soul and body!"

"No—ah—good to mine," said Galusha.

CHAPTER VI

IT was not settled that evening. Martha declared she must have at least a few hours in which to think it over and Galusha, of course, agreed.

"It won't take too long," she said. "Naturally, you want to know so that you can make your plans."

Galusha smiled. "Please take as much time as you need, Miss Phipps," he urged. "If you permit me to remain here while you are—ah—endeavoring to reach a decision I shall be quite satisfied, really. In that case, you know, I should be willing to wait for the decision until spring. Dear me, yes—even until summer."

Martha laughed and declared she should decide long before that. "I think breakfast time to-morrow will settle it," she added.

It did. After breakfast she informed him that he might stay if he wished.

"Though *why* you want to I can't understand," she said. "And of course it is part of the agreement that you'll feel free to give it up and go any time you wish; as soon as you begin to get tired of the place and us, I mean."

He beamed satisfaction. "I shall not be the one to tire first," he declared. Then he added, earnestly, "Of course, Miss Phipps, you will be perfectly frank and tell me at once if you change *your* mind. And if I should become a —ah—well, a sort of nuisance, be irregular at meals, or noisy or—— What is it? I beg your pardon?"

She had laughed outright. She was still smiling when she apologized.

"Please excuse me for laughin', Mr. Bangs," she said, "but don't you think yourself that that is funny? The idea of your bein' noisy, I mean."

He stroked his chin.

"We-ll," he admitted, "perhaps it is. But sometimes I am quite boisterous, really I am. I remember once, years ago, I was in an old cemetery in New Hampshire and I suddenly discovered an inscription which pleased me *very* much. *Most* quaint and unusual it was—dear me, yes. And quite unconsciously I burst into a shout—a cheer, as one may say. The old sexton was quite scandalized and warned me not to do it again. He said it would disturb people. I don't know whom he meant, there were no living people to be disturbed."

The question of terms was the cause of a supplementary discussion. Mr. Bangs insisted upon continuing the three dollars a day rate and Miss Martha declared he should do nothing of the kind.

"That three dollars a day was just a temporary thing," she said. "I said it just because I was sure you would go over to Elmer Rogers' if I didn't. Elmer Rogers is a robber and always was. Father used to say he was the forty-first member of the Forty Thieves and that they didn't boil him because he wasn't enough account to waste hot oil on."

"But—ah—it seems to me that if the Rogers' House board is worth three dollars a day yours should be worth five at least."

"Maybe so, but I never heard anybody but Elmer say his board was worth one dollar, let alone three."

They compromised on a daily rate of two and a half per day, which each declared to be ridiculous.

Thus Galusha Cabot Bangs became no longer a transitory but a regular boarder and lodger at the Phipps' place. The fact became known to Miss Primrose Cash that forenoon, to the driver of the grocer's cart one hour later, and to all of East Wellmouth before bedtime. It was news and, in October in East Wellmouth, one item of local news is a rare and blessed dispensation.

Before another day had passed the news item had been embellished. Mr. Bangs visited the general store of Erastus Beebe to purchase headgear to replace the brown derby. Erastus happened to be busy at the moment—there were two customers in his store at the same time, an event most unusual—so Galusha's wants were supplied by no less a person than Mr. Horatio Pulcifer.

Raish's greeting was condescendingly genial.

"Well, well!" he exclaimed, pumping the little man's arm up and down with one hand and thumping his shrinking shoulder blades with the other. "If it ain't the perfessor himself! How are you this mornin', Mr. Bangs? Right up and comin', eh?"

Galusha would have withdrawn his hand from the Pulcifer clutch if withdrawal had been possible. It being quite impossible, he murmured that he was—"ah—quite well" and, conscious that the eyes of Mr. Beebe and his two customers were fixed upon him, fixed his own gaze upon Mr. Pulcifer's assortment of watch charms and shivered with embarrassment.

"Ain't it funny, now?" queried Raish, addressing the world in general. "Ain't it funny how things happen? When I fetched you over in my car t'other night didn't I say I hoped you and me'd meet again? That's what I said. And now we've met twice since. Once in the old boneyard and now here, eh? And they tell me you like East Wellmouth so much you're goin' to stick around for a spell. Good business! Say, I'll be sellin' you a piece of Wellmouth property one of these days to settle down on. That's the kind of talk, eh, Perfessor? Haw, haw, haw!"

He pounded the Bangs' shoulder blades once more. Mr. Beebe and his two customers echoed the Pulcifer laugh. Galusha smiled painfully—as the man in the operating chair smiles at the dentist's jokes.

"I—I—excuse me," he faltered, turning to the grinning Erastus, "can I—— That is, have you a—ah—hat or—or cap or something I might buy?"

Before the proprietor of the general store could answer,

Mr. Pulcifer answered for him. Again the hand descended upon the Bangs' shoulder.

"Haw, haw!" roared Raish, joyfully. "I get you, Mr. Bangs. The old lid blew out to sea and we've got to get a new one. Say, that was funny, wasn't it; that hat goin' that way? I don't know's I ever laughed more in my life. One minute she was jumpin' along amongst them gravestones like a hoptoad with wings, and then—— Zing! Fsst! away she went a half mile or so down into the breakers. Haw, haw, haw! And to see your face! Why——"

Galusha interrupted.

"*Please* don't do that," he said, nervously.

"Hey? Do what?"

"Ah—slap my back. I'd rather you wouldn't, if you don't mind. And—oh—I should like to see a—a cap or something."

The last sentence was addressed to Mr. Beebe, who cleared his throat importantly.

"Jest a minute, jest a minute," said Erastus. "Soon's I get through waitin' on these customers I'll 'tend to you. Jest a minute. Yeast cake, did you say, Mrs. Blount?"

"Oh—oh, pardon me," faltered Galusha. "I'll wait, of course."

"Wait?" It was Mr. Pulcifer who spoke. "You don't have to wait. I know Ras's stock as well as he does, pretty nigh. *I'll* show you a cap, Mr. Bangs."

"Oh—oh, I couldn't think of troubling you, really I couldn't."

"No trouble at all. What's a little trouble amongst neighbors, eh? And that's what we are now—neighbors, eh? Sure, Mike! You and me are goin' to see a lot of each other from now on. There! There's a good, stylish cap, if I do say it. Try it on? What's your size, Perfessor?"

Five minutes later Galusha descended the steps of the Beebe store, wearing a cloth cap which was, to say the very least, out of the ordinary. Its material was a fuzzy frieze of nondescript colors, a shade of dingy yellow predominating, and its shape was weird and umbrellalike.

With it upon his head little Galusha resembled a walking toadstool—an unhealthy, late-in-the-season toadstool.

The quartet in the Beebe store watched his departure from the windows. All were hugely amused, but one, Mr. Pulcifer, was hilarious.

"Haw, haw, haw!" roared Raish. "Look at him! Don't he look like a bullfrog under a lily pad? Eh? Don't he now? Haw, haw, haw!"

Erastus Beebe joined in the laugh, but he shook his head.

"I've had that cap in stock," he said, "since—well, since George Cahoon's son used to come down drummin' for that Boston hat store, and he quit much as eight year ago, anyhow. How did he ever come to pick *that* cap out, Raish?"

Mr. Pulcifer regarded the questioner with scornful superiority.

"Pick it out!" he repeated. "He never picked it out, I picked it out for him. You don't know the first principles of sellin', Ras. If you had me to help around here you wouldn't have so many stickers in your stock."

Beebe, gazing after the retreating figure of Mr. Bangs, sniffed.

"If I had your brass, Raish," he observed, calmly, "I'd sell it to the junk man and get rich. Well, maybe I won't have so many stickers, as you call 'em, if that little critter comes here often. What's the matter with him; soft in the head?"

"Isn't this his hat—the one he wore when he came in here?" queried Mrs. Jubal Doane, one of the two customers.

Mr. Beebe picked it up. "Guess so," he replied. "Humph! I've seen that hat often enough, too. Used to belong to Cap'n Jim Phipps, that hat did. Seen him wear it a hundred times."

Mrs. Becky Blount, the other customer, elevated the tip of a long nose. "Well," she observed, "if Martha Phipps is lendin' him her pa's hats *so* early, I must say——"

She did not say what it was she must say, but she had said quite enough.

Martha herself said something when her boarder appeared beneath his new headgear. When he removed it, upon entering the dining room, she took it from his hand.

"Is *this* the cap you just bought, Mr. Bangs?" she asked.

"Yes," said Galusha, meekly. "Do you like it?"

She regarded the fuzzy yellow thing with a curious expression.

"Do you?" she asked.

The reply was astonishingly prompt and emphatic.

"I loathe it," said Galusha.

She transferred the stare from the cap to its owner's face.

"You do!" she cried. "Then why in the world did you buy it?"

Mr. Bangs squirmed slightly. "He said I ought to," he answered.

"Who said so?"

"That man—that Mr. Pulcifer. Mr.—ah—Deedee—Beebe, I mean—was busy, and Mr. Pulcifer insisted on showing me the caps. I didn't like this one at all, but he talked so much that—that I couldn't stay and hear him any longer. He makes me very nervous," he added, apologetically. "I suppose it is my fault, but—ah—he does, you know."

"And do you mean to say that you took this—this outrage because Raish Pulcifer talked you into it?"

Galusha smiled sadly. "Well, he—he talked me into it— yes," he admitted. "Into the—ah—cap and out of the store. Dear me, yes."

Miss Martha drew a long breath.

"My heavens and earth!" she exclaimed. "And what did you do with father's hat, the one you wore down there?"

Her lodger gasped. "Oh, dear, dear!" he exclaimed. "Oh, dear me! I must have left it in the shop. I'm *so* sorry. How could I do such a careless thing? I'll go for it at once, Miss Phipps."

He would have gone forthwith, but she stopped him.

"I'm goin' there myself in a little while," she said. "I've got some other errands there. And, if you don't mind," she added, "I'd like to take this new cap of yours with me. That is, if you can bear to part with it."

She went soon afterward and when she returned she had another cap, a sane, respectable cap, one which was not a "sticker."

"I took it on myself to change the other one for this, Mr. Bangs," she said. "I like it lots better myself. Of course it wasn't my affair at all and I suppose I ought to beg your pardon."

He hastened to reassure her.

"Please don't speak so, Miss Phipps," he begged. "It was very, very kind of you. And I like this cap *very* much. I do, really. . . . I ought to have a guardian, hadn't I?" he added.

It was precisely what she was thinking at the moment and she blushed guiltily.

"Why, what makes you say that?" she asked.

"Oh, I'm not saying it, not as an original thought, you know; I'm merely repeating it. Other people always say it, they've said it ever since I can remember. Thank you very much for the cap, Miss Phipps."

He was sunnily cheerful and very grateful. There was not the slightest resentment because of her interference. And yet if she had not interfered he would have worn the hideous yellow cap and been as cheerful under that. Pulcifer had imposed upon him and he realized it, but he deliberately chose being imposed upon rather than listening to the Pulcifer conversation. He was certainly a queer individual, this lodger of hers. A learned man evidently, a man apparently at home and sure of himself in a world long dead, but as helpless as a child in the practical world of to-day. She liked him, she could not help liking him, and it irritated her exceedingly to think that men like Raish Pulcifer and Erastus Beebe should take advantage of his childlike qualities to swindle him, even if the swindles were but petty.

"They shan't do it," she told Lulie Hallett, the next morning. "Not if I can help it, they shan't. Somebody ought to look out for the poor thing, half sick and with nobody of his own within goodness knows how many miles. I'll look out for him as well as I can while he's here. My conscience wouldn't let me do anything else. I suppose if I pick out his other things the way I picked out that cap the whole of East Wellmouth will be talkin'; but I can't help it, let 'em."

For the matter of that, the Beebes and the Blounts and Doanes were talking already. And within a fortnight Miss Phipps' prophecy was fulfilled, the whole of East Wellmouth *was* talking of Galusha Bangs. Some of the talk was malicious and scandalous gossip, of course, but most of it was fathered by an intense and growing curiosity concerning the little man. Who was he? What was his real reason for coming to East Wellmouth to live—in the *winter* time? What made him spend so many hours in the old cemetery? Was he crazy, as some people declared, or merely "kind of simple," which was the opinion of others? Mr. Pulcifer's humorous summing-up was freely quoted.

"He may not be foolish now," observed Raish, "but he will be if he lives very long with that bunch down to the lighthouse. Old Cap'n Jeth and Zach and Primmie Cash are enough to start anybody countin' their fingers. My opinion is, if you want to know, that this Bangs feller is just a little mite cracked on the subject of Egyptians and Indians and gravestones—probably he's read a lot about 'em and it's sprained his mind, as you might say. That would account for the big yarns he tells Prim about Africa and such. As to why he's come here to live, I cal'late I've got the answer to that. He's poorer'n poverty and it's cheap livin' down at Martha Phipps's. How do I know he's poor? Cripes t'mighty, look at his clothes! Don't look much like yours or mine, do they?"

They certainly did not look much like Mr. Pulcifer's. Galusha's trunk had arrived at last, but the garments in it were as drab and old-fashioned and "floppy" as those he wore on his arrival. Horatio was invariably arrayed like a lily of the field—if by that term is meant a tiger lily. Raish generally finished his appraisal by adding, patronizingly:

"He's all right, though, old Galushy is. Nothin' harmful about him. See how easy I get along with him. I shake hands with him and hit him a clip on the back, and, gosh t'mighty, he thinks I'm his best friend on earth. He'd do anything for me, that old owl would."

And, perhaps, because it was given forth with such authority from the Pulcifer Mount Sinai, the fact that Bangs was very poor and was living at Gould's Bluffs because of that poverty came to be accepted in East Wellmouth as a settled fact. So quickly and firmly was it settled that, a month later, Erastus Beebe, leaning over his counter in conversation with a Boston traveling salesman, said, as Galusha passed the store:

"Queer-lookin' customer, ain't he? One of our town characters, as you might say. Pretends he's been all over creation, but the truth is he lives down here by the lighthouse and is poorer than the last pullet in Job's coop. Kind of an inventor, or book writer, or some such crazy thing. Queer how that kind get that way, ain't it?"

"Is that all he does for a living?" asked the salesman.

"Don't do much of that, seems so, nowadays. Spends most of his time copyin' off tombstone-writin' over in the old Baptist graveyard. Seems to *like* to be there, he does. Thunder sakes! a graveyard is the last place I'd spend *my* time in."

The Bostonian made the obvious retort that it was probably the last place Mr. Beebe *would* spend his time in.

Galusha, of course, was not in the least aware of the East Wellmouth estimate of himself, his fortune and his activities. He would not have been interested had he known. He was enjoying himself hugely, was gaining daily in health, strength, and appetite, and was becoming thoroughly acquainted with Gould's Bluffs, its surroundings, and its people.

He made many calls at the lighthouse nowadays. These calls were not especially for the purpose of cultivating Captain Jethro's acquaintance, although the rugged, bigoted old light keeper afforded an interesting study in character. The captain's moods varied. Sometimes he talked freely and interestingly of his experiences at sea and as keeper of the light. His stories of wrecks and life-saving were well told and Galusha enjoyed them. He cared less for Jethro's dissertations on investments and deals and shrewd trades. It was plain that the old man prided himself upon them, however. On one occasion Mr. Bangs happened to mention Martha Phipps and hinted at his own fear that his lodging at the Phipps' home was in the nature of an imposition upon the lady's good nature. The light keeper shook his shaggy head impatiently.

"No, no, no," he growled, " 'tain't any such thing. Your boardin' there's a good thing for Martha. She needs the money."

Galusha was troubled.

"I'm sorry to hear that," he said. "She is not—ah—not pinched for means, I hope. Not that that is my business, of course," he added, hastily.

Captain Jeth's reply was gruff and rather testy.

"She'll come out all right," he said, "if she's willin' to do as I do and wait. I know I'll come out right. Julia told me so, herself."

Galusha had forgotten, momentarily.

"Julia?" he repeated.

"My wife."

"Oh—oh, yes, yes, of course."

In these conversations Bangs learned to steer the talk as far as possible from the subjects of life beyond the grave or of spirit communications. The slightest touch here and the captain was off, his eyes shining beneath his heavy brows, and his face working with belligerent emotion. A hint of doubt or contradiction and trouble followed immediately.

"Don't argue with me," roared Cap'n Jethro. "I *know*."

Lulie and Galusha had many chats together. He had liked her at first sight and soon she came to like him.

"He's as funny and odd as can be," she told Martha, "and you never can tell what he may say or do next. But he's awfully nice, just the same."

Little by little she confided to him her hopes and doubts and fears, the hopes of her own love story and the doubts and fears concerning her father.

"He isn't well," she said, referring to the latter. "He pretends he is, but he isn't. And all this consulting with mediums and getting messages and so on is very bad for him, I know it is. Do you believe in it at all, Mr. Bangs?"

Galusha looked doubtful.

"Well," he replied, "it would be presumptuous for one like me to say it is all nonsense. Men like Conan Doyle and Lodge and Doctor Hyslop are not easy dupes and their opinions are entitled to great respect. But it seems—ah—well, I am afraid that a majority of the so-called mediums are frauds."

"*All* of father's mediums are that kind," declared Lulie, emphatically. "I know it. Most of them are frauds for money, but there are some, like that ridiculous Marietta Hoag, who pretend to go into trances and get messages just because they like to be the center of a sensation. They like to have silly people say, 'Isn't it wonderful!' Marietta Hoag's 'control,' as she calls it, is a Chinese girl. She must speak spirit Chinese, because no Chinese person on earth ever talked such gibberish. Control! *She* ought to be controlled—by the keeper of an asylum."

The indignation expressed upon Lulie's pretty face was so intense that Galusha suspected an especial reason.

"Is—ah—is this Marietta person the medium who—who——" he began.

"Who set father against Nelson? Yes, she is. I'd like to shake her, mischief-making thing. Father liked Nelson well enough before that, but he came home from that séance as bitter against him as if the poor boy had committed murder. Marietta told him that a small dark man was

trying to take away his daughter, or some such silliness.
Nelson isn't very small nor *very* dark, but he was the only
male in sight that came near answering the description. As
a matter of fact——"

She hesitated, colored, and looked as if she had said more
than she intended. Galusha, who had not noticed her embarrassment, asked her to go on.

"Well," she said, in some confusion, "I was going to say
that if it hadn't been Nelson it would probably have been
some one else. You see, I am father's only child and so—
and so——"

"And so he doesn't like the idea of giving you up to
some one else."

"Yes, that's it. But it wouldn't be giving me up. It would
be merely sharing me, that's all. I never shall leave father
and I've told him so ever so many times. . . . Oh, dear!
If you could have known him in the old days, Mr. Bangs,
before he—well, when he was himself, big and strong and
hearty. He used to laugh then; he hardly ever laughs now.
He and Cap'n Jim Phipps—Martha's father—were great
friends. You would have liked Cap'n Jim, Mr. Bangs."

"Yes, I am sure I should."

"So am I. Martha is very much like him. She's a dear,
isn't she?"

Galusha nodded. "She has been very kind to me," he
said. "Indeed, yes."

"Oh, she is to every one. She is always just like that.
I am very glad you have decided to board with her this
winter, Mr. Bangs. I have an idea that she has been—well,
troubled about something; just what, of course, I don't
know, although I think—but there, I mustn't guess because
it is not my business."

Galusha expressed a wish that he might become better
acquainted with Nelson Howard.

"I am sure I should like him," he said. "He seems like
a very nice young man."

Lulie nodded radiantly.

"Oh, he is," she cried. "Truly he is, Mr. Bangs. Why,

every one says——" Then, becoming aware of her enthusiasm, she blushed and begged pardon. "You see, I hear so much against him—from father, I mean—that I couldn't help acting silly when you praised him. Do forgive me, won't you, Mr. Bangs?"

He would have forgiven her much more than that.

"I shall make it a point to go over to the South Wellmouth station and call upon him," he told her. She thanked him.

"I am hoping that you and Martha and Nelson and I may spend an evening together pretty soon," she said. "You see, father—but there, that's another secret. I'll tell you in a little while, next week, I hope."

He learned the secret from Martha. On a day in the following week Miss Phipps informed her lodger that he and she were to have supper at the light keeper's that evening.

"It's a real sort of party," declared Martha. "Small but select, as they used to say in books when I was a girl. There will be four of us, you and I and Nelson Howard and Lulie."

Galusha was surprised.

"Nelson Howard!" he repeated. "Why, dear me, I thought—I understood that Mr. Howard was *persona non grata* to Captain Hallett."

Martha nodded. "Well, if that means what I suppose it does, he is," she replied. "If Cap'n Jeth knew Nelson was goin' to eat supper in his house he'd go without eatin' himself to stop it. But, you see, he doesn't know. Jethro is goin' spiritualizin' to-night. Marietta Hoag and Ophelia Beebe and their crowd of rattleheads have dug up a brand new medium who is visitin' over in Trumet and they've made up a party to go there and hold a séance. When they told Cap'n Jeth, of course nothin' would do but he must go, too. So, *while* he is gone Nelson is comin' over to supper. It's deceivin' the old man, in one way, of course, but it isn't doin' him a bit of harm. And it does give the young folks a pleasant time, and I think they deserve it. Lulie has been as kind and forbearin' with her father as a daughter could be, and Nelson has been more patient than the average young fellow, by a good deal."

Late that afternoon two automobiles laden with humanity, male and female, drove past the Phipps' gate, and Primmie, from the window, announced that it was "Marietta and 'Phelia and the rest of 'em. My savin' soul, ain't they talkin' though! Cal'late the sperits 'll have busy times this evenin', don't you, Miss Martha?" A few minutes later she proclaimed that Cap'n Jeth had just climbed aboard and that the autos were coming back.

"See! See, Mr. Bangs!" she cried, pointing. "There's Cap'n Jeth, settin' between Marietta and 'Phelia Beebe. There's the three of 'em on the back seat. Cap'n Jeth's the one with the whiskers."

At six o'clock Martha and her lodger walked over to the Hallett house. Miss Phipps was dressed in her best gown and looked the personification of trim, comfortable New England femininity. Galusha was garbed in the suit he wore the evening of his arrival, but it had been newly sponged and pressed.

"It looks lots better," observed Martha, inspecting him as they walked along. "It wouldn't have, though, if Primmie had finished the job. I was so busy that I let her start on it, but when I saw what a mess she was makin' I had to drop everything else and do it myself."

Galusha looked puzzled.

"Yes?" he said, politely. "Oh, yes, yes. Yes, indeed."

She shook her head.

"I do believe you don't know what I'm talkin' about," she said. "Now, do you?"

"Why—ah—why, Miss Phipps, I confess I—I——"

"Well, I declare! I never saw a person like you in my life. Didn't you notice *any* difference in that suit of clothes?"

Mr. Bangs, looking downward, suddenly became aware of his immaculate appearance. He was very much upset.

"I—I don't know what you must think of me," he stammered. "I have been—that is, I was thinking of other things and I—— Dear me! Oh, dear! I am *very* grateful to you. But you shouldn't take so much trouble."

"It wasn't any trouble. The suit was hangin' in your closet and I noticed how wrinkled and out of shape it was. And the stains on the trousers—my!"

"Yes—ah—yes. I wore it over at the cemetery the other day and I—ah—imagine I must have gotten down on my knees to examine the tombstones."

"I guess likely. It looked as if you might have crawled from here to the cemetery and back. Now don't say any more, Mr. Bangs. It was no trouble at all. I always used to take care of father's clothes. He used to say I kept him all taut and shipshape."

Lulie met them at the door.

"Where is Primmie?" she asked.

"She'll be over pretty soon," replied Martha. "I knew you wouldn't need her yet to help with the supper and the longer she stays away the more talk there will be for the rest of us. She is to eat in the kitchen, Lulie, remember that. I *won't* have her chatterin' all through our meal."

"She and Zacheus are to eat together," replied Lulie. "It is all settled. Now if Nelson will only come. He is going to get away just as soon as the down train leaves."

He arrived soon afterward, having bicycled over from South Wellmouth. Primmie arrived also and bursts of her energetic conversation, punctuated by grumblings in Mr. Bloomer's bass, drifted in from the kitchen. Supper was a happy meal. Young Howard, questioned by Martha and Lulie—the latter evidently anxious to "show off" her lover —told of his experiences aboard one of Uncle Sam's transports and the narrow escape from a German submarine. Galusha, decoyed by Miss Phipps, was led into Egypt and discoursed concerning that marvelous country. Lulie laughed and chatted and was engagingly charming and vivacious. Martha was her own cheerful self and the worried look disappeared, for the time, from her face.

After supper was over, the ladies helped Primmie clear the table while the men sat in the sitting room and smoked. The sitting room of the light keeper's home was even more nautical than that at the Phipps' place. There was no less than six framed paintings of ships and schooners on the walls, and mantel and what-not bore salt-water curios of many kinds handed down by generations of seafaring Halletts—whales' teeth, little ships in bottles, idols from the South Sea islands, bead and bone necklaces, Eskimo lanceheads and goodness knows what. And below the windows, at the foot of the bluff on the ocean side, the great waves pounded and muttered and growled, while high above the chimneys of the little house Gould's Bluffs light thrust its flashing spear of flame deep into the breast of the black night.

It was almost half past eight when Martha Phipps, whose seat was near the front window of the sitting room, held up a warning hand.

"Listen!" she cried. "Isn't that an automobile comin'?"

It undoubtedly was. Apparently more than one motor car was approaching along the sandy road leading from the village to the lighthouse.

"Who in the world is it?" asked Martha, drawing aside the window shade and trying to peer out. "Lulie, you don't think it can be——"

Lulie looked troubled, but she shook her head.

"No, it can't be," she declared. "The séance was to be away over in Trumet and it is sure to last hours. They couldn't have gone as far as that and——

She was interrupted. From the dining room came the sound of rushing feet. Primmie burst into the room. She was wildly excited.

"My Lord of Isrul, Miss Martha!" she cried. "It's them come back. It is, it is, it is!"

"Who? Who, Primmie?" demanded Miss Phipps. "Stop flappin' your wings—arms, I mean. Who's come back?"

"The sperit folks. All hands of 'em, Marietta and 'Phelia Beebe and Abe Hardin' and Cap'n Jeth and all. And——

and they're comin' in here—and here's Nelson right where
Cap'n Jeth can catch him. Oh, my savin' soul!"

From behind her agitated shoulder peered the countenance
of Mr. Bloomer.

"She's right, Lulie," observed Zach, with calm emphasis.
"The whole crew of ghost seiners is back here in port again,
Cap'n Jeth and all. Better beat for open water, hadn't you,
Nelse, eh? Be the divil to pay if you don't. . . . Godfreys,
yes!"

CHAPTER VII

THE announcement exploded like a bomb in the midst of the little group in the light keeper's sitting room. Lulie turned a trifle pale and looked worried and alarmed. Martha uttered an exclamation, dropped the window shade and turned toward her young friend. Mr. Bangs looked from one to the other and was plainly very anxious to help in some way but not certain how to begin. Of the four Nelson Howard, the one most concerned, appeared least disturbed. It was he who spoke first and his tone was brisk and businesslike.

"Well, Lulie," he said, "what do you want me to do? Shall I stay and face it out? I don't mind. There's nothing for us to be ashamed of, you know."

But Lulie shook her head. "Oh, no, no, Nelson," she cried, "you mustn't. You had better go, right away. There will be a scene, and with all those people here——"

Miss Phipps put in a word. "But perhaps Nelson's right, after all, Lulie," she said. "There is no reason in the world why he shouldn't come to see you, and maybe he and Cap'n Jeth might as well have a plain understandin' now as any time."

Miss Hallett's agitation increased. "Oh, no," she cried, again. "Don't you see it mustn't happen, on father's account? You know how he—you know how excited and—and almost violent he gets when any one crosses him nowadays. I'm afraid something might happen to him. I'm afraid. Please go, Nelson, for my sake."

The young man nodded. "Of course, Lulie," he declared. "You're perfectly right. I'm off. Good-night."

He was hastening toward the dining room door, but Primmie, dancing up and down like a jumping jack, barred his way.

"No, no, no," she squealed, "you can't—you can't. They're almost to the door now. He'll catch you sure. He *will*. Oh, my Lord of Isrul!"

Sure enough, the latch of the door leading from the side porch to the dining room was rattling at that moment. Fortunately the door itself was hooked on the inside. Nelson hesitated.

"Humph!" he grunted. "Could I get through to the kitchen and out that way, do you think, Zach?"

"Godfreys, no! Not with them winder curtains strung up higher'n Haman the way they be. No, no! Godfreys!"

Martha stepped across the sitting room and flung open another door on the opposite side. As she did so there sounded a prodigious thumping from the side porch and the bull-like voice of Captain Hallett bellowed his daughter's name.

"Go let 'em in, Lulie," whispered Martha. "I'll look out for things here. Quick, Nelson, out this way, through the front hall and out the front door. *Quick!*"

Captain Jeth was accompanying his shouts by thumping upon the side of the house. Lulie, after one desperate glance at her lover, hurried to the dining room. Young Howard hesitated a moment.

"My hat and coat?" he whispered. "Where are they?"

They were hanging in the entry upon the door of which the captain was thumping. Zach hastened to get them, but before he reached the dining room they heard the outer door open and Jeth's voice demanding to know why Lulie had kept him waiting so long. Nelson, with a somewhat rueful smile and a wave of the hand to Martha and Galusha, dodged into the blackness of the front hall. Miss Phipps closed the door after him. The conspirators looked at each other. Primmie's mouth opened but the expansive hand of Mr. Bloomer promptly covered it and the larger part of her face as well.

"This ain't no time to holler about your savin' soul," whispered Zacheus, hoarsely. "This is the time to shut up. And *keep* shut up. You be still, Dandelion!"

Primmie obeyed orders and was still. But even if she had shrieked it is doubtful if any one in the dining room could have heard her. The "ghost seiners," quoting from Mr. Bloomer, were pouring through the entry and, as all were talking at once, the clatter of tongues would have drowned out any shriek of ordinary volume. A moment later the Halletts, father and daughter, led the way into the sitting room. Lulie's first procedure was to glance quickly about the apartment. A look of relief crossed her face and she and Martha Phipps exchanged glances.

"Father has—he has come back," was her somewhat superfluous explanation. Captain Jethro noted the superfluity.

"Cal'late they can see that for themselves, Lulie," he observed. "How are you, Martha? Evenin', Mr. Bangs. Everything all right about the light, Zach?"

"Ay, ay, sir," was Mr. Bloomer's nautical reply. The captain grunted.

"Better go look at it," he said. Turning, he called over his shoulder, "Come in, all hands."

"All hands," that is, the company in the dining room— came in. There were fourteen of them, all told, and, as Martha Phipps told Galusha Bangs afterward, "If you had run a net from one end of Ostable County to the other you wouldn't have landed more freaks than there were in that house at that minute." The majority were women and the few men in the party looked as if each realized himself a minority at home and abroad.

"Set down, everybody," commanded Captain Jethro. "Lulie, you better help me fetch in them dining-room chairs. We'll need 'em."

"But, father," begged Lulie, "what are you going to do?"

"Do? We're goin' to have a meetin', that's what we're goin' to do. Set down, all of you that can. We'll have chairs for the rest in a minute."

"But, father——" began Lulie, again. The captain interrupted her. "Be still," he ordered, irritably. "Marietta, you set over here by the melodeon. That'll be about right for you, will it?"

Miss Marietta Hoag was a short, dumpy female with a face which had been described by Zach Bloomer as resembling a "pan of dough with a couple of cranberries dropped into it." She wore a blue hat with a red bow and a profusion of small objects—red cherries and purple grapes —bobbing on wires above it. The general effect, quoting Mr. Bloomer again, was "as if somebody had set off a firecracker in a fruit-peddler's cart." The remainder of her apparel was more subdued.

She removed the explosive headgear and came forward in response to the light keeper's command. She looked at the chair by the ancient parlor organ and announced: "Yes, indeed, it'll do real well, thank you, Cap'n Jethro." Her voice was a sharp soprano with liquid gurgles in it—"like pourin' pain-killer out of a bottle," this last still another quotation from the book of Zacheus.

"All right," said Captain Jeth, "then we'll begin. We've wasted enough time cruisin' way over to Trumet and back for nothin'. No need to waste any more. Set down, all hands, and come to order. Lulie, you and Martha and the rest of you set down, too."

"But, father," urged his daughter again, "I don't understand. What are you going to do?"

"Goin' to have a meetin', I tell you."

"But what sort of a meeting?"

"A séance. We cruised clear over to Trumet to hear that Brockton medium that was stayin' at Obed Taylor's there and when we got to Obed's we found she'd been called back home unexpected and had left on this afternoon's train. So we came back here and Marietta's goin' to try to get in communication herself. That's all there is to it. . . . Now don't waste any more time askin' fool questions. Set down. Martha Phipps, what are you and Mr. Bangs standin' up for?"

Martha's answer was quietly given.

"Why, good gracious, Jethro!" she observed, "why shouldn't we stand up? Mr. Bangs and I came over to spend the evenin' with Lulie. We didn't know you and Marietta and Ophelia and the rest were goin' to hold any —er—what do you call 'em?—séances. We'll run right along and leave you to enjoy yourselves. Come, Mr. Bangs."

For some reason or other this reply appeared to irritate the light keeper exceedingly. He glared at her.

"Set down, both of you," he ordered. "I want you to. 'Twill do you good. No, you ain't goin', neither. Lulie, you tell 'em to stay here."

His manner was so determined and the light in his eye so ominous that his daughter was alarmed.

"Oh, do stay, Martha," she pleaded. "Won't you please stay, you and Mr. Bangs? I think it will be for the best, truly I do. Please stay."

Martha looked at her lodger. Galusha smiled.

"I shall be very glad to remain," he observed. "Indeed yes, really."

Miss Phipps nodded. "All right, Lulie," she said, quietly. "We'll stay."

They took chairs in the back row of the double circle. Primmie, eyes and mouth open and agog with excitement, had already seated herself. Captain Jethro looked about the room.

"Are we all ready," he growled. "Eh? Who's that comin'? Oh, it's you. Well, set down and keep quiet."

It was Mr. Bloomer who had reëntered the room and was received so unceremoniously. He glanced at Galusha Bangs, winked the eye which the captain could not see, and sat down next to Primmie.

"Now then," said Captain Jeth, who was evidently master of ceremonies, "if you're all ready, Marietta, I cal'late we are. Cast off! Heave ahead!"

But Miss Hoag seemed troubled; evidently she was not ready to cast off and heave ahead.

"Why—why, Cap'n Jeth," she faltered, "I *can't*. Don't you *know* I can't? Everybody's got to take hands—and the lights must be turned way down—and—and we've *got* to have some music."

The captain pulled his beard. "Humph!" he grunted. "That's so, I forgot. Don't know what's the matter with me to-night, seem to be kind of—of upset or somethin'. Zach, turn them lamps down; more'n that, way down low. . . . That'll do. Now all hands hold hands. Make a—a kind of ring out of yourselves. That's it. Now what else was it, Marietta?"

"Music," faltered Miss Hoag, who seemed rather over-awed by the captain's intensity and savage earnestness. "We always have music, you know, to establish the—the contact. Have somebody play the organ. 'Phelia, you play it; you know how."

Miss Ophelia Beebe, sister of the village storekeeper, was a tall, angular woman garbed in black. Her facial expression was as mournful as her raiment. She rose with a rustle and moved toward the ancient melodeon. Lulie spoke hurriedly.

"No, no, Ophelia," she protested, "it isn't any use. That old thing has been out of order for—why, for years. No one could possibly play on it. No one has for ever and ever so long. Father knows it perfectly well."

Again Captain Jethro tugged at his beard.

"Humph!" he grunted. " 'Tis out of order; I remember now. . . . Humph! I—I forgot that. Well, we'll have to have some sort of music. Can anybody that's here play on anything?"

There was silence for a moment. Then a thin masculine voice from the dimness made proclamation.

"I can play on the fiddle," it said; and then added, as if in afterthought, "some."

There was a rustle in the corner from which the voice had come. Mutterings and whisperings arose. "Don't talk so foolish!" "Well, Sary, he asked if anybody could play on anything and I——" "Be still, I tell you! I declare if there's any chance for a person to make a jumpin' numbskull out of himself in front of folks I'll trust you to be right on deck." "Now, Sary, what are you goin' on like this for? I only just——"

The dispute was growing louder and more violent. Captain Jethro roared a command for silence.

"What's all this?" he demanded. "Silence there for'ard!" He waited an instant and then asked, "Who was it said they could play the fiddle? Was it you, Abel Hardin'?"

Mr. Abel Harding, clam digger and fish purveyor, resident in South Wellmouth, acknowledged his identity.

"Yus, Cap'n Jeth," he declared. "I said I could play the fiddle, and I can, too. Sary B., she says——"

"Sarah B."—otherwise Mrs. Abel Harding—interrupted. "He can't play nothin' but two jig tunes and he plays them like the very Old Scratch," she snapped, with emphasis.

"Well, I never said I was anything great at it, did I? I said I can play some, and I can. If you'd just keep your tongue to home and leave me be I——"

"*Silence!*" shouted the light keeper again. The domestic squabble broke off in the middle and some irreverent giggles from other sections of the circle subsided. Captain Jethro's indignant gaze swept the group. Primmie said afterward, "You couldn't see him glare at you, but you could *feel* him doin' it." When the stillness was absolute the captain asked, "Where is your fiddle, Abel?"

"Eh?" Mr. Harding paused and cleared his throat. "Why," he stammered, "it's—it's to home. Er—er—that's where I keep it, you know."

"Humph!" Captain Jethro's scorn was withering. "And home is eleven mile away or such matter. How much good is your bein' able to play on it goin' to do us when 'tain't here for you to play on?"

There were discreet snickers from the dimness. Mrs. Hardin's voice was audible, saying, "There, I told you so, foolhead." The captain once more ordered and obtained silence.

"We've had enough of this," he growled. "This ain't a

play-actin' show to laugh at. If we can't behave accordin'
as we should we'll give it up. Marietta says she can't get
into contact with the sperit world without music. Would
it do if we was to sing somethin', Marietta?"

Miss Hoag faltered that she didn't know's she hardly believed 'twould. "I always *have* had some sort of instru-
mental music, Cap'n Jethro. Don't seem to me's if I could
hardly get along without it."

The captain grunted again. "Can't anybody play *anything?*" he demanded. "Anything that's within hailin' distance, I mean."

Another silent interval. And then a voice said, timidly,
"I can play the mouth organ."

It was Primmie's voice and as she was sitting next Zach
Bloomer, who was next Galusha Bangs, the unexpectedness
of it made the latter jump. Miss Phipps, next in line on
Galusha's left, jumped likewise.

"Primmie," she said, sharply, "don't be silly."

"But I *can,* Miss Martha. You know I can. Zach knows
it, too. You've heard me, ain't you, Zach? Ain't you?
Ain't you?"

Thus urged, Mr. Bloomer answered, "I've heard you," he
said. And added, fervently and under his breath, "Godfreys!"

"Primmie," began Martha, again, but Captain Jethro
broke in.

"Quiet, Martha Phipps," he ordered. "Stop your talkin',
all hands. Marietta, do you cal'late you could get under
way with mouth organ music?"

"Why—why, I don't know. Maybe I could if—if it
played church tunes."

"Can you play hymn tunes, Primmie?"

"Yes, sir. I can play 'Sweet By and By' and 'Brighten
the Corner Where You Be' and 'Pack up Your Troubles in
Your Old Kit Bag.' No, that ain't one, is it? But I can
play——"

"Where's your mouth organ now?"

"It's in my jacket pocket out yonder in the kitchen."

"Go fetch it."

Sounds as of one individual falling over others, accompanied by exclamations and confusion, indicated that Miss Cash was going in search of the instrument. Lulie made one more attempt at persuasion.

"Father," she pleaded, "what makes you try to hold a séance to-night? You've been 'way over to Trumet and back and you must be tired. You aren't very well, you know, and all this excitement isn't good for you. Won't you please——"

Her father stamped his foot. "Set down," he shouted. "I know what I'm doin'. This is my house and I'll do as I please in it. Stop! I don't want to hear any more. Where's that Cash girl?"

Primmie was returning bearing the mouth organ. She plowed through the circle like an armored tank through a wire entanglement and reached the light keeper's side.

"Here I be," she announced, "and here 'tis. Shall I commence to begin now? Where do you want me to set?"

She was given a seat in the front row, facing the medium. Captain Hallett, after some final instructions to Zacheus concerning the turning lower of one of the lamps and a last order for stillness, gave the command.

"All ready! Heave ahead!"

Miss Hoag leaned back in her rocking-chair and closed her eyes. Primmie drew a long breath and the first bars of the "Sweet By and By" were forcibly evicted from the harmonica. Zach Bloomer, the irrepressible, leaned over and breathed into his neighbor's ear.

"Say, Mr. Bangs," he whispered, "if you was a sperit would you leave a comf'table berth up aloft to come and anchor alongside *that* noise?"

The "noise" became more enthusiastic as the musician warmed to her work. Miss Hoag stirred uneasily in her chair. Captain Jethro bent toward her.

"Tell her not to play so *loud*," whispered Marietta. The captain obeyed.

"Come, come, Primmie," he said, irritably. "Go easy on

it, soften her down. Play low. And stop stompin' out the
time with your foot."

Thus cautioned Miss Cash played low, very low, and also
very slowly. "The Sweet By and By" droned on, over and
over, in the dark stuffiness of the crowded room. Galusha
Bangs, who had been at first much amused, began to be
bored. Incidentally he was extremely sorry for Lulie, poor
girl, who was compelled to be present at this ridiculous
exhibition of her father's obsession. Heavy breathing
sounded near at hand, growing steadily heavier until it became a snore. The snore broke off in the middle and with
a sharp and most unchurchly ejaculation, as if the snorer
had been awakened suddenly and painfully. Galusha fancied
he recognized Mr. Harding's voice. Primmie ended her
thirty-second rendition of the "Sweet By and By" chorus
and began the thirty-third.

Then Miss Hoag began to groan. The first groan was
so loud and unexpected that Miss Cash gasped "My savin'
soul!" into the mouth organ. Marietta continued to groan,
also to pound the floor with her heels. In her capacity as
"medium" she, like other mediums—mediums of her stripe,
that is—was "getting under control."

Then followed the usual sort of thing which follows at
this sort of séance. Miss Hoag, through her "control," began to receive and transmit "messages." The control spoke
in a kind of husky howl, so to speak, and used a lingo most
unusual on this plane, however common it may be elsewhere.

Mr. Bangs was startled when first favored with a sample
of this—literally—unearthly elocution.

"Oh, dear me!" he exclaimed. "Oh, dear! *Why* does she
do that? Is—is she ill?"

Miss Beebe answered, from her place in the circle. "It's
her sperit control talkin' now," she whispered. "She's controlled by a China woman."

"Name of Little Cherry Blossom," whispered Mr. Harding.

"Sshh!" said several voices, indignantly.

"Allee samee comee manee namee Johnee," announced Little Cherry Blossom. "Anybody heree knowee manee Johnee?"

Several did, of course, and John was soon undergoing cross-examination. He proved to be the cousin of Mrs. Hannah Peters' first husband who was drowned on the Grand Banks fifteen or sixteen years before. "John-ee" was, like so many of his kind, a bit shaky on names and dates but strong on generalities. However, everybody except the few skeptics from the Phipps' place seemed satisfied and made no embarrassing comments.

Everybody but Mr. Bloomer, that is; Zacheus, the philosopher who had studied his profession aboard a lightship, commented on everything. Sitting next Mr. Bangs, he put his lips close to the ear of the last-named gentleman and breathed caustic sarcasm into it. Galusha found it distracting and, at times, annoying, for Mr. Bloomer's mustache was bristly.

"Little Cherry Blossom talks's if she had a cold," whispered Zach. "Better take a little cherry rum, hadn't she, eh?"

The control was loudly paging a person named Noah.

"Sperit heree wantee talkee with Noah," she cried. "Wheree isee Noah?"

"'Board the Ark, most likely," whispered Mr. Bloomer. "Be hollerin' for Jonah next, won't she? Cal'late so. Yus, yus."

Message after message came and was recognized and acknowledged by the devout. The group from the Phipps' house had so far been slighted, so, too, had Captain Jethro Hallett. There was a slight hubbub in the circle, owing to the fact that two of its members simultaneously recognized and laid claim to the same spirit, each declaring him to be or have been an entirely different person when living. During this little controversy Zacheus whispered in his neighbor's ear.

"Say, Mr. Bangs," he whispered, "this is gettin' kind of tiresome, ain't it? Must be worse for Nelse, though, eh?"

Galusha did not catch his meaning. "For—for whom?" he asked. "I beg your pardon."

"Oh, you're welcome. Why, I mean Nelse Howard must be gettin' more tired than we be, shut up in that front hall the way he is."

"Shut up— Why, really, I—— Mr. Howard left the house long ago, didn't he? By the front door, you know."

Zach chuckled. "That front door is locked and the key's been lost for more'n a fortn't. Cal'late Lulie forgot that when she told him to skip out that way. He can't *get* out. He's in that front entry now and he'll have to stay there till all hands have gone and the cap'n gone to bed. That's a note, ain't it! . . . Sshh! They're goin' to begin again."

The identity of the spiritual visitor having been tentatively established, the "communications" continued. Galusha paid little heed to them. The thought of young Howard a prisoner in the front hall was uncomfortable of itself, but still more uncomfortable was the mental picture of what might happen should his presence there be discovered by Captain Hallett. The old light keeper was bigoted and absurdly prejudiced against his daughter's lover at all times. An encounter between them would always be most unpleasant. But this evening, when the captain was in his most fanatical mood, for him to find Nelson Howard hiding in his own house—well, the prospect was almost alarming.

Galusha, much troubled in mind, wondered if Lulie had remembered the locked door and the lost key. Did she realize her fiancé's plight? If so, she must be undergoing tortures at that moment. Nelson, of course, could take care of himself and was in no danger of physical injury; the danger was in the effect of the discovery upon Captain Jethro. He was not well, he was in a highly nervous and excited state. Galusha began to fidget in his chair. More than ever he wished the séance would end.

However, it did not end. The messages continued to come. Apparently the line of spirits waiting to communicate was as long as that at the ticket office of a ball park on a pleasant Saturday. And suddenly Mr. Bangs was startled out of his fidgets by the husky voice of Little Cherry Blossom calling the name which was in his mind at the moment.

"Jethro," wheezed Little Cherry Blossom. "Jethro. Some one heree wantee talkee Jethro."

Martha Phipps, sitting next to Galusha, stirred and uttered an impatient exclamation under her breath. From beyond, where Lulie sat, Galusha caught a quick gasp and a frightened "Oh, dear!" Zacheus whispered, "Godfreys!" Primmie bounced up and down with excitement. The circle rustled and then grew very still.

"Well," growled Captain Jethro, a quaver in his deep voice, "I'm here. It is—is it you, Julia?"

Little Cherry Blossom said that it was. Mr. Bangs heard another sniff of disgust from Miss Phipps. He was himself thoroughly disgusted and angry. This mockery of a great sorrow and a great love seemed so wicked and cruel. Marietta Hoag and her ridiculous control ceased to be ridiculous and funny. He longed to shake the fat little creature, shake her until her silly craze for the limelight and desire to be the center of a sensation were thoroughly shaken out of her. Marietta was not wicked, she was just silly and vain and foolish, that was all; but at least half of humanity's troubles are caused by the fools.

"Julia," said Captain Jethro, his big voice trembling as he said it, "I—I'm here, Julia. What is it?"

"Julia she say she gladee you heree," gurgled Little Cherry Blossom. Martha Phipps drew a breath between her teeth as if in pain. Her hand squeezed Lulie's tight. She was suffering with the girl. As for Galusha, sensitive soul that he was, he blushed all over in sympathetic embarrassment.

"I'm glad to be here, Julia," said the captain. "You know it, too, I guess likely. Is all well with you, Julia?"

Cherry Blossom in horrible pidgin English affirmed that all was well, all was happiness and delight and bliss in the realm beyond. Galusha did not hear much of this, he was suffering too acutely to listen. Then he heard Captain Jethro ask another question.

"Is there any special message you've got for me, Julia?"

Yes, there was. "Daughter, daughter." There was some message about a daughter.

"Lulie? Is there somethin' you want to tell me about Lulie, Julia?"

"Father!" It was Lulie herself who uttered the exclamation. "Father," she cried. "Don't! Oh, don't! Please don't!"

Her father's reply was a furious roar.

"Stop!" he thundered. "Be still! Don't you say another word!"

"But, father, *please*——"

"Stop! . . . Julia, Julia . . . are you there? What is it about Lulie? Tell me."

Little Cherry Blossom herself seemed a bit nervous, for her next message was given with a trifle less assurance. It was an incoherent repetition and re-repetition of the word "daughter" and something about "looking out" and "danger."

Captain Jethro caught at the word.

"Danger?" he queried. "Danger for Lulie? Is that what you mean, Julia? I'm to look out on account of danger comin' for Lulie? Is that it, Julia?"

Lulie made one more desperate plea.

"Father," she begged, "please don't! Of course there isn't any danger for me. This is *so* ridiculous."

"Be still, I tell you. . . . Is that it, Julia? Is it?"

Little Cherry Blossom with some hesitation indicated that that was it. A rustle of excitement stirred the circle.

"What kind of danger?" demanded the light keeper, eagerly. "Can't you tell me that, Julia?"

Apparently she could not, for there was no reply. The captain tried to help by suggestion.

"Danger from—from her bein'—er—hurt?" he suggested. "Bein' run over—or—or—drowned or somethin'?"

No, that was not it.

"Danger from somebody—some person?"

"Yes." Another rustle of excitement in the circle. The light keeper caught his breath.

"Julia," he demanded, "do you mean that—that our girl's in danger from some—some *man?*"

"*Father!* I won't stand this. It's perfectly——"

"Lulie Hallett, you set down! Set *down!*"

Martha Phipps laid a hand upon the girl's arm. "Don't excite him," she whispered. "I'd sit down if I were you, Lulie."

Lulie, trembling with indignation, subsided under protest. Little Cherry Blossom burst out with a gush of gibberish concerning some man, "bad, wicked manee," who was trying to influence "daughter" in some way or other, just how was not particularly intelligible. Captain Jethro offered another suggestion.

"Julia," he demanded, "is it the outsider, the small, dark man you said afore? Is it him?"

Yes, it was. The rustle in the circle was now so pronounced as to amount almost to a disturbance. Mr. Abel Harding whispered audibly, "It's Nelson Howard she means, don't she?" His wife even more audibly ordered him to "shut up, for the land sakes." Primmie dropped the mouth organ on the floor with a metallic clatter. Startled, she made her customary appeal to the ruler of Israel.

"It's him, eh?" growled the light keeper. "I thought so. I've got my eye on him, Julia, and he knows it. What's he up to now? Where is he?"

"Near her."

"Near her? Here? . . . In this *house,* do you mean?"

A moment's hesitation, and then, "Ye-es, I—I shouldn't wonder."

This bit of information, even though unusually qualified considering its spirit source, caused a genuine sensation. Almost every one said something. Zach Bloomer whistled shrilly in Mr. Bangs' ear and said, "Godfreys!" Galusha said, "Oh, dear me!" with distressful emphasis. Martha Phipps and Lulie clutched each other and the latter uttered a faint scream. Primmie Cash, who had stooped to pick up the dropped harmonica, fell on her knees beside it. Captain Jethro stamped and roared for silence.

"Be still!" he shouted. "Stop! *Stop!* By the ever-lastin', I'll—I'll—— Julia! Julia!"

But Julia did not answer this time. Neither did Little Cherry Blossom. Whether Miss Hoag was frightened at the effect of her message or whether she figured that she had caused sensation sufficient for one day are matters for conjecture. At all events she stirred in her chair and announced faintly, and in her natural, everyday tones and accent, that she wished a drink of water.

"Where—where be I?" she gasped. "I—— Oh, fetch me a drink, somebody, won't you, please?"

The light keeper, paying no need whatever, was shouting his wife's name.

"Julia! Julia!" he cried. "Don't go! I want you! I need you!"

Lulie called "Father" and hastened toward him. Zacheus whispered in Galusha's ear that he cal'lated 'twouldn't do no harm to turn on the glim and proceeded forthwith to turn up the wick of one of the lamps. The sudden illumination showed Captain Jethro standing in the middle of the floor, his face flushed, his brows drawn together and his lips twitching. He was glaring about the room and the expression upon his face was so fierce that Mr. Bangs said, "Oh, dear me!" again when he saw it.

Lulie put her arm about the light keeper's shoulder. "Father, father," she pleaded, "please don't look that way. Come and sit down. Please do!"

But sitting down was far from the captain's thoughts just then. He impatiently tossed his daughter's arm aside.

"So he's here, is he," he growled, between his teeth. "He's in my house, is he? By the everlastin', I'll show him!"

Martha Phipps pushed her way toward the pair.

"There, there, Jethro," she said, quietly, "don't act this way. Don't you see you're frightenin' Lulie half out of her wits? There's nothin' for you to look so savage about. Come over and sit down and rest. You're tired."

"No, I ain't tired, either. Be quiet, woman. By the Lord, if he's in this house I'll find him. And *when* I find him——"

"Sshh, sshh! What in the world are you talkin' about? Marietta didn't say——"

"Julia—my spirit wife—told me that that skulkin' swab of a Nelse Howard was here in this house. You heard her. Let go of me, both of you! Now where is he?"

He was turning directly toward the door leading to the front hall. Lulie was very white and seemed on the point of collapse. Even Miss Phipps, usually so calm and equal to the emergency, appeared to find this one a trifle too much for her, for she glanced desperately about as if in search of help. Zach Bloomer repeated "Godfreys" several times and looked, for him, almost excited. As for Primmie, she was so frightened as to be speechless, a miracle far more amazing than any other which the séance had thus far produced. The remaining members of the circle were whispering in agitation and staring wide-eyed at the captain and those about him.

Then a masculine voice, a very soft, gentle masculine voice, said, "I beg your pardon, Captain Hallett, but may I —ah—ask a question?"

The very gentleness of the voice and the calmness of its tone had more effect in securing the light keeper's attention than any shout could possibly have done. Captain Jethro stopped in his stride.

"Eh?" he grunted. "Eh? What's that?"

Galusha Bangs moved forward, quietly elbowing his way from the back row of the circle to the open space before the inner line of chairs and their excited occupants.

"It is—ah—I, Captain Hallett," he observed, calmly, "I wished to ask a question. You see, I have been very much interested by the —ah—manifestations here this evening. Very much so, really—indeed, yes."

The light keeper interrupted. "Don't bother me!" he ordered, savagely. "I'm goin' to find that sneakin' rascal, and—— Get out of my way, will you?"

Somehow or other the little Egyptologist had moved forward until, without appearing to have made an effort to do so, he was directly in the captain's way—that is, between the latter and the door of the front hall. The command to get out of the way he acknowledged politely and with caution.

"Yes, yes, of course," he said, hastily. "I'm very sorry. Very sorry indeed. I beg your pardon, Captain Hallett. Now there is one point in this lady's—ah—messages—ah—communications, you know—which puzzles me somewhat. You see——"

"I can't stop to talk to you now. I'm goin' to—— *Will* you get out of my way?"

"Was I in your way? I *beg* your pardon. How clumsy of me! I—ah—— You see, this lady's last message seemed to point so directly in my direction that I felt constrained to speak. You see, when she, or her—control, is it?—mentioned my being here in your house and accused me of having an evil influence upon your daughter, I—well, I was surprised and—ah—hurt."

A general gasp of astonishment from the circle behind him interrupted. Mr. Abel Harding shouted "Eh!" and, for a wonder, his wife did not take him to task for it. For the matter of that, she had uttered an exclamation also. So had Ophelia Beebe and many others. Zacheus whistled. Primmie once more referred to her saving soul. Martha Phipps cried out.

As for Jethro Hallett, he stared uncomprehendingly at the Bangs' face which looked so earnestly and gravely up into his. He drew a hand across his forehead and breathed heavily.

"Wha—what are you talkin' about?" he demanded. "Who—who said anything about you?"

Galusha transferred his gaze from the light keeper's countenance to that of Miss Marietta Hoag. The medium's moonlike visage bore an expression of intense surprise.

"Why—ah—she did," replied Galusha, gently. "This lady here. She said that an outsider, a small, dark man, was exerting an evil influence upon Miss Lulie—upon your daughter. Then she said this person was here in your house. Now, as I am the only person present who answers to that description, naturally I—well, I—really, I must protest. I have the highest respect and regard for your daughter, Captain Hallett. I should be the last, the very last, to wish to exert any such influence."

"Nonsense!" The amazed captain shouted the word. "What are you talkin' about? 'Twan't you she said. 'Twas that Howard swab. He's been hangin' around Lulie for more'n a year."

"Ah—pardon me, Captain Hallett, but really I must make my point. It could not have been Mr. Howard to whom the—ah—control referred. Mr. Howard is somewhat dark, perhaps, but he is not small. I am both dark and small. And I am here, whereas Mr. Howard apparently is not. And I am, beyond question, an outsider. Therefore——"

"Nonsense, I tell you! She said Nelson Howard was in this house."

"Pardon me, pardon me, Captain Hallett. She said a small, dark man, an outsider, was in this house. She mentioned no names. You mentioned no names, did you, Miss —ah—Hoag?"

Marietta, thus unexpectedly appealed to, gasped, swallowed, turned red and stammered that she didn't know's she did; adding hastily that she never remembered nothin' of what she said in the trance state. After this she swallowed again and observed that she didn't see *why* she couldn't have that drink of water.

"So you see, Captain Hallett," went on Mr. Bangs, with the same gentle persistence, "being the only person present answering the description given by the medium I feel somewhat—ah—distressed. I must insist that I am unjustly accused. I must ask Miss Phipps here and your daughter herself to say whether or not my conduct toward Miss Lulie has not been quite—ah—harmless and without—ah—malevolence. I shall be glad to leave it to them."

Of the pair to whom this appeal for judgment was made Martha Phipps alone heeded it. Lulie, still white and trembling, was intent only upon her father. But Martha rose to the occasion with characteristic promptness.

"Of course, Mr. Bangs," she declared, "you've behaved just as nice as any one could be in this world. I could hardly believe my ears when Marietta said you were an evil influence towards Lulie. You ought to be careful about sayin' such things, Marietta. Why, you never met Mr. Bangs before this evenin'. How could you know he was an evil influence?"

Miss Hoag, thus attacked from an unexpected quarter, was thrown still more out of mental poise. "I never said he was one," she declared, wildly. "I only just said there was a—a—— I don't know what I said. Anyhow *I* never said it, 'twas my control talkin'. I'll leave it to 'Phelia Beebe. You know I don't know what I'm sayin' when I'm in the trance state, don't you, 'Phelia? Anyhow, all I said was. . . . Oh, 'Phelia," wildly, "why don't you help me out? . . . And—and I've asked no less'n four mortal times for that drink of water. I—I—— Oh, oh——"

She became hysterical. The circle ceased to be a circle and became a series of agitated groups, all talking at once. Mr. Bloomer seized the opportunity to turn up the wick of another lamp. Lulie, clinging to her father's arm, led him toward a chair in a secluded corner.

"Sit down, father," she urged. "Sit down, and rest. Please do!"

The old light keeper's fiery rage seemed to be abating. He passed his hand across his forehead several times and his expression changed. He looked like one awakening from a bad dream.

"I—I cal'late I will set down for a minute or so, Lulie," he faltered. "I do feel sort of tired, somehow or 'nother. I don't want to talk any more, Mr. Bangs," he added, wearily. "I—I'll have to think it all out. Lulie, I cal'late they'd better go home. Tell 'em all to go. I'm tired."

Martha Phipps passed from group to group whispering.

"I guess we'd better go," she suggested. "He's pretty well worn out, I'm afraid. Everybody's things are there in the dinin' room or in the side entry. We'd better go right away, it seems to me."

Galusha had gotten his "things" already, his coat was over his arm. The others followed his example. A few minutes more and the last of the "ghost seiners" had left the house and were climbing into the automobiles in the yard. Marietta Hoag's voice was the last distinctly audible.

"I can't help it," she wailed. "It wasn't my fault anyway. And—and, besides, that Bangs man hadn't any right to say 'twas him I meant. . . . I mean the control meant. It wasn't him at all. . . . I mean I don't believe 'twas. Oh, dear! I *wish* you'd stop askin' questions, Abe Hardin'. *Can't* you stop?"

Galusha and Primmie set out for the Phipps' homestead ahead of its owner, but she caught up with them at the gate.

"He's goin' right up to bed," she said. "Zach will look out for the light to-night."

"And——" asked Galusha, with significant emphasis.

Martha did not reply. She waited until they were in the sitting room and alone, Primmie having been sentenced to go to her own room and to bed. Miss Cash had no desire for bed; her dearest wish was to remain with her mistress and their lodger and unload her burden of conversation.

"My savin' soul!" she began. "My savin' soul! Did you ever in your born days! When that Marietta Hoag—or that Chinee critter—or Cap'n Jeth's ghost's wife—or whoever 'twas talkin' that spirit jabber—when she—them, I mean—give out that a small, dark man was right there in that house, I thought——"

"Primmie, go to bed."

"Yes'm. And when I remembered that Nelse Howard was——"

"Go to bed this minute!"

"Yes'm. But how do you 'spose he's goin' to——"

Miss Phipps conducted her to the foot of the back stairs and, returning, closed each door she passed through behind her. Then she answered her lodger's unspoken question.

"Lulie will go with her father and help him up to his room," she said. "After he is out of the way Nelson can come out and Zach, I suppose, will let him out by the side door."

Galusha smiled faintly. "The poor fellow must have been somewhat disturbed when that—ah—medium person announced that the 'evil influence' was in the house," he observed.

Martha sniffed. "I guess likely we were all disturbed," she said. "Especially those of us who knew. But how did Marietta know? That's what I can't understand. Or did she just guess?"

Before Bangs could answer there was a rap on the windowpane. Martha, going to the door, admitted Nelson Howard himself. The young man's first speech was a question.

"Do you know what became of my hat?" he asked. "Like an idiot I hung my hat and coat in that entry off the dining room when I went in. When I came out just now the hat was gone."

Martha looked troubled.

"It wasn't that cap you wear so much, at the station and everywhere?" she asked. "I hope no one took *that;* they'd know whose 'twas in a minute."

"Yes, that's what I'm afraid of. I . . . Eh? Why, there it is now."

The cap was lying on the couch beside Mr. Bangs' overcoat. Howard picked it up with an air of great relief.

"You brought it over for me, Mr. Bangs, didn't you?" he cried.

"Why—why, yes, I—I did," stammered Galusha. "You see, I——"

The young man broke in enthusiastically. "By jingo, that was clever of you!" he cried. "I was afraid some one had got that cap who would recognize it. Say," he went on, "I owe you about everything to-night, Mr. Bangs. When Marietta gave out her proclamation that the 'small dark man' was in that house I came nearer to believing in her kind of spiritualism than I ever thought I should. I was scared—not on my own account, I hope—but for Lulie and her father. If the old cap'n had found me hiding in that front hall I don't know what he might have done, or tried to do. And I don't know what effect it might have had on him. He was—well, judging from what I could hear, he was in a state that was—that was pretty near to—to——"

While he was hesitating Martha Phipps finished the sentence. "To what they put people in asylums for," she said, emphatically. "He was, there is no doubt about that. It's a mercy he didn't find you, Nelson. And if I were you I wouldn't take any such chances again."

"I shan't, you needn't worry. When Lulie and I meet after this it will be—— Humph! well, I don't know where it will be. Even the graveyard doesn't seem to be safe. But I must go. Tell Lulie I got away safe and sound, thanks to Mr. Bangs here. And tell her to 'phone me to-morrow. I'm anxious about Cap'n Jeth. Sometimes I think it might be just as well if I went straight to him and told him——"

Again Martha interrupted.

"My soul, no!" she exclaimed. "Not now, not till he gets that 'small dark man' notion out of his head."

"I suppose you're right. And Mr. Bangs has set him guessing on that, too. Honestly, Mr. Bangs, you've just about saved—well, if you haven't saved everybody's life you've come pretty near to saving the cap'n's reason, I do believe. How Lulie and I can ever thank you enough I don't know."

Galusha turned red. "Ah—ah—don't—ah—please don't," he stammered. "It was just—ah—a silly idea of mine. On the spur of the moment it came to me that—ah—that the medium person hadn't said *who* the small, dark man was. And as I am rather dark perhaps—and small, certainly— it occurred to me to claim identity. Almost every one else had received some sort of—ah—spirit message and, you see, I didn't wish to be neglected."

"Well, it was the smartest dodge that I ever heard of. By jingo, it was! Say, you don't suppose Cap'n Jeth will take it seriously and begin to get down on *you*, do you?"

Martha looked grave. "I was wonderin' that myself," she said.

Galusha smiled. "Oh, dear no," he said. "I think there

is no danger of that, really. But, Mr. Howard, in regard to that—ah—cap of yours, I . . . Eh? . . . Um . . . Why, dear me, I wonder——"

"Why is it you wonder, Mr. Bangs?" asked Martha, after a moment's wait.

"Why—ah—considering that that cap of Mr. Howard's is one which, so you and he say, he is in the habit of wearing, and that many people have often seen him wear, I was wondering—— Dear me, yes, that might explain."

"Explain what?"

"Why, it occurred to me that as that cap was hanging in the—ah—entry—the little hall off Captain Hallett's dining room—when the people came in, and as the medium person —Miss—ah—bless me, what *is* her name?—as she came in with the rest, it occurred to me that she might have seen the cap and——"

Miss Phipps clapped her hands. "She saw it and knew whose it was," she cried, excitedly. "Of course she did! *That's* how she guessed the small, dark man was in the house. *That's* how 'Little Toddy Blossom,' or whatever her name is, got so smart all at once. Well, well! Of course, of course!"

"It—ah—occurred to me that that might possibly explain," observed Galusha, placidly.

"It does. But, Nelson, what set Marietta and her spirits after you in particular? Has she got any grudge against you?"

"Not that I know of, Martha. She knows I don't take any stock in her kind of spirit messages. I don't think she likes me very well on that account."

"Well, perhaps, that is reason enough. Or perhaps she just happened the first time to mention the small dark man hit or miss and Cap'n Jethro pinned the tag to you; after that she did her best to keep it there. Well, thanks to Mr. Bangs, the cap'n isn't as sure as he was, that's some comfort."

Martha accompanied Nelson to the door. After he had gone and she returned to the sitting room she found her lodger standing, lamp in hand, at the foot of the stairs.

"Goin' to turn in, Mr. Bangs?" she asked. "Goin' to bed, I mean? Father always used to call it turnin' in; it's a salt-water way of sayin' it, just as so many of his expressions were. I guess you must be pretty tired. I know I am. Take it by and large—that is another of father's expressions —we've had an excitin' evenin'."

Galusha admitted the fact. His landlady regarded him with an odd expression.

"Do you know," she said, suddenly, "you are the most surprisin' person I ever met, Mr. Bangs? . . . There! I didn't mean to say that," she added. "I was thinkin' it and it sort of spoke itself, as you might say. I beg your pardon."

"Oh, that's quite all right, quite, Miss Phipps," Galusha assured her. "I have no doubt you are perfectly correct. No doubt I am surprising; at least most people seem to find a peculiar quality in most of my—ah—actions." He smiled his gentle smile, and added, "I presume it must be a part of my profession. In books, you know—in novels—the few I have read—the archæologist or the scientific man or the college professor is always peculiar."

She shook her head. "That isn't just what I meant," she said. "So far as that goes I've generally noticed that folks with little brains are fond of criticizin' those with bigger ones. Part of such criticisms is 'don't understand' and the rest is plain jealousy. But what I meant by callin' you sur-prisin' was—was—— Well," with a half laugh, "I might just as well say it plain. Ever since you've been here, Mr. Bangs, the feelin' has been growin' on me that you were probably the wisest man in the world about some things and the most simple and impractical about others. Over there in Egypt you know everything, I do believe. And yet right down here on Cape Cod you need somebody to keep Ras Beebe and Raish Pulcifer from cheatin' you out of your last cent. That's what I thought. 'Mr. Bangs is wonder-ful,' I said to myself, 'but I'm afraid he isn't practical.' And yet to-night, over there, you were the only practical one amongst us."

Galusha protested. "Oh, no, Miss Phipps," he said. "Dear me, no. My claiming to be the small, dark man was, as I said, merely a silly notion which came to me. I acted on the spur of the moment. It was nothing."

"It was about everything," stoutly. "It was your notion, as you call it, that saved Cap'n Jethro from findin' Nelson Howard in that front hall; and savin' him from that saved us from havin' a crazy man on our hands, I truly believe. And you did it so right on the instant, so matter of fact and common sense. Really, Mr. Bangs, I—I don't know what to say to you."

Galusha smiled. "You said it before," he observed, "when you said you were surprised. I am surprised myself. Dear me, yes."

"Don't! That was a foolish thing for me to say and you mustn't take it the wrong way. And your bringing Nelson's hat over here instead of leavin' it in that entry for more of Marietta's crowd to notice and, ten to one, recognize! We all knew it was hangin' there. I saw Nelson hang it there, myself, when he came in. But did *I* think to take it out of sight? Did *I*—— Why, what is it? What's the matter?"

Her lodger was protesting violently. "Don't, don't, don't, Miss Phipps," he begged. "Please don't! You see, that hat —that cap of Mr. Howard's——"

"Yes, you brought it over here."

"Yes, I—I brought it over. I brought it—but——"

"But what?"

"But I didn't know that I did. I must have been thinking of something else when I went after my things and it is a mercy that I took my own coat. It was only by accident that I took the—ah—young man's cap. I was under the impression that it was my own. I presume my own cap is hanging in the Hallett entry at this moment. . . . Ah— good-night, Miss Phipps. Good night. I have had a very pleasant evening, very pleasant indeed."

CHAPTER VIII

MARTHA PHIPPS and her lodger, to say nothing of Lulie Hallett, were fearful of the effect which the eventful séance might have upon the light keeper. It was with considerable foreboding that Martha called Lulie up on the telephone the next morning. But the news she received in answer to her call was reassuring. Captain Jethro, so Lulie said, was apparently quite himself again, a little tired and a trifle irritable, but otherwise all right.

"The only unusual thing about him," said his daughter, "is that he has not once mentioned the séance or anything that happened there. If it wasn't too ridiculous to be possible I should almost think he had forgotten it."

"Then for the land sakes don't remind him," urged Martha, eagerly. "So long as *he* is willin' not to remember you ought to be. Yes, and thankful," she added.

"I guess likely he hasn't forgotten," she said afterwards, in conversation with her lodger. "I imagine he is a good deal upset in his mind; your bouncin' in and claimin' to be the 'evil influence' put him 'way off his course and he hasn't got his bearin's yet. He's probably tryin' to think his way through the fog and he won't talk till he sees a light, or thinks he sees one. I wish to goodness the light would be so strong that he'd see through Marietta Hoag and all her foolishness, but I'm afraid that's too much to expect."

Her surmise was correct, for a few days later the captain met Galusha on the road leading to the village and, taking the little man by the arm, became confidential.

"Mr. Bangs," he said, "I cal'late you must think it's kind of queer my not sayin' a word to you about what happened t'other night over to the house."

Galusha, who had been thinking of something else and was mentally thousands of miles away—on the banks of the Nile, in fact—regarded him rather vacantly.

"Eh? Oh—um—yes, of course," he stammered. "I beg your pardon."

"No reason why you should beg my pardon. I don't blame you for thinkin' so. It's natural."

"Yes—yes, of course, of course. But I don't know that I quite comprehend. Of what were you speaking, Captain Hallett?"

The captain explained. "Of course you think it's queer that I haven't said a word about what Julia told us," he went on. "Eh? Don't you?"

"What—ah—what Miss Hoag said, you mean?"

"Plague take Marietta!" impatiently. "She wan't nothin' but the go-between. 'Twas my wife that said it. You understand 'twas Julia, my wife, talkin', don't you?"

"Why—ah—why—I suppose——"

"Suppose? Don't you *know* 'twas?"

"Why—ah—no doubt, no doubt."

"Course there ain't any doubt. Well then, Julia said there was a dark man heavin' a sort of evil influence over Lulie."

"She said a *small* dark man, a stranger. And she said he was present among us. So far as I can see I was the only small dark stranger."

"But you ain't an evil influence, are you?"

"Well, I—ah—hope not. Dear me, no!"

"I hope not, too, and I don't believe you are. No, there is some mistake somewheres. 'Twas Nelson Howard she must have meant."

"But, Captain Hallett, Mr. Howard is not small."

"No, and he wan't there that evenin', neither. But I'm bettin' 'twas him she meant just the same. Just the same."

"Do you think that is quite fair to Mr. Howard? If he

isn't small, nor very dark, and if he was not in your house that evening, how——"

"I don't know—I don't know. Anyhow, I don't believe she meant you, Mr. Bangs. She couldn't have."

"But—ah—why not?"

"Because—well, because you couldn't be an evil influence if you tried, you wouldn't know how. *That* much I'll bet on. There, there, don't let's talk no more about it. Julia and me'll have another talk pretty soon and then I'll find out more, maybe."

So that was the end of this portion of the conversation. The light keeper positively refused to mention the subject again. Galusha was left with the uneasy feeling that his brilliant idea of claiming to be the small, dark influence for evil had not been as productive of good results as he had hoped. Certainly it had not in the least shaken the captain's firm belief in his spirit messages, nor had it, apparently, greatly abated his prejudice against young Howard. On the other hand, Lulie found comfort in the fact that in all other respects her father seemed as rational and as keen as he had ever been. The exciting evening with the Hoag spook had worked no lasting harm. For so much she and her friends were grateful.

The autumn gales blew themselves out and blew in their successors, the howling blasts of winter. Winter at Gould's Bluffs, so Galusha Bangs discovered, was no light jest of the weather bureau. His first January no'theaster taught him that. Lying in his bed at one o'clock in the morning, feeling that bed tremble beneath him as the wind gripped the sturdy gables of the old house, while the snow beat in hissing tumult against the panes, and the great breakers raved and roared at the foot of the bluff—this was an experience for Galusha. The gray dawn of the morning brought another, for, although it was no longer snowing, the wind was, if anything, stronger than ever and the seaward view from his bedroom window was a picture of frothing gray and white, of flying spray and leaping waves, and on the landward side the pines were bending and threshing as if they were being torn in pieces. He came downstairs, somewhat nervous and a trifle excited, to find Mr. Bloomer, garbed in oilskins and sou'wester, standing upon the mat just inside the dining room door. Zacheus, it developed, had come over to borrow some coffee, the supply at the light having run short. As Galusha entered, a more than usually savage blast rushed shrieking over the house, threatening, so it seemed to Mr. Bangs, to tear every shingle from the roof.

"Goodness gracious!" exclaimed Galusha. "Dear me, what a terrible storm this is!"

Zacheus regarded him calmly. "Commenced about ten last night," he observed. "Been breezin' on steady ever since. Be quite consider'ble gale if it keeps up."

Mr. Bangs looked at him with amazement.

"If it keeps up!" he repeated. "Isn't it a gale now?"

Zach shook his head.

"Not a reg'lar gale, 'tain't," he said. "Alongside of some gales I've seen this one ain't nothin' but a tops'l breeze. Do you remember the storm the night the *Portland* was lost, Martha?"

Miss Phipps, who had come in from the kitchen with a can of coffee in her hand, shuddered.

"Indeed I do, Zacheus," she said; "don't remind me of it."

"Why, dear me, was it worse than this one?" asked Galusha.

Martha smiled. "It blew the roof off the barn here," she said, "and blew down both chimneys on the house and both over at Cap'n Jeth's. So far as that goes we had plenty of company, for there were nineteen chimneys down along the main road in Wellmouth. And trees—mercy! how the poor trees suffered! East Wellmouth lost thirty-two big silver-leafs and the only two elms it had. Set out over a hundred years ago, those elms were."

"Spray from the breakers flew clear over the top of the bank here," said Zach. "That's some h'ist for spray, hundred and odd feet. I wan't here to see it, myself, but Cap'n Jeth told me."

"You were in a more comfortable place, I hope," observed Galusha.

"Um—we-ell, that's accordin' to what you call comf'table. I was aboard the Hog's Back lightship, that's where I was."

"Dear, dear! Is it possible?"

"Um-hm. Possible enough that I was there, and one spell it looked impossible that I'd ever be anywheres else. Godfreys, what a night that was! Whew! Godfreys domino!"

Primmie, who had also come in from the kitchen, was listening, open-mouthed.

"I bet you that lightship pitched up and down somethin' terrible, didn't it, Zach?" she asked.

Zacheus looked at her solemnly. "Pitched?" he repeated, after a moment's contemplation. "No, no, she didn't pitch none."

"Didn't? Didn't pitch up and down in such a gale's that? And with waves a hundred foot high? What kind of talk's that, Zach Bloomer! How could that lightship help pitchin', I'd like to know?"

Mr. Bloomer adjusted the tin cover on the can in which Martha had put the coffee, then he put the can in the pocket of his slicker.

"We-ll, I tell you, Primmie," he drawled. "You see, we had pretty toler'ble long anchor chains on that craft and when the captain see how 'twas blowin' he let them chains out full length. The wind blowed so strong it lifted the lightship right out of the water up to the ends of them chains and kept her there. Course there was a dreadful sea runnin' underneath us, but we never felt it a mite; that gale was holdin' us up twenty foot clear of it!"

"Zacheus Bloomer, do you mean to say——"

"Um-hm. Twenty foot in the air we was all that night and part of next day. When it slacked off and we settled down again we was leakin' like a sieve; you see, while we was up there that no'thwester had blowed 'most all the copper off the vessel's bottom. Some storm that was, Posy, some storm. . . . Well, so long, all hands. Much obliged for the coffee, Martha."

He tugged his sou'wester tighter on his head, glanced at
Miss Cash's face, where incredulity and indignation were
written large and struggling for expression, turned his head
in Mr. Bangs' direction, winked solemnly, and departed.
The wind obligingly and enthusiastically saved him the
trouble of closing the door.

Galusha was not called upon to endure any such experiences as those described by the veracious Mr. Bloomer
in his record-breaking gale, but during that winter he learned
a little of what New England coast weather could be and
often was. And he learned, also, that that weather was, like
most blusterers, not nearly as savage when met squarely face
to face. He learned to put on layer after layer of garments,
topping off with oilskins, sou'wester and mittens, and tramp
down to the village for the mail or to do the household
errands. He was growing stronger all the time and if the
doctor could have seen him plowing through drifts or
shouldering his way through a driving rain he would have
realized that his patient was certainly obeying the order to
"keep out of doors." Martha Phipps was perfectly certain
that her lodger was keeping out of doors altogether too
much.

"You aren't goin' out to-day, Mr. Bangs, are you?" she
exclaimed. "It's as cold as the North Pole. You'll freeze."

Galusha smiled beneath his cap visor and between the earlaps.

"Oh, no, indeed," he declared. "It's brisk and—ah—
snappy, that's all. A smart walk will do me good. I am
accustomed to walking. In Egypt I walk a *great* deal."

"I don't doubt it; but you don't have much of this sort of
weather in Egypt, if what I've heard is true."

Mr. Bangs' smile broadened. "I fear I shall have to admit
that," he said; "but my—ah—physician told me that a change
would be good for me. And this *is* a change, now isn't it?"

"I should say it was. About as much change as a plate
of ice cream after a cup of hot coffee. Well, if you're bound
to go, do keep walkin' fast. Don't forget that it's down to
zero or thereabouts; don't forget that and wander over to

the old cemetery and kneel down in front of a slate tombstone and freeze to death."

"Oh, I shall be all right, Miss Phipps. Really I shall. Don't worry, I beg of you."

He had begged her not to worry on many other occasions and she had been accustomed to answer him in a manner half joking and half serious. But this time she did not answer at all for a moment, and when she did there was no hint of a joke in her tone.

"No," she said, slowly. "I won't. I couldn't, I guess. Don't seem as if I could carry any more worries just now, any more than I am carryin', I mean."

She sighed as she said it and he looked at her in troubled alarm.

"Oh, dear me!" he exclaimed. "I—I'm so sorry. Sorry that you are worried, I mean. Is there anything I can do to—to—— I should be very glad to help in any way if——"

He was hesitating, trying to say the right thing and very fearful of saying too much, of seeming to be curious concerning her personal affairs, when she interrupted him. She was standing by the kitchen door, with one hand upon the knob, and she spoke without looking at him.

"There is nothin' you or anybody can do," she said. "And there isn't a single bit of use talkin' about it. Trot along and have your walk, Mr. Bangs. And don't pay any attention to what I said. It was just silliness. I get a little nervous, sometimes, but that's no reason for my makin' other people that way. Have a good walk."

He did not have a very good walk and his thoughts while walking were not as closely centered about ancient inscriptions, either Egyptian or East Wellmouthian, as was usually the case upon such excursions. Miss Martha Phipps was worried, she had said so, herself. Yes, and now that he thought of it, she looked worried. She was in trouble of some sort. A dreadful surmise entered his mind. Was it possible that he, his presence in her house, was the cause of her worry? He had been very insistent that she take him as boarder and lodger. The sum he paid each week was ridiculously small. Was it possible that, having consented to the agreement, she had found it a losing one and was too kind-hearted and conscientious to suggest a change? He remembered agreements which he had made, and having made, had hesitated to break, even though they turned out to be decidedly unprofitable and unpleasant. He had often been talked into doing things he did not want to do, like buying the yellow cap at Beebe's store. Perhaps he had talked Miss Phipps into taking him as boarder and lodger and now she was sorry.

By the time Galusha returned from his walk he was in what might be described as a state of mind.

As he entered the Phipps' gate he met some one coming down the path toward it. That some one, it developed, was no less a person than Mr. Horatio Pulcifer. Raish and Galusha had not encountered each other for some time, weeks, in fact, and Mr. Bangs expected the former's greeting to be exuberant and effusive. His shoulders and his spirit were alike shrinking in anticipation.

But Raish did not shout when he saw him, did not even shake hands, to say nothing of thumping the little man upon the back. The broad and rubicund face of East Wellmouth's leading politician and dealer in real estate wore not a grin but a frown, and when he and Galusha came together at the gate he did not speak. Galusha spoke first, which was unusual; very few people meeting Mr. Horatio Pulcifer were afforded the opportunity of speaking first.

"Ah—good-morning, Mr. Pulcifer," said Galusha, endeavoring to open the gate.

"Huh!" grunted Raish, jerking the gate from Mr. Bangs' hand and pushing it somewhat violently into the Bangs' waistcoat. "Mornin'."

"It is a nice—ah—cool day, isn't it?" observed Galusha, backing from the gateway in order to give Horatio egress. Mr. Pulcifer's answer was irrelevant and surprising.

"Say," he demanded, turning truculently upon the speaker, "ain't women hell?"

Galusha was, naturally, somewhat startled.

"I—I beg your pardon?" he stammered.

"I say ain't women hell? Hey? Ain't they, now?"

Galusha rubbed his chin.

"Well," he said, doubtfully, "I presume in—ah—certain instances they—— My experience has been limited, but——"

"Humph! Say, they make me sick, most of 'em. They haven't any more business sense than a hen, the heft of 'em ain't. Go into a deal with their eyes open and then, when it don't turn out to suit 'em, lay down and squeal. Yes, sir, squeal."

"Ah—I see. Yes, yes, of course. Squeal—yes. The—the hens, you mean."

"*Hens?* No, women. They make me sick, I tell you. . . . And now a lot of dum fools are goin' to give 'em the right to vote! Gosh!"

He strode off along the road to the village. Galusha wonderingly gazed after him, shook his head, and then moved slowly up the path to the house. Primmie opened the door for him. Her eyes were snapping.

"Hello, Mr. Bangs!" she said. "I 'most wisht he'd drop down dead and then freeze to death in a snowbank, that's what I wish."

Galusha blinked.

"Why, bless my soul!" he exclaimed. "Of whom are you speaking?"

"That everlastin' Raish Pulcifer. I never did like him, and now if he's comin' around here makin' her cry."

"Eh? Making her cry?"

"Sshh! She'll hear you. Makin' Miss Martha cry. She's up in her room cryin' now, I'll bet you on it. And he's responsible. . . . Yes'm, I'm comin'. Don't say nothin' to her that I told you, will you, Mr. Bangs?"

She hurried away in response to her mistress' hail. Galusha said nothing to Miss Phipps, nor to any one else, but during the rest of that day he did a great deal of thinking. Martha Phipps was worried, she was troubled, she had been crying; according to Primmie Horatio Pulcifer was responsible for her tears. Galusha had never fancied Mr. Pulcifer, now he was conscious of a most extraordinary dislike for the man. He had never disliked any one so much in all his life, he was sure of that. Also he was conscious of a great desire to help Martha in her trouble. Of course there was a certain measure of relief in learning that Pulcifer and not he was responsible for that trouble, but the relief was a small matter in comparison with the desire to help.

He could think of but one way in which Horatio Pulcifer could cause worry for Martha Phipps and that was in connection with some business matter. Certain fragments of conversations occurred to him, certain things she had said to him or to Captain Hallett in his hearing which were of themselves sufficient to warrant the surmise that her trouble was a financial one. He remembered them now, although at the time they had made little impression upon his mind. But Raish Pulcifer's name was not mentioned in any of those conversations; Captain Jethro's had been, but not Raish's. Yet Primmie vowed that the latter had made Miss Martha cry. He determined to seek Primmie and ask for more particulars that very evening.

But Primmie saved him the trouble of seeking her. Miss Phipps and her maid left him alone in the sitting room as soon as supper was over and neither came back. He could hear the murmur of voices in the kitchen, but, although he sat up until ten o'clock, neither Primmie nor her mistress joined him. So he reluctantly went up to his room, but had scarcely reached it when a knock sounded on the door. He opened it, lamp in hand.

"Why, Primmie!" he exclaimed.

Primmie waved both hands in frantic expostulation.

"Sshh! shh! shh!" she breathed. "Don't say nothin'. I don't want her to hear you. *Please* don't let her hear you, Mr. Bangs. And *please* come right downstairs again. I want to talk to you. I've *got* to talk with you."

More bewildered than he had before been, even on that bewildering day, Galusha followed Miss Cash down the stairs, through sitting room and dining room to the kitchen.

Then Primmie put down the lamp, which she had taken from his hand, carefully closed the door behind them, turned to her companion and burst out crying.

"Why—why, Primmie!" exclaimed Galusha. "Oh, dear me! What is it?"

Primmie did not answer. She merely waved her hands up and down and stood there, dripping like a wet umbrella.

"But—my soul, Primmie!" cried Mr. Bangs. "Don't! You—you mustn't, you know."

But Primmie did, nevertheless. Galusha in desperation turned toward the door.

"I'm going to call Miss Phipps," he declared. Primmie, the tears still pouring down her cheeks, seized him by the arm.

"Don't you do it!" she commanded. "Don't you dast to do it! I'll—I'll stop cryin'. I—I'm goin' to if you'll only wait and give me a chance. There! There! See, I'm—I'm stoppin' now."

And, with one tremendous sniff and a violent rub of her hand across her nose, stop she did. But she was still the complete picture of misery.

"Why, what *is* the matter?" demanded Galusha.

Primmie sniffed once more, gulped, and then blurted forth the explanation.

"She—she's canned me," she said.

Galusha looked at her uncomprehendingly. Primmie's equipment of Cape Cod slang and idiom, rather full and complete of itself, had of late been amplified and complicated by a growing acquaintance with the new driver of the grocery cart, a young man of the world who had spent two hectic years in Brockton, where, for a portion of the time, he worked in a shoe factory. But Galusha Bangs, not being a man of the world, was not up in slang; he did not understand.

"What?" he asked.

"I say she's canned me. Miss Martha has, I mean. Oh, ain't it awful!"

"Canned you? Really, I——"

"Yes, yes, yes! Canned me, fired me. Oh, *don't* stand there owlin' at me like that! Can't you see, I—— Oh, please, Mr. Bangs, excuse me for talkin' so. I—I didn't mean to be sassy. I'm just kind of loony, I guess. Please excuse me, Mr. Bangs."

"Yes, yes, Primmie, of course—of course. Don't cry, that's all. But what is this? Do I understand you to say that Miss Phipps has—ah—*discharged* you?"

"Um-hm. That's what she's done. I'm canned. And I don't know where to go and—and I don't want to go any-wheres else. I want to stay here along of her."

She burst into tears again. It was some time before Galusha could calm her sufficiently to get the story of what had happened. When told, flavored with the usual amount of Primmieisms, it amounted to this: Martha had helped her with the supper dishes and then, instead of going into the sitting room, had asked her to sit down as she had something particular to say to her. Primmie obediently sat and her mistress did likewise.

"But she didn't begin to say it right off," said Primmie. "She started four or five times afore she really got a-goin'. She said that what she'd got to say was dreadful unpleasant and was just as hard for her to say as 'twould be for me to hear. And she said I could be sartin' sure she'd never say it if 'twan't absolutely necessary and that she hadn't made up her mind to say it until she'd laid awake night after night tryin' to think of some other way out, but that, try as she could, she didn't see no other way. And so then— so then she said it. Oh, my savin' soul! I declare I never thought——"

"Hush, hush, Primmie. Ah—control yourself, please. You promised not to cry, you know."

"Cry! Well, ain't I tryin' not to cry, for mercy sakes? She was cryin', too, I tell you, afore she finished. If you'd seen the pair of us settin' there bellerin' like a couple of young ones I cal'late you'd a thought so."

"Bellowing? Miss Phipps?"

"Oh, I don't mean bellerin' out loud like a—like a heifer.

I guess likely I was doin' that, but she wan't. She was just
cryin' quiet, you know, but anybody could see how terrible
bad she was feelin'. And then she said it—oh, dear, dear!
How *can* I tell it? How *can* I?"

Galusha groaned, in harassed desperation.

"I don't know," he admitted, "But I—really I wish you
would."

Miss Phipps had, it seemed, told her maidservant that,
owing to the steadily increasing cost of living, of food and
clothes and every item of daily expense, she was finding it
more and more hard to get along. She said her income was
very small and her bills continually growing larger. She
had cut and scrimped in every possible way, hoping against
hope, but at last she had been driven to the point where even
the small wage she was paying Primmie seemed more than
she could afford. Much as she hated to do it, she felt compelled to let the girl go.

"She said she'd help me get another place," said Primmie,
"and that I could stay here until I did get one, and all sorts
of things like that. I told her I didn't want no other place
and I didn't care a bit about the wages. I said I'd rather
work here without a cent of wages. She said no, she
wouldn't let me do that. If she couldn't pay me I couldn't
work here. I said I could and I should and she said I
couldn't and shouldn't. And—and we both cried and—and
that's the way it ended. And that's why I come to you, Mr.
Bangs. I *can't* go away and leave her. I *can't*, Mr. Bangs.
She can't keep this whole house a-goin' without somebody
to help. I've *got* to stay. You make her keep me, Mr.
Bangs. I don't want no pay for it. I never was no hand
to care for money, anyhow. Pa used to say I wan't. None
of our folks was. Matter of that, we never had none to care
for. But you make her keep me, Mr. Bangs."

She began to sob once more. Poor Galusha was very
much distressed. The cause of Martha Phipps' worry was
plain enough now. And her financial stress must be very
keen indeed to cause her to take such drastic action as the
discharge of Primmie the faithful.

"You'll make her keep me, won't you, Mr. Bangs?" pleaded Primmie, once more.

Galusha rubbed his chin. "Dear me," he said, perplexedly, "I—— Well, I shall be glad to do all I can, of course, but how I can make her keep you when she has made up her mind not to, I—really, I don't see. You don't think, do you," he added, "that my being here is in any way responsible for a portion of Miss Phipps' financial trouble? You don't think it might be—ah—easier for her if I was to—ah—go?"

Primmie shook her head. "Oh, no, no," she declared, with decision. "You ain't a mite of bother, Mr. Bangs. I've heard Miss Martha say more'n a dozen times what a nice man you was and how easy 'twas to provide for you. She likes you, Miss Martha does, and I do, too. Even when we thought you was an undertaker huntin' 'round for remains we liked you just the same."

Galusha could not help feeling a certain satisfaction in this whole-hearted declaration. It was pleasant to learn that he was liked and that his hostess considered him a nice man.

"Thank you, Primmie," he said. "But what I meant was —was—— Well, I pay what seems to me a ridiculously small sum for board and lodging. I begged to be allowed to pay more, but Miss Phipps wouldn't permit it. Now I am sure she must be losing money in the transaction and if I were to go—ah—elsewhere perhaps it might be—ah—easier for her. Candidly, don't you think so, Primmie?"

Miss Cash appeared to consider. Then she shook her head again. "No," she said, "I don't. You pay your board and I've heard her say more'n once that she felt as if you was payin' too much. No, 'tain't that. It's more'n that. It ain't anything to do really with you or me, Mr. Bangs. Miss Martha's lost some money somehow, I believe. She ain't got enough to get along on, 'cause she told me she hadn't. Now, she used to have and I believe she's lost some of it somewheres. And I believe that——"

Galusha felt it his duty to interrupt.

"Primmie," he continued, "you mustn't tell me anything which Miss Phipps wouldn't wish told. I wouldn't for the world have you think that I am unduly curious concerning her personal affairs. If there is any trait which I—ah—detest above others it is that of unwarranted curiosity concerning the—ah—private affairs of one's acquaintances. I . . . Why do you look at me like that? Were you about to speak?"

Primmie was staring at him in what seemed to be awe-stricken admiration. She drew a long breath.

"My Lord of Isrul!" she exclaimed, fervently, "I never heard anybody string talk along the way you can in all my born days, Mr. Bangs. I bet you've said as many as seven words already that I never heard afore, never heard ary one of 'em, I ain't. Education's wonderful, ain't it? Pa used to say 'twas, but all he had he had picked up off fishin' and clammin' and cranberrin' and around. All our family had a kind of picked-up education, seemed so."

"Yes, yes, Primmie, but——"

"But why don't I mind my own business and stick to what I was goin' to say, you mean? All right, I will. I was goin' to say that I believe Miss Martha's lost money some-how and I believe that dressed-up stuffed image of a Raish Pulcifer is responsible for her losin' it, that's what I believe."

"Mr. Pulcifer! Why, Primmie, why do you say that? What proof have you?"

"Ain't got no proof. If folks could get proof on Raish Pulcifer he'd have been in jail long ago. Zach Bloomer said that only the other day. But a body can guess, can't they, even if they ain't got proof, and that's what I'm doin' —guessin'. Every once in a while Miss Martha goes up to the village to see this Pulcifer thing, don't she? Yes, she does. Went up twice inside of a fortni't that I know of. Does she go 'cause she likes him? I cal'late she don't. She likes him about the way I do and I ain't got no more use for him than a hen has for a toothbrush. And t'other day she sent for him and asked him to come here and see her. How do I know she did? 'Cause she telephoned him and I heard her doin' it, that's how. And he didn't want to come and she just begged him to, said she would try not to bother

him again if he would come that once. And he came and
after he went away she cried, same as I told you she did."

"But, Primmie, all that may be and yet Mr. Pulcifer's
visit may have no connection with Miss Martha's monetary
trouble."

"I want to know! Well, if that's so, why was she and him
talkin' so hard when he was here this afternoon? And why
was she askin' him to please see if he couldn't get some sort
of an offer? I heard her ask that."

"Offer for what?"

"Search me! For somethin' she wanted to sell, I presume
likely. And he says to her, 'No, I can't,' he says. 'I've told
you so a dozen times. If I could get anybody to buy I'd
sell my own, wouldn't I? You bet your life I would!' And
she waited a minute and then she says, kind of low and more
as if she was talkin' to herself than to him, 'What *shall* I
do?' she says. And he heard her and says he—I'd like to
have chopped his head off with the kindlin' hatchet when I
heard him say it—says he, '*I* don't know. How do you s'pose
I know what you'll do? I don't know what I'll do, myself,
do I?' And she answered right off, and kind of sharp, 'You
was sure enough what was goin' to be done when you got
father into this thing.' And he just swore and stomped out
of the house. So *that* sounds as if he had somethin' to do
with it, don't it?"

Galusha was obliged to admit that it did so sound. And
when he remembered Mr. Pulcifer's remark at the gate, that
concerning women and business, the evidence was still more
convincing. He did not tell Primmie that he was convinced,
however. He swore her to secrecy, made her promise that
she would tell no one else what she had told him or even that
she had told him, and in return promised to do what he could
to bring about her retention in the Phipps' home.

"Although, as I said, Primmie," he added, "I'm sure I
can't at present see what I can do."

Another person might have found little encouragement in
this, but Primmie apparently found a good deal.

"You'll see a way, I'll bet you you will, Mr. Bangs," she

declared. "Anybody that's been through the kind of times you have, livin' along with critters that steal the shirt off your back, ain't goin' to let a blowed-up gas balloon like Raish Pulcifer stump you. My savin' soul, no!"

Mr. Bangs smiled faintly.

"The shirt wasn't on my back when it was stolen," he said.

Primmie sniffed. "It didn't have no chance to be," she declared. "That camel thing got it onto *his* back first. But, anyhow, I feel better. I think now we're goin' to come out all right, Miss Martha and me. I don't know why I feel so, but I do."

Galusha was by no means as confident. He went back to his room and to bed, but it was long before he fell asleep. Just why the thought of Martha Phipps' trouble should trouble him so greatly he still did not understand, exactly. Of course he was always sorry for any one in trouble, and would have gone far out of his way to help such a person, had the latter appealed to him. But Martha had not appealed to him; as a matter of fact, it was evident that she was trying to keep knowledge of her difficulty from him and every one else. Plainly it was not his business at all. And yet he was filled with an intense desire, even a determination, to make it his business. He could not understand why, but he wasted no time trying to understand. The determination to help was strong when at last he did fall asleep and it was just as strong when he awoke the next morning.

CHAPTER IX

H E endeavored, while dressing, to map out a plan of campaign, but the map was but a meaningless whirligig of lines leading nowhere when Primmie called from the foot of the stairs that breakfast was ready. During breakfast he was more absent-minded than usual, which is saying a good deal, and Martha herself was far from communicative. After the meal he was putting on his hat and coat preparatory to going out for his usual walk when Primmie came hurrying through the hall.

"She wants you," said Primmie, mysteriously, her eyes shining with excitement. "She wants to see you in the settin' room. Come on, come on, Mr. Bangs! What are you waitin' for?"

As a general rule Galusha's thoughts started upon the morning ramble some little time before he did and recalling them was a rather slow and patience-taxing process. In this case, however, they were already in the sitting room with Martha Phipps and so had a shorter road home. But they came slowly enough, for all that.

"Eh?" queried Galusha, peering out between the earlaps of his cap. "Eh? What did you say, Primmie?"

"I say Miss Martha wants to see you a minute. She's in there a-waitin'. I bet you she's goin' to tell you about it. Hurry! hurry!"

"Tell me? . . . About what?"

"Why, about what 'tis that's worryin' her so. About that Raish Pulcifer and all the rest of it. . . . Oh, my Lord of Isrul! Don't you understand *now?* Oh, Mr. Bangs, won't you *please* wake up?"

But Galusha was beginning to understand.

"Dear me! Dear me!" he exclaimed, nervously. "Do you think that—— Did she say she wished to see me, Primmie?"

"Ain't I been tellin' you she did? Now you talk right up to her, Mr. Bangs. You tell her I don't want no wages. Tell her I'll stay right along same as ever and—— You *tell* her, Mr. Bangs."

Martha was standing by the stove in the sitting room when her lodger entered. She turned to greet him.

"I don't know as I'm doin' right to keep you from your walk, Mr. Bangs," she said. "And I won't keep you very long. But I did want to talk with you for just a minute or two. I wanted to ask your advice about—about a business matter."

Now this was very funny indeed. It would have been hard to find a richer joke than the idea of consulting Galusha Bangs concerning a matter of business. But both parties to this consultation were too serious to see the joke at that moment.

Galusha nodded solemnly. He faltered something about being highly honored and only too glad to be of service. His landlady thanked him.

"Yes," she said, "I knew you would be. And, as I say, I won't keep you very long. Sit down, Mr. Bangs. Oh, not in that straight up-and-down thing. Here, in the rocker."

Galusha lifted himself from the edge of the straight-backed chair upon which he had perched and sat upon the edge of the rocking-chair instead. Martha looked at him sitting there, his collar turned up, his cap brim and earlaps covering two thirds of his face and his spectacles at least half of the remaining third, his mittened hands twitching nervously in his lap, and, in spite of her feelings, could not help smiling. But it was a fleeting smile.

"Take off your things, Mr. Bangs," she said. "You'll roast alive if you don't. It's warm in here. Primmie forgot and left the dampers open and the stove was pretty nearly red-hot when I came in just now. Yes, take off your over-coat and cap, and those mittens, for mercy sakes."

Galusha declared that he didn't mind the mittens and the rest, but she insisted and he hastily divested himself of his wrappings, dropping them upon the floor as the most convenient repository and being greatly fussed when Miss Phipps picked them up and laid them on the table.

"I—I beg your pardon," he stammered. "Really, I *don't* know why I am so thoughtless. I—I should be—ah—hanged or something, I think. Then perhaps I wouldn't do it again."

Martha shook her head. "You probably wouldn't in that case," she said. "Now, Mr. Bangs, I'm going to try to get at that matter I wanted to ask your opinion about. Do you know anything about stocks—stockmarket stocks, I mean?"

Her lodger looked rather bewildered.

"Dear me, no; not a thing," he declared.

She did not look greatly disappointed.

"I didn't suppose you did," she said. "You—well, you don't look like a man who would know much about such things. And from what I've seen of you, goodness knows, you don't *act* like one! Perhaps I shouldn't say that," she added, hastily. "I didn't mean it just as it sounded."

"Oh, that's all right, that's all right, Miss Phipps. I know I am a—ah—donkey in most matters."

"You're a long way from bein' a donkey, Mr. Bangs. And I didn't say you were, of course. But—oh, well, never mind that. So you don't know anything about stocks and investments and such?"

"No, I don't. I am awfully sorry. But—but, you see, all that sort of thing is so very distasteful to me. It bores me —ah—dreadfully. And so I—I dodge it whenever I can."

Martha sighed. "Some of the rest of us would like to dodge it, too," she said, "if we only could. And yet——" she paused and regarded him with the odd expression she had worn more than once when he puzzled her—"and yet I —I just can't make you out, Mr. Bangs. You say you don't know anything about money and managin' money, and yet those Egypt trips of yours must cost a lot of money. And somebody must manage them. *Somebody* must 'tend to payin' the bills and the wages and all. Who does that?"

Galusha smiled. "Why, I do," he admitted, "after a fashion. But it is a very poor fashion. I almost never—I think I may safely say never come in from one of those trips without having exceeded the—ah—estimate of expenses. I always exceed it more or less—generally more."

He smiled again. She looked more puzzled than ever.

"But some one has to pay the extra, don't they?" she asked. "Who does pay it, the museum people?"

"Why—ah—no, not exactly. It is—ah—ah—generally provided. But," he added, rather hastily, as if afraid she might ask more questions along this line, "if I might make a suggestion, Miss Martha—Miss Phipps, I mean——"

"Plain Martha will do well enough. I think you're the only one in East Wellmouth that calls me anything else. Of course you can make a suggestion. Go ahead."

"Well—ah—well, Miss Phipps—ah—Miss Martha, since you permit me to call you so. . . . What is it?"

"Oh, nothin', nothin'. I was goin' to say that the 'Miss' wasn't necessary, but never mind. Go on."

"Well—ah—Mar—ah—Miss Martha, I was about to suggest that you tell me what you intended telling me. I am very anxious to help—ah—even if I can't, you know. Only I beg of you not to think I am actuated by idle curiosity."

She shrugged her shoulders.

"Even if you were I don't know that I shouldn't want to tell you, just the same," she observed. "The fact is I've just *got* to talk this over with some one. Mr. Bangs, I am so worried I don't know what to do. It is a money matter, of course, that's worryin' me, an investment father made a little while before he died. Mr. Bangs, I don't suppose it's likely that you ever heard of the Wellmouth Development Company? No, of course you haven't."

And yet, as she looked into her lodger's face, she was surprised at its expression.

"Why, you never have heard of it, have you?" she demanded.

Galusha stroked his chin. "That day in the cemetery," he murmured. "That day when I was—ah—behind the tomb and heard Captain Hallett and Mr. Pulcifer speaking. I may be mistaken, but it seems to me that they mentioned the name of—ah—ah——"

"The Development Company? Of course they did and you told me so when you got home. I remember now. Well, Cap'n Jeth and Raish were both mixed up in it along with father. Yes, and Doctor Powers and a lot more, though not so much. Raish, of course, was at the back of it in the beginnin'. He got 'em all in it, got himself into it, as far as that goes. You see, it was this way."

She told the story of the Wellmouth Development Company. It—the story—began when the Eagle Fish Freezing Company of Denboro, a concern then running and operating one large cold storage plant in that village, were looking about for a favorable spot upon which to build a second. The spot which appealed to their mind to purchase was the property at the mouth of Skoonic Creek in East Wellmouth.

"It's a real pretty place," said Martha, "one of the prettiest spots alongshore, and the view from the top of the bluff there is just lovely. You can see miles and miles out to sea and all up and down the shore—and back over the village, for that matter. But, come to think of it, you know the place, Mr. Bangs. It's only a little way from the old Baptist buryin' ground."

Galusha nodded. "Isn't it where my—ah—late lamented hat set sail?" he asked.

"Why, of course it is. Just there. Well, the Eagle Fish folks made their plans to buy all that property, the hills on both sides, and the low land down by the creek. It was just the place for 'em, you see. And they were quietly makin' arrangements to pick up the different parcels of land from the owners here and there, when Raish Pulcifer got wind of it. There's precious little goin' on down this part of the Cape that Raish doesn't get wind of, particularly if it's somebody else's secret. He's got a reg'lar pig's nose for rootin' up other people's private concerns. Well, Raish found out what the Eagle Company was up to and he started bein' up to somethin' himself."

Mr. Pulcifer, so Miss Phipps went on to say, conceived the idea of buying the Skoonic Creek property before the Eagle Company could do so. The principal difficulty was that just then his own limited capital was tied up in various ways and he lacked ready money. So, being obliged to borrow, he sought out Captain Hallett, got the shrewd old light keeper's cupidity aroused—not a very difficult task at any time—and Captain Jethro agreed to help finance the deal.

"It didn't need a whole lot of real money," explained Martha. "Most folks that owned that land had owned it for mercy knows how long and had done nothin' but pay taxes on it, so they were glad enough to sell for somethin' down to bind what Raish and Jethro called 'options.' Anyhow, when the Eagle people finally started in to put their grand plan into workin', they bumped bows on into a shoal, at least that's the way father used to tell about it. They found that all that Skoonic Creek land was in the hands of Raish Pulcifer and Cap'n Jeth Hallett; those two either owned it outright or had options where they didn't own."

At first the Eagle Company declined to have anything to do with the new owners. They declared the whole affair off, so far as the Skoonic Creek location was concerned, and announced their intention of going elsewhere. But there was no sufficiently attractive "elsewhere" to go. There followed much proposing and counter-proposing and, at last, an entirely new deal. A new corporation was formed, its name The Wellmouth Development Company.

"I don't know a great deal about it," confessed Martha, "that is, not about the reasons for it and all, but, as near as I can make out, Raish and Jethro wouldn't sell outright to the Eagle Company, but wanted to come in on the profits from the cold storage business, which were pretty big sometimes. And they couldn't get into the reg'lar Eagle Fish Freezing Company, the old one. So they and the Eagle folks together undertook to form this new thing, the Development Company, the name meanin' nothin' or a whole lot, 'cordin' to how the development developed, I presume likely. The capital stock—I know all this because Cap'n Jethro and father used to talk it over so much between 'em and Cap'n Jeth and I have talked so much since—was fifty thousand. An awful lot of money, isn't it, Mr. Bangs?"

Her tone was awe-stricken as she mentioned the amount. Galusha gravely admitted that it was an "awful lot of money." All sums were awful to him; he would have agreed if the Wellmouth Development Company had been capitalized from one thousand to a million. Miss Phipps went on.

"They put out the stock somethin' like this: The Eagle folks took pretty near half, somewhere around twelve hundred shares, I think they had. And Raish he took five hundred shares, and Cap'n Jeth four hundred, and father—after listenin' to Jethro and Raish talk about dividends and profit sharin' and such till, as he said, the tar on his top riggin' began to melt, he drew out money from the savin's bank and sold some other bonds and stocks he had and went in for two hundred and fifty shares. Twenty dollars a share it was; did I tell you that? Yes, five thousand dollars father put into that Development Company. It seemed like a lot even then; but, my soul and body, *what* a lot it seems to me now!"

She paused for an instant, then sighed, and continued.

"If you've figured this all out in your head, Mr. Bangs," she said, "which I suppose you haven't——?"

Galusha, surprised by the direct question, started, colored, and guiltily admitted the correctness of her supposition.

"I—I haven't," he faltered. "Dear me, no. In fact I—ah—doubt if I am capable of doing such a thing."

"Well, never mind, you don't have to. What it amounted to was that the Eagle folks had twelve hundred shares and Raish and Jeth and father had eleven hundred and fifty together. You see, neither side would let the other have more'n half, or even quite half, because then whichever had it could control things. So the remainin' one hundred and fifty shares was sold around Wellmouth and Trumet. Doctor Powers has a few shares and Eben Taylor's got some, and so have lots of folks, scattered around here. You see, all hands were anxious to get in, it looked like a real good investment.

" 'But,' says father—right here in this very room I heard him say it one night—'it's that one hundred and fifty shares that worry me. If the Eagle crowd ever *could* buy up those shares they would control, after all, and freeze us out. Freezin' is their business, anyhow,' he said, and laughed that big laugh of his. Seems as if I could hear him laugh now. Ah, hum! . . . But there, let's get under way again or you'll go to sleep before the ship makes port. I declare, that was father's word, too, I'm always quotin' him. . . . Let me see. . . . Oh, yes. . . . When father said that about the one hundred and fifty shares controllin' Cap'n Jethro looked at Raish and Raish looked at him. Then Raish laughed, too, only his laugh isn't much like father's.

" '*I* got those extra shares taken up,' he said, 'and I was particular who took 'em. There's mighty few of those shares will be sold unless I say the word. Most of the folks that bought those shares are under consider'ble obligation to me.' Just what he meant by that I don't know, of course, but I can guess. Raish makes it a point to have people under what he calls 'obligations' to him. It comes in handy for him, in politics and other ways, to have 'em that way. He lends money and holds mortgages and all that, and that's where the obligations come in. . . . Well, anyhow, that's what he said and, although father didn't look any too happy at the time and wouldn't talk about it afterward, it seemed to settle the objection about the hundred and fifty shares. So the new company got under way, the stockholders paid their money in, old Cap'n Ebenezer Thomas of Denboro was made president and Raish Pulcifer was vice president and Judge Daniel Seaver of Wellmouth Centre was secretary and treasurer. The Judge was Wellmouth Centre's biggest gun, rich—at least, that's what everybody thought then—

and pompous and dignified and straight-backed as an old-fashioned church pew.

"Well, I'm pretty near to the end, although it may not seem that way. For the first few months all hands were talkin' about what great things the Wellmouth Development Company was goin' to do. Then Judge Seaver gave 'em somethin' else to talk about. He shot himself one night, and they found him dead and all alone in the sittin' room of his big house. And when they came to look over his papers and affairs they found that, instead of bein' rich, he hadn't a cent in the world. He had lost all his own money gamblin' in stocks, and, not only that, but he'd lost all that other folks had given him to take care of. He was treasurer of the Eagle Fish Freezin' Company and he'd stolen there until that company had to fail. And, bein' secretary and treasurer of the Wellmouth Development Company, he had sent the fifty thousand its stockholders paid in after the rest of his stealin's. All there was left of that new Development Company was the land over here by Skoonic Creek. He couldn't steal that very well, although, when you think of the stealin' he did do, it's a wonder he hadn't tried to carry it off by the wheelbarrow load.

"It isn't worth while my tellin' you all the hullabaloo that came after the smash. It would take too long and I don't know the ins and outs of it, anyway. But the way it stands now is this: The Eagle Fish Freezin' Company is out of business. Their factory is run now by another concern altogether. The Wellmouth Development Company is still alive—at least it's supposed to be, but nobody but a doctor could tell it wasn't dead. The Denboro Trust Company has the Eagle Company's twelve hundred shares—I don't know how it got 'em; a long snarled-up tangle of loans, and security for loans, and I don't know what—and the rest of us have got ours. All that's back of those shares—all that the Development Company owns—is that Skoonic Creek property and that is goin' to be worth a lot some day—maybe. But I guess likely the some day will be a long, long time after *my* day. There, Mr. Bangs, that's the story of the

Wellmouth Development Company. And I presume likely you're wonderin' why I tell it to you."

Galusha, who had been faithfully endeavoring to grasp the details of his hostess' narrative, passed a hand in bewildered fashion across his forehead. He murmured that the story was—ah—very interesting, very interesting indeed —yes. Martha smiled faintly.

"I'm glad you think so," she said. "It is interestin' enough to some of us here in Wellmouth, those of us who have our money tied up in it, but I shouldn't think a stranger would find much in it to amuse him. But, you see, Mr. Bangs, I didn't tell it to amuse you. I told it because—because—well, because, I—I wondered if in any way you knew, or could find out, how I could sell my two hundred and fifty shares. You see, I—I've *got* to sell 'em. At least, I've got to get more money somehow or—or give up this house. And I can't tell you what it would mean to me to do that."

Galusha murmured something, something meant to be sympathetic. Miss Phipps' evident distress and mental agitation moved him extraordinarily. He wanted to say many things, reassuring things, but he could not at the moment think of any. The best he could do was to stammer a hope that she would not be obliged to sell the house.

She shook her head. "I'm afraid I shall," she said. "I don't see how I can possibly keep it much longer. When father died he left me, so he thought, with enough income to get along on. It wasn't much—fact is, it was mighty little—but we could and did get along on it, Primmie and I, without touchin' my principal. But then came the war and ever since livin' costs have been goin' up and up and up. Now my income is the same as it was, but what it will buy is less than half. It doesn't cost much to live down here, but I'm afraid it costs more than I can afford. If I begin to take away from my principal I'll have to keep on doin' it and pretty soon that will be all gone. After that—well, I don't want to look any further than that. I shouldn't starve, I presume likely; while I've got hands I can work and I'd manage to keep alive, if that was all. But it isn't all. I'd like to keep on livin' in my own home. And I can't do that, Mr. Bangs. I can't do that, as things are now. I must either get some more money somehow, or sell this house, one or the other."

Galusha leaned eagerly forward. He had been waiting for an excuse and now he believed he saw one.

"Oh, Miss Phipps," he cried, "I—I think I can arrange that. I do indeed. You see, I have—ah—more money than I need. I seldom spend my money, you know, and——"

She interrupted him and her tone was rather sharp.

"Don't, Mr. Bangs," she said. "Don't say any more. If you've got the idea that I'm hintin' for you to *lend* me money—you or anybody else—you never was more mistaken in your life. Or ever will be."

Galusha turned red. "I beg your pardon," he faltered. "Of course I know you were not hinting, Miss Martha. I— I didn't dream of such a thing. It was merely a thought of my own. You see, it would be such a favor to me if you would permit me to—to——"

"Don't."

"But, Miss Phipps, it would be doing me such a *great* favor. Really, it would."

He was so very much in earnest that, in spite of her own stress of mind, she could not help smiling.

"A great favor to help you get rid of your money?" she asked. "You havin' such a tremendous lot of it, I presume likely."

"Yes—ah—yes, that's it, that's it."

Her smile broadened. "And 'twas because you were so dreadfully rich that you came here to East Wellmouth to live, I suppose. Mr. Bangs, you're the kindest, best-hearted man that ever stepped, I do believe, but truly I doubt if you know whether you're worth ten dollars or ten hundred. And it doesn't make the least difference, so far as I am concerned. I'll never borrow money while I'm alive and I'll try to keep enough one side to bury me after I'm dead. So don't say any more about lendin'. That's settled."

Galusha reluctantly realized that it was. He tried a new idea.

"I fear," he stammered, "that my being here may have been a contributory cause to your—ah—difficulties. Dear me, yes! I have realized since the beginning that the amount I pay you is ridiculously small."

"*What?* The board you pay *small?* Rubbish! You pay me altogether too much and what I give you to eat isn't worth half of it. But there, I didn't mean to go into all this at all. What I told you all this long rigmarole for was to see if you could think of any way for me to turn those Development Company shares of mine into money. Not what father paid for them, of course, or even half of it. But *some* money at least. If I thought they weren't worth anything I shouldn't think of tryin' to sell 'em. I don't want to cheat—or steal. But they tell me they are worth somethin', maybe will be worth quite a good deal some day and I must wait, that's all. But, you see, that's what I can't do —wait."

She had been, she said, to every one she could think of, to Pulcifer, who would not give her any encouragement, declaring that he was "stuck" worse than she was and was only hoping some one might make a bid for his holdings; to Captain Jethro, who, relying as usual upon his revelations from the beyond, blandly told her to wait as he was waiting. It had been communicated to him that he was to sell his own shares at a profit; if she waited she might do likewise. The president of the Denboro Trust Company had been very kind, but his counsel was not too encouraging. The Development shares were nonsalable at the present time, he said, but that did not mean that they were valueless. The Skoonic Creek property was good. Shore land on the Cape was becoming more valuable every year. Some time—perhaps ten years from now—she might——

"And where will I be in ten years?" asked Martha, sadly. "Goodness knows, Mr. Bangs, I don't. I tried to get the Trust Company man to take my shares at almost any price and do the waitin' for me, but he didn't see it that way.

Said the bank was goin' to hold on to what it had, but it certainly didn't want any more. So there I am. . . . And yet, and yet if I *could* sell—if I *could* get two thousand dollars, yes, or even fifteen hundred just now, it might tide me over until the cost of livin' comes down. And everybody says they *are* comin' down. Mr. Bangs, can you see any way out for me? Can you think of any one who would know about—— Oh, my soul and body! Look *out!*"

She sprang to her feet with a little scream. Her lodger's rocking-chair, with its occupant, had suddenly tilted over backward. Fortunately his proximity to the wall had prevented a complete overturn, but there sat Galusha, the back of the chair against the wall and his knees elevated at a very acute angle. The alarming part of it was that he made no effort to regain his equilibrium, but remained in the unusual, not to say undignified, posture.

"What *is* the matter?" demanded Miss Phipps, seizing him by the arm and pulling him forward. "What was it? What happened?"

Galusha's face was beaming. His eyes shone with excitement.

"It—it struck me at that moment," he cried. "At that very moment."

"Struck you?" Miss Phipps looked about the room. "What struck you? Where? Are you hurt?"

Mr. Bangs' beaming smile broadened.

"I mean the idea struck me," he declared. "Dear me, how odd that it didn't do so before. Yes, he is exactly the right person. Exactly. Oh, dear me, this is *very* good!"

Martha said afterward that she never in her life felt more like shaking a person.

"What do you mean?" she demanded. "What was it that struck you?"

"Why, Cousin Gussie," announced Galusha, happily. "Don't you see? He will be *exactly* the one."

CHAPTER X

WHEN, at last—and it took some time—Martha Phipps was actually convinced that her lodger's "Cousin Gussie" was no less a person than the senior partner of the famous banking firm of Cabot, Bancroft and Cabot, she was almost as excited as he.

"Cabot, Bancroft and Cabot," she repeated. "Why, everybody knows about them! They are the biggest bankers in New England. I have heard father say so ever so many times. And this Mr. Cabot, is he really your cousin?"

Galusha nodded. "Oh, yes," he said. "He is my cousin—really he is. I have always called him Cousin Gussie; that is," he added, "except when I worked for him, of course. Then he didn't like to have me."

"Worked for him?"

"Yes, in his office, in the—ah—banking house, you know."

"Do you mean to say you used to work for Cabot, Bancroft and Cabot? Were you a banker?"

Galusha shook his head. "No," he said. "Dear me, no! But once I tried to be."

"Oh! And you gave it up?"

"*I* was given up—as a bad job. If you don't mind," he added, apologetically, "I'd rather not talk about that. I've gotten over it a long while ago, or I thought I had, but for a time I—I felt very badly—ah—ungrateful, you know."

Martha didn't know, nor did she in the least understand, but she did not, of course, press the subject.

"Why, I can hardly believe it," she said. "That about your bein' that Mr. Cabot's cousin, I mean. But of course I do believe it, if you say so, Mr. Bangs. And you think he would tell me what to do with this Development stock of mine, whether it is worth anything or not? He would know, if anybody did, that's a fact."

Galusha nodded assent.

"He knows all about everything," he declared; "everything of that kind, I mean. He is used to making all sorts of—ah—investments for people, and taking care of their money, and all that sort of thing. Why," he added, as a final clincher, "he takes care of all my money, really, he does."

Miss Phipps laughed.

"And that I suppose is enough to keep one man busy," she observed.

Galusha was too much in earnest to notice the sarcasm.

"I'm sure it must be," he said. "I never could do it myself."

"I can believe that without any trouble. Now what is your idea, Mr. Bangs; to write to your cousin, tell him everything I've told you, and then ask his advice? Is that it?"

That was not exactly it, apparently. Galusha thought that perhaps he might go to Boston forthwith, on the very next train, and consult Cousin Gussie in person. But Martha did not think this advisable.

"I certainly shouldn't put you to all that trouble," she said. "No, I shouldn't, so please don't let's waste time arguin' about it. And, besides, I think a letter would be a great deal better."

Galusha said that a letter was so slow.

"Maybe so, but it is sure. Truly now, Mr. Bangs, do you believe if you went to your cousin that you could tell him this Development Company yarn without gettin' it all tangled up? I doubt if you could."

He reflected for a moment, and then ruefully shook his head.

"I'm afraid you are right," he admitted. "I presume I could learn it—ah—by rote, perhaps, but I doubt if ever I could understand it thoroughly."

"Well, never mind. My plan would be to have you write your cousin a letter givin' him all the particulars. I'll help you write the letter, if you'll let me. And we'll ask him to write right back and tell us two things: Number One—Is the Development stock worth anything, and what? Number Two—If it is worth anything, can he sell it for that? What do you think of that idea?"

Naturally, Galusha thought it a wonderful idea. He was very enthusiastic about it.

"Why, Miss Phipps—Miss Martha, I mean," he declared, "I really think we—ah—may consider your troubles almost at an end. I shouldn't be in the least surprised if Cousin Gussie bought that stock of yours himself."

Martha smiled, faintly. "I should," she said, "very much surprised. But perhaps he may know some one who will buy it at some price or other. And, no matter whether they do or not, I am ever and ever so much obliged to you, Mr. Bangs, for all your patience and sympathy."

And, in spite of her professed pessimism she could not help feeling a bit more hopeful, even sharing a bit of her lodger's confidence. And so when Primmie, in tears, came again that afternoon to beg to be retained in service, Martha consented to try to maintain the present arrangement for a few weeks more, at least.

"Although the dear land knows I shouldn't, Primmie," she said. "It's just postponin' what is almost sure to come, and that isn't right for either of us."

Primmie's grin extended from ear to ear.

"You bet you it's right for one of us, Miss Martha," she declared. "And you ain't the one, neither. My Lord of Isrul, if I don't feel some better'n I did when I come into this room! Whew! My savin' soul! Zach Bloomer he says to me this mornin'. 'What's the matter, Posy?' he says. 'Seems to me you look sort of wilted lately. You better brace up,' he says, 'or folks'll be callin' you a faded flower.' 'Well,' says I, 'I may be faded, but there's one old p'ison ivy around here that's fresh enough to make up.' Oh, I squashed *him* all righty, but I never took no comfort out of doin' it.

I ain't took no comfort for the last two, three days. But now—— Whew!"

The letter to Cousin Gussie was written that very afternoon. Mr. Bangs wrote it, with helpful suggestions, many of them, from Miss Phipps. At Martha's suggestion the envelope was marked "Personal."

"I suppose it is foolish of me," she said, "but somehow I hate to have my affairs talked all over that office. Even when I was a little girl, and things went wrong in school, I used to save up my cryin' until I got home. I'm the same now. This Development Company milk is spilled, and, whether any of it can be saved or not, there is no use callin' a crowd to look at the puddle. If your cousin thinks it's necessary to tell other Boston folks, I presume he will, but *we* won't tell anybody but him."

Galusha hoped to receive an answer the following day, but none came. Nor did it come the next day, nor the next. That week passed and no reply came from Cousin Gussie. Galusha began to worry a little, but Miss Phipps did not.

"Perhaps he's away for a day or two, sick or somethin'," she suggested. "Perhaps he's lookin' up some facts about the Development Company. Perhaps he hasn't had time to read the letter at all yet. Mercy me, you mustn't expect as busy a man as the head of Cabot, Bancroft and Cabot to drop everything else and run around in circles attendin' to my little two-for-a-cent business!"

The relative of the great man admitted that there was reason in this line of argument, but he was impatient, nevertheless. His daily walks now included trips to the post office. On one of those trips he caught a glimpse of Mr. Pulcifer's hemispherical countenance through its wearer's office window, and, on the spur of the moment's impulse, went in.

Horatio, who was smoking his customary cigar, reading a political circular and humming "Beautiful Lady" all at the same time, looked up from the reading and greeted him boisterously.

"Well, well, well!" exclaimed Raish. "If it ain't the Perfessor again! Welcome to amongst our midst, as the feller said. Have a chair, Perfessor. How's things in the graveyard these days? Kind of dead around there, eh? Haw, haw, haw!"

He enjoyed his joke and laugh and Galusha smiled because he felt that politeness required it. When the laugh and smile had run their course, he endeavored to come to the point.

"Mr. Pulcifer," he said, "I—if you are not too greatly occupied I should like to ask—ah—a business question. Ah —may I?"

He most assuredly could. In fact, he was urged to ask it then and there.

"Never too busy to talk business, a feller usually ain't; eh, Perfessor? Haw, haw! I'd say he wan't, eh? Set down, set down and ease your mind. What's the business question? Let 'er go."

Mr. Bangs let her go to the extent of stammering a request to be given his companion's candid opinion concerning the shares of the Wellmouth Development Company. He was—ah—somewhat interested in them, so he said.

Raish leaned back in his chair and scrutinized the questioner. He shot at least five deep-drawn puffs of smoke into the already murky air of the little office before replying.

"Humph!" he grunted, after the fifth puff. "Wellmouth Development Company, eh? You're interested in that, are you?"

"Why—ah—yes, yes. To a certain extent, yes, Mr. Pulcifer."

"Humph! What d'you mean, interested? How interested?"

"Why, as—ah—as an investment, you know. As something to put one's money into."

"Humph! Was you thinkin' of puttin' some of yours into it?"

"Why, not exactly. But, you see, a friend of mine——— But, really, I think I shouldn't give any further particulars at the present time. You'll excuse me under the circumstances, Mr. Pulcifer, I'm sure. Dear me, I hope you will."

He was forgiven. Mr. Pulcifer assured him to that effect. But Raish was still uncertain just how to proceed. He continued to puff and scrutinize.

"What I wish to know," continued his caller, after another moment's interval, "is—well, in short, I should like to know your opinion of Wellmouth Development shares as an investment security."

"Um—ye-es. Well, you said that before."

"Did I? Dear me, I believe I did. Well, then, suppose, just suppose that I actually did wish to buy some of those shares. Would you consider it a good thing for me to do?"

Here at last was something tangible—and promising. Mr. Pulcifer's puffy lids drew nearer together to hide the gleam behind them. He took the cigar from his mouth and held it between the fingers of his right hand. During his next speech he gesticulated with it.

"Would I consid——" he began, and then paused, apparently overcome by his feelings. The pause was not long, however. "Would I consider Wellmouth Development a good thing for you to put your money in? *Would* I?"

"Ah—yes. Would you?"

"Say, Perfessor, you listen to me. *I* know all about Wellmouth Development. You've come to the right place. You listen."

Galusha listened, listened for a long time. The red of the Pulcifer cigar tip died out and that of the Pulcifer face brightened.

"And so I say," vowed Raish, in conclusion, "with all that property behind it and all that future ahead of it, if Development ain't a good investment, what is?"

"I don't know, I'm sure," confessed Galusha. "But——"

"Don't know? You bet you don't know! Nor nobody else. Not for quick returns, maybe—though you can't never tell. But for a feller that's willin' to buy and put away and hang on—say, how can you beat it?"

"I don't know, but——"

"You bet you don't know! The main thing is to buy right. And I'm goin' to put you wise—yes, sir, wise to somethin' I wouldn't let every Tom, Dick, and Harry in on, by a consider'ble sight. I think I can locate a fair-sized block of that stock at—well, at a little bit underneath the market price. I believe—yes, sir, I believe I can get it for you at—at as low as eighteen dollars a share. I won't swear I can, of course, but I *may* be able to. Only you'll have to promise not to tell anybody how you got it."

"Eighteen dollars a share? Is that a fair price, do you think, Mr. Pulcifer?"

"*Fair* price?" Mr. Pulcifer was overcome by the absurdity of the question. "A fair price!" he repeated. "Man alive, it's a darned *low* price! You buy Wellmouth Development at that price and then set back and hang on. Yes, sir, that's all you'll have to do, just hang on and wait."

To his surprise, Mr. Bangs seemed to find something humorous in this suggestion. Instead of appearing thrilled, as he certainly should, he smiled.

"Ah—yes," he observed, quietly. "That is what my friend has been doing, I believe. Yes, indeed, just that."

Raish did not smile. He looked puzzled and a bit perturbed.

"What friend?" he demanded. "Been doin' what?"

"Hanging on and waiting, as you advise, Mr. Pulcifer. She has had—ah—several shares of the Development stock and she——"

"Hold on! Did you come here to *sell* somebody's stock for 'em?"

"Why, no, not exactly. But, as I say, a friend of mine has some and she was anxious to know what it was worth at the present time. When I tell her that you will give eighteen dollars a share for it——"

"Here!" Raish's smile and his urbanity had vanished. "Here," he demanded, "what are you talkin' about? Who the devil said anything about my givin' eighteen dollars a share?"

"Why, I understood you to say that the—ah—shares were

cheap at that figure, that it was a very low price for them. You did say that, didn't you?"

Mr. Pulcifer seemed to find articulation difficult. He blew and sputtered like a stranded porpoise and his face became redder than ever, but he did not answer the question.

"I understood——" began Galusha, again, but a roar interrupted him.

"Aw, you understand too darn much," shouted Raish. "You go back and tell Martha Phipps I say I don't know what them shares of hers are worth and I don't care. You tell her I don't want to buy 'em and I don't know anybody that does. Yes, and you tell her that if I did know anybody that was fool enough to bid one dollar of real money for 'em I'd sell him mine and be darn glad of the chance. And say, you tell her not to bother me no more. She took her chance same as the rest of us, and if she don't like it she can go—— Eh? What is it?"

His caller had risen, rather suddenly for him, and was standing beside the desk. There was a peculiar expression on his thin face.

"What's the matter?" demanded Mr. Pulcifer. Galusha's gaze was very direct.

"I wouldn't say that," he said, quietly.

"Eh? Say what? I was just goin' to say that if Martha Phipps didn't like waitin' same as the rest of us she——"

"Yes, yes," hastily, "I know. But I shouldn't say it, if I were you."

"You wouldn't. Why not, for thunder sakes?"

"Because—well, I am sure you were speaking hastily—without thinking."

"Is that so?" How do *you* know I wasn't thinkin'?"

"Because I am sure no one who had stopped to think would send that sort of message to a lady."

"Humph! . . . Well, I swear! . . . Wouldn't send—I want to know!"

"Yes—ah—and now you do know. Good-day, Mr. Pulcifer."

He was at the door when the surprised and, to tell the truth, somewhat disconcerted Horatio called after him.

"Here! Hold on, Perfessor," he hailed; "don't go off mad. I didn't mean nothin'. Er—er—say, Perfessor, I don't know's there's any use in your tellin' Martha what I said about them Development shares bein' cheap at eighteen. Of course, that was all—er—more or less of a joke, you understand, and—— Eh? What say?"

"I said I understood, Mr. Pulcifer."

"Yes—er—yes, yes. Glad you do; I thought you would. Now I tell you what to do: You tell Martha . . . you tell her . . . say, what *are* you goin' to tell her?"

"Nothing. Good-day, Mr. Pulcifer."

Galusha did not tell Martha of the interview in the real estate dealer's office, but the recollection of it did not tend to make him more easy in his mind concerning her investment in Wellmouth Development Company. And, as another week went by and still Cousin Gussie did not reply to the letter of inquiry, his uneasiness grew with his impatience. Another and more practical person would have called the Boston bankers by telephone, but Galusha did not think of that. Martha offered no suggestions; her advice was to wait.

"I don't think we ought to hurry your cousin, Mr. Bangs," she said. "He's probably lookin' into things, and he'll write when the time comes."

Galusha devoutly wished the time would come soon. He somewhat felt a great responsibility in the matter. This sense of responsibility caused him to assume more and more optimism as his nervousness increased. Each day of waiting found him covering his disappointment and anxiety with a more cheerful prophecy.

"I've been thinking, Miss Martha," he said, "that Cousin Gussie must be *most* interested in the—ah—Development Company. I really believe that he may be considering going into it himself—ah—extensively, so to speak. The more he delays replying to our letter, the more certain I am that this is the case. You see, it is quite logical. Dear me, yes.

If he were not interested at all he would have replied at once, any one would. And if only a little interested, he would have replied—say, at the end of a week. But now he has taken almost three weeks, so—so—well, *I* think we may infer *great* interest, personal interest on his part. Now, don't you think so, Miss Martha?"

Martha shrugged. "Accordin' to that reasonin," she said, "if he never answers at all it'll be because he's interested to death. Well, it begins to look as if that might be it. There, there, Mr. Bangs, I mustn't talk that way, must I? We won't give up the ship as long's the pumps work, as father used to say."

It was the first symptom of discouragement she had shown. The next morning Galusha crept downstairs before daylight, left a note on the dining table saying he would be back next day, and started on his long tramp to the railway station. At noon of that day he entered the Boston office of Cabot, Bancroft and Cabot.

Disappointment met him at the threshold, so to speak. The young, extremely young, gentleman at the desk by the door, informed him that Mr. Augustus Cabot was not in. Pressed still further, he admitted that he would not be in that day. No, he would not be in that week. No, he was not in Boston. Where was he? Well, he had gone away and the date of his return was extremely uncertain.

Galusha, his spirits at a low ebb, stroked his chin in sad perplexity.

"Dear me! Dear me!" he observed. And then added: "Is—is anybody in?"

Considering that the space behind the mahogany and brass railings was crowded with clerks and that from the various inner offices people were constantly coming and going, the question was peculiar. The young guardian of the portal seemed to find it so. He regarded Mr. Bangs with the puzzled stare of one not certain whether he has to do with a would-be joker or an imbecile.

"Say, who do you want to see?" he demanded.

"Why, Mr. Cabot—Mr. Augustus Cabot."

"Mr. Cabot's away, I tell you. He's out of town."

A tall, thin man of middle age, who had just emerged from one of the private offices, paused beside them. He looked at Galusha through his eyeglasses, and then held out his hand.

"Why, Bangs!" he exclaimed. "It *is* Bangs, isn't it? Glad to see you. Don't you know me? I'm Minor. How are you?"

Galusha remembered him, of course. Minor had been a young assistant bookkeeper in those far-off and dismal days when he, Galusha, had worked—or attempted to work—in that very office. That was—mercy, that was a great many years ago! Minor had changed very much.

They shook hands and Galusha was invited to come into Mr. Minor's private office.

"Let me see," said the latter, "you are—you are—— What is your business now? I did hear, but I've forgotten."

Galusha told of his connection with the National Institute.

"I do—ah—archæological work," he added. "Egyptology is my specialty."

Minor nodded. "Yes, yes," he said, doubtfully. "Just so."

Plainly he regarded it as a weird sort of business.

"And you are still a—ah—banker?" queried Galusha.

"Yes. Very much so. I'm second vice president here now."

"Dear me! dear me! You have been in this place ever since? Well, well!"

A pause, during which each regarded the other, trying not to show the pity they felt. Then Minor asked if there was anything he could do for his former associate. Galusha explained that he had come to town to see his cousin, Mr. Augustus Cabot, on a business matter. Mr. Minor was surprised, momentarily.

"That's so," he said, "he is a relative of yours, isn't he? I had forgotten."

"Yes, yes, he is. He—ah—you see, he looks after things for me—investments and—all that."

"Humph! Well, if you wanted to see him personally, you're out of luck. He is away out in the Sierras, somewhere. Been there for a month and he won't come back till the doctors tell him he may. Goodness knows when that will be."

Cousin Gussie had, it appeared, suffered a severe nervous breakdown. The physicians had ordered immediate dropping of business and business cares.

"He must drop everything, they said, and cut, if he wanted to head off something a good deal more serious. He must get out of doors and stay there; go to bed early at night—instead of early in the morning, which had been more in his line—and rough it generally."

"Why—yes, yes, indeed. That was almost precisely what the doctors told me I must do. Rest and—ah—good air, you know, and pleasant people. *I* was very fortunate, really. I am at—ah—Gould's Bluffs, Cape Cod, you know."

"Yes? Well, he's away out in California or Nevada or thereabouts. His secretary is with him—Thomas, the fellow he's had so many years; you remember him. Thomas has gone along to see that the chief—Mr. Cabot, I mean—doesn't get any business letters or wires or anything of that sort. He looks out for those that do come, the personal matters."

"Oh! Then perhaps my letter has been forwarded out there. That would explain why I have received no answer. Yes, of course."

"Sure! Thomas will write you by and by, no doubt. But now that you are here, why don't you see Barbour? Barbour is in charge of the chief's outside affairs while Thomas is away. That is, he is in charge of everything that can be handled here. The most important stuff goes to Thomas, of course. But come in and see Barbour. Perhaps he can tell you what you want to know."

Mr. Barbour was a bald-headed, worried-looking little man, who, in the seclusion of a rear office, sat behind a big desk. Minor introduced Galusha and Mr. Barbour extended a moist and flabby hand. Minor excused himself and hastened out to the really important matters of life. Galusha told Barbour the story of his letter to Cousin Gussie. He did not tell what was in the letter, further than to say that it was an inquiry concerning a certain investment security.

Barbour shook his head.

"Everything marked 'Personal' I forward to Thomas," he said. "He'll write you pretty soon, although I'm pretty sure he won't trouble the chief with your question. Doctors are mighty strict about that. Nothing we here can do to help, is there? Perhaps Mr. Minor might answer your question."

Galusha was thinking of Minor that very moment, but he shook his head. Martha had asked that no one but Cousin Gussie be told of her trouble. No, he would wait, at least until he heard from the secretary in the West.

"Why, thank you, Mr. Barbour," he said, rising. "I—I will wait, I think."

"All right, sir. Sorry, but you see how it is. Drop in again, Mr.—er—Barnes. Barnes was the name, wasn't it?"

"Why, not exactly. My name is Bangs, but it really doesn't matter in the least. Dear me, no. I am a relative of Mr. Cabot's. But that doesn't matter either. Good-morning, Mr. Barbour."

But it did seem to matter, after all. At any rate, Mr. Barbour for the first time appeared actually interested.

"Eh?" he exclaimed. "Bangs? Oh, just a minute, Mr. Bangs. Just a minute, if you please. Bangs? Why, are you—— You're not the—er—professor? Professor Ga—Ga——"

"Galusha. Yes, I am Galusha Bangs."

"You don't mean it! Well, well, that's odd! I was planning to write you to-day, Professor. Let me see, here's the memorandum now. We look after your business affairs, I believe, Professor?"

Galusha nodded. He was anxious to get away. The significance of Cousin Gussie's illness and absence and what those might mean to Martha Phipps were beginning to dawn upon him. He wanted to get away and think. The very last thing he wished to do was to discuss his own business affairs.

"Yes," he admitted; "yes, you—ah—do. That is, Cousin Gussie—ah—Mr. Cabot does. But, really, I——"

"I won't keep you but a moment, Professor. And what I'm going to tell you is good news, at that. I presume it *is* news; or have you heard of the Tinplate melon?"

It was quite evident that Galusha had not heard. Nor, hearing now, did the news convey anything to his mind.

"Melon?" he repeated. "Ah—melon, did you say?"

"Why, yes. The Tinplate people are——"

It was a rather long story, and telling it took longer than the minute Mr. Barbour had requested. To Galusha it was all a tangled and most uninteresting snarl of figures and stock quotations and references to "preferred" and "common" and "new issues" and "rights." He gathered that, somehow or other, he was to have more money, money which was coming to him because the "Tinplate crowd," whoever they were, were to do something or other that people like Barbour called "cutting a melon."

"You understand, Professor?" asked Mr. Barbour, concluding his explanation.

Galusha was at that moment endeavoring to fabricate a story of his own, one which he might tell Miss Phipps. It must not be too discouraging, it must——

"Eh?" he ejaculated, coming out of his daydream. "Oh, yes—yes, of course."

"As near as I can figure, your share will be well over twelve thousand. A pretty nice little windfall, I should say. Now what shall I do with it?"

"Yes. . . . Oh, I beg your pardon. Dear me, I am afraid I was not attending as I should."

"I say what shall I do with the check when it comes. That was what I intended writing you to ask. Do you wish me to reinvest the money, or shall I send the check to you?"

"Yes—ah—yes. If you will be so kind. You will excuse me, won't you, but really I must hurry on. Thank you very much, Mr. Barbour."

"But I don't quite understand which you wish me to do, Professor. Of course, Thomas usually attends to all this—your affairs, I mean—but I am trying not to trouble him unless it is absolutely necessary. Shall I send the check direct to you, is that it?"

"Yes—yes, that will do very nicely. Thank you, Mr. Barbour. Good-morning."

He hurried out before Barbour could say any more. He cared nothing about Tinplate melons or checks; in fact, he forgot them both almost before he reached the street. But Martha Phipps—he had assured and reassured Martha Phipps that Cousin Gussie would help her out of her financial difficulties. And Cousin Gussie had not as yet learned of those difficulties, nor, in all probability, would he be permitted ever to learn of them.

Galusha Bangs' trip back to East Wellmouth was by no means a pleasure excursion. What should he say to Martha? How could he be truthful and yet continue to be encouraging? If he had not been so unreasonably optimistic it would be easier, but he had never once admitted the possibility of failure. And—no, he would not admit it now. Somehow and in some way Martha's cares must be smoothed away. That he determined. But what should he say to her now?

He was still asking himself that question when he turned in at the Phipps' gate. And Fate so arranged matters that it was Primmie who heard the gate latch click and Primmie who came flying down the path to meet him.

"Mr. Bangs! Oh, Mr. Bangs!" she cried, breathlessly. "It's all right, ain't it? It's all right?"

Galusha, startled, stared at her.

"Dear me, Primmie," he observed. "How you do—ah—bounce at one, so to speak. What is the matter?"

"Matter? I cal'late we both know what's the matter, but

what *I* want to know is if it's goin' to keep *on* bein' the matter. Is it all right? Have you fixed it up?"

"Fixed what up? And *please* speak lower. Yes, and don't—ah—bounce, if you don't mind."

"I won't, honest I won't. But have you fixed up Miss Martha's trouble; you and them Bancroft folks, I mean? Have you, Mr. Bangs?"

"Bancroft folks? . . . How did you know I——"

"I seen it, of course. 'Twas in that note you left on the table."

"Note? Why, Primmie, that note was for Miss Phipps. Why did you read it?"

"Why wouldn't I read it? There 'twas laid out on the table when I came down to poke up the fire and set the kettle on. There wasn't no name on it, so 'twan't till I'd read it clear through that I knew 'twas for Miss Martha. It said: 'Have gone to Boston to see—er—what's-his-name and Somebody-else and——' Never mind, Bancroft's all I remember, anyhow. But it said you'd gone to them folks to see about 'stock matter.' Well, then I knew 'twas for Miss Martha. *I* didn't have no stock matters for folks to see about. My savin' soul, no! And then you said, 'Hope to settle everything and have good news when I come back.' I remember *that* all right. . . . Oh, Mr. Bangs, have you settled it? *Have* you got good news for her?"

By this time she had forgotten all about the request to speak in a low tone. Galusha glanced fearfully at the open door behind her.

"Sshh! shh, Primmie," he begged.

"But have you? Have you, Mr. Bangs?"

"Why—why, perhaps, Primmie. I mean—that is to say——"

He stopped. Miss Phipps was standing in the doorway.

"Why, Mr. Bangs!" she exclaimed. "Are you here so soon? I didn't expect you till to-night. What are you standin' out there in the cold for? Come in, come in!"

And then Primmie, to make use of the expressive idiom of **her** friend, the driver of the grocery cart, Primmie "spilled the beans." She turned, saw her mistress, and ran toward her, waving both hands.

"Oh, Miss Martha!" she cried, "he—he's done it. He says it's all right. He does! he does!"

"Primmie!"

"He says he's been to them—them Bancroft what's-his-name folks and he's got the good news for you. Oh, ain't it elegant! Ain't it!"

This wild perversion of his guarded statement took Galusha completely by surprise. He started forward aghast. And then he saw Martha Phipps' face. Upon it were written such hope and relief and joy that the words of expostulation and protest remained unspoken. And it was Martha who spoke first.

"Oh, Mr. Bangs!" she gasped. "Oh, Mr. Bangs!"

Galusha's chin quivered. His face became very red.

"Why—why—why, Miss Martha, I—I——"

His agitation caused his teeth actually to chatter. Martha noticed the chatter and misinterpreted the cause.

"Mercy me!" she cried. "You're standin' out there and freezin' to death. Of course you are. Come right in! Primmie, open those stove dampers. Put the kettle on front where it will boil quick. . . . No, Mr. Bangs, you mustn't tell me a word until you're warm and rested. You would like to go to your room, wouldn't you? Certainly you would. Primmie will bring you hot water as soon as it's ready. No, don't try to tell me a word until after you are rested and washed up."

It was a welcome suggestion, not because Galusha was so eager to "wash up," but because he was eager, very eager, to be alone where no one could ask more embarrassing questions. Yet the last thing he saw as he closed his room door was the expression upon Miss Phipps' face. Hope, relief, happiness! And what he had to tell would change them all.

Oh, if he had not been so foolishly optimistic! What should he say? If he told the exact truth—the whole truth——

But there, what was the whole truth? After all, he did not *know* that nothing would come of his letter to Cousin Gussie. Something might come of it. Yes, even something very good might come. If Cousin Gussie himself never saw the letter, Thomas, the secretary, would see it and very likely he would write encouragingly. He might—it was quite likely that he would—give the names of other Boston financiers to whom Wellmouth Development might be of interest. In this case, or even the probability of such a case, he, Galusha, would certainly not be justified in making his story too discouraging.

When, at last, he did descend to the sitting room, where Miss Phipps was awaiting him, the tale he told her bore very little resemblance to the hopeless, despairful narrative he had, while on the way down in the train, considered inevitable and the telling of which he had so dreaded. In fact, when it was finished Martha's expression had changed but little. She still looked happy.

She drew a long breath. "Well!" she exclaimed, "I can hardly believe it; it seems almost too good to believe. And so that secretary man told you that he felt sure that your cousin, or his other secretary—how many secretaries does one man have to have, for mercy sakes?—would attend to the Development thing and it would be all right if we would just wait a little longer? Was that it?"

Galusha, who, in his intense desire not to be discouraging, had not until now realized how far he had gone in the other direction, blinked and wiped his forehead with his handkerchief.

"That was it, wasn't it?" repeated Martha.

"Why—why—ah—yes, about that, as—ah—one might say. Yes."

It was the first lie Galusha Bangs had told for many, many years, one of the very few he had ever told. It was a very white lie and not told with deliberation or malice aforethought. But, as so often happens, it was destined to be the father of a pestilential pack which were neither white nor unintentional.

CHAPTER XI

ABOUT the Phipps' home hung now the atmosphere of expectancy. It had so hung for several weeks, ever since the first letter to Cousin Gussie had been posted, but now there was in it a different quality, a quality of brightness, of cheer. Martha seemed more like herself, the capable, adequate self which Galusha had met when he staggered into that house out of the rain and wind of his first October night on Cape Cod. She was more talkative, laughed more frequently, and bustled about her work with much, if not all, of her former energy. She, herself, was quite aware of the change and commented upon it rather apologetically in one of her talks with her lodger.

"It's ridiculous," she said, "and I know it, but I can't help it. I'm as excited as a child and almost as sure everything is goin' to come out right as—well, as Primmie is. I wasn't so at all in the beginnin'; when we first sent that letter to your cousin I didn't think there was much more than one chance in a thousand that he would take any interest in Wellmouth Development stock. But since you got back from your Boston cruise, Mr. Bangs, I've felt altogether different. What the Cabot, Bancroft and Cabot folks said wasn't any too definite; when I sit right down and think about it I realize it wasn't. But it was encouraging, real encouraging. And that bit of real encouragement has made me over, like an old dress. Which reminds me that I've got to be makin' over some of *my* old dresses pretty soon, or summer'll be here and I won't have a thing fit to wear. I declare," she added, with a laugh, "this is the first time I've even thought about clothes since last fall. And when a woman forgets to be interested in dressmakin' she's pretty far gone. . . . Why, what makes you look so sorrowful? Is anything wrong?"

Galusha replied that nothing whatever was wrong; there was, he said, no reason in the world why he should appear sorrowful. Yet, this answer was not the exact truth; there were reasons, and speeches such as Miss Martha's reminded him of them. They awoke his uneasy conscience to the fear that the encouragement she found in his report from Cabot, Bancroft and Cabot was almost entirely due to his interpretation of that report and not to the facts behind it. However, as she must on no account guess this to be the case, he smiled and assumed an air more than ever carefree.

One afternoon, when, on his way home after an unusually lengthy walk, he stopped at the post office, he found that the Phipps' mail had already been delivered.

"Zach Bloomer stopped along in and took it," explained Miss Tamson Black, the postmaster's sister-in-law. "I told him I presumed likely you'd be here after it yourself pretty soon, but it didn't make no difference. He said—but maybe I better not tell you."

"Oh, yes—no doubt," observed Galusha, who was, as usual, paying little attention.

Tamson, plainly disappointed at his lack of curiosity, elevated her thin nose.

"Well," she observed, "what he *said* was that, fur's things bein' here was concerned, Christmas would be here, give it time enough. Pretty sassy kind of talk, *I* call it, but maybe you ain't so partic'lar, Mr. Bangs."

"Dear me! Of course. Well, well! . . . Oh, were there any letters for—ah—for me, may I ask?"

"Why, yes, there was, two of 'em. That's what made me cal'late you might like to get 'em first yourself. I knew you didn't get letters very often, Mr. Bangs; that is, I've noticed you ain't since I've been helpin' in this office. Anyhow, 'most anybody would rather get their own mail private than have Zach Bloomer cartin' it from land-knows-where to never-and-gone, smellin' it all up with old tobacco pipes and fish or whatever else he carries 'round in his pockets. Course I don't mean he lugs fish around in his pocket, 'tain't likely—— He, he, he—but that old coat of his always smells like a—like a porgie boat. And I don't know's I mean that those letters of yours were any more 'special private than common; anyhow, both envelopes was in *male* handwritin'—— He, he, he! But I noticed one was stamped from way out in—in Nevada, seems if 'twas, so——"

"Eh?" Galusha came to life with astonishing quickness. "From—from Nevada, did you say?"

"Um-hm. I remember it real plain now. You see, it kind of caught my eye as I was sortin.' We don't never get much mail from Nevada—not in this office we don't never hardly. So when I see . . . Well, my good land!"

The exclamation was caused by the unceremonious suddenness of Mr. Bangs' exit. He was well across the road by the time Miss Black reached the window.

"My good land!" exclaimed Tamson again. Later she told her brother-in-law that she cal'lated that Nevada letter was maybe more private than she cal'lated first, and that she bet you she was goin' to look pretty hard at the handwritin' on the *next* one that come.

Primmie, apparently, had been watching through the kitchen window for Galusha to appear. At any rate, she opened the door for him. Her mouth opened also, but he, for perhaps the first time in their acquaintanceship, spoke first.

"I know—I know, Primmie," he said, hastily; "or if I don't know you can tell me later on. Ah—please don't delay me now."

Primmie was struggling between surprise and disappointment.

"Well," she observed, as the little man hurriedly shed his hat and coat; "well, all right, Mr. Bangs. Only Zach, he told me to be sure and tell you, and tell you how sorry he was that it happened, and that he can't exactly figger out just how it did come to happen, neither."

"Eh?" Galusha paused, with one arm still in the sleeve of his overcoat. "Happen? What has happened to—ah—Mr. Bloomer?"

"Ain't nothin' happened to him. 'Twas him that made it happen to your letter. And *that* letter of all letters! You see, Zach he don't exactly remember when 'twas he got it from the post office, but it must have been much as a week ago, sartin sure. Anyhow, when he took out the lighthouse mail he left this letter in the pocket, and to-day, just now, when he got them other letters of yours and put 'em in the same pocket, he found the first one. And when I see that 'Cabot, What-d'ye-call-it and Cabot' name printed out right on the envelope and it come over me that 'twas *that* letter he'd forgot and had been totin' 'round with him, '*Well*,' says I. 'My Lord of Isrul!' I says——"

"Primmie! Primmie, stop! Stop—please! And tell me: Where are those letters?"

"Hey? I was goin' to tell you. *I* put 'em right here on the dinin' room table, but Miss Martha she carted 'em off upstairs to your bedroom. Said she presumed likely you'd want to open 'em by yourself. *I* don't see why——"

"Hush! Hush! Where is—ah—Miss Phipps?"

"She's in the settin' room. Told me not to disturb her, she wanted to be alone. I——"

Galusha hastened away, leaving the excited Miss Cash still talking. From the foot of the stairs he caught a glimpse of Martha in the chair by the front window of the sitting room, looking out. She must have heard him, but she did not turn her head. Nor did he speak to her. Time enough for that when he had read what was in those letters.

There they were, three of them, upon his bureau. He picked up the one on top. It bore upon the envelope the words "National Institute, Washington, D. C.," and was, he knew, merely a monthly report. Usually such reports were of great interest to him; this one was not. He had really important matters to claim his attention.

The second letter was, obviously, that which the forgetful Zacheus had carried about with him for a week. In the

corner was the Cabot, Bancroft and Cabot name.   He tore
it open.   An oblong slip of paper fell to the floor.   He did
not even stoop to pick this up, for there was a letter, too.
It began:

"*Prof. Galusha Bangs,
  East Wellmouth, Mass.*
"DEAR SIR:
"Pursuant to your instructions in our conversation of recent date I am enclosing check representing your share of
the new Tinplate re-issue, sale of rights, transfer of old stock,
bonus, etc.   The transfer has been, as I told you I felt sure
it would be, very advantageous and profitable to stockholders like yourself.   The amount due you, as shown in statement attached, is——"

Galusha read no further.   What did he care for Tinplate,
profits, business, or anything like that!   There was not a
word in the letter concerning Wellmouth Development.   It
was a bitter disappointment.

But there was the third letter, the letter from Nevada.
He opened that.   The first page which he looked at was that
bearing the signature.   Yes, the letter was from George L.
Thomas, and George L. Thomas was Cousin Gussie's private
secretary.   At last!

The letter shook in Galusha's fingers as he began to read.
Mr. Thomas was glad to hear from him, glad to learn that
he was in better health, etc. . . . All right enough, this beginning, but not at all important.   Thomas also felt sure that
he, Professor Bangs, would be grateful to know that Mr.
Cabot's condition was, so his physician seemed to think,
steadily improving.   The improvement was slow, of course,
which was to be expected, but . . . a long paragraph here
which Galusha skipped.   He was highly pleased to know that
Cousin Gussie was better, but at present that was sufficient;
he could not waste time in reading details of the convales-
cence.   *Why* didn't the man get down to business?

Ah, here it was!   Mr. Thomas wrote:

"In your letter to Mr. Cabot I note your inquiry concerning the stock of the Wellmouth Development Company, its desirability as an investment, the likelihood of present sale, and so on. I know nothing of the matter personally, and am not in a position to ascertain at the present time. Speaking in a general way, however, and with my only knowledge of the facts in the case that supplied by your letter, I should suggest that your friend keep his stock and await developments. I am quite sure that a forced sale— if such a sale could now be made at any price, which I doubt —would involve the sacrifice of almost the entire amount invested. I should suggest holding on and waiting."

Galusha passed his shaking hand across his perspiring forehead.

"Oh, dear me!" he said aloud.

"This would be my advice," went on the letter, "but if you wish a more positive answer I suggest your writing Mr. Minor at our Boston office. He will be very glad to look into the matter for you, I am sure, although I am practically certain his views will agree with mine. Of course, as you will understand, it is quite impossible to mention your inquiry to Mr. Cabot. He is here to regain his health, which is still very far from normal, his doctor is with him, and the one word which is positively forbidden is 'Business.' Mr. Cabot is supposed to forget that there is such a thing. By the way he spoke of you only the other day, and jokingly said he wondered how mummies and quahaugs were mixing. The fact that he is beginning to joke once more we all consider most encouraging. . . ."

A paragraph or two more of this sort of thing and then Mr. Thomas' signature. Galusha stared at the letter dully. This—this was what he and Martha Phipps had awaited so long! This was the outcome of his brilliant idea which was to save the Phipps' home . . . and its owner's peace of mind . . . and Primmie . . . and . . . .

Oh, dear me! dear me!

Galusha walked slowly across the room to the chair by the window, and, sitting down, continued to stare hopelessly at the letter in his hand. He read it for the second time, but this rereading brought no comfort whatever. Rather, it served to bring home to him the hard realities of the whole wretched affair. Cousin Gussie's interest was what he had banked on, and that interest was absolutely unapproachable. To write Minor at the Boston office was a possibility, of course, but, in his present frame of mind Galusha felt no hope that such a proceeding would help. Thomas had written what amounted to that very thing; Thomas was "practically certain" that Minor's views would agree with his. And, besides, to write Minor meant another long wait, and Martha Phipps must be very close to her limit of waiting. How could he summon the courage to descend to the sitting room and tell her that she must prepare for another period of waiting, with almost certain disappointment at the end?

A temperament like Galusha Bangs' is capable of soaring to the heights and descending to the depths. Just now the elevator was going down, and down it continued to go to the very subcellar. It was dark in that subcellar, not a ray of light anywhere. Galusha realized now, or thought he did, that all his great scheme for helping Martha to dispose of her Development shares had been based upon nothing substantial, nothing but rainbow-tinted hopes which, in turn, were based upon nothing but wishes. Omitting the hopes and wishes, what was there left? Just what the president of the Trumet Trust Company had told Martha and what Raish Pulcifer, when angered into truthtelling, had told him. That is, that the shares of the Wellmouth Development Company might be worth something some day, but that now they were worth nothing, because no one would buy them.

Yes . . . yes, that was the truth. . . . But how could he go down to the sitting room and tell Martha Phipps that truth, having already told her so much that was quite different?

If she would only let him lend her the five thousand dollars, or whatever it was. He did not know how much Cousin Gussie was taking care of for him at present, but there had been a large sum at the time of Aunt Clarissa's death. He remembered that the figures had quite frightened him then. He had not thought much about them since, because they did not interest him. He always had enough for his needs and more than enough, and dividends, and interests, and investments and all such things bored him and made him nervous. But, now that he *was* interested in an investment—Martha Phipps' investment—it brought home to him the undisputable fact that he, Galusha Bangs, had plenty of money to lend, if he wished to lend it.

And if Cousin Gussie, or Cousin Gussie's representatives, would let him have it for such a purpose! Cousin Gussie always made such an unpleasant disturbance when he expressed a desire for any of his money, asked so many embarrassing questions as to what was to be done with it, and the like. If he should go now and ask for five thousand dollars to lend Martha Phipps, what . . .

But Martha Phipps would not accept a loan, anyway. She had told him that very thing, and he knew her well enough by this time to know she meant what she said.

Yet there remained the imminent and dreadful question: How, how, *how* could he go down to where she was sitting waiting and tell her that her hopes, hopes which he had raised, were based solely upon the vaporings of an optimistic donkey?

In his wrathful disgust with that donkey he shifted angrily in his chair and his foot struck a bit of paper upon the floor. It rustled and the rustle attracted his attention. Absently he stepped and picked up the paper. It was the slip which had fallen from the Cabot, Bancroft and Cabot letter and was a check drawn to his order for fourteen thousand, three hundred and ten dollars and thirty-eight cents, his share of the Tinplate "melon."

Fifteen more minutes passed before Mr. Bangs came down to the sitting room, but when he did he came in a great hurry. He dashed into the apartment and announced his intention of starting for Boston at once.

"And—and if you will be so kind as to let me have those —ah—shares of yours, Miss Martha," he said.

Martha looked at him. She had been rather pale when he entered, but now the color rushed to her face.

"Shares?" she repeated. "Do you mean——"

"Those—ah—Development shares of yours—yes. If you will be good enough to let me take them with me——"

"Take them with you? . . . Oh, Mr. Bangs, you don't mean you have heard from your cousin and that he is goin' to——"

"Yes—ah—yes," broke in Galusha, hastily. "I have heard. I am to—that is, I must take the shares with me and go to Boston at once. If you will be willing to entrust them to me, Miss Martha."

"I'll get 'em this minute." She started toward the stairs, but paused and turned.

"Is it really settled, Mr. Bangs?" she asked, as if scarcely daring to believe in the possibility. "Are they really goin' to buy that Wellmouth stock of mine?"

"Why—why——" Galusha was yawing badly, but he clutched the helm and kept on the course; "I—ah—hope so, Miss Martha, I hope so."

"And pay me—pay me *money* for it?"

"I presume so. I hope so. If you will——"

"I declare, it doesn't seem possible! Who, for mercy sakes, is goin' to buy it? Mr. Cabot, himself?"

He had been expecting this and was prepared for it. He had rehearsed his answer many times before coming downstairs. He held up a protesting hand.

"I am very sorry," he said, "but—but, you see, that is a—ah—secret, I understand. Of course, they did not write me who was to buy the stock and so—and so——"

"And so you don't know. Well, it doesn't make a bit of difference, really. The Lord knows I shouldn't care so long as I sell it honestly and don't cheat anybody. And a big house like Cabot, Bancroft and Cabot ought to know what they're doin' when they buy, or let any of their customers buy. I'll get the certificate this very minute, Mr. Bangs."

She hastened up the stairs. Galusha wiped his forehead and breathed heavily. There was a knock on the door leading to the dining room; it opened and Primmie's head appeared.

"I heard her go upstairs," she whispered, hoarsely. "Is it all right, Mr. Bangs? Was there good news in that What-you-call-it-Bancroft letter, Mr. Bangs? Was there?"

"Go away, Primmie! Go *away!*"

"I'm a-goin'. But was there?"

"Yes—ah—no—I—I guess so."

"Lord everlastin' of Isrul! My savin' soul!"

Martha's footsteps on the stairs caused the head to disappear and the door to close. Miss Phipps appeared, her hand clasping a highly ornate document.

"Here's the certificate," she said, breathlessly. "I'm so upset and excited I don't know hardly whether I'm in the channel or hard aground, as father used to say, but I've signed my name on the back. Once when I sold two shares of railroad stock he left me I had to sign on the back there. I *hope* I've done it in the right place."

Galusha declared the signature to be quite right, yes. As a matter of fact, he could not have told for certain that there was a signature there. He crammed the certificate into his pocket.

"Oh, my sakes!" protested Martha, "you aren't goin' to just put it loose into that pocket, are you? Don't you think it ought to go in your—your wallet, or somewhere?"

"Eh? Why—why, I presume it had. . . . Dear me, yes. . . . It would be a—a joke if I lost it, wouldn't it?"

"A *joke!* Well, it wouldn't be my notion of a joke, exactly."

"Oh, dear, dear! Did I say 'joke'? I didn't mean that it would actually be—ah—humorous, of course. I meant . . . I meant . . . Really, I don't think I know what I meant."

"I don't believe you do. Mr. Bangs, I truly think you are more excited about all this than I am, and all on my account. What can I ever say—or do—to——"

"Please, please, Miss Martha! Dear me, dear me, *don't* speak in that way. It's so—ah—nonsensical, you know. Now if—if I may have my coat and—ah—cap——"

"Cap! Goodness gracious, you weren't plannin' to wear that old cap, earlaps and all, to Boston, were you? And—mercy me! I didn't think of it until this minute—the train doesn't go for 'most two hours."

She burst out laughing and, because she was overwrought and a trifle hysterical, she laughed a good deal. Galusha laughed even longer than she did, not because he was hysterical, but because laughing was very much easier and safer than answering embarrassing questions.

When it really was time to leave for the railroad station and Galusha, *not* wearing the earlapped cap, but hatted and garbed as became his rank and dignity, was standing on the stone step by the outside door, she said:

"Now do be careful, Mr. Bangs."

"Yes—yes, I will, I promise you. I shall keep one hand in my pocket, holding the pocketbook with the certificate in it, until I get to the office. I shall think of nothing else."

"Mercy me, think of *somethin'* else, please! Think of yourself when you're goin' across those Boston streets or you'll be run over. I declare, I don't know as I ought to let you go."

"Oh, I shall be quite safe, quite. But, really," he added, with a puzzled smile, "I can't tell you how odd this seems. When I was a boy my Aunt Clarissa, I remember, used to caution me about—about crossing the streets, and so on. It makes me feel quite young again to have you do it, Miss Martha. I assure you it does."

Martha regarded him gravely.

"Hasn't anybody since ever told you to be careful?" she asked; "anybody since your aunt died, I mean?"

"Why, no, I think not. I presume," he added, with the air of one suggesting a happy explanation, "I presume no one has—ah—been sufficiently interested. It would have been peculiar if they had been, of course."

"Hum! . . . Well, I hope you won't think I am impudent for remindin' you to look out."

"Oh, no, indeed. It is very nice of you to take the trouble. I like it, really I do."

The office of Cabot, Bancroft and Cabot was closed when his train reached Boston, so he went to a hotel and remained there over-night. But he was on hand at the banking office early the next morning. In the interval he had time for more reflection and, as a result, he determined not to go to Mr. Barbour with his business. The fear that knowledge of what he was about to do would reach Cousin Gussie's ears was strong upon him. Doubtless it was a fact that he had a right to do what he pleased with his own money, but it was also a fact that Cousin Gussie seemed to think he had no such right. Barbour was the Cabot secretary, or assistant secretary, so decidedly it was best not to go to Barbour.

It was Minor whom he saw as he entered the banking house and to Minor he divulged his business. Taking from his pocketbook the Tinplate check, he asked if he might have it—ah—broken up, so to speak.

"You see," he explained, "I want to get—ah—five thousand dollars."

Minor appeared rather puzzled at first, and Mr. Bangs' tangled and nervous explanations did not seem to enlighten him greatly. At last, however, he caught the idea.

"I see," he said. "You don't want to deposit and draw against it; you want two checks instead of one. One check for five thousand and the other for the balance."

"Yes, yes, yes," assented Galusha, much relieved. "That is it, exactly. I am very much obliged to you—indeed I am—yes."

Minor took him to one of the windows and introduced him to the clerk at the desk behind it.

"Give Mr. Bangs whatever he wants," he said.

Galusha explained. The clerk asked how he would have the five-thousand-dollar check made out.

"In your own name?" he asked.

Mr. Bangs reflected. "Why—ah——" he stammered, "I should prefer it in—ah—some other name, if possible. I should prefer that my name was not connected with it, if you don't mind."

"In the name of the person you intend paying it to?" inquired the clerk.

Galusha reflected again. If Martha Phipps' name were written on that check it would be possible that, some day or other, Cousin Gussie might see it. And if he saw it, questions would be asked, embarrassing questions.

"No-o," he said, hesitatingly; "no, I think I should not care to have her—that is, to have that person's name appear, either. Isn't there some way by which the sum could be paid without any one's name appearing? A check to—to— oh, dear me! why *can't* I think of it?"

"To bearer, you mean?"

"That's it, that's it. A check to bearer would be very satisfactory, very satisfactory, indeed. Thank you very much."

The clerk, who was a painstaking young man, destined to rise in his profession, inspected the odd individual outside the railing.

"A check to bearer is almost the same as cash," he said. "If you should lose it, it would be negotiable—practically the money itself, or pretty near it."

Galusha started. He looked radiantly happy.

"That's it!" he exclaimed. "That's it, of course. Thank you for the suggestion. The money will be the very thing. It will be such a delightful surprise. And there will be no one's name upon it at all. I will take the money, of course."

It took some time to convince the astonished clerk that Mr. Bangs actually wished five thousand dollars in currency, but he finally was convinced.

"How will you have it?" he asked. "Small bills or large?"

Galusha apparently did not care. Any denominations would be quite satisfactory, he affirmed. So, when the transaction was finished, and he left the Cabot, Bancroft and Cabot office, it was with a new check for nine thousand, three hundred and ten dollars and thirty-eight cents in his pocketbook and in his trousers' pocket a roll of bills as thick as his wrist. By way of modification to this statement, it may be well to explain that Galusha Bangs' wrists, considered *as* wrists, were by no means thick.

The clerk stared after him as he departed and a fellow clerk paused to ask questions.

"Who was the old guy?" he inquired.

"Name's Bangs."

"What is he?"

"A nut," was the reply, given with the assurance of absolute conviction.

The "nut" traveled back to East Wellmouth upon the afternoon train and, back once more in the Phipps' sitting room, "shelled out" upon the center table. Martha stared at the heap of bills and caught her breath with a gasp.

Galusha deposited the last bank note upon the table.

"There!" he exclaimed, with satisfaction; "that is all, I believe. And I have actually gotten it here—all of it. I am quite sure I haven't lost a—a penny. Dear me, that is a very remarkable thing to do—for me to do, I mean."

Miss Phipps did not answer and, turning, he saw that she was sitting in the rocking-chair, her hand to her forehead. Her face was white.

"Dear me!" he exclaimed, in alarm. "Miss Martha, are you ill?"

Still she did not answer and, very much frightened, he hastened to the door, opened it, and shouted for Primmie. The summons for her handmaiden acted as a complete restorative. Martha came to life at once.

"*What* in the world are you callin' Primmie for?" she demanded. "I don't want her. I wouldn't have her see all that. . . . Oh, good heavens and earth!"

Primmie was already in the room. She, as Mr. Bangs would have described it, bounced in.

"Yes'm—I mean yes, sir," was her salutation. "Here I be. . . . Oh, my savin' soul of Isrul!"

She had seen the mound of money upon the table.

Two minutes later Martha and her lodger were again alone in the sitting room. Primmie had been, gently but firmly, escorted to outer darkness and the door closed behind her. She was still asking questions and calling for her ransomed spirit and the ruler of Israel; they could hear her do so even through the door. The exclamations died away in the direction of the kitchen. Miss Phipps, who had done escort duty, turned toward Galusha and ruefully shook her head.

"I *guess* there isn't anybody I'd rather should not have been here just now than Primmie Cash," she observed. "If there is I can't think of their names. Mr. Bangs, I know you meant well, because you couldn't mean any other way, but would you mind tellin' me *why* you called for her?"

Galusha blinked in bewildered fashion behind his spectacles.

"Why—why," he stammered, "you—you see—why, I spoke to you several times and you did not answer—and you were so pale, I thought—I thought——"

"You thought I was sick and so you sung out for Primmie. Humph! that's a good deal like jumpin' into the well to get out of the rain. But there, never mind. So I looked pale and didn't answer when you spoke? Do you wonder? Mr. Bangs," she moved to the table and laid a hand, which trembled a good deal, upon the pile of bills, "is this money really mine?"

"Yes—oh, yes, indeed. It is yours, of course."

"All of it? It doesn't seem possible. How much is there here?"

He told her. She lifted the topmost bills from the heap and reverently laid them down again.

"Five thousand dollars!" she repeated. "It's like—it's like somethin' in a dream, or a book, isn't it? I can hardly believe I am Martha Phipps. So they did think Wellmouth Development was worth somethin', after all. And they paid—why, Mr. Bangs, they paid the full price, didn't they! Twenty dollars a share; as much as father paid in the first place."

"Yes—ah—yes, of course. Yes, indeed. Are you sure you feel quite well again, Miss Martha?"

"I'm sure. But what did they say when they bought it, Mr. Bangs?"

"Say? Ah, say? . . . Why, they said—ah—um—they said there was the money and—and I counted it, you know, and——"

"Yes, yes. But didn't they say anything about the stock; about why they bought it, and like that?"

"Why, no . . . no, I think nothing was—ah—so to speak —ah—said. They—ah—— Won't you sit down again, Miss Martha? I think you had better."

"Sit down! Mr. Bangs, I'm too excited to sit down. I could fly, I think, a good deal easier than I could sit; at least, I feel as if I could. And so they just bought that stock and said nothing more than that? Just bought it?"

"Yes—ah—yes, that's it. They—ah—bought it, you know."

"It seems strange. What did your cousin say?"

"Ah—my cousin? Cousin Gussie, you mean. Yes, yes, of course. Oh, he said—ah—all sorts of things."

"Did he? About the stock?"

"Oh, no, not about the stock so much. No, not so much about that, about . . . a sort of general conversation it was, about—about the weather, and—and the like."

"The weather? Did he write about the weather in his letter?"

He had for the moment forgotten that his relative was an invalid in the Far West and that Miss Phipps knew it. He turned red, coughed, stammered and then broke out in a series of fragmentary and involved explanations to the effect that Cousin Gussie was—ah—naturally much interested in the weather because of his state of health and—and—— She paid little heed, for in the midst of his explaining she interrupted.

"Oh, never mind, never mind," she said. "It doesn't make one bit of difference and why I asked about it I don't know. You see, Mr. Bangs, I'm not back on earth yet, as you might say, and I don't suppose I shall be for a little while, so you'll have to be patient with me. All I can think of is that now I can live here in this house, for a while longer anyhow, and perhaps always. And I sha'n't have to turn Primmie away. And—and maybe I won't have to lie awake night after night, plannin' how I can do this and do without that —and—and——"

She stopped, her sentence unfinished. Galusha said nothing. A moment later she turned to him.

"Should I write your cousin a letter and thank him, do you think?" she asked.

Galusha's reply was hurriedly given and most emphatic.

"Oh, no, no," he protested. "It will be quite unnecessary, quite. Indeed, no. He—ah—he would not expect it."

"No, I presume likely he wouldn't. And, after all, it was just a matter of business with his firm. But it wasn't a matter of business with you, Mr. Bangs. And if it hadn't been for you, I—I—— Well, I mustn't say any more or— or . . . Oh, you understand what I want to say, don't you?"

"Now—now, Miss Martha, please. I have done nothing, really, nothing but what any friend would have done."

"Any friend like you, you mean. I don't know where there are any more such friends, Mr. Bangs."

"Now, *please*. Miss Martha, I—I *hope* you won't mention this again. It will oblige me greatly if you will not. Really, I—I mean it."

She nodded, slowly. "Yes," she said, "bein' you, I think you do mean it. So I won't say any more; but I shall think a great deal, Mr. Bangs, and I never shall stop thinkin'. . . . There! And now what shall I do with all this money? Of course, I'll put it in the bank to-morrow, but what will I do with it to-night? By the way," she added, "it seems queer they should have paid you in cash instead of a check. Why did they, I wonder?"

Here was a demand for more explaining. Galusha plunged headlong, foundered, and then emerged, like a dog, with an explanation, such as it was, between his teeth.

"They—ah—they thought the money would be safer," he said.

Martha laughed aloud. "Safer?" she repeated. "Why, that's funny. Perhaps they're right, but I know the only way I shall feel safe between now and bankin' time to-morrow is to stay awake and watch every minute. Oh, I sha'n't do that exactly, of course, but I'm beginnin' to realize the responsibility of havin' riches. Ah hum! I laugh, Mr. Bangs, but you mustn't think it's because I don't realize what you—I mean . . . well, I guess I laugh because I'm kind of hysterical and—happy. I haven't been so happy for a long, long time. I won't say it again because you don't want me to, but for this once more, thank you, Mr. Bangs."

As Galusha left her to go to his room, she said: "Now I must go out and get after Primmie again. I'm scared to death that she'll tell everybody from here to Provincetown about my bein' worth a million dollars. She won't make it any *less* than a million, and the chances are it will be consider'ble more."

"But, Miss Martha, you have already told her not to tell about the money. I heard you tell her just now when you sent her out of the room."

Martha shrugged her shoulders.

"When you pour water into a sieve," she said, "it doesn't do much good to tell the sieve not to leak. Father used to say that some folks' heads were built so that whatever was poured into their ears ran right out of their mouths. Primmie's is made that way, I'm afraid. She'll swear she won't tell, and she won't mean to tell, but . . . Well, good-night, Mr. Bangs."

CHAPTER XII

MISS PHIPPS had prophesied that the cares attending the possession of wealth might interfere with her sleep that night. Concerning his own slumbers Galusha made no prophecy, but the said slumbers were broken and scanty, nevertheless. Martha's happiness, her relief, and the kind things she had said to him, all these were pleasant to reflect upon and to remember. Not so pleasant was the thought of the deception he had practiced. Of course, he had deceived for a good purpose and certainly with no idea of personal gain, quite the contrary. But he had been deceitful—and to Martha Phipps, of all people. What would she say if she ever found it out? He reflected upon the amazing number of—ah—fibs he had told her, and the question what would she say if she ever learned of these was even more terrifying in its possibilities. She must not learn of them, she must never, never know that it was his own money which he had brought from Boston, that he, and no one else, had bought that stock of hers.

Here he sat up in bed, having suddenly remembered the certificate for two hundred and fifty shares of Wellmouth Development Company stock which she had handed him when he started for Boston. He had folded it lengthwise and crosswise and had put it in his pocket—and had not thought of it since, until that moment. A cold chill ran down his back. What if——

He scrambled out of bed and, the room being distinctly cool, chills immediately ran up and down other portions of his anatomy. He did not mind those, however, but finding the matches, lighted the lamp and began pawing over his garments, those which he had worn upon his Boston pilgrimage.

The certificate was not in the coat pocket. Galusha gasped. Had he dropped it in the train? Or in the office of Cabot, Bancroft and Cabot? Why, if the last were true, it would be found and traced to him, and Minor and Barbour and, eventually, Cousin Gussie would learn that he . . . .

Here he remembered that Martha had urged him not to put it in his coat pocket but in his pocketbook. Oh, joy! He delved for the pocketbook, opened it—and found no certificate therein.

Oh, dear, dear! Oh, dear! Suppose he had not lost it in Boston. Suppose he had that very evening dropped it in the house here at home, in the sitting room, or the dining room. Suppose Primmie should find it, or Miss Phipps herself. Then she would *know* that he had deceived her— and lied to her——

And then he remembered that, instead of putting the certificate in his pocketbook, he had found the latter too small for the purpose, and had put the document in the inside pocket of his waistcoat. And in that waistcoat pocket he found it.

So that was all right, all right so far; but the fact remained that, instead of the troublesome thing—damning evidence of his guilt and deception—reposing safely in the vaults of a Boston bank, where he had intended putting it, it was here, in the house, in the house of Miss Martha Phipps, who might find it at any time.

He tried various hiding places, the drawers of his bureau, the table drawer, under the straw matting in the corner, but none seemed satisfactorily secure. Under the matting was, at first thought, ideal, but, after secreting it there and getting into bed, he remembered that Martha had declared his room needed new matting and, if ever she could afford that cost, new matting it should have. Having come into possession of five thousand dollars, she might feel that she could now afford it. He climbed, shivering, out of bed again, resurrected the certificate and hid it under his pillow, an orthodox but safe hiding place for that night only. The next morning he wrapped it in a summer undergarment and placed the said garment at the bottom of a pile of similar intimacies in his bureau drawer. And each night of the following week, before retiring, he dug it out to make sure of its safety.

The day after her boarder's return from Boston, Martha went over to Wellmouth Centre. The bank there had charge of her account, such as it was, and she wished to have it take charge of the, to her, huge sum of real money which Mr. Bangs had brought. She told the cashier that she was desirous of speaking with him on a matter of business, and he invited her into his little room at the end of the counter. There she took from her "Boston bag" a brown paper parcel and, unwrapping the brown paper, disclosed the five thousand dollars.

Cashiers of small town banks know the true financial strength and weakness of dwellers in those towns, just as the doctors know their physical ones. Mr. Edgar Thacher, which was the cashier's name in this instance, knew how much of an estate Cap'n Jim Phipps had left his daughter and how that estate was divided as to investments. So he was surprised when Martha revealed the money.

"Good land, Martha!" he exclaimed. "What's happened? Haven't gone into the counterfeiting trade, have you?"

Martha smilingly shook her head. "No, Edgar," she said. "It's too late in life for me to begin learnin' new trades, I guess. Just count that, will you, please? I want to make sure it's all there and that I didn't really have only half of it and dream the rest."

The cashier counted the money. "Five thousand, I make it," he said.

"That's what it ought to be. Now will you put that to my account? I don't know how long it'll stay there—the whole of it not very long, I'm afraid—but it will be earnin' a little interest while it does stay."

"Yes, sure. Well, Martha, it's none of my business, of course, but, as long as you say you haven't been counterfeiting, I wish you would give me your receipt for making money. Anybody that can make five thousand in one lump these hard times is doing well."

Martha shook her head once more. She and the cashier were old friends. "No receipt to give, Edgar," she said. "I wish there was; I'd be busy usin' it, I tell you. I just sold somethin' I owned, that's all, and got a good deal better price than I ever expected to. In fact, I had about given up hope of ever gettin' a cent. But there, I mustn't talk so much. You'll deposit that to my account, won't you, Edgar? And, if you *should* see your way clear to pay seven or eight per cent interest instead of four, or whatever you do pay, don't bother to write and ask me if I'll take it, because you'll only be wastin' your time. . . . Eh? Why, good gracious, Jethro! What are you doin' over here?"

The captain's big frame blocked the doorway of the cashier's office. He had opened that door without knocking, because it was his habit to open doors that way. Captain Jethro Hallett's position as keeper of the Gould's Bluffs light was not an exalted or highly paid one, but his influence in Wellmouth and its vicinity was considerable, nevertheless. He was accounted a man of means, he had always been— more especially in the years before his wife's death and the break in health which followed it—a person of shrewd business ability and keenness in a trade, and even now, when some of the townsfolk grinned behind his back and told stories of his spiritualistic obsessions, they were polite and deferential to his face. As a matter of fact, it would have been extremely impolitic to be otherwise than deferential to him. Captain Jeth was quite aware of his worth and expected deference.

He was as surprised to see his neighbor as she was to see him.

"Why, hello, Martha!" he grunted. "What fetched you here?"

"I asked you first, Cap'n Jeth, but it doesn't make any difference. My feet brought me as far as the corner and Ras Beebe's grocery cart brought me the rest of the way. I had

planned to come in the train, but Ras saved me the trouble—
and the fare. He's goin' back in a few minutes, so I've got
to hurry."

"Humph! But what did you come here *for?*"

"Oh, I had a little business with Edgar and the bank.
Excuse me, Jethro. Edgar . . ."

She stooped and whispered to the cashier. He nodded.

"Yes, Martha, of course," he said. "You've got your
book? All right. Back in a minute, Cap'n."

He picked up the pile of money from the desk, took from
Miss Phipps' hand the pass book she handed him, and together they stepped out into the public room. Captain
Jethro, whose eyes had caught sight of the bills, leaned
forward and peered through the little grating above Mr.
Thacher's desk. He saw the cashier and Martha standing
by the teller's window. The former said something and
handed the teller the bank book and the roll of bills. A
moment later the teller, having counted the money and
made an entry in the book, handed the latter back to the
lady.

"Five thousand," he said, and his tone was not low.
"There you are, Miss Phipps. Thank you."

When, having escorted the lady to the door, Thacher
came back to his private office, he found the light keeper
sitting in the armchair reserved for customers and pulling
thoughtfully at his beard.

"Well, Cap'n," said Mr. Thacher, "what can I do for
you?"

Captain Jethro crossed his legs. "I come over to cash a
couple of checks I got by mail," he said. "Had plenty of
time so I thought I'd drop in and see you a minute."

"Oh, yes, yes. Glad to see you."

"Um-hm. Ain't so glad to see me as you was to see
Martha Phipps, I guess likely. *I* ain't depositin' any five
thousand dollars. 'Twas five thousand she just deposited,
wasn't it?"

The cashier was rather annoyed. He did **not** answer at
once. His visitor repeated the question.

"Martha just put five thousand in the bank, didn't she?"
he asked.

"Why—yes. Did she tell you she was going to?"

"No. I heard Eldridge say five thousand when he give
her back her bank book. Five thousand is a lot of money.
Where'd she get it from?"

"I don't know, Cap'n, I'm sure. Little more springlike
out to-day, isn't it?"

"Um-hm. Martha been borrerin' from the bank, has
she?"

"No."

"Didn't know but she might have mortgaged the Phipps'
place. Ain't done that, you say?"

"No. At least, if she has she didn't tell me of it. How
are things over at the lighthouse?"

"All right enough. I don't hardly believe she could raise
more'n three thousand on a mortgage, anyhow. . . . Humph!
Five thousand is a sight of money, too. . . . Didn't she tell
you nothin' about how she got it?"

Thacher's annoyance increased. The ordinary caller dis-
playing such persistent curiosity would have been dismissed
unceremoniously; but Jethro Hallett was not to be dismissed
that way. The captain owned stock in the bank and, before
his illness, his name had been seriously considered to fill the
first vacancy in its list of directors.

"Must have told you *somethin'* about how she got hold of
all that money," persisted the light keeper. "What did she
say to you, anyway, Ed?"

"She said—she said—— Oh, well, she said she had sold
something she owned and had got the five thousand for
it."

"Humph! I want to know! Sold somethin', eh? What
was it she sold?"

"She didn't say, Cap'n. All she said was that she had sold
it and got the five thousand. Oh, yes, she did say that it
was a bigger price than she ever expected to get and that
there was a time when she never expected to get a cent."

"Humph! I want to know! Funny she should sell anything without comin' to me first. She generally comes to ask my advice about such things. . . . Humph! . . . She didn't sell the house? No, I'd a-known if she had done that. And what else. . . . Humph! . . ."

He pulled at his beard in silence for a moment. The teller, a brisk young man, possessed of a profound love of mischief and a corresponding lack of reverence, entered the office.

"Oh, excuse me," he said. "I thought you was alone, Mr. Thacher." Then, with a wink at his superior over the light keeper's tousled gray head, he observed, "Well, Cap'n Jeth, what's this I hear about Marietta Hoag? They tell me she's left the Spiritualists and gone over to Holiness chapel. Is it so?"

Jethro came out of his reverie. His deep-set eyes flashed and his big fist pounded the office table. No, it was not so. It was a lie. Who said it? Who was responsible for starting such sacrilegious, outrageous yarns? Marietta Hoag was a woman called and chosen to receive and give out revelations from on high. The Holiness crowd was a crew of good-for-nothin', hollerin' hard-shells. By the ever-lastin'——

He blew out of the office and out of the bank, rumbling and spitting fire like a volcano. The teller and the cashier watched him go. Then the former said:

"That's the way to get rid of him, Mr. Thacher. He'll set 'round and talk you to death if you give him half a chance. When you want him to go, tell him somebody at the other end of the town has been running down the Spiritualists. He'll be so anxious to get there and heave 'em overboard that he'll forget to stop and finish what he was saying here."

Which may or may not have been true, but the fact remains that the light keeper did not entirely forget what he and the cashier said concerning Martha Phipps' surprising bank deposit. And the next morning, as Martha was walking up the lane from the village, where she had been on a supply-purchasing excursion, she heard heavy footsteps and, turning, saw her neighbor tramping toward her, his massive figure rolling, as it always did when in motion, from side to side like a ship in a seaway.

"Why, hello, Jethro!" she exclaimed. Captain Jethro merely nodded. His first remark was a question, and very much to the point.

"Look here, Martha," he demanded. "Have you sold that Development stock of yours?"

Martha stared at him. For a moment she was inclined to believe in the truth of the light keeper's "spirit revelations."

"Why—why, Jethro!" she gasped. The captain, gazing at her keenly beneath his shaggy brows, seemed to find his answer in her face.

"Humph!" he observed. "You have sold it, ain't you? Well, by the everlastin'!"

"Why—why, Jethro! What are you talkin' about?"

"About that two hundred and fifty shares of Wellmouth Development of yours. You've sold it, ain't you, Martha? And you must have got par for it, too. Did the Trumet Trust Company folks buy it?"

But Miss Phipps was recovering from her surprise. She waited a moment before replying and, when she did reply, her tone was as crisp, if not as domineering, as her interrogator's.

"See here, Jethro," she said; "you're takin' a good many things for granted, aren't you?"

"No, I don't cal'late I am. I know you've sold somethin' and got five thousand dollars for it. I see you deposit the five thousand, myself, and Ed Thacher told me, after I pumped it out of him, that you said you'd sold somethin' you owned and got a good price when you didn't know as you'd ever get a cent. Now, you ain't sold your place because I'd know if you had, and it ain't worth five thousand, anyway. The other stocks and bonds you've got ain't——"

But Martha interrupted.

"Jethro," she said, sharply, "I just said that you were takin' a good many things for granted. You are. One of 'em is that you can talk to me as if I was Zach Bloomer or a fo'masthand on your old schooner. I'm neither of those and I don't care to be talked to in that way. Another is that what I chose to do with my property is your business. It isn't, it's mine. I may have sold that stock or any other, or the house or the barn or the cat, as far as that goes, but if I have or haven't it is my affair. And I think you'd better understand that before we talk any more."

She turned and walked on again. Captain Jethro's eyes flashed. It had been some time since any one had addressed him in that manner. However, women were women and business was business, and the captain was just then too intent upon the latter to permit the whims of the former to interfere. He swallowed his temper and strode after his neighbor.

"Martha," he said, complainingly, "I don't see as you've got any call to talk to me that way. I've been a pretty good friend to you, seems to me, and I was your father's friend, his chum, as you might say. Seems as if I had—well, a right to be interested in—in what you do."

Martha paused. After all, there was truth in what he said. He had been her father's close friend, and, no doubt, he meant to be hers. And he was Lulie's father, and not well, not quite his old self mentally or physically. Perhaps she should make allowances.

"Well, all right, Cap'n Jeth," she said. "It wasn't what you said so much as it was how you said it. Now will you tell me why you're so dreadfully anxious to know how I got that five thousand dollars I deposited over to the bank yesterday?"

The light keeper pulled at his beard; the latter was so thick as to make a handful, even for one of his hands. "Well," he said, somewhat apologetically, "you see, Martha, it's like this: *If* you sold them Development shares of yours —and I swan I can't think of anything else you own that would sell for just that money—*if* you sold 'em, I say, I'd like to know how you done it. I've got four hundred shares of that stock I'd like to sell fust-rate—fust-rate I would."

She had not entirely forgiven him for his intrusion in her

affairs and his manner of the moment before. She could not resist giving him a dig.

"Cap'n Jeth," she said, "I don't see why you need to worry. I've heard you say a good many times that you had promises from—well, from the spirits that you were goin' to sell your Development stock and at a profit. All you had to do, you said, was wait. Now, you see, *I* couldn't wait."

The captain nodded in satisfaction. "So *'twas* the Development you sold," he growled. "I figgered out it couldn't be nothin' else."

Martha scarcely knew whether to frown or laugh. Some of her pity concerning the old man's mental state had been, obviously, unnecessary. He was still sharp enough in business matters.

"Well," she said, with both laugh and frown, "suppose it was, what of it?"

"Why, just this, Martha: If there's anything goin' on on the inside of the Development Company I want to know it."

"There isn't anything goin' on so far as I know."

"Then who bought your stock? The Denboro Trust Company folks?"

"No. They don't know a thing about it."

"'Twan't that blasted Pulcifer?"

"No. I should hope not. Now don't ask any more, because I sha'n't tell you. It's a secret, that's all, and it's got to stay that way."

He looked at her. She returned his look and nodded. She meant what she said and he reluctantly recognized the fact.

"Humph! Well, all right, Martha," he growled. "But —but will you do this much for me? Will you ask these folks—whoever 'twas bought your two hundred and fifty— if they don't want my four hundred? If they're really buyin', I shouldn't be surprised if they would want it. If they bought it just as a favor to you, and are goin' to hang on and wait—why—why then, maybe they'd do a favor to a friend of yours and your father's afore you. Maybe they will, you can't tell. And you can tell 'em I've had word from —from over yonder that it's all goin' to turn out right. You ask 'em if they don't want to buy my stock, will you, Martha?"

Martha took time for reflection. Then she said: "Cap'n Jeth, if I do ask 'em that, will you promise not to tell a soul a word about my sellin' my stock, or about the money, or anything of the kind? Will you promise that?"

The light keeper nodded. "Sartin sure," he said. "I'll promise you, Martha."

"All right, I'll ask, but you mustn't count on anything comin' from it."

The captain's brows drew together. "What I count on," he said, solemnly, "is a higher promise than yours or mine, Martha Phipps. What we do down here will only be what them up aloft want us to do. Don't you forget that."

They parted at the Phipps' gate. Captain Jethro walked moodily home. Lulie met him at the door. She was wearing her hat and coat.

"I'm going up to the village, father," she said. "I have some errands to do. I'll be back pretty soon."

Her father watched her as she walked away. The thought crossed his mind that possibly Nelson Howard might be visiting the village that forenoon. He called her name, and she turned and came back.

"What is it, father?" she asked.

Jethro hesitated. He passed a hand across his forehead. His head felt tired. Somehow he didn't want to talk any more. Even as important a topic as Nelson Howard did not arouse his interest.

"Oh, nothin', nothin'," he assured. "Cal'late maybe I'll lay down and turn in a little spell afore dinner. Is Zach on deck?"

"Yes, he is out in the kitchen, or was a minute ago. Primmie was over on an errand and I heard their tongues going. Shall I speak to Zach, father?"

He told her no, and went into the house. There was a couch in the dining room and he stretched himself upon it.

The head of the couch was near the door leading to the kitchen. That door was closed, but from behind it sounded voices, voices which were audible and distinct. A dispute seemed to be in progress between Mr. Bloomer and Miss Cash and, although Zacheus continued to grumble on in an even key, Primmie's tone became higher and shriller with each retort.

"I tell you 'tis so, Zach Bloomer. . . . Well, maybe 'twan't a hundred and fifty thousand, but I bet you 'twas more money than you ever see in *your* life. So now!"

The assistant light keeper was heard to cough. Primmie seemed to discern a hint of skepticism even in the cough.

"Oh, you can set there and keep on turnin' up your nose and—and coughin'," she declared, "but——"

Zacheus interrupted to say that he hardly ever turned up his nose when he coughed.

"Seems to come handier to turn it down, Posy," he said.

"Oh, be still, foolish! Well, anyhow, it's true, every word of it. I see more money at one time and in one—er—er junk, as you might say, than ever I see afore—yes, or I bet you ever see neither, Zach Bloomer."

"We-ll, course what I ever see never amounted to much, but if it's more than *you* see, Rosebud, then it must have been consider'ble of a lot. Over in them Mashpaug woods, where you hail from, money kind of grows on the bushes, like huckleberries, I presume likely. Martha Phipps been over there berryin', has she?"

"No, she ain't. Besides, I never said Miss Martha brought the money into the house. All's I said was that 'twas in there and I see it with my own eyes."

"Sho! With your own eyes, eh? Well, well! What do you cal'late 'twould have looked like if you'd borrered somebody else's eyes? Say, Posy, was it you fetched the billion and a half, or whatever 'twas, into the house?"

"Me? *Me* with all that money? My savin' soul!"

"Well, who did fetch it? Santy Claus?"

"I sha'n't tell you. I promised Miss Martha I wouldn't tell one word about that money and I ain't goin' to."

"Hooray, Posy! That's the way to talk! Well, now, be honest about it: What did you have for supper night afore last? Mince pie, was it? Why didn't you eat another slice? Then you'd have dreamed about a mackerel keg full of di'monds, most likely."

Captain Jethro, trying to fall asleep on the couch in the dining room, turned over in disgust and raised himself upon an elbow preparatory to shouting an order for silence. But Primmie's next speech caught his attention and the order was not given.

"Dreamed!" retorted the indignant young woman. "Are you tryin' to tell me I only dreamed about that money, Zacheus Bloomer? Huh! My Lord of Isrul! If you'd seen that great big piled-up heap of bills layin' right there on the table in our settin' room where Mr. Bangs put 'em, I guess you'd have said 'dreams' and more, too. Ten dollar bills there was and twenties and—and thirties and forties, for all I know."

"That so? Right where Mr. Bangs put 'em, eh? Now I *know* you was dreamin', Pansy Blossom. That little dried-up Bangs man ain't worth more'n ten cents, if that."

"He ain't? How do you know he ain't?"

"Same as I know when that Lucy Larcom tomcat of Martha's has been in a fight, by the looks of him. Look at the Bangs man's clothes, and—and his hat—and—why, Godfreys mighty, he can't afford to get his hair cut oftener than once in three months! Anyhow, he don't. And you stand there and tell me he come cruisin' in t'other night and commenced sheddin' million dollar bills all over the furniture. Where'd he get 'em to? Dig 'em up over in the Baptist graveyard?"

"No, he never. He got 'em up to Boston. Leastways, I guess he did, 'cause that's where he went. And, besides, what do you know about how much he's worth? He may look kind of—of ratty, but all the same he's got rich relations. Why, one of his relations is head of the biggest broke —I mean, brokin' and bank place there is in Boston. Cabot,

Bancroft and—and Thingumbob is the name of it. And Miss Martha told me 'twas——"

There was much more of this and the listener on the dining room couch heard it all. He remained on that couch until Miss Cash, at the back door of the kitchen, delivered her triumphant farewell.

"So there now, Zach Bloomer," she said, "I guess you believe now I didn't dream it. And you needn't ask any more questions because I sha'n't tell you a single word. I promised Miss Martha I wouldn't never tell and I'm goin' to keep my promise."

That evening Martha approached her lodger on the subject of the possibility of selling the light keeper's Development holdings for him. To say the least, she received no encouragement. Galusha was quite emphatic in his expression of disbelief in that possibility.

"Oh, dear me, no, Miss Martha," he stammered. "I—ah —I feel quite sure it would be unwise to—ah—attempt such a thing. You see—ah—you see—my cousin is—is——"

"I know, he's sick, poor man, and shouldn't be disturbed. You're right, of course, Mr. Bangs. It was only that Cap'n Jeth had always been a good friend of father's and mine and I thought if Cabot, Bancroft and Cabot really were buyin' the stock perhaps they might like to buy his. But I can see why you wouldn't want to trouble Mr. Cabot again just now. I'm sorry I mentioned it to you; I'm afraid I have made you nervous."

Galusha was nervous, certainly, and showed it. He protested, however, that he was quite all right really, and, as his landlady did not mention the subject again, he recovered a portion of his equilibrium. And during the following week he gradually gained more and more confidence. The telltale certificate hidden in his bureau drawer was, of course, a drawback to his peace of mind, and the recollection of his recent outbreak of prevarication and deception was always a weight upon his conscience. But, to offset these, there was a changed air about the Phipps' home and its inmates which was so very gratifying that, if it did not deaden that conscience, it, at least, administered to it an effective dose of soothing syrup.

Primmie wept no more into the dishwater nor sighed despairingly when serving breakfast. She sang now and, although an unprejudiced person might not have found the change an unmixed delight, Galusha did. Miss Phipps sang, too, occasionally, not with the camp-meeting exuberance of her maid, but with the cheery hum of the busy bee. She was happy; she said so and looked so, and, in spite of his guilty knowledge of the deceit upon which that happiness was founded, her lodger was happy because she was.

"Do you know," he observed, on Saturday morning of that week, as, coated and capped for his daily walk, he stood by the door of the dining room, "it's quite extraordinary, really. I have been thinking, you know, and it really is quite extraordinary."

Martha was sitting in the rocker by the window, the morning sunshine streaming in through the leaves and blossoms of the potted plants on the brackets dappling her hair and cheek with cheery splashes of light and shade. She was consulting the pages of her cookbook, as a preliminary to preparing a special dessert for Sunday's dinner, and was humming as she did so.

She looked up when he spoke.

"What is extraordinary?" she asked. "Your thinkin', do you mean? I don't see anything very extraordinary about that. You're thinkin' most of the time, seems to me."

"Oh, I don't mean that. I meant what I was thinking was extraordinary. Or not precisely that, either. I—ah—I mean —well, you see, when I was in Washington—at the Institute, you know—it used to annoy me—ah—extremely, to have any one sing or whistle in my vicinity. Really, it did. I sometimes spoke very sharply—ah—irritably to any one who did that. And now, as I stood here and heard you singing, Miss Martha, it suddenly came over me that I do not mind it at all. I—ah—actually like to hear you. I do, very much, indeed. Now, isn't that extraordinary!"

Martha laughed aloud. "Why, yes," she declared; "I

think it is. Anybody likin' to hear me sing is about as extraordinary as anything that ever was, I guess. Mr. Bangs, you're awfully funny."

Galusha nodded. "Yes," he said, "I am sure I must be. I think if I were any one else I should laugh at myself a great deal. I mean—ah—I mean in that case I should laugh, not at myself, but at me. Good gracious, I haven't made that very clear, have I?"

His smile was so contagious that she laughed again.

"I didn't mean you were funny to laugh at, but to laugh with," she said. "You're goin' to have an especially nice walk this mornin'. It's such a lovely forenoon I almost wish I was goin' with you."

Galusha beamed. "Why—why, so do I!" he exclaimed, in delighted surprise. "Yes, I do, I do, indeed! Ah—ah— why don't you?"

"Mercy me, I couldn't think of it! I must stay here and get to cookin' or we'll have no puddin' to-morrow noon. I'll be with you in spirit, as the books say; how will that do?"

Whether or not she was with him in spirit, she was very much in her lodger's thoughts as he walked down the path to the gate. It was such a beautiful forenoon, with the first promise of spring in the air, that, instead of starting toward the village, as was his usual custom, he turned in the other direction and strolled toward the lighthouse. The sea view from the cliff edge should be magnificent on a morning like this.

But it was not of the view, or the beauty of the morning, that he thought as he wandered slowly on. His mind, for some reason or other, seemed to be filled with the picture of Martha Phipps as she sat in the rocking-chair, with the background of old-fashioned plants and blossoms, and the morning sunshine illumining her pleasant, comely face. He could visualize every feature of that face, which fact was extremely odd, for it had been many years since he had noticed a female face sufficiently for that face to impress itself upon his memory. Years and years before Galusha

Bangs had been forced to the conclusion that the interest of attractive feminity was not for him and he had accepted the inevitable and never permitted his own interest to stray in that direction. A few feminine faces he could, of course, recall; the face of his Aunt Clarissa, for instance, and—dear me, yes! that of the pestiferous Mrs. Worth Buckley, his —ah—not his "old man of the sea" exactly, but his equally troublesome, middle-aged woman of the mountains. Mrs. Buckley had not attracted his notice, she had seized it, served a subpoena upon it, and his provokingly contrary memory persisted in recalling her face, probably because he so earnestly desired to forget it.

But he found a real pleasure in visualizing the face of Miss Martha Phipps. Her eyes now—her eyes were—ah— um—they were blue; no, they were gray—or a sort of gray-blue, perhaps, or even a shade of brown. But the precise color made no real difference. It was the way they looked at one, and—ah—smiled, so to speak. Odd, because he had never before realized that one could—ah—smile with one's eyes. Attractive, too, that smile of hers, the eyes and the lips in combination. A sort of cheerful, comfortable smile —yes, and—ah—attractive—ah—inviting, as one might say; a homelike smile; that was the word he wanted—"homelike." It had been a long, long time since he had had a home. As a matter of fact, he had not cared to have one. A tent in Egypt or Syria, furnished with a mummy or two, and with a few neighborly ruins next door—this had been his idea of comfort. It was his idea still, but nevertheless——

And then he became aware that from somewhere, apparently from the heavens above, a voice was shouting—yes, roaring—his name.

"Mr. Bangs! . . . Hi-i, Mr. Bangs!"

Galusha came out of his walking dream, stared about him, found that he had walked almost to the fence surrounding the light keeper's home and would have collided with that fence in another stride or two, looked around, down, and finally up—to see Captain Jethro leaning over the iron rail surrounding the lantern room at the top of the lighthouse.

"Oh! Why—ah—good gracious!" he exclaimed. "Were you calling me, Captain Hallett?"

Captain Jethro shook his big head. "Callin'!" he repeated. "I've been bellerin' like the foghorn for five minutes. A little more of it and I'd have run out of steam or bust a b'iler, one or t'other. Ain't been struck deef, have you, Mr. Bangs?"

"No—ah—no, I trust not. I was—ah—thinking, I presume, and I did not hear you. I'm very sorry."

"That's all right. Glad you was only thinkin' and no worse. I didn't know but you'd been struck by walkin' paralysis or somethin'. Say," he leaned further over the rail and lowered his voice. "Say," he said again, "would you mind comin' up here a minute? I want to talk to you."

Mr. Bangs did not mind and, entering the round tower, he climbed the spiral stair to the little room at the top. The great lantern, with its glittering facets and lenses filled that room almost entirely, and the light keeper's great form filled it still more. There was scarcely space for little Galusha to squeeze in.

Jethro explained that he had been cleaning the lantern.

"It's Zacheus' job really," he observed, "but I have to do it myself once in a while to keep it shipshape. Say," he added, opening the door which led to the balcony, "look out yonder. Worth lookin' at, ain't it?"

It was. The morning was dry and clear, a brisk wind from the west, and not a cloud. The lighthouse, built as it was upon the knoll at the edge of the bluff, seemed to be vastly higher than it actually was, and to tower far above all else until the view from its top was almost like that from an aëroplane. The horizon swept clear and unbroken for three quarters of a circle, two of those quarters the sharp blue rim of the ocean meeting the sky. The white wave-crests leaped and twinkled and danced for miles and miles. Far below on the yellow sand of the beach, the advancing and retreating breakers embroidered lacy patterns which changed constantly.

"Worth looking at, ain't it?" repeated the captain.

Galusha nodded. "Indeed it is," he said, with emphasis. Yet it surprised him slightly to find the gruff old light keeper enthusiastic concerning a scene which must be so very much a matter of course to him.

"The Almighty done a good job when He built that," observed Captain Jethro, waving his hand toward the Atlantic. "Don't never get tired of lookin' at salt water, I don't, and yet I've been in it or on it or around it pretty much all my life. And now I'm up above it," he added, thoughtfully. "We're pretty high up where we are now, Mr. Bangs. I like to set up here and—er—well, kind of think about things, sometimes. . . . Humph! . . . Do you cal'late we're any nigher when we're up aloft here than we are down on the ground yonder; nigher to *them,* I mean?"

His visitor was puzzled. "I—I beg your pardon?" he stammered. "Nigher—ah—nearer to—ah—what?"

"Nigher to them—them that's gone afore. Seems sometimes, when I'm alone up here, particular of a foggy day, as if I was consider'ble nigher to them—to *her,* especial— than when I'm on the ground. Think there's anything in it, do you?"

Galusha said he didn't know; we know so little about such things, really. He wondered what the captain had invited him up there to talk about. Some spiritualistic subject, very likely; the conversation seemed to be tending that way. Jethro appeared to have forgotten altogether the séance and his, Galusha's, assumption of the character of the small, dark "evil influence." It looked very much as if that assumption—so far as it entailed the permanent shifting of prejudice from Nelson Howard to himself—had been effort wasted.

Captain Jeth pulled at his beard and seemed to be dreaming. Galusha pitied the old fanatic as he stood there, massive, rugged, brows drawn together, sturdy legs apart as if set to meet the roll of a ship at sea—a strong figure, yet in a way the figure of a wistful, dreaming child, helpless——

"Mr. Bangs," said the light keeper, "don't you cal'late, if you set out to, you could sell my four hundred Wellmouth

Development same as you sold Martha's two hundred and fifty?"

Galusha would have sat down, if there had been anything except the floor to sit down on. As a matter of fact, even that consideration might not have prevented his sitting; his knees bent suddenly and he was on his way to the floor, but his shoulders struck the wall behind him and furnished the support he so very much needed. So far as speech was concerned, that was out of the question. His mouth opened and shut, but nothing audible issued therefrom. Mr. Bangs, at that moment, gave a very good imitation of a fish unexpectedly jerked out of deep water to dry, very dry land.

Captain Jethro did not seem to realize the effect of his question upon his visitor. His big fist moved downward from his chin to the tip of his beard, only to rise and take a new hold at the chin again. His gaze was fixed upon the rolling sea outside.

"You see," he went on, "I kind of figger it out this way: If them folks who bought Martha's stock are cal'latin' to buy up Development they'll want more'n two hundred and fifty. I'll sell 'em mine at a reasonable figger; sha'n't ask much over what I paid for it, I sha'n't. If they ain't buyin' for anything 'special, but just 'cause they think it's a good thing to keep—well, then——"

Galusha interrupted. The faculty of framing words and uttering them was returning to him, albeit slowly and jerkily.

"Why—why, Captain Hallett," he faltered. "How—how —who—who——"

"Martha didn't tell me nothin' except that she had sold her stock," broke in the light keeper. "I guessed that, too, afore she told me. She never mentioned your name, Mr. Bangs, nor where she sold it, nor nothin'. But, of course, when I found out 'twas you who went to Boston and fetched home the five thousand dollars I didn't need to be told— much. Now, Mr. Bangs, I wish you'd see if you can't sell my four hundred shares for me. It'll be consider'ble of a favor if you will. You see, them shares——"

But Galusha did not wait for him to finish. His alarmed protests fairly tumbled over each other.

"Why—why, Captain Hallett," he cried, "really I—I . . . ah . . . What you ask is quite impossible. Oh, very much so—ah—very. You see . . . Well, really, I . . . Captain Hallett, this entire matter was supposed to be a secret, an absolute secret. I am surprised—and—ah—shocked to learn that——"

The captain's big paw was uplifted as a signal. "Sshh! Heave to! Come up into the wind a minute, Mr. Bangs. 'Tis a secret, fur's I'm consarned, and 'twill be just the same after I've sold my stock. I realize that business men don't want business matters talked about, 'tain't likely. All I'd like to have you do is just see if you can't dispose of that four hundred of mine, same as you done with Martha's. Just as a favor I'm askin' it."

Galusha shook his head violently. His agitation was as great as ever. After going through the agony of the frying pan and congratulating himself that that torment was over, then to find he had escaped merely into the fire was perfectly maddening—not to say frightening—and—oh, dear, dear, dear!

"Really, I'm very sorry, very," he reiterated. "But I am *quite* sure I can do nothing with your shares, Captain Hallett. It—it—such a thing would be absolutely impossible. I'm sorry."

Captain Jethro's calm was unshaken. "We-ll," he said, slowly, "I ain't altogether surprised. Course I could see that maybe you wouldn't want to go cruisin' up to them folks again, 'specially they bein' relations. I don't blame you for that, Mr. Bangs. But, in case you did feel that way, I'd made up my mind I'd go up there myself and see 'em."

"Eh? Ah—ah—— See? See whom?"

"Why, them relations of yours. Them Cabot, Bancroft and Cabot folks. I know *of* 'em; everybody that knows anything about bankin' does, of course. I don't know any of 'em personal, but I cal'lated maybe you'd be willin' to give me a note, a letter introducin' me, you see. Then I could tell 'em why I come, and how I wanted to talk with 'em about sellin' some more of the same stock they sold for you. That would be all right, wouldn't it, Mr. Bangs?"

Galusha did not answer. The absolute hopelessness of the situation was beginning to force itself upon his understanding. Whether or not he gave the letter of introduction, the light keeper would go to Cabot, Bancroft and Cabot— oh, how on earth did he ever learn that *they* had anything to do with it?—and begin talkin' about Martha Phipps' stock; and they would deny knowing anything of it; and then the captain would persist, giving details; and Barbour and Minor and the rest would guess the truth and probably write Thomas, who would eventually tell Cousin Gussie; and the light keeper would return home and tell Martha, and she would learn that he had lied to her and deceived her——

"Well, what do you say, Mr. Bangs?" inquired Captain Jethro.

Bangs turned a haggard gaze in the speaker's direction. The latter was standing in exactly the same attitude, feet apart, hand to beard, sad eyes gazing out to sea; just as he had stood when Galusha's sympathy had gone out to him as a "helpless, dreaming child."

"What are you laughin' at?" asked Captain Jeth, switching his gaze from old ocean to the face of the little archæologist.

Galusha had not laughed, but there was a smile, a wan sort of smile, upon his face.

"Oh, nothing in particular," he replied. "I was reflecting that it seemed rather too bad to waste pity in quarters where it was not—ah—needed, when there was such a pressing demand, as one might say, at home."

CHAPTER XIII

THE earnest young man behind the counter in the office of Cabot, Bancroft and Cabot—the young man who had so definitely classified Galusha Bangs as a "nut" —was extremely surprised when that individual reappeared before his window and, producing the very check which he had obtained there so short a time before, politely requested to exchange it for eighty-two hundred dollars in cash and another check for the balance.

"Why—why—but——!" exclaimed the young man.

"Thank you. Yes, if—ah—if you will be so good," said Galusha.

The young man himself asked questions, and then called Mr. Minor into consultation, and Mr. Minor asked more. The answers they received were not illuminating, but in the end the transaction was made as requested.

"But, Bangs," said Minor, laughing, "what I can't understand is why you want to bother with the check for eleven hundred and odd—whatever it is. Why not take the whole amount in cash and be done with it?"

Galusha shook his head. "I prefer it the—ah—other way. If you don't mind," he added, politely.

"Oh, we don't mind. But—well, it seems rather funny, that's all. Ha, ha!"

"Does it? Yes, I—ah—dare say it does."

"Ha, ha! Yes, rather. Of course, it is your business, you know, but——"

He laughed again. The harassed Galusha waited until the laugh was over. Then he said, gently, "Yes, I was under that impression."

233

"Eh? What impression?"

"That it was, as you say, my—ah—business."

"Yes. Why . . . Eh? Oh! . . . Humph! . . . Why, yes, surely, certainly. Here," turning briskly to the clerk, "give Mr. Bangs what he wishes at once."

He walked away, pulling thoughtfully at his mustache. Galusha, rubbing his chin, looked gravely after him. The clerk began making out the check. This done and the check entrusted to a messenger to be taken to the private office for signing, the next business was the counting of the money.

"Eighty-two hundred, you said?" asked the clerk.

"Eighty-two hundred—ah—yes," said Galusha.

Eight thousand was, of course, the price at par of Jethro Hallett's four hundred shares of Wellmouth Development stock. The additional two hundred was a premium paid, so to speak, to the departed spirit of the late Mrs. Jethro Hallett. She, by or through the Chinese control of Miss Marietta Hoag, had notified her husband that he was destined to sell his Development shares at a profit, a small profit perhaps, but *a* profit, nevertheless.

So, when at that point of their conversation in the lantern room of the Gould's Bluffs light, Galusha, recognizing his helpless position and the alternative of buying the Hallett holdings or being exposed to Cousin Gussie as a sentimental and idiotic spendthrift and to Martha Phipps as a liar and criminal—when Galusha, facing this alternative, stammered a willingness to go to Boston and see if he could not dispose of Jethro's stock as he had Martha's, the captain added an additional clause.

"I won't sell for par," he declared stubbornly. "Julia revealed to me that I wouldn't, and so I sha'n't. I'll sell for fifty cents a share extry, but I won't sell for twenty flat. Rather than do that I'll go to them Cabot folks myself and see if I can't find out who's buyin' and why. Then I'll go to the real buyers and make the best trade I can with them. If they really want to get hold of that stock, fifty cents a share won't stand in their way, I'll bet you."

It did not stand in Galusha's way, either. In his desper-

ate position he would have paid any amount obtainable
rather than have the light keeper go to Boston on such an
errand.

Leaving the clerk's window with his pocket bulging with
bank notes, Mr. Bangs proceeded sadly, but with determination, to the private office of Mr. Barbour, his cousin's
"second secretary." There, producing from another pocket
a huge envelope, portentously daubed and sealed with red
wax, he handed it to Barbour. It contained the two stock
certificates, each signed in blank, Martha's for two hundred
and fifty shares, Captain Jethro's for four hundred. The
envelope and the wax he had procured at a stationer's near
the South Station. The obliging salesman had permitted
him to do the sealing on the premises.

"Mr. Barbour," he faltered, "I should like to leave this
with you, if—if quite convenient, that is to say."

Barbour turned the big envelope over.

"Yes, Mr. Bangs, surely," he said, but he looked puzzled.
"What is it?"

Galusha blushed and stammered. "Why—why——" he
began; "I—ah—you see—it is—ah—something of mine."

"Something you wish me to take care of?" asked Barbour,
still looking at the envelope.

His caller grasped at the straw.

"Yes—yes, that is it," he said, eagerly. "Dear me, yes.
If you will be so kind."

"Yes, indeed, Mr. Bangs. No trouble at all. I'll put
it——"

But the little man stopped the sentence in the middle.

"If—if you please," he protested. "Ah—please don't. I
don't wish to know where you put it. Really, I don't, not
in the least. I very much prefer not to know where it is. . . .
Ah—good-day, Mr. Barbour. Thank you very much."

The general opinion in the office of Cabot, Bancroft and
Cabot concerning the senior partner's queer cousin was
strengthened by this visit. The surmise that Galusha Bangs
was a "nut" became a conviction.

But, for the "nut" himself, life during the coming weeks

and months became a much less worrisome struggle. Returning to East Wellmouth, for the second time laden with legal tender, he delivered his burden to Captain Jethro, who, in return, promised faithfully never to reveal a word concerning the sale of his Development stock or drop a hint which might help to locate its purchasers.

"Course I won't say nothin'," vowed the captain. "I realize that business men don't want their business talked about. And if them Cabot, Bancroft and Cabot folks are tryin' to buy in the stock, whether it's for themselves or somebody else, they'll want it kept dark. No, I ain't told a soul on this earth and I *won't* tell one. That is satisfactory, ain't it?"

The shadow of a smile passed across Galusha's face. "Quite, quite," he replied. "Nothing could be more so unless——"

"Well, unless what?"

"Oh, nothing, nothing. Thank you—ah—thank you very much."

It had occurred to him that, considering the light keeper's peculiarities, the promise not to tell a soul on earth might be stretched to include those elsewhere; but he kept the thought to himself. Captain Jethro did not press his question. The shrewd old captain was so thoroughly delighted at having sold, and at the prophesied profit, his troublesome holdings in the Wellmouth Development Company, that his mood was neither combative nor inquisitive.

Galusha did not tell Miss Phipps of his business deal with the light keeper. In the first place, his telling her would involve more deception and, also, might lead to more possibilities of discovery. The average, well-meaning person, having been driven by relentless fate to the committing of murder, could scarcely have felt more conscience-stricken and depraved than did little Galusha Bangs at having lied to Martha Phipps. Of course, the lies and deceit had resulted in a distinct benefit to her and had been perpetrated solely with that idea, but this fact he ignored entirely. And no murderer could have been more anxious to hide his guilty secret than was he. So, for the first few days after his return with the light keeper's money, he was inclined to be thoughtful and nervous, to fall into troubled trances at table or in the middle of a conversation, and to start rather violently when aroused from those trances. Primmie was disposed to attribute these lapses to disease. She confided her fears to her employer.

"You know what I think 'tis makes him act so, Miss Martha?" she asked, on one occasion.

"Makes who act how?"

"Makes Mr. Bangs set there and go moonin' off and not pay no attention and then jump when you wake him up as if you'd stuck a pin in him. You know what I think 'tis? I think maybe it's dropsy."

"What?"

"Um-hm. I had a great-aunt once; had a slew of 'em, fur's that goes, 'cause my grandmother on the starboard side——"

"What side?"

"Eh! Oh, that's what pa used to call his side of the family, the starboard side. All ma's folks was port side, 'cordin' to his tell. He'd worked aboard vessels, pa had; that is, as much as he ever worked anywheres. Well, anyhow, his grandmother she had eight sisters and three brothers, so I had great-aunts thicker'n miskeeters in a swamp hole—my savin' soul, yes! Well, anyhow, one of 'em, Aunt Lucifer 'twas——"

"Primmie! What was her name?"

"Lucifer. Ma and us children always called her Aunt Lucy, though; she liked it better."

"Heavens and earth! I should think she might. *What* possessed anybody to name a child Lucifer? And a girl-child at that!"

"Does sound kind of funny, don't it? Folks 'most always used to laugh when they heard what her name was. That is, fust along they did; but they never laughed but once when she was around. Talk about makin' anybody mad! And temper—my Lord of Isrul! Why, if they laughed at her name she was li'ble to grab hold of the fust thing come to hand, flatiron or frying pan or chunk of stove wood or anything, and let 'em have it rattley-bang-jing. *I* never seen her do it, of course—all that was afore *my* time—but pa used to say it never made no difference whether 'twas the man come tryin' to collect the store bill or the minister or anybody, she'd up and flatten him just the same. Course pa said 'twas a whole lot more li'ble to be the bill man than the minister 'cause there was precious few ministers ever——"

"There, there, Primmie! I can't stop to listen any longer, I'm busy. But do tell me why they named the poor thing Lucifer? How did they ever hear the name, anyway; way over in those Mashpaug woods?"

"Oh, there was a story about that, kind of a pretty story 'twas, too. 'Cordin' to pa's tell, the fust time Aunt Lucy's ma—my great grandmother, and the land knows what *her* name was, *I* don't—the fust time she went out after the baby was born she went to camp meetin'. And one of the ministers there he talked some consider'ble about a critter name of Lucifer that was a fallen-down angel, whatever that is. Well, my great-grandmother she didn't understand much about what he was talkin' about—I cal'late none of 'em did fur's that goes, and no wonder—but the name of Lucifer sort of stuck in her head 'cause she thought 'twas kind of pretty. And when she got back home they told her the baby had fetched loose from the bed where it had been asleep and fell onto the floor and pretty nigh busted itself in two. And it never hardly cried at all—was a reg'lar angel they said—and that made her think about the fallen-down angel she'd just heard tell of to camp meetin' and its name was Lucifer. And they hadn't named the baby yet, so——"

"I see. Ha, ha! Primmie, you are—well, there aren't many like you, I'm sure. Now I must go. Well, what is it?"

"Oh, nothin', only I ain't told you why I think Mr. Bangs may be comin' down with dropsy. You see, Aunt Lucy—this Lucifer one I've been tellin' you about—she had it.

I only remember her 'long towards her last. She wan't heavin' any teakittles at folks then; my savin' soul, no! She used to set in a big rockin'-chair over by the stove and was all puffed-up like—like a featherbed, you might say; and she'd kind of doze along and doze along and you could holler your head off and she wouldn't pay no attention, and then she'd kind of wake up, as you might say, and sing out, 'Hey? What say?' just like Mr. Bangs, for all the world. And 'twas dropsy she had, so now you see, don't you, Miss Martha?"

"Yes, yes, Primmie, I see. Tut, tut, tut! You certainly have a great imagination, of its kind. I shouldn't worry about Mr. Bangs' disease, if I were you. The poor man isn't really strong yet and he has been runnin' back and forth to Boston lately altogether too much for his own good. He is tired and his nerves are tired, too; so we must make it as easy as we can for him, Primmie, you and I."

"Yes'm. He's a good man, ain't he?"

"Indeed he is!"

"Yes'm. Even if he is so kind of—of funny."

Often, in earlier conversations with her housemaid, Miss Phipps had agreed that her lodger was, to say the least, "funny"; but now she seemed to resent the word.

"Humph!" she observed, crisply, "if he is, I presume likely he has the right to be. And I know this, if there were more 'funny' people like him in this world it would be a big improvement. Primmie, go and do your sweepin'."

CHAPTER XIV

WITH the end of the following week spring came in earnest to Gould's Bluffs, not yet as a steady boarder—spring in New England is a young lady far too fickle for that—but to make the first of her series of ever-lengthening visits. Galusha found her, indeed, a charming young person. His walks now were no longer between snowdrifts or over frozen fields and hills. Those hills and fields were still bare and brown, of course, but here and there, in sheltered hollows, tiny bits of new green began to show. In April, by disturbing the layers of dead leaves and sodden vegetation through which these hints of greenness peeped, one was likely to come upon fragrant treasures, the pink and white blossoms of the trailing arbutus.

There was a superfluity of mud, of course, and as Miss Phipps often informed him, Galusha's boots and lower trouser legs were "sights to see" when he came back from those walks. He expressed contrition and always proclaimed that he should be much more careful in future— much more, yes. But he was not, nor did he care greatly. He was feeling quite well again, better than he had felt for years, and spring was in his middle-aged blood and was rejuvenating him, just as it was rejuvenating the world and its creatures about him, including Lucy Larcom, Martha's ancient and rheumatic Thomas cat. Lucy—an animal as misnamed as Primmie's "Aunt Lucifer"—instead of slumbering peacefully and respectably in his cushioned box in the kitchen, which had been his custom of winter nights, now refused to come in at bedtime, ignored his mistress'

240

calls altogether, and came rolling home in the morning with slit ears and scarred hide and an air of unrepentant and dissipated abandon.

Galusha, inspecting the prodigal's return one morning, observed: "Luce, when I first met you, you reminded me strongly of my Aunt Clarissa. The air of—ah—dignity and respectable disapproval with which you looked me over was much like hers. But now—now, if you wore a hat on one side and an—ah—exuberant waistcoat, you would remind me more of Mr. Pulcifer."

With April came the fogs, and the great foghorn bellowed and howled night after night. Galusha soon learned to sleep through the racket. It was astonishing, his capacity for sleep and his capability in sleeping up to capacity. His appetite, too, was equally capable. He was, in fact, feeling so very well that his conscience began troubling him concerning his duty to the Institute. He wrote to the directors of that establishment suggesting that, as his health was so greatly improved, perhaps he had better return to his desk. The reply was prompt. The directors were, so the letter said, much pleased to hear of his improved health, but they wished him to insure the permanence of that improvement by remaining away for another six months at least. "We have," the writer added, "a plan, not yet definite and complete, although approaching that condition, which will call for your knowledge and experienced guidance. Our plan will probably materialize in the fall or winter. I can say no more concerning it now, except to add that we feel sure that it will be acceptable to you and that you should take every precaution to gain strength and health as a preparatory measure."

Galusha could not guess what the plan might be, but he was a bit surprised to find himself so willing to agree to the directors' mandate that he remain in East Wellmouth for the present. His beloved desk in his beloved study there in Washington had been torn from him, or rather he had been torn from it, and for a time it had really seemed as if the pangs of severance might prove fatal. By all that was fit and proper he should fiercely resent the order to remain away for another six months. But he did not resent it fiercely; did not resent it at all; in fact, to be quite honest, he welcomed it. He was inwardly delighted to be ordered to remain in East Wellmouth. Such a state of mind was surprising, quite nonunderstandable.

And, day by day and week by week, the fear that his guilty secret concerning the Wellmouth Development stock might be discovered became less and less acute. Captain Jethro never mentioned it; Martha Phipps, when she found that he preferred not to discuss it, kept quiet, also. Perhaps, after all, no one would ever know anything about it. And the change in Martha's spirits was glorious to see.

He and Lulie Hallett had many quiet talks together. Ever since the evening of the séance when, partially by craft and partially by luck, he had prevented her father's discovering young Howard's presence in the house, she had unreservedly given him her friendship. And this gift Galusha appreciated. He had liked her when they first met and the liking had increased. She was a sensible, quiet, unaffected country girl. She was also an extremely pretty girl, and when a very pretty girl—and sensible and unaffected and the rest—makes you her confidant and asks your advice concerning her love affair and her heart's most precious secrets, even a middle-aged "mummy duster," whose interest in the female sex has, until very recently, centered upon specimens of that sex who have been embalmed several thousand years—even such a one cannot help being gratified by the subtle flattery.

So when Lulie asked his advice Galusha gave it, such as he happened to have in stock, whole-heartedly and without reserve. He and she had many chats and the subjects of these chats were almost invariably two—her father and Nelson Howard. How could she reconcile the one with and to the other? Mr. Bangs' council was, of course, to wait and hope, but a council of procrastination is, to say the most, but partially satisfying.

One afternoon, in the middle of May, he met her on the way back from the village and, as they walked on together, he asked her if there were any new developments in the situation. She looked troubled.

"I don't exactly know what you mean by developments," she said. "If you mean that father is any more reconciled to Nelson, he isn't, that's all. On any other subject he is as nice as he can be. If I wanted anything in the world, and he had money enough to buy it, I do believe I could have it just for the asking. That is a good deal to say," she added, with a half smile, "considering how fond father is of money, but honestly, Mr. Bangs, I think it's true."

Galusha declared that he had no doubt of its truth, indeed, no.

"But, you see," continued Lulie, "the one thing I do want —which is for father to like Nelson—can't be bought with money. I try to talk with him, and argue with him; sometimes when he is especially good-natured and has been especially nice to me, I try to coax him, but it always ends in one way; he gets cross and won't listen. 'Don't talk to me about that Howard swab, I won't hear it.' That's what he always says. He always calls Nelson a 'swab.' Oh, dear! I'm so tired of it all."

"Yes—ah—yes, I'm sure you must be. Ah—um—swab? Swab? It doesn't sound agreeable. What is a—ah—swab, may I ask?"

"Oh, I believe it's a kind of mop that the sailors use aboard ship to clean decks with. I believe that is what it is."

"Indeed? Yes, yes, of course. Now that is quite interesting, isn't it? A mop—yes. But really, I don't see why Mr. Howard should be called a—ah—mop. There is nothing about him which suggests a mop to me. Now in my case —why, this very morning Miss Mar—Miss Phipps suggested that my hair needed cutting very badly. I hadn't noticed it, myself, but when she called my attention I looked in the mirror and—ah—really, I was quite a sight. Ah—shaggy, you know, like a—like a yak."

"A what?"

"A yak. The—ah—Tibetan animal. I spent a season in

Tibet a number of years ago and they use them there for beasts of burden. They have a great deal of hair, you know, and so did I—ah—this morning. Dear me, yes; I was quite yaklike."

Lulie turned an amused glance at him. "So Martha tells you when——" she began, and then stopped, having spoken without thinking. But her companion was not offended.

"Oh, yes, yes," he said cheerfully. "She tells me many things for my own good. She quite manages me. It is extremely good of her, for goodness knows I need it. Dear me, yes!" He thoughtfully rubbed his shorn neck and added, "I told that barber that my hair needed cutting badly. I—ah—fear that is the way he cut it. . . . I read that joke in the paper, Miss Lulie; it isn't original, really."

He smiled and she burst out laughing. But she did not laugh long. When she next spoke she was serious enough.

"Mr. Bangs," she said, "you don't think it dishonorable, or mean to father, for me to keep on seeing Nelson, do you? Father keeps ordering me not to, but I never say I won't. If he asked me I should tell him that I did."

Galusha's answer was promptly given.

"No, I don't think it dishonorable," he said. "Of course, you must see him. It is too bad that you are obliged to see him in—ah—ah—dear me, what is the word I want? Clan—clan—— sounds Scottish, doesn't it?—oh, yes, clandestine! It is too bad you are obliged to see him clandestinely, but I suppose your father's attitude makes anything else impossible. I am very sorry that my claiming to be the evil influence has had so little effect. That was a mistake, I fear."

"Don't say that, Mr. Bangs. You saved us all from a dreadful scene, and father himself from—I hate to think what. Don't ever say that it was a mistake, please. But I do so hate all this hiding and pretending. Some day it will have to end, but how I don't know. Nelson comes first, of course; but how can I leave father? I shall see him—Nelson, I mean—to-night, Mr. Bangs. He has written me saying he is coming over, and I am going to meet him. He says he has good news. I can't think what it can be. I can't think of any good news that could come for him and me, except that father has stopped believing in Marietta Hoag's spirits and has gotten over his ridiculous prejudice; and that *won't* come—ever."

"Oh, yes, it will! I'm sure it will. Dear me, you mustn't lose heart, you know."

"Mustn't I? No, I suppose I mustn't. Thank you, Mr. Bangs. Nelson and I are ever and ever so much obliged to you. You are a great comfort to me. I told Martha that very thing yesterday," she added.

Galusha could not help looking pleased. "Did you, indeed?" he observed. "Well, well—ah—dear me, that was a rather rash statement, wasn't it?"

"Not a bit. And do you want to know what she said? She said you were a great comfort to a good many people, Mr. Bangs. So there; you see!"

That evening the moon rolled, like a silver bowl, over the liquid rim of the horizon, and, upsetting, spilled shimmering, shining, dancing fire in a broad path from sky edge to the beach at the foot of Gould's Bluffs. At the top of that bluff, in the rear of a clump of bayberry bushes which shielded them from the gaze of possible watchers at the lighthouse, Nelson Howard and Lulie, walking slowly back and forth, saw it rise.

Nelson told her the good news he had mentioned in his letter. It was that he had been offered a position as operator at the great wireless station in Trumet. It was what he had been striving for and hoping for and his war record in the radio service had made it possible for him to obtain it. The pay was good to begin with and the prospect of advancement bright.

"And, of course, the best of it is," he said, "that I shall be no further away from you than I am now. Trumet isn't a bit farther than South Wellmouth. There! Don't you think that my good news *is* good news?"

Of course she did and said so.

"And I'm awfully proud of you, too," she told him.

"Nothing to be proud of; I'm lucky, that's all. And don't

you see, dear, how this is going to help us? I shall be earning good pay and I shall save every cent possible, you can bet on that. Rooms are furnished by the company for single men, and houses, nice, comfortable houses, for the married ones. In three months, or in six at the most, I shall have added enough to what I have saved already to make it possible for us to be married. And we *will* be married. Just think of you and me having one of those pretty little houses for our own, and being there together, in our home! Just think of it! Won't it be wonderful!"

He looked down into her face and smiled and she, looking up into his, smiled, too. But she shook her head, nevertheless.

"Yes, dear," she said, "it would be wonderful. But it's too wonderful to be true, I'm afraid."

"Why? Nonsense! Of course it can be true. And it's going to be, too, in six months, perhaps sooner."

But still she shook her head.

"It can't be, Nelson," she said, sadly. "Don't you see it can't? There is father."

"Your father will be all right. That's one of the good things about this new job of mine. You will be only a little way from him. He'll be here at the light, with Zach to look after him, and you can come over every few days to make sure things are going as they should. Why——"

She touched his lips with her fingers.

"Don't, dear," she begged. "You know you're only talking just because it is nice to make-believe. I like to hear you, too; but what is the use when it's *only* make-believe? You know what father's health really is; you know how nervous he is. Doctor Powers told me he must not be overexcited or—or dreadful things might happen. You saw him at that horrid séance thing."

He shrugged. "If I didn't see I heard," he admitted.

"Yes, you heard. And you know how near—— Now suppose I should tell him that you and I intended getting married and going to Trumet to live; what do you think would happen?"

"But, look here, Lulie: You've got to tell him some time, because we *are* going to be married, you know."

"Are we? Yes, I—I hope we are. But, oh, Nelson, sometimes I get almost discouraged. I *can't* leave him in that way, you know that. And, in a sense, I don't want to leave him, because he is my father and I love him."

"But, confound it, you love me, too, don't you?"

"You know I do. But—but—oh, dear! What can I do?"

He did not answer at once. After a moment he said, rebelliously: "You have got your own life to live. Your father has lived the biggest part of his. He hasn't any right to prevent your being happy. It would be different if he had any excuse for it, reasonable excuse. I'm a—well, I'm not a thief—or a fool, quite, I hope. I can provide for you comfortably and I'll do my level best to be a good husband to you. If there was any excuse for his hating me, any except that idiotic spirit craziness of his. And what right has he to order you around? A hundred years or so ago fathers used to order their sons and daughters to marry this one or the other, and if they didn't mind they disinherited 'em, or threw 'em out of doors, or some such stuff. At least, that's the way it worked, according to the books and plays. But that doesn't go nowadays. What right has he——"

But again she touched his lips.

"Don't, Nelson, please," she said, gently. "Rights haven't anything to do with it, of course. You know they haven't, don't you? You know it's just—just that things are *as* they are and that's all. If father was as he used to be, his real self, and he behaved toward you as he is doing, I shouldn't hesitate at all. I should marry you and feel I was doing exactly right. But now——"

She stopped and he, stooping, caught a gleam of moisture where the moonlight touched her cheek. He put his arm about her waist.

"Don't, dear," he said, hastily. "I'm sorry. Forgive me, will you? Of course you're dead right and I've been talking like a jackass. I'll behave, honest I will. . . . But what *are* we going to do? I won't give you up, you know, no matter if every spirit control in—in wherever they come from orders me to."

She smiled. "Of course we're not going to give each other up," she declared. "As for what we're going to do, I don't know. I suppose there is nothing to do for the present except to wait and—and hope father may change his mind. That's all, isn't it?"

He shook his head. "Waiting is a pretty slow game," he said. "I wonder, if I pretended to fall in love with Marietta Hoag, if those Chinese spooks of hers would send word to Cap'n Jeth that I was really a fairly decent citizen. Courting Marietta would be hard medicine to take, but if it worked a cure we might try it. What do you think?"

"I should be afraid that the remedy might be worse than the disease. Once in Marietta's clutches how would you get away?"

"Oh, that would be easy. I'd have Doctor Powers swear that I had been suffering from temporary softening of the brain and wasn't accountable for what I'd been doing."

"She might not believe it."

"Maybe not, but everybody else would. Nothing milder than softening of the brain would account for a fellow's falling in love with Marietta Hoag."

A little later, as they were parting, she said, "Nelson, you're an awfully dear fellow to be so thoughtful and forbearing and—and patient. Sometimes I think I shouldn't let you wait for me any longer."

"Let me! How are you going to stop me? Of course I'll wait for you. You're the only thing worth waiting for in the world. Don't you know that?"

"I know you think so. But, oh, dear, it seems sometimes as if there never would be any end to the waiting, and as if I had no right to ask——"

"There, there! Don't *you* begin talking about rights. There's going to be an end and the right kind of end. No Chinese spooks are going to keep us apart, my girl, not if I can help it."

"I know. But can you help it? . . . I must go now. Yes,

I must, or father will wonder where I am and begin looking for me. He thinks I am over at Martha Phipps', you
know. Good-night, dear."

"Good-night, girlie. Don't worry, it's coming out all
right for us, I'm sure of it. This new job of mine is the
first step in that direction. There! Kiss me and run along.
Good-night."

They kissed and parted, Lulie to hasten back along the
path to the light and Nelson to stride off in the opposite
direction toward South Wellmouth. Neither of them saw
two figures which had, the moment before, appeared upon
the summit of the knoll about thirty yards from the edge of
the bluff and directly behind them. But the pair on the
knoll saw them.

Martha Phipps had been standing by the window of the
sitting room in her home looking out. She had been standing there for some minutes. Galusha Bangs, in the rocking-
chair by the center table, was looking at her. Suddenly
Martha spoke.

"I declare!" she exclaimed. "I do believe that's the love-
liest moon I ever saw. I presume likely," she added, with a
laugh, "it's the same moon I've always seen; it just looks
lovelier, that's all, seems to me. It will be beautiful to
look at from the top of the bluff, the light on the water, I
mean. You really ought to walk over and see it, Mr.
Bangs."

Galusha hesitated, rubbed his spectacles, and then was
seized with an inspiration.

"I—I will if you will go, too," he said.

Martha turned to see if he was in earnest.

"Mercy me!" she exclaimed. "Why should I go? I've
seen that moon on that same water more times than I like to
count."

"But you haven't seen it—ah—recently. Now have you?"

"Why, no, I don't know as I have. Come to think of it,
I don't believe I've been over to the top of the bank to see
the moonlight since—well, since father died. Father loved
to look at salt water by sunlight or moonlight—or no light.

But, good gracious," she added, "it seems awfully foolish, doesn't it, to go wading through the wet grass to look at the moon—at my age?"

"Why, not at all, not at all," persisted Galusha. "I must be—ah—vastly older than you, Miss Phipps, and——"

"Nonsense!"

"Oh, but I am, really. One has only to look at me to see. And there are times when I feel—ah—incredibly ancient; indeed, yes. Now in your case, Miss Martha——"

"In my case I suppose I'm just a slip of a girl. For mercy sakes, don't let's talk ages, no, nor think about 'em, either. . . . Do *you* want to go out to-night to look at that moon, Mr. Bangs?"

"Why, yes—I—if you——"

"Then get your rubbers and cap. I'll be ready in a minute."

The moon was well up now and land and sea were swimming in its misty radiance. There was not a breath of wind and the air was as mild as if the month had been June and not May. Under their feet the damp grass and low bushes swished and rustled. An adventurous beetle, abroad before his time, blundered droning by their heads. From the shadow of a bunch of huckleberry bushes by the path a lithe figure soared lightly aloft, a furry paw swept across, and that June bug was knocked into the vaguely definite locality known as the "middle of next week."

Martha uttered a little scream. "Goodness gracious me!" she exclaimed. "Lucy Larcom, you bad cat, how you did scare me!"

Lucy leaped soundlessly over the clump of huckleberry bushes and galloped gayly into the distance, his tail waving like a banner.

"*Well!*" observed his mistress; "for a cat as old as you are I must say!"

"He feels young to-night," said Galusha. "It must be the —ah—moonlight, I think. Really, I—ah—I feel surprisingly young, myself. I do, indeed!"

Martha laughed blithely. They came to the abrupt little

slope at the southwestern edge of the government property and when he offered to help her down she took his hand and sprang down herself, almost as lightly and easily as Lucy could have done it. Galusha laughed, too, light-heartedly as a boy. His spectacles fell off and he laughed at that.

The minute afterward they arrived at the crest of the knoll. Another moment and the silhouetted figures of Lulie Hallett and Nelson Howard appeared from behind the clump of bayberry bushes and walked onward together, his arm about her waist. The pair on the knoll saw the parting.

Lulie ran up the path and the door of the light keeper's cottage closed behind her. Howard disappeared around the bend of the hill. Martha and Galusha turned hastily and began walking toward home. Neither spoke until they were almost there. Then Miss Phipps, apparently feeling that something should be said, observed: "The moon was—was real pretty, wasn't it, Mr. Bangs?"

Galusha started. "Eh?" he queried. "Oh, yes! yes, indeed! Ah—quite so."

He made the next remark also; it was quite irrelevant.

"Youth," he said, musingly. "Youth is a wonderful thing, really it is."

Possibly his companion understood his thought, or had been thinking along the same line herself. At all events she agreed. "Yes, it is," she said. "It is so. And most of us don't realize how wonderful until it's gone."

From the shadows by the gate Lucy Larcom sprang aloft to knock another beetle galley-west. Lucy was distinctly a middle-aged cat, but he did not allow the fact to trouble him. He gathered his June bugs while he might and did not stop to dream vain dreams of vanished youth.

CHAPTER XV

EARLY June came to Gould's Bluffs. The last of the blossoms fell from the apple and pear trees in the Phipps' orchard, there were young swallows in the nests beneath the eaves of the shed, and tulips and hyacinths gave color and fragrance to the flower beds in the front yard. Down in the village Ras Beebe began his twice-a-year window dressing, removing the caps, candy, sweaters, oil heaters, patent medicines and mittens to substitute bathing suits, candy, straw hats, toy shovels, patent medicines and caps. Small boys began barefoot experiments. Miss Tamson Black departed for Nantucket to visit a cousin. Mr. Raish Pulcifer had his wife resurrect his black-and-white striped flannel trousers from the moth chest and hang them in the yard. "No use talkin'," so Zach Bloomer declared, "summer is headin'. down our way. She'll be here afore we know it."

She was. One pleasant morning Galusha, emerging from the Phipps' "side door," saw workmen about the premises of the Restabit Inn. For a week thereafter the neighborhood echoed with hammer blows and reeked with the smell of new paint. The Restabit Inn, shaking off its winter shabbiness, emerged scrubbed, darned, patched and pressed, so to speak, in its last—and several "lasts before that"— summer suit made over, ready to receive callers.

On the twentieth of the month the callers began to arrive. East Wellmouth broke out, as a child breaks out with the measles, in brilliant speckles, the disease in this instance being unmistakably a pronounced case of summer boarders.

252

The "speckles" were everywhere, about the post office, in Ras Beebe's store, about the lighthouse, on the beaches, and far and wide over the hills and hollows. They picknicked in the pine groves, they giggled in the back seats on prayer meeting nights, they sang noisily on the way back to the hotel after evening mail sorting, they danced jazzily in the hotel parlor and on the porches.

Martha did not mind them; she said they were rather nice, on the whole, because they helped to remind her that all creation wasn't East Wellmouth. Galusha didn't object to them, except when they were *too* noisy at midnight or thereabouts and interfered with his slumbers. Primmie condescended to them and aired her knowledge of local celebrities and traditions. Captain Jethro ignored them utterly and Lulie was popular among them. Only Zacheus, the philosopher, seemed to find them unmitigated nuisances. Somehow or other the summer visitor got under Mr. Bloomer's hard shell and upon his salt-seasoned nerves.

"Blast 'em!" grumbled Zach, "I don't know why 'tis, but they rile me like fury. Prob'ly it's because I ain't never been much used to 'em the way I would have been if I'd been keepin' light ashore all my days. Out on the old Hog's Back we never had no visitors to speak of and we used to hanker for 'em. Here, by Godfreys, they don't give us no time to hanker for nothin'. And they ask such foolhead questions! One woman, she says to me yesterday, she says —I was showin' her the foghorn, and says she: 'Do you have to turn a crank to make it go?' Think of that! A hand crank to make the fourth highest-power foghorn on the coast blow! I lost my patience. 'No ma'am,' says I, 'a crank ain't necessary. I just put my mouth to the touch-hole,' I says, 'and breathe natural and she chirrups.' She believed it, too. I cal'late I'll catch thunder from Cap'n Jeth if he finds out what I told her, but I can't help it; there's limits, by Godfreys domino, limits!"

Galusha found, except for the slight annoyance of too many of these sojourners, that summer at Gould's Bluffs and vicinity was even more delightful than the fall and spring had been. His friends, the Halls, whose invitation to their cottage at Wellmouth had been the cause of his coming to the Cape, were not occupying that cottage this summer; they had rented it for the season and gone abroad. So he had no old friends to call upon. But his new friendships were enjoyable and dependable. His health improved steadily; he gained in strength, and the fear that his guilt in the affair of the Wellmouth Development stock might be discovered grew less and less. Only one thing troubled him, and that was so vague that it was scarcely a trouble. The Institute people had written him of some great plan for his professional services, a plan which was to develop in the fall. Now, by all that was right and proper, he should have been tremendously curious concerning that plan, should have been eagerly guessing what it might be and counting the days until the time came for his return to work and its immediate development. But he was not curious, he did not count the days; for some weird and unnatural reason—or for no reason whatever—he was not eager to return to work. He, Galusha Bangs, whose life had been devoted to his pet science, who had had no thought except for that science, had labored for it and in it every day for twenty years and had dreamed about it at night—he did not seem to care to go back to it. He did not seem to want to go anywhere. Contentment for him was apparently right there at Gould's Bluffs and nowhere else. Amazing but true. And no less disgraceful than amazing. It was a state of mind, of course, a psychological state due to physiological causes and doubtless was but temporary. Nevertheless, it troubled him a bit.

One morning in July he received a shock. Zacheus, returning from the post office, met him at the Phipps' gate and handed him a letter.

"Come in last night's mail," explained Zach. "I happened to be cruisin' up to the village so I thought I might as well fetch it down to you, Mr. Bangs."

Galusha thanked him and put the letter in his pocket. After dinner, having gone to his room, he was searching his pockets for a handkerchief; finding his handkerchief invariably entailed a search, because he was quite as likely to have put it in his waistcoat pocket as in those of his trousers, and just as likely to find it at last in the pocket of his overcoat downstairs on the rack. In this case he did not find it at all, having dropped it on the road, but he did find the letter. Still wondering where he could have put the handkerchief, he absently tore open the envelope and began to read, as follows:

"*Professor Galusha C. Bangs,*
  East Wellmouth, Mass.
DEAR SIR:
  "Mr. Augustus Cabot wishes me to inform you that he has returned to this office, having, so he feels, quite regained his health. He sends his regards to you and hopes that you, too, are getting on toward complete recovery."

Galusha, having read so far, leaned back in his chair. Cousin Gussie well again! Back again at his Boston office! Why, this was unexpected news! He was gratified and pleased, of course. Nevertheless, coupled with the gratification was a slight feeling of uneasiness. Nevada—well, Nevada was such a long and safe way off; whereas Boston was so very and dangerously near. To a person with a guilty conscience, one with a secret to conceal, the advantages of Nevada as a residence for a possibly inquisitive relative were obvious. And was Thomas writing merely to impart the news of his employer's return? Or were there other reasons?

"You will remember" [began the next sentence of the letter], "writing him some time ago, while he and I were in Nevada, asking his advice concerning some corporation, the stock of which a friend of yours was considering, either as a purchase or sale, I do not remember which."

Galusha closed his eyes and passed an agitated hand across his forehead. His question was answered; there *were* other reasons.

"You may not be aware" [the letter continued], "of the forest fire which, on April seventeenth, destroyed the sanitarium and camps in which Mr. Cabot and I were staying. The entire institution, including our own camp, was burned and with it were destroyed all my business records, letters received, copies of letters sent, etc. At the time we were not at all concerned with this loss, being fearful of the effect which the excitement might have upon Mr. Cabot's health. I am glad to say, however, that the effect, if any, was not injurious. But the loss of all correspondence, including that with you, is now causing some annoyance. My recollection is that I advised your friend not to buy any stock of the nature you described, or, if he owned any, not to attempt a forced sale. As we have heard nothing further from you since, and as neither our Mr. Minor nor Mr. Barbour report your consulting them on the subject, I take it your interest in the matter is closed."

Again Galusha leaned back in his chair. But this time he drew a long breath of relief. Mr. Thomas "took it" that his interest in the matter was closed, did he? Well, it was, indeed it was. The sole interest he now had in the Wellmouth Development Company was to forget it utterly. . . . And yet, if it was not concerning the Development matter that Thomas was writing, what was it? The beatific smile which had followed the sigh of relief faded from his face and he began to read again.

"In looking over your affairs which, among others, have kept me very busy since my return, I find," wrote Thomas, "that Mr. Barbour, at your request, sent you a check on March 13th, for fourteen thousand three hundred and ten dollars and thirty-eight cents, the same being your share of the Tinplate reorganization profits. On March 15th, you came personally to this office and exchanged that check for five thousand dollars in cash and another check for ninety-three hundred and ten dollars and thirty-eight cents. On March 24th, according to our records, you again came in person and exchanged this new check for eighty-two hundred dollars in cash and a third check for eleven hundred and ten dollars and thirty-eight cents. This third check we do not find has as yet been presented for payment nor has it been deposited to your account with us. Considering the lapse of time since the check was drawn, this seems somewhat unusual and so I am writing to ask concerning it. Mr. Cabot wishes me to add, also, that as thirteen thousand, two hundred dollars, the amount of cash drawn by you on the two occasions mentioned, is a large sum, he is, as your financial guardian—this is the term he requests me to use—a trifle anxious concerning it. He cannot, he says, conceive of a use to which you could put such a sum, particularly in your present location on the Cape. He wishes me to ask you to write him particulars in the matter. To his request I am adding my own concerning the missing check. A prompt reply will greatly oblige us both. Apologizing for the inconvenience which this may cause you, and with Mr. Cabot's sincere regards and good wishes, I am,

"Yours respectfully,

"George L. Thomas."

Mr. Bangs' smiles, beatific or otherwise, had so far vanished by this time that he could not summon them again that day. He attempted to appear cheerful during supper that evening and breakfast next morning, but it was a sorrowful cheer. Martha asked if he was sick. He said he was not, indeed no, really, but she looked as if she did not believe him. Primmie's suspicions of dropsy, or some equally distressing ailment, revived. She watched him for signs of relapse.

The letter requested an immediate reply. That reply was neither written nor sent. Mr. Bangs could not think of a reply which would embrace the two elements, safety and sanity. It was impossible to tell the truth and dangerous to attempt to tell anything else. So he did not answer the Thomas letter.

In a week he received a second one, asking if he had gotten the first. This simply *had* to be acknowledged, so he did so. He wrote that his friend was no longer interested in the stock concerning which he had inquired. Also he returned

the check for the balance of the Tinplate payment—it had
been lying in his bureau drawer ever since he brought it
from Boston—but he made no mention of what he had done
with the eighty-two hundred dollars in cash nor the five
thousand which he had previously drawn. He did not refer
to these sums at all. He requested that the check for the
Tinplate balance be deposited to his account and sent it in
the envelope with his letter to Thomas. Then he fearfully
awaited the next blow.

It came, and in a new fashion, about a week later. He
and Martha were in the sitting room after supper when the
telephone bell rang.

"Pardon me, Miss Martha," said Galusha, "but wasn't
that our—I should say your ring?"

Martha smiled. "I didn't notice," she said. "You're always thinkin' you hear our ring, Mr. Bangs. The last time
you heard it and called me to the 'phone, it turned out to
be Emulous Dodd, the undertaker. He said, 'I don't want
you.' I told him I was thankful for that."

Her lodger shook his head. "I'm very sorry," he said.
"These telephone calls down here—'Two long and three
short' and—ah—the like—they do confuse me, I admit. I
really can't seem to get accustomed to them. Now . . . Oh,
but that *is* your ring, isn't it, Miss Martha?"

It was. Martha took down the receiver.

"Yes . . . yes," she said. "Yes, this is Phipps. . . . Oh,
all right. . . . The girl says it's a long-distance call," she
added, turning to Galusha. "Who can be callin' *me* from
long distance? . . . Yes . . . yes. . . . This is Miss Phipps
speakin' now. . . . Who? . . . Oh, Mr. Bangs? Yes, he's
right here. It's for you, Mr. Bangs."

Galusha took the receiver from her hand. "Ah—hello!"
he hailed. The wire buzzed and sang. Then, in his ear and
with surprising clearness and nearness, a voice said,
brusquely: "Hello! Hello, there! Is that you, Loosh?"

Galusha recognized the voice. He had not heard it for
a long time, but he recognized it at once. And, recognizing
it, something like panic seized him.

"Hello!" shouted the voice again. "Hello, Galusha! Is that you?"

Galusha glanced fearfully over his shoulder. Martha was gazing at him. She looked alarmed.

"Oh, what is it, Mr. Bangs?" she asked. "It—it's not bad news, is it?"

"No—ah—no," he faltered. "I—I——"

"Eh? What's that?" demanded the voice in the receiver, impatiently. "Hello! Who is this, anyway?"

"Is there somebody sick or—or anything?" asked Martha.

"No—no, Miss Martha. It's all right, really. Yes, indeed, I—— Oh, quite right. Yes."

"But you look so frightened."

"Do I? Oh, not in the least. That is, I . . . Yes, yes, I hear. Yes, this is Bangs speaking."

"Oh, it is! Well, I'm glad you're speaking at last. You're Galusha Bangs, you say?"

"Yes. Yes, I—I think so."

"You *think* so! That's good! Don't you know whether you are or not?"

"I meant I—I thought I said so. I am Galusha Bangs. Yes."

"Good! Then we've settled so much. You know who I am, of course?"

Did he? Oh, if he only did not! He cast another alarmed glance in his landlady's direction. He wondered if the voice which was so distinctly audible in his ear could be he heard and understood in the room. Oh, this was dreadful, dreadful!

"*Hello!*" roared the voice again. "Hello, Bangs! Are you there?"

"Oh, yes—ah—yes. I am here. Quite so—yes."

"Well, I'm glad. I thought you might have gone clamming or something. Well, I asked if you knew who this was? Do you?"

Galusha swallowed, shut his eyes, and then faced the inevitable.

"It—it is Cousin Gussie, isn't it?" he faltered.

He heard, or imagined that he did, a little gasp of surprise from Miss Phipps. He did not dare look again in her direction.

"That's right," said the voice. "You're a good guesser. How are you, anyway?"

Galusha stammered that he was very well. He added that he was glad to see his relative. The relative promptly observed that his eyesight must be remarkably good.

"You know what I've called you up for, of course?" he added.

Martha had risen and was leaving the room on tiptoe.

"You and your cousin can talk better alone, I know," she whispered. "I want to see Primmie a minute, anyway."

Her lodger regarded her mutely. The expression of dumb misery on his face caused her to pause for an instant.

"You're *sure* there's no bad news, Mr. Bangs?" she asked, anxiously.

He managed to smile, but the smile was not a convincing success. "Oh, yes—ah—quite, quite," he protested. "It—it is—ah—extremely pleasant, really. . . . Yes—yes, Cousin Gussie, I am—I am still here."

"Oh, you are! Fine! I thought probably you had gone to dig another quahaug. Why don't you answer letters?"

Galusha glanced desperately at the kitchen door. Thank heaven, it was closed.

"I answered yours," he declared.

"You did not. You only half answered it. That idiot Barbour sent you a check for over fourteen thousand dollars. Of course, if I had been well and here he wouldn't have done any such fool thing. He says you told him to."

"Ah—did I?"

"Did you? Don't you know whether you did or not? Well, never mind. You came up here on two separate occasions, so they tell me, and drew thirteen thousand of that in cash and took it away with you. Now what on earth did you do that for?"

Galusha did not answer. Cabot immediately demanded to

know if he was still there. Assured of this, he repeated his question.

"I—I wanted it," faltered Galusha.

"You *wanted* it! Wanted thirteen thousand two hundred dollars in cash down there on the clam flats? What did you want it *for?*"

"I—I—— Well, you see—you see——"

"No, I don't see. Now, look here, old man: I realize you're of age and that your money is your own, and all that. It isn't, legally speaking, one single bit my business if you take every cent you've got and sink it in the middle of Cape Cod Bay. But I promised your aunt before she died that I would try and see that you didn't do that kind of thing. She knew you couldn't take care of money; I knew it; why, confound it, you knew it, too! You and I talked that whole matter over and we agreed I wasn't to give you any large sums of your money, no matter how hard you begged for them, unless you told me why you wanted them and I was satisfied it was all right. Didn't we agree to that? Isn't that so?"

"Why—why, yes, Cousin Gussie. You have been very kind. I appreciate it, I assure you."

"Oh, be hanged! I haven't been kind. I've only been trying to keep you from being *too* kind to people who work you for a good thing, that's all. Look here, Loosh: *I* know what you've done with that thirteen thousand dollars."

Galusha shot one more pitiful glance in the direction of the kitchen.

"Ah—ah—do you?" he stammered.

"Yes. You've given it away, haven't you?"

"Well—well, you see——"

"You have? I knew it! And I know whom you've given it to."

There was no answer to be made to this appalling assertion. Poor Galusha merely clung to the receiver and awaited his death sentence.

"You've given it to some mummy-hunter to fit out another grave-robbing expedition. Now, haven't you?"

"Why—why——"

"Be a sport now, Loosh! Tell me the truth. That's what you've done, isn't it?"

Galusha hesitated, closing his eyes, struggled with his better nature, conquered it, and faltered: "Why—why—in a way of speaking, I suppose——"

"I knew it! I bet Minor a dinner on it. Well, confound you, Loosh; don't you realize they're only working you for what they can get out of you? Haven't I told you not to be such an ass? You soft-headed old . . . Here! What's the matter with this wire? Hello, Central! Hello! . . ."

The Cabot oration broke off in the middle and was succeeded by a series of rattles and thumps and jingles like a barrel of kitchenware falling downstairs; this was followed by a startling stillness, which was, in turn, broken by an aggrieved voice wailing: "Say, Central, why can't I get that twenty-seven ring fourteen Bayport? I bet you you've given me every other d— number on Cape Cod!"

Galusha hung up the receiver. Then he sat down in the rocker and gazed at the opposite wall. His secret was safe. But that safety he had bought at the price of another falsehood—told to Cousin Gussie this time. He did not seem to be the same Galusha Cabot Bangs at all. That Galusha— the former Galusha—had considered himself a gentleman and would no more have told a lie than he would have stolen his neighbor's spoons. This one—his present self— lied not only once but twice and thrice. He told one untruth to cover another. He lived in an atmosphere of blackest falsehood and deception. The sole ray of light in the darkness was the knowledge that Martha Phipps did not know his real character. She considered him honest and truthful. In order that she might continue to think him so, he would go on prevaricating forever, if necessary.

It preyed upon his conscience, nevertheless. The thought uppermost in his mind was expressed in a reply which he made to a question asked by Mr. Bloomer on an afternoon of that week. Zach and Primmie were, as so often happened, involved in an argument and, as also so often happened, they called on him to act as referee.

"We was talkin' about names, Mr. Bangs," explained Primmie. "He's always makin' fun of my name. I told him my name was pretty enough to get put into poetry sometimes. You know——"

"I told her," broke in Zach, solemnly, but with a wink at Galusha, "that the only thing I could think of to rhyme with 'Primrose' was 'Jim Crows.'"

"I never said it rhymed," protested Miss Cash, hotly. "You can have your name in poetry without its rhymin', I guess likely. You're always tellin' me about how 'Zacheus he, climbed up a tree——' Now if your name had to rhyme 'twould have to be—er—er—well, nothing'," triumphantly; "'cause nothin' *could* rhyme with Zacheus."

Mr. Bloomer, solemn as ever, shook his head.

"Yes, it could," he declared. "What's the name of that plant Lulie's got in the settin' room window over home? The one with the prickers on it. Cat-tailed—no, rat-tailed —um——"

"Cactus." Galusha supplied the word.

"That's it," said Zach. "That would do it.

> 'Old man Zach'us
> Shinned up a cactus—'

Have to step lively, wouldn't he?" he added, with a chuckle.

Primmie sniffed. "Silly!" she retorted. "What was that pretty piece of poetry you told me the other day that had my name in it, Mr. Bangs? The one about it bein' so and so and not much else? You know the one."

Galusha obliged.

> "'A primrose by the river's brim
> A yellow primrose was to him,
> And it was nothing more.'"

"There!" said Primmie, triumphantly. "Do you hear that, Zach Bloomer? That's poetry, the real kind. And it's got my name in it, too."

Zach shook his head.

"You ain't a yellow primrose, Posy," he said. "You're a red one—red and speckled. Mr. Bangs," he added, before the outraged Primmie could reply, "I think consider'ble about names, havin' such a out-of-common sort of a one myself. I never heard your name afore. . . . Galusha. . . . Godfreys! Was you named for somebody in the family?"

"Yes."

"I see. Yes, yes. Most generally names like that, the tough ones, come out of the Bible in the fust place. Is your name in Scriptur' anywheres?"

"I don't know. I—ah—presume I should, but I don't."

"Um-hm. Queer names in the Bible. . . . Um-hm. And some good ones, too. . . . I've always been a good deal interested in names. Used to set around hours at a stretch, when I was aboard the old lightship, and try to pick out what name in Scriptur' I cal'lated I'd ruther be called. Finally I got down to two—John and Paul. Both of 'em short and sensible, no frills to 'em. Of the two I figgered maybe Paul would fit me best. Paul, he was shipwrecked one time, you remember, and I've been wrecked no less'n three. . . . Paul. . . . Um-hm. . . . Say, Mr. Bangs, have you ever tried to fit yourself with a Bible name?"

Galusha smiled and said he never had. Primmie, who had been silent for almost three minutes, could remain so no longer.

"I think Solomon would be the right name for you, Mr. Bangs," she cried, enthusiastically. "You know such a terrible lot—about some kinds of things." This last a hasty addition.

Zach snorted. "Solomon!" he repeated. "Dan Beebe— Ras Beebe's cousin over to Trumet—named his boy Solomon, and last week they took the young-one up to the State home for feeble-minded. What name would you pick out of the Bible for yourself, Mr. Bangs?"

It was then that Galusha made the reply to which reference has been made. His smile changed and became what Primmie described as "one of his one-sided ones."

"Ah—um—well—Ananias, perhaps," he said, and walked away.

Zach and Miss Cash stared after him. Of course, it was the latter who spoke first.

"Ananias!" she repeated. "Why, Ananias was the feller that—that lied so and was struck down dead. I remember him in Sunday school. Him and his wife Sophrony. Seems to me 'twas Sophrony; it might have been Maria, though. But, anyhow, they died lyin'."

"That so? I thought they lied dyin'."

"Oh, be still! But what did Mr. Bangs pick out *that* name for—of all names? Can you tell me that?"

Zacheus could not, of course, nor did he attempt it. Instead, he rose and gazed sadly at his companion.

"He said it for a joke, Buttercups," he observed. "Joke. *You* know, a joke. One of them things that—— I tell you what: You look up 'joke' in the dictionary and then, after you've found out what 'tis, I'll lend you a patent-medicine almanac with one or two of 'em in it. . . . Well, I've got to be gettin' under way. So long, Posy."

Possibly Primmie might have inquired further into the reasons which led the Phipps' lodger to select for himself the name of the person who "died lying," but that very afternoon, while on an errand in the village, she heard the news that Nelson Howard had been offered a position as operator at the Trumet wireless station, had accepted and was already there and at work. Every professional gossip in East Wellmouth was talking about it, not only because of its interest as a piece of news, but because of the astonishing fact that no one but those intimately interested had previously known of the offer.

"Why in the world," said Becky Blount, expressing the opinion of what Captain Jethro Hallett would have called her "tribe," "he felt 'twas necessary to hide it as if 'twas something to be ashamed of, *I* don't see. Most folks would have been proud to be offered such a chance. But that Nelse Howard's queer, anyhow. Stuck-up, I call him; and Lulie Hallett's the same way. She nor him won't have anything

to do with common folks in *this* town. And it'll be worse
now."

This was quite untrue, of course, for Lulie and Nelson
were extremely friendly with all except the Blounts, Marietta Hoag, and a few more of their kind. The solid, substantial people in the village liked them, just as they liked
and respected Martha Phipps. These people took pains to
congratulate young Howard and to whisper a hope to Lulie
that her father's unreasonable opposition to the former
might be lessened by the news of his advancement.

Primmie, returning home with the sensation, was disappointed to find it no sensation at all. Lulie had told both
Miss Phipps and Galusha shortly after Nelson told her.
She had told her father also, but he had not expressed gratification. Instead, the interview between them had ended unpleasantly.

"The first thing he did," said Lulie, when telling the story
to her confidants at the Phipps' home, "was to ask me how
I knew about it. I told him that Nelson told me."

Martha lifted her brows. "My!" she exclaimed. "You
did?"

"Yes, I did. I don't know why exactly. Somehow I felt
just then as if I didn't care."

"And what did he say?"

"He didn't say as much as I thought he would. He
turned and stared at me under those big eyebrows of his,
and then he said: 'When did you see him?' I said, 'Yesterday.' 'When did you see him before that?' I said, 'About
a week ago. Nelson and I usually see each other about once
a week, father,' ı told him."

"My!" exclaimed Martha, again. "That was plain enough,
to be sure."

"Yes, wasn't it? I wonder now that I had the courage.
He didn't flare up as I expected he would, as I am sure he
would have done last fall, for instance. He just looked and
looked at me. Then he said: 'Are you really planning to
marry that fellow, Lulie?' I thought that, as I had gone
so far, I might as well go the rest, so I said: 'Yes, father,

some day. Not as long as you want me or need me, but some day, if he is willing to wait for me.' He just kept on pulling his beard and looking at me. At last, when he did speak, he asked, 'In spite of me and—and your mother?' It made me feel dreadfully wicked; I almost cried, I guess. But I had to go through with it then, so I said: 'I don't want to marry "in spite" of any one, father. You know I don't. And I shall never leave you—never. But can't you *please* see Nelson as he is and not—and not——' He interrupted me there; in fact, I doubt if he heard me. 'Your mother has warned me against that young fellow,' he said. 'You know she has, Lulie.' 'I know you *think* she has, father,' I said."

Martha's hands fell in her lap. Galusha shook his head. "Dear me!" he observed. "Dear me!"

Lulie nodded. "Yes, I know," she said. "As soon as I said it I thought 'Dear me,' too. But I don't believe he heard that, either. He seemed to be thinking and didn't speak for ever so long. Then he said, 'The revelations from above ain't to be set aside. No, no, they lay a duty on us.' Then he stopped again and turned and walked away. The last words he said, as he was going out of the room, were, 'Don't let me ever see that Howard around this house. You hear me?' And that is the way it ended. He hasn't mentioned the subject since. But, at least," said Lulie, with an attempt at a smile, "he didn't call Nelson a 'swab.' I suppose that is some comfort."

Martha and Galusha agreed that it was. The latter said: "It seems to me that you may consider it all quite encouraging, really. It is only the—ah—spirits which stand in the way now."

"Yes, but oh, Mr. Bangs, they always will stand in the way, I'm afraid. Other things, real things or real people we might change or persuade, but how can you change a— a make-believe spirit that isn't and never was, except in Marietta Hoag's ridiculous imagination? Oh, Martha," she added, "you and Mr. Bangs don't think I'm horrid to speak like this, do you? Of course, if I believed, as father

does, that it was really my mother's spirit speaking, I should
—well, I should be. . . . But what is the use? I *can't* believe such a thing."

"Of course you can't, child," said Martha. "I knew your
mother and if she was comin' back to this earth she wouldn't
do it through Marietta Hoag's head. She had too much
self-respect for that."

Galusha stroked his chin. "I suppose," he said, "if there
were some way in which we might influence that imagination of Miss—ah—Hoag's, a change might be brought about.
It would be difficult to reach the said imagination, however,
wouldn't it? I once found a way to reach a tomb of the
XIIIth Dynasty which had been buried for thousands of
years under thirty-three feet of rock and sand. I located it
by accident—that is, in a way, it was an accident; of course,
we had been searching for some time. I happened to strike
the earth at a certain point with my camera tripod and it
sounded quite hollow. You see, there was a—ah—sort of
shaft, as one might say, which came quite close to the sur-
face at that point. It sounded surprisingly hollow, like a—
like something quite empty, you know. Yes."

Martha nodded. "If you struck Marietta's head anywhere," she observed, "it would sound the same way. She's
got about as much brains as a punkin lantern."

"Yes—ah—yes, but I fear we should gain little by doing
that. We shouldn't get at our 'spirit' that way. But perhaps we may find a way. There are obstacles, but there
were obstacles above and about that tomb also. Dear me,
yes. We must consider, Miss Lulie; we must, so to speak,
consider."

His advice to Nelson was similar.

"I should say the situation was a bit more encouraging,
Mr. Howard," he said. They had been discussing Lulie's
talk with her father. Nelson nodded.

"Perhaps it is, a little bit," he admitted. "It seems barely
possible that the old man is not quite as bitter against me as
he was. For instance, I met him yesterday at the post office
and said 'Good-morning, Cap'n Jeth.' I always speak to

him whenever I meet him, make it a point to, but he never speaks to me. He didn't speak yesterday, but he did bow. It was more of a bob than a bow and he looked savage enough to bite me; but, at least, he went so far as to show he knew I was on earth. That was rather funny, too, his doing that. I wonder why he did."

Galusha reflected a moment. Then he said: "I shouldn't be greatly surprised if your new position at the radio station may be the cause. Captain Hallett is—ah—not unmindful of success in business. Miss Mar—ah—that is, Miss Phipps says he is a very shrewd business man. My own experience," he added, meditatively, "would lead me to that conclusion, also."

Nelson was surprised.

"Have you had business dealings with the cap'n?" he asked. "I never thought of you as a business man, Mr. Bangs."

Galusha started and seemed embarrassed.

"Oh—ah—ah—I'm not, Mr. Howard," he declared, hastily. "Indeed, no."

"But you spoke of your business experience with Cap'n Jeth; or I thought you did."

The little archæologist looked very solemn.

"Such experiences as I have had with Captain Hallett," he observed, "have been—ah—most unbusinesslike."

They parted a few minutes later. Said Nelson, gloomily: "I'm afraid the situation hasn't changed a whole lot, after all, Mr. Bangs. Cap'n Jeth may think more of my new job than he did of my old one, but he doesn't think any better of me as a son-in-law. And he won't, so long as he believes in that fool spirit stuff."

Galusha stroked his chin. "We must consider those spirits, Mr. Howard," he said. "Dear me, yes; we must seriously consider those spirits."

CHAPTER XVI

AUGUST is the banner month at all northern seaside resorts. August at East Wellmouth crowded the Restabit Inn to overflowing. On pleasant Sundays the long line of cars flying through the main road of the village on the way to Provincetown met and passed the long line returning Bostonward. The sound of motor horns echoed along the lane leading to Gould's Bluffs. Galusha found it distinctly safer and less nerve-racking to walk on the grass bordering that lane than in the lane itself, as had hitherto been his custom. The harassed Zacheus led more visitors than ever up and down the lighthouse stairs, expressing his opinion of those visitors, after their departure, with fluency and freedom. Mr. Bloomer's philosophy helped him through most annoyances, but it broke down under the weight of the summer boarder and his—or—her questions.

Galusha, in his daily walks, kept far afield, avoiding the traveled ways. His old resort, the Baptist cemetery, he seldom visited now, having examined and reëxamined all the interesting stones within its borders. He had discovered another ancient burial ground, over on the South Wellmouth road, and occasionally his wanderings took him as far as that. The path to and from this cemetery led over the edge of the bluff and wound down to the beach by the creek and landlocked harbor where his hat—the brown derby—had put to sea that Sunday morning in the previous October. The path skirted the creek for a little way, then crossed on a small bridge and climbed the pine-clad hills on the other side.

Late one afternoon in August, Galusha, returning along this path, met a man coming in the other direction. The man was a stranger to him and obviously not a resident of East Wellmouth. He was a stout, prosperous-looking individual, well-dressed and with a brisk manner. When Mr Bangs first saw him he was standing at a point near the foot of the bluff, and gazing intently at the view. Galusha turned the corner above the bridge where the path reëntered the pine grove. When he emerged again the man had walked on to the little rise by the farther edge of the creek. He was standing there, as he had stood at the point where Galusha first noticed him, looking about, up and down the creek, across the little harbor, at the beaches, the sand cliffs, the pines and the sea.

Galusha crossed the bridge and approached along the path. The stranger heard his step and turned.

"Good-afternoon," said Galusha.

The man nodded and returned the greeting.

"Nice view from here," he observed. Galusha agreed that the view was very nice, indeed. He passed on and turned to climb the bluff. Then the stranger called to him.

"Excuse me," he said. "But may I ask you a question or two? Don't want to keep you if you are in a hurry, though."

Galusha declared himself to be not in the least hurried. The man walked toward him.

"Are you acquainted about here?" he asked.

"Why—why—ah—yes, to some extent. Yes."

"I mean do you know the lay of the land in this vicinity?"

"Why—ah—yes, I think so. Fairly well."

"I see. Can you tell me how much water there is in that channel out yonder?" He pointed toward the mouth of the inlet, where the two lines of creaming breakers approached each other, but did not meet.

"No—no, I am sorry, but I can't."

"How deep is it off here opposite where we're standing?"

"Dear me! I'm afraid I don't know that, either. When

you asked concerning the lay of the land I didn't understand you meant the—ah—lay of the water. I'm very sorry."

The man laughed. "That's all right," he said. "Asked my question the wrong way, didn't I? Well, tell me a little about the land, then. Are the woods the other side of that hill or only on this?"

Galusha informed him concerning the extent of the pine grove. The stranger asked some questions about the course of the creek above the bridge, the distance from the main highway, whether the land beyond the hill was settled or unoccupied. His final question was concerning the Restabit Inn.

"Any other hotels around here within ten miles?" he asked. When told there were not, he merely nodded, making no comment.

"Well, I'm much obliged," he said. "I was just loafing around and a little curious, that's all. Thanks. Hope I haven't kept you too long. Good-day."

Galusha followed the winding path up the face of the high bluff. When, having reached its top, he paused to get fresh breath in place of that he had lost, he looked down and saw his questioner standing where he had left him and, apparently, still admiring the view.

The following afternoon they saw each other again. This time the stranger was on the other side of the creek, wandering about at the edge of the pine grove. He acknowledged Galusha's bow with a wave of the hand, but he did not come nearer to ask more questions.

That evening, at the supper table, Mr. Bangs mentioned the meeting. Primmie, who prided herself upon knowing every visitor in town and where he or she came from, was ready with the information in this case.

"I know who he is," she declared. "His name's Williams and him and his wife's stoppin' at the Restabit. They never meant to stay there only one night, but his automobile blowed up or busted out somethin' and they had to send to Boston to get a new one. It's a dreadful expensive kind of a one, the auto is, one of them—them Pieced-Arrows, all upholstery and drapery window curtains and places to put bouquets and your feet in winter to warm 'em—your feet, I mean, not the bouquets—and——"

"There, there, Primmie," said Martha. "That will do. For mercy sakes, how did you find out all that?"

"Their chauffeur told me. I know him, too. Him and me was introduced last night when he stopped in to get a drink of water. His name is Kelly, and he——"

"Wait a minute. When you and he were introduced, you say? Who introduced you?"

"Why, he did, Miss Martha. You see, he was comin' along by and he see me out settin' on the side steps, you know. And he stopped and he says: 'You look lonesome,' he says. 'Well,' says I, 'I may *look* so, but I ain't; my savin' soul, no!' Then he wanted to know if he couldn't have a drink of water and, of course——"

"Yes, I see—of course. I think you had better sit in the house this evenin', Primmie."

The "Pieced-Arrow" car, with Mr. Kelly on the driver's seat and Mr. and Mrs. Williams inside, left East Wellmouth at the end of that week. Yet once more before the season closed Galusha fancied that he caught a glimpse of that car's owner. The time was the first week in September and Galusha, returning later than usual along the path from South Wellmouth, saw two figures walking along the beach of the inlet. They were a good way off, but one certainly did resemble Williams as he remembered him. The brisk step was like his and the swing of the heavy shoulders. The other figure had seemed familiar, too, but it disappeared behind a clump of beach-plum bushes and did not come out again during the time that Galusha remained in sight. On reflection the latter decided that he was mistaken. Of course, Williams could not be one of the pair, having left the Cape. It was too dark to see plainly; and, after all, it made little difference whether it was he or not. Mr. Bangs stopped speculating on the subject and promptly forgot it entirely.

On the morning after Labor Day there was a general exodus of city sojourners from the Inn and on September

15 it closed its doors. The weather was still beautiful and mild, even more so than during the previous month, but East Wellmouth's roads and lanes were no longer crowded. The village entered upon its intermediate season, that autumn period of quiet and restful beauty, which those who know and love the Cape consider most delightful of the year.

Galusha enjoyed its beauties hugely. He could stroll where he pleased now and no charging and bellowing motor car was likely to awaken him from his daydreams and cause him to leap frantically into the gutter. Sunsets over the western dunes and the Bay were hazily wonderful fantasies of crimson and purple and gold and sapphire, with the nets and poles of the distant fish weirs scattered here and there about the placid water like bits of fairy embroidery. And then to end his walk by turning in at the Phipps' gate; the lamplight in the cozy dining room shining a welcome and Martha's pleasant, attractive face above the teacups. It was like coming home, like coming to a real home, his home. He dreaded to think of leaving it—even for his loved science and the promised "great plan" which the Institute people were to present him that very fall or winter.

He had heard nothing further from them concerning the plan, but he knew he was likely to hear at any moment. He was well, perfectly well now, and stronger than he had been for a long, long time. He felt himself abundantly able to take charge of an exploring expedition, or to reorganize a department, to do anything which the Institute might ask him to do. His guess was that the plan was for another archæological expedition, one to go farther afield and equipped for more thorough research than any yet sent out. He himself had urged the need of such an expedition many times, but when the war came all such ideas were given up. The giving up had been, on his part, although he realized the necessity which prompted it and even urged the yielding to that necessity, a bitter disappointment.

And now—well, now he could not seem to arouse an atom of real enthusiasm. He should be too excited to sleep, but he did sleep well. When he dreamed of Egypt and the tombs of the Ptolemies, there was always a Cape Cod cottage in the foreground. And the cottage never varied in design; it was always the "Phipps' place," and its mistress was always standing in the doorway. That was the great trouble, he knew it. He was going to be homesick for that cottage and its contents. If they might only be transferred with him to Egypt, then the land of the Pharaohs would be even more paradisical than he used to think it.

He told Martha of the promised plan and its call to duty. Oddly enough, thereafter they discussed it but little. Other subjects, although mere commonplaces, they seemed to find more interesting. One evening, however, they were together in the sitting room and Martha said:

"I noticed you got a letter from Washin'ton to-day, Mr. Bangs."

Galusha nodded. "Yes," he said. "It wasn't a letter exactly. Merely another of the regular reports, that is all."

"I see. . . . Well, I suppose you will be hearin' from them pretty soon about—about that other matter. The plan they told you they had for you."

He nodded again. "Dear me, yes," he agreed. "I suppose I shall."

"Why do you say 'Dear me'? You want to hear, don't you? It will be a wonderful thing for you, I should think. It is sure to be somethin' you will like, because they said so in their letter."

"Yes—ah—yes."

Both were silent for a brief interval, then Martha said: "I presume likely I shall be sittin' here in this very room this winter, doin' just the very same thing I'm doin' now, knittin' or sewin', with everything just as it is, cat and plants and Primmie and all the everyday things I've been amongst all my life. And you'll be away off, goodness knows where, among goodness knows what sorts of queer people and queer places. . . . Well," she added, with a smile, "you won't have any one to fret you about whether you put on rubbers or not. That'll be a comfort for you, at any rate."

He did not seem to find great comfort in the prospect.

"I shall not put them on," he said. "I know I sha'n't. I shall forget all about them, and forget to eat at regular times, and to—ah—keep my head covered in the sun. Why, do you know," he added, in a burst of confidence and quite as if he had not said the same thing before, "when I am by myself I always forget things like that, things that real people—ah—normal people, remember. Then I have—ah—indigestion and headaches and all sorts of miserable ailments. I shall forget again, of course, and my friends, the normal ones, will tell me, as they always do, that I need a—ah—keeper, so to speak. Oh, dear, yes."

She was indignant. "A keeper!" she repeated. "The idea! I do wish you wouldn't keep speakin' of yourself as simple-minded or crazy, Mr. Bangs. You are absent-minded, I know, but what of it? Whose business is that?"

He rubbed his chin. "Why, here," he observed, smiling slightly, "you have been kind enough to make it *your* business, Miss Martha. The reason I do not have—ah—sunstrokes and colds and headaches here is that you take pains to see that I am protected against their causes. I realize that. And I realize, too," he added, "that in Egypt I shall miss your—your great kindness. I shall miss all this—this room and all—very much, indeed. I think—no, I know I have never spent such a pleasant year as this has been. And I fear I shall never spend another as pleasant."

She laughed, but she looked pleased, nevertheless.

"Nonsense!" she exclaimed. "You'll have many more a great deal pleasanter, of course. You're well now, Mr. Bangs, and good health makes such a difference. You will enjoy your work more than ever."

"Will I? I don't believe I shall. That is very odd, I know, but I think it is true. I have been thinking about it a great deal of late and—ah—I—well, you know, I am very sure I shall be lonely."

"Lonely? You! Lonesome over in Egypt, after all you've told me about your lovin' it so, Mr. Bangs! Lonesome for what, for mercy sakes?"

"Why, for—for the Cape, you know; and this house and this pleasant room and—and the kindness which has been shown me here."

"Don't. What do what you call kindnesses amount to— the little things Primmie and I have been able to do for you —what do they amount to compared to what you did for me? I shouldn't be in this house, I shouldn't own it, if it wasn't for the interest you took and the trouble you went to. Lonesome! I think *I'm* goin' to be the real lonesome one this winter. Since you've been livin' here, Mr. Bangs, I've had a chance to talk of somethin' beside the little two-for-a-cent things that most of us Gould's Bluffs people have to talk about from December to June. I've had the chance to talk about somethin' besides Primmie's foolishness or Cap'n Jethro's 'spirits,' or the post office gossip. It has been wonderful for me. When father was alive no gale that ever blew could keep him from trampin' up to the office after his mornin' paper. He used to say that readin' the paper was the only way he could keep enough canvas drawing to pull him out of the doldrums. More of his sea talk, that was, of course, but you understand what he meant."

Galusha understood. "We all have our—ah—doldrums," he observed.

"Yes, seems as if we did. But, there!" briskly picking up her knitting, "I don't know as it does us much good to sit and talk about 'em. Primmie had a book around here last week, an old thing, one of Mrs. Southworth's it was; Primmie borrowed it somewhere. I looked it over one afternoon, that was as much as I wanted to do with it, and I remember there was an old woman in it who seemed to spend most of her time dreamin' of her 'vanished past.' She seemed to worry over that vanished past a good deal, but, so far as I could see, she didn't gain much by it. She might have done some plain sewin' and gained more. I can't see that you and I gain much by sittin' here and frettin' about next winter, Mr. Bangs. I suppose when winter is really here you will be trottin' around Egypt on a camel, or some sort of menagerie animal, and I shall be sweepin' and dustin' and makin' pies. And we both will be too busy to remember we're lonesome at all. I—— Yes, Primmie, what is it?"

Miss Cash's head and shoulders appeared between the door and the jamb.

"Miss Martha," she whispered, hoarsely, "there's somebody come to see you."

"Come to see me? Who is it; Cap'n Jethro?"

"No'm. It's Raish—I mean Mr. Pulcifer. And," confidentially, "he won't tell what he's come for, neither."

"And I presume likely you asked him that very thing. Well, bring him into the dinin' room and tell him I'll be right there. Humph!" she added, after Primmie had departed, "I wonder what Raish Pulcifer wants to see me about. I can't imagine, but I guess it isn't likely to be very important. I'll be back in a few minutes, Mr. Bangs."

It was, however, a full half hour before she reëntered the sitting room, and when she did so there was a puzzled expression on her face.

"Now, that's funny," she observed, musingly; "that certainly is funny. What is he drivin' at, I wonder?"

"Mr. Pulcifer?" inquired Galusha.

"Why, yes. He didn't say so in so many words; in fact, he didn't really say much of anything right out. He wouldn't be Raish Pulcifer if he was straight and plain. He talked about the weather and how he hadn't seen me for some time and just thought he'd call, and so on. That was just greasin' the ways for the launchin', as father would have said. He edged around and edged around and finally brought up the thing I'm pretty sure he came to see me about, my two hundred and fifty shares of Wellmouth Development Company stock."

Galusha caught his breath. "Eh?" he exclaimed.

"Yes; I think he came to see me about just those shares. Of course, he thinks I've still got them. He talked about his own shares and about the company in general and how it wasn't likely to amount to much and—oh, well, never mind; he talked a mile before he gained a foot. But I think, Mr. Bangs, I *think* he came to see if I would sell him that stock of mine, and, if I would, what I would sell it for. Considerin' that only a little while ago he told you he wouldn't touch the Wellmouth Development stock with a ten-foot pole, that's kind of funny, isn't it?"

CHAPTER XVII

G ALUSHA had some difficulty in falling asleep that
night. The habit of dropping into a peaceful and
dreamless slumber within five minutes after blowing out his lamp, a habit which had been his for the past
month, was broken. He had almost succeeded in forgetting
the Wellmouth Development Company. His distress of
mind and conscience concerning his dealings with it had
very nearly vanished also. He had been forced into deceit
to save Martha Phipps from great trouble, and the end justified the means. Having reached that conclusion in his
thinking, he had firmly resolved to put the whole matter
from his mind.

His one plunge into the pool of finance he had come to
believe destined never to be revealed. No one had mentioned the Development Company or its stock for weeks. It
was, apparently, dead and satisfactorily buried, and the
Bangs' secret was entombed with it.

And now, if Martha's surmise was correct, here was a
"resurrection man," in the person of Mr. Horatio Pulcifer.
hanging about the cemetery. The capacity for hating was
not in Galusha's make-up. He found it difficult to dislike
any one strongly. But he could come nearer to disliking
Raish Pulcifer than any one else, and now to dislike was
added resentment. Why in the world should this Pulcifer
person interfere with his peace of mind?

In the morning, and with the bright September sunshine
streaming into the room, his disquietude of the previous
night seemed rather foolish. No doubt Miss Martha had

been mistaken; perhaps Horatio had not had any idea of
buying her shares. Martha herself seemed a little doubtful.

"I've been thinkin' it over," she said, "and I wonder if I
just imagined that's what he was after. It seems almost as
if I must have. I can't think of any sensible reason why a
man who was so dreadfully anxious to sell, and only a little
while ago, should be wantin' to buy now. Perhaps he didn't
mean anything of the kind."

Galusha comforted himself with the thought that this was,
in all probability, the truth: Miss Martha had misinterpreted the Pulcifer purpose; Raish had not meant anything
of the kind.

But the comfort was short-lived. A few days later Doctor
Powers called at the Phipps' home. After he had gone
Martha came to the sitting room, where her lodger was read-
ing the paper, and, closing the door behind her, said:

"Mr. Bangs, I guess I was right, after all. Raish Pulcifer *was* hintin' at buyin' my Wellmouth Development stock."

Galusha dropped the paper in his lap. "Oh, dear! I—
I mean, dear me!" he observed.

"Yes, I guess there isn't much doubt of it. Doctor Powers came here to tell me that he had sold his shares to him
and that Eben Snow and Jim Henry Willis have sold theirs
in the same place. He says he doesn't know for certain,
but he thinks Raish has bought out all the little stockholders.
He's been quietly buyin' the Development stock for the last
week."

Mr. Bangs took off his spectacles and put them on again.
"Good gracious!" he stammered.

"That's what Doctor Powers says. He stopped in, just as
an old friend, to drop the hint to me, so that I could be
ready when Raish came to buy mine. I asked him what the
Pulcifer man was payin' for the stock. He said as little as
he had to, as near as he could find out. Of course, no one
was supposed to tell a word about it—Raish had asked 'em
not to do that—but *somebody* told, and then it all began to
come out. As a matter of fact, you might as well ask water
to run up hill as to ask Jim Willis to keep quiet about his

own business or keep out of any one else's. The price paid,
so the doctor says he's heard, runs all the way from eight
dollars a share up to fourteen and a half. Poor old Mrs.
Badger—Darius Badger's widow—got the eight dollars. She
was somethin' like me, I guess—had given up the idea of
ever gettin' a cent—and so she took the first offer Raish
made her. Eben Snow got the fourteen and a half, I believe, the highest price. He needed it less than anybody
else, which is usually the way. Doctor Powers sold his for
twelve and a half. Said he thought, when he was doin' it,
that he was mighty lucky. Now he wishes he hadn't sold
at all, but had waited. 'Don't sell yours for a penny less
than fifteen, Martha,' he told me. 'There's somethin' up.
Either Raish has heard somethin' and is buyin' for a specu-
lation, or else he's actin' as somebody else's agent.' What
did you say, Mr. Bangs?"

Galusha had not said anything; and what he said now
was neither brilliant nor original.

"Dear me, dear me!" he murmured. Martha looked at
him, keenly.

"Why, what is it, Mr. Bangs?" she asked. "Raish's buyin'
the stock won't make any difference to you, will it?"

"Eh? . . . To *me?* Why—why, of course not. Dear me,
no. Why—ah—how could it make any difference to me?"

"I didn't mean you, yourself. I meant to the Cabot, Bancroft and Cabot people, or whoever it was that bought my
stock."

"Oh—oh, oh! To them? Oh, yes, yes! I thought for the
moment you referred to me personally. Ha, ha! That
would have been very—ah—funny, wouldn't it? No, I
don't think it will make any difference to Cousin—ah—I
mean to the purchasers of your shares. No, no, indeed—
ah—yes. Quite so."

If Miss Phipps noticed a slight incoherence in this speech,
she did not comment upon it. Galusha blinked behind his
spectacles and passed a hand across his forehead. His
landlady continued her story.

"I asked Doctor Powers what reason Raish was givin'

people for his buyin'. The doctor said he gave reasons
enough, but they weren't very satisfyin' ones to a thinkin'
person. Raish said he owned a big block of the stock himself and yet it wasn't big enough to give him much say as
to what should be done with the company. Of course,
nothin' could be done with it at present, but still some time
there might and so he thought he might as well be hung for
an old sheep as a lamb and buy in what he could get, provided he could get it cheap enough. He had come to the
doctor first, he said. Ha, ha! That was kind of funny."

"Eh? . . . Oh, yes, certainly. . . . Of course."

"But I haven't told you yet why it was funny. It seems
he told every person he went to that he or she was the first.
Doctor Powers prides himself on bein' a pretty good business man and I guess it provoked him to find that Raish
had fooled him into takin' a lower price than some of the
rest got. He said as much to me. He said that he agreed
with what Raish said, that about he might as well be hung
for an old sheep as a lamb. So long as he *was* hung, so the
doctor said, he didn't care what it was for."

She laughed again and her lodger smiled, although rather
feebly. He murmured that it was very amusing.

"Yes, wasn't it?" said Martha. "Well, the doctor was
very anxious that I should not sell at a cent less than fifteen
dollars a share. I wonder what he, or Raish Pulcifer either,
would say if they knew I *had* sold already, and for as much
as father paid, too. Oh, I wonder if Raish has been to see
Cap'n Jeth yet. He won't buy *his* shares for any eight dollars a piece, he can be sure of that."

Galusha nodded; he was sure of it, too.

"But," said Martha, ending the conversation for the time,
"why do you suppose Raish is buyin' at all? What is goin'
on, anyway?"

She was by no means the only one who was asking that
question. Three days later Captain Jethro asked Galusha
the same thing. They met in the lane leading to the village
and the light keeper approached the subject without pre-
amble.

"Say, Mr. Bangs," he demanded, "what's Raish Pulcifer cal'late he's doin'?"

Galusha smiled. "I thank you for the compliment, Captain Hallett," he said, "but my intuition cannot keep pace with Mr. Pulcifer's—ah—calculations. No, indeed."

Jethro pulled his beard. "I asked you," he said, solemnly, "what Raish Pulcifer cal'lated he was doin' buyin' up Development stock? Do you know?"

"No. Is he buying it?"

"If you ain't heard that he is, you're about the only one in East Wellmouth. Ain't you heard it?"

Galusha would have liked to change the subject, but with Jethro Hallett that was not an easy task, as he knew from experience. He did not immediately make the attempt.

"Why—ah—yes," he admitted. "I have heard that he has bought—ah—some."

"Um-hm. Who told you; Martha?"

"Why—why—really, Captain, I don't know that I ought—— You'll pardon me, but——"

"Been tryin' to buy Martha's, has he?"

Galusha sighed. "Have you noticed," he suggested, "what a remarkable view one gets from this point? The village and the bay in front, and, in the rear, the—ah—light and the —ah—rest. Quite remarkable, don't you think so, Captain?"

Captain Jethro looked gravely at the view.

"Raish been to see Martha about buyin' her stock, has he?" he asked.

Galusha rubbed his chin. "I have often wondered," he said, "why no summer cottage has been built just here. The spot would seem to possess very marked advantages. Very —ah—very much so."

The light keeper cleared his throat. "Zach said he see Raish comin' out of your gate t'other day," he said. "Been to see Martha about her shares then, had he?"

"The—ah—proximity to the main road is an advantage in particular," Galusha continued. "One would be near it and yet, so to speak, secluded from it. Really, a very exceptional spot, Captain Hallett."

Captain Jethro stroked his beard, frowned, and gazed steadily at the face of the little archæologist. Galusha gazed serenely and with a pleased interest at the view. After a moment the light keeper said: "He's been after mine, too."

"Eh? . . . Oh, indeed? You mean——"

"I mean Raish Pulcifer's been tryin' to buy my Development stock same as he has Martha's. Hey? What say?"

"I said nothing, Captain. Not a word, really."

"Humph! . . . Well, he's been tryin' to buy mine, anyway. And, nigh's as I can find out, he's bought every loose share there is. All hands are talkin' about it now; some of 'em are wonderin' if they hadn't better have hung on. Eben Snow came to me this mornin' and he says, 'I don't know whether I did right to let go of that stock of mine or not,' he says. 'What do you think, Jeth?' I haven't got much use for Eben. and ain't had for years; I went to sea with him one v'yage and that generally tells a man's story. I've seen him at church sociables—in the days when I wasted my time goin' to such things—spend as much as five minutes decidin' whether to take a doughnut or a piece of pie. He couldn't eat both, but he was afraid whichever he took the other might turn out to be better. So when he asked me my opinion about his sellin' his Development, I gave it to him. 'You've been wantin' to sell. ain't you?' says I. 'I've heard you whinin' around for months because you couldn't sell. Now you *have* sold. What more do you want?' He got mad. 'You ain't sold *your* holdin's at any fourteen dollars a share, have you?' he says. I told him I hadn't. 'No, and I'll bet you won't, either,' says he. I told him he'd make money if he could get somebody to take the bet. Humph! the swab!"

For the first time Galusha asked a direct question.

"Did—ah—Mr. Pulcifer actually—ah—bid for your Development shares, Captain Hallett?" he inquired.

"Oh, he come as nigh to doin' it as I'd let him. Hinted maybe that he'd give me as much as he did Snow, fourteen fifty. I laughed at him. I asked him what made him so reckless, when, the last time he and I talked, he was tryin' to sell me his own shares for ten. And now he wanted to *buy* mine at fourteen and a half!"

"And—ah—what reason did he give for his change of heart? Or didn't he give any?"

"Humph! Yes, he gave a shipload of reasons, but there wouldn't any one of 'em float if 'twas hove overboard. He ain't buyin' on his own account, that I *know.*"

"Oh—ah—do you, indeed. May I ask why you are so certain?"

"For two reasons. First, because Raish ain't got money enough of his own to do any such thing. Second, and the main reason why I know he ain't buyin' for himself is because he says he is. Anybody that knows Raish knows that's reason enough."

Galusha ventured one more question.

"When he—ah—approached you, did you—that is, what excuse did you give him for—for your lack of interest, so to speak?"

"Hey? I didn't give him any. And I didn't tell him I wasn't interested. I am interested—to see how far he'll go. I sha'n't tell him I've sold already, Mr. Bangs; your Boston friends needn't worry about that. When I sign articles I stick to my contract."

They had reached the Phipps' gate by this time and there they parted. The light keeper strode off, rolling heavily, his beard blowing across his shoulder. He had been, for him, remarkably good-humored and talkative. Galusha was inclined to attribute the good humor to the fact that Captain Jethro considered he had made a good bargain in selling his own shares at a price so much higher than that obtained by Snow and the rest. The next time they conversed the good humor was not as apparent. But that occasion was almost a fortnight later.

And, meantime, Mr. Pulcifer had become the center of interest in East Wellmouth and its neighborhood. An important figure he always was, particularly in his own estimation, but now the spotlight of publicity which beat upon his ample figure had in its rays the blue tinge of mystery. The question which all Wellmouth was asking was that which Captain Jethro had asked Mr. Bangs: "What is Raish up to now?"

And Mr. Pulcifer firmly refused to answer that question. Or, to be more exact, he always answered it, but the answers were not considered convincing. Some pretended to be satisfied with his offhand declaration that he "had a little chunk of the stock and just presumed likely I might as well have a little more. Ain't nothin' to make a fuss about, anyhow." A few pretended to accept this explanation as *bona fide,* but the remainder, the majority, received it with open incredulity.

The oddest part of it all was the fact that the great Horatio appeared to dislike the prominent position which his activities held in the community mind. Ordinarily prominence had been the delight of his soul. In every political campaign, wherever the limelight shone brightest there had strutted Mr. Pulcifer, cigar in mouth, hat over one eye, serene self-satisfaction in the possession of mysterious knowledge radiating from his person. He loved that sort of thing; to be the possessor of "inside information," however slight, or even to be popularly supposed to possess it, had hitherto been the meat upon which this, Wellmouth's, Cæsar, fed and grew great.

But Raish was not enjoying this particular meal. And his attitude was not pretense, either; it was obvious that the more East Wellmouth discussed his buying the Development stock the less he liked it. When his fellow townsmen questioned him he grew peevish.

"Oh, forget it!" he exclaimed to one of the unfortunate who came seeking information. "You make me tired, Jim Fletcher, you and Ras Beebe and the whole gang. By cripes, a feller can't as much as take a five cent cigar out of his pocket without all hands tryin' to make a—a molehill out of it. Forget it, I tell you!"

Mr. Fletcher was a simple soul, decidedly not one of East

Wellmouth's intellectual aristocracy, but he was persistent.

"Aw, hold on, Raish," he expostulated, "I never said a word about your takin' a five cent cigar out of your pocket. . . . Er—er—you ain't taken one out, have you?"

"No, and I ain't goin' to—not now."

"All right—all right. *I* never asked you. All I said was——"

"I know what you said."

"Why, no, you don't neither. You're all mixed up. Nobody's said anything about cigars, or makin'—er—er—— What was it you said they made?"

"Oh, nothin', nothin'. A molehill is what I said."

"What kind of a hill?"

"A molehill. Didn't you ever hear of a ground mole, for heaven sakes?"

"Course I've heard of a ground mole! But what's a ground mole got to do with a cigar, I want to know? And you said a mole*hill*. What's a ground mole doin' up on a hill?"

"Not up *on* one—*in* one. A molehill is what a ground mole lives in, ain't it? It's just a sayin'. . . . Oh, never mind! Go on! Take a walk."

"*I* don't want to walk. And a ground mole lives in a hole, not a hill, like a—like a ant. You know that as well as I do. And, anyhow, nobody said anything about ground moles, or—or mud turtles neither, far's that goes. No, nor five cent cigars. Now, Raish, I'll tell you what they're sayin'; they say——"

"And I'll tell *you!* Listen! Listen, now, because this is the last time I'll tell anybody anything except to go——"

"Sshh, shh, Raish! Alvira's right in the kitchen and the window's open. . . . No, 'tain't, it's shut. Where will they go?"

"Listen, you! I've bought those few extra shares of Development because I had some myself and thought I might as well have a few more. I bought 'em and I paid for 'em. Nobody says I ain't paid for 'em, do they?"

"No, no. Don't anybody say that. All they say is——"

"Be still! Now I bought those shares. What of it? It's my business, ain't it? Yes. And I haven't bought any more. You can tell 'em that: *I haven't bought any more.*"

"Oh, all right, Raish, all right. I'll tell 'em you ain't. But——"

"That's all. Now forget it! For-*get* it!"

Which should, perhaps, have been sufficient and convincing. But there were still some unconvinced. For example, Martha happened to meet one morning, while on an errand in the village, the president of the Denboro Trust Company. He explained that he had motored over, having a little matter of personal business to attend to.

"I haven't seen you for some time, Miss Phipps," he observed. "Not since our—er—little talk about the Wellmouth Development stock. That was the last time, wasn't it?"

Martha said that it was. He lowered his voice a very little and asked, casually: "Still holding on to your two hundred and fifty shares, are you?"

"Why, that was what you told me to do, wasn't it?"

"Yes, yes. I believe it was. Humph! Just so, yes. So you've still got those shares?"

Martha smiled. "I haven't sold 'em to Raish Pulcifer, if that's what you're hintin' at," she said.

He seemed a bit embarrassed. "Well," he admitted, with a laugh, "I guess I'll have to own that I did mean that. There seems to be a good many who have sold to Pulcifer. All the little fellows, the small holders. You haven't, you say?"

"I haven't sold a share to him."

"Humph! Neither has Cap'n Jeth Hallett; he told me so just now. . . . Hum! . . . What is Raish buying for? What's the reason he's buying? Have you heard?"

"I've heard what he's told other folks; that's all I know about it."

"Hum. . . . Yes, yes. Well, here's my advice, Miss Phipps: If I were you—if I were you, I say, and he came to me and wanted to buy, I shouldn't be in too big a hurry to sell. Not in too big a hurry, I shouldn't."

"Why not?"

He glanced at her quickly. "Oh, he *has* been to see you about buying your shares, then?" he suggested.

She shook her head. "I didn't say he had," she replied. "I just asked why I shouldn't sell if he wanted to buy, that's all. Why shouldn't I?"

He seemed more embarrassed and a trifle irritated.

"Why—why—— Oh, well, I suppose you should, perhaps, if he offers you enough. But I wish you wouldn't until—until—— Well, couldn't you let me know before you give him his answer? Would you mind doing that?"

And now she looked keenly at him. "What would I gain by that?" she asked. *"You* aren't thinkin' of buyin' more of that stock are you? The other time when we talked, you told me the Trust Company had all they cared to own and were keepin' it because they had to. I would have been glad —yes, awfully glad, to sell you my shares. But you wouldn't even consider buyin'. Do you want to buy now?"

He frowned. "I don't know what I want," he said, impatiently. "Except that the one thing we want to find out is why Pulcifer is buying. The Trust Company holds a big block of that stock and—and if there is anything up we want to know of it."

"What do you mean by 'anything up'?"

"Oh, I mean if some other people are trying to get—er— into the thing. Of course, it isn't likely, but——"

He did not finish the sentence. She asked another question.

"Has Raish been to see you about buyin' the Trust Company stock?" she asked.

"No. He hasn't been near us."

"Perhaps he would if you told him you wanted to sell."

"I don't know that we do want to sell. That's a pretty good piece of property over there and some day—— Ahem! Oh, well, never mind. But I wish you would let us know before you sell Pulcifer your holdings. It might—I can't say positively, you know—but it *might* be worth your while."

Martha, of course, made no promise, but she thought a

good deal during her walk homeward. She told her lodger
of the talk with the Trust Company official, and he thought
a good deal, also.

His thoughts, however, dealt not with the possible rise in
value of the six hundred and fifty shares which, endorsed
in blank, reposed, presumably, somewhere in the vaults of
Cabot, Bancroft and Cabot. He thought not at all of anything like that. He had gotten rid of those certificates and
hoped never to hear of them again. But now, with all this
stir and talk, there was distinct danger that not only he but
others might hear of them. Galusha Bangs and Raish Pulcifer had, just now, one trait in common, both detested the
publicity given their dealings in the securities of the Wellmouth Development Company.

But, in spite of this detestation, Horatio still seemed
anxious to deal in those securities. He visited the Phipps'
home twice that week, both times after dark and, as the
watchful Primmie observed and commented upon, each time
coming not by the lane, but across the fields. And when he
left, at the termination of his second visit, the expression
upon his face was by no means one of triumph.

And Martha, of course, told her lodger what had trans-
pired.

"I declare," she said, after her caller had gone, "I shall
really begin to believe somethin' *is* up in that Development
Company, just as the Trust Company man said. Raish certainly wants to buy the two hundred and fifty shares he
thinks I've got. This is the third time he's been to see me,
sneakin' across lots in the dark so nobody else would see
him, and each time he raised his bid. He got up to eighteen
dollars a share to-night. And, I do believe, if I had given
him the least bit of encouragement, he would have gone
higher still. What do you think of that, Mr. Bangs?"

Galusha did not know what to think of it; he found it extremely unpleasant to think of it at all.

"Have you—ah—have you told him you do not intend selling?" he asked.

"Why, no, I haven't. You see, if I do he'll think it's

awfully queer, because he knows how anxious I was, a while ago, *to* sell. I just keep puttin' him off. Pretty soon I suppose I shall *have* to tell him I won't sell no matter what he offers; but we'll try the puttin' off as long as possible." She paused, and then added, with a mischievous twinkle, "Really, Mr. Bangs, I am gettin' a good deal of fun out of it. A few months ago I was the one to go to him and talk about that stock. Now he comes to me and I'm just as high and mighty as he ever was, you can be sure of that. 'Well, Raish,' I said to him to-night, 'I don't know that I am very much interested. If the stock is worth that to you, I presume likely it's worth it to me.' Ha, ha! Oh, dear! you should have seen him squirm. He keeps tryin' to be buttery and sweet, but his real feelin's come out sometimes. For instance, to-night his spite got a little too much for him and he said: 'Humph!' he said, 'somebody must have willed you money lately, Martha. Either that or keepin' boarders must pay pretty well.' 'Yes,' said I, 'it does. The cost of livin' is comin' down all the time.' Oh, I'm havin' a beautiful game of tit-for-tat with Raish."

She laughed merrily. Galusha did not laugh. The game was altogether too risky for him to enjoy it. A person sitting on a powder barrel could scarcely be expected to enjoy the sight of a group of children playing with matches in close proximity. An explosion, sooner or later, might be considered certain. But the children continued to play and day after day went by, and no blow-up took place. Galusha sat upon his barrel pondering apprehensively and—waiting. There were times when, facing what seemed the inevitable, he found himself almost longing for the promised summons from the Institute. An expedition to the wilds of—of almost anywhere, provided it was remote enough—offered at least a means of escape. But, to offset this, was the knowledge that escape by flight involved giving up East Wellmouth and all it had come to mean to him. Of course, he would be obliged to give it up some day and, in all probability, soon— but—well, he simply could not bring himself to the point of hastening the separation. So he shifted from the powder barrel to the sharp horn of the other dilemma and shifted back again. Both seats were most uncomfortable. The idea that there was an element of absurdity in his self-imposed martyrdom and that, after all, what he had done might be considered by the majority as commendable rather than criminal, did not occur to him at all. He would not have been Galusha Cabot Bangs if it had.

He meditated much and Primmie, always on the lookout for new symptoms, noticed the meditations. When Primmie noticed a thing she never hesitated to ask questions concerning it. She was dusting the sitting room one morning and he was sitting by the window looking out.

"You're thinkin' again, ain't you, Mr. Bangs?" observed Primmie.

Galusha started. "Eh?" he queried. "Thinking? Oh, yes—yes!—I suppose I was thinking, Primmie. I—ah—sometimes do."

"You 'most always do. I never see anybody think as much as you do, Mr. Bangs. Never in my born days I never. And lately—my savin' soul! Seems as if you didn't do nothin' *but* think lately. Just set around and think and twiddle that thing on your watch chain."

The thing on the watch chain was a rather odd charm which Mr. Bangs had possessed for many years. "Twiddling" it was a habit of his. In fact, he had twiddled it so much that the pivot upon which it had hung broke and Martha had insisted upon his sending the charm to Boston for repairs. It had recently been returned.

"What is that thing, Mr. Bangs?" asked Primmie. "I was lookin' at it t'other day when you left your watch chain layin' out in the sink."

"In the sink? You mean *by* the sink, don't you, Primmie?"

"No, I don't, I mean *in* it. You'd forgot your watch and Miss Martha she sent me up to your room after it. I fetched it down to you and you and her was talkin' in the kitchen and you was washin' your hands in the sink basin. Don't you remember you was?"

"Was I? I—I presume I was if you say so. Really I—I have forgotten."

"Course you have. And you forgot your watch, too. Left it layin' right alongside that tin washbasin full of soapsuds. 'Twas a mercy you didn't empty out the suds on top of it. Well, I snaked it out of the sink and chased out the door to give it to you and you was halfway to the lighthouse and I couldn't make you hear to save my soul. 'Twas then I noticed that charm thing. That's an awful funny kind of thing, Mr. Bangs. There's a—a bug on it, ain't there?"

"Why—ah—yes, Primmie. That charm is a very old scarab."

"Hey? A what? I told Miss Martha it looked for all the world like a pertater bug."

Galusha smiled. He held out the charm for her inspection.

"I have had that for a long time," he said. "It is a—ah—souvenir of my first Egyptian expedition. The scarab is a rather rare example. I found it myself at Saqqarah, in a tomb. It is a scarab of the Vth Dynasty."

"Hey? Die—what?"

"The Vth Dynasty; that is the way we classify Egyptian —ah—relics, by dynasties, you know. The Vth Dynasty was about six thousand years ago."

Primmie sat down upon the chair she had been dusting.

"Hey?" she exclaimed. "My Lord of Isrul! Is that bug thing there six thousand year old?"

"Yes."

"My savin' soul! *What* kind of a bug did you say 'twas?"

"Why, I don't know that I did say. It is a representation of an Egyptian beetle, *Ateuchus Sacer,* you know. The ancient Egyptians worshiped the beetle and so they——"

"Wait! Wait a minute, Mr. Bangs. *What* did you say they done to it?"

"I said they worshiped it, made a god of it, you understand."

"A god! Out of a—a pertater bug! Go long, Mr. Bangs! You're foolin', ain't you?"

"Dear me, no! It's quite true, Primmie, really. The ancient Egyptians had many gods, some like human beings, some in the forms of animals. The goddess Hathor, for example, was the goddess of the dead and is always represented in the shape of a cow."

"Eh! A cow! Do you mean to sit there and tell me them folks—er—er—went to church meetin' and—and flopped down and said their prayers to a *cow?*"

Galusha smiled. "Why, yes," he said, "I presume you might call it that. And another god of theirs had the head of a hawk—the bird, you know. The cat, too, was a very sacred animal. And, as I say, the beetle, like the one represented here, was——"

"Hold on, Mr. Bangs! *Ho-old* on! Don't say no more to me *now*. Let me kind of—of settle my stomach, as you might say, 'fore you fetch any more onto the table. Worshipin' cows and—and henhawks and—and cats and bugs and—and hoptoads and clams, for what *I* know! My savin' soul! What made 'em do it? What did they do it *for?* Was they all crazy?"

"Oh, no, it was the custom of their race and time."

"Well!" with a heartfelt sigh, "I'm glad times have changed, that's all I've got to say. Goin' to cow meetin' would be too much for *me!* Mr. Bangs, where did you get that bug thing?"

"I found it at a place called Saqqarah, in Egypt. It was in a tomb there."

"A tomb! What was you doin' in a tomb, for the land sakes?"

"I was opening it, looking for mummies and carvings, statues, relics, anything of the kind I might find. This scarab was in a ring on the finger of the mummy of a woman. She was the wife of an officer in the royal court. The mummy case was excellently preserved and when the mummy itself was unwrapped——"

"Wait a minute! Hold on just another minute, won't you, Mr. Bangs? You're always talkin' about mummies. A mummy is a—a kind of an image, ain't it? I've seen pictures of 'em in them printed report things you get from that Washin'ton place. An image with funny scrabblin' and pictures, kind of, all over it. That's a mummy, ain't it, Mr. Bangs?"

"Why, not exactly, Primmie. A mummy is——"

He proceeded to tell her much concerning mummies. From that he went on to describe the finding of the particular mummy from whose finger the scarab had been taken. Miss Cash listened, her mouth and eyes opening wider and wider. She appeared to be slowly stiffening in her chair. Galusha, growing interested in his own story, was waxing almost eloquent, when he was interrupted by a gasp from his listener. She was staring at him, her face expressing the utmost horror.

"Why, dear me, Primmie, what is it?" he begged.

Primmie gasped again. "And you set there," she said, slowly, "and tell me that you hauled that poor critter that had been buried six thousand years out of—of—— My Lord of Isrul! Don't talk no more to me now, Mr. Bangs. I sha'n't sleep none *this* night!" She marched to the door and there, turning, looked at him in awe-stricken amazement.

"And to think," she said, slowly, "that I always cal'lated you was meek and gentle and—and all like that—as Moses's grandmother. *Well,* it just shows you can't tell much by a person's *looks.* Haulin' 'em out of their graves and—and unwrappin' 'em like—like bundles, and cartin' 'em off to museums. And thinkin' no more of it than I would of— of scalin' a flatfish. My savin' soul!"

She breathed heavily once more and departed. That evening she came to her mistress with a new hint concerning the reason for the Bangs' absent-mindedness.

"It's his conscience," she declared. "He's broodin', that's what he's doin'. Broodin' and broodin' over them poor remains in the showcases in the museums. He may be a good man; I don't say he ain't. He's just lovely *now,* and that's why his conscience keeps a-broodin', poor thing. Oh, I know what I'm talkin' about, Miss Martha. You ask him

some time where he got that bug thing—a Arab, he calls it—
that he wears on his watch chain. Just ask him. You'll
hear somethin' *then,* I bet you! Whew!"

Galusha found considerable amusement in talks like those.
Primmie was a distinct relief, for she never mentioned the
troublesome Development Company. Talk in the village
concerning it was dying down and Mr. Pulcifer's assertion
that he had bought only the shares of the small holders
was becoming more generally believed. But in the Gould's
Bluffs settlement this belief was scoffed at. Captain Jeth
Hallett told Galusha the truth and his statement was merely
a confirmation of Martha Phipps'.

"Raish is hotfoot after that stock of mine," growled the
light keeper. "He's 'round to see me every day or two.
Don't hint any more neither; comes right out and bids for
it. He's got to as high as nineteen a share now. And he'd
go higher, too. *How* far he'll go I don't know, but I cal'late
I'll keep him stringin' along till I find out."

He pulled at his beard for a moment and then added:

"It's plain enough, of course, that Raish is agent for
somebody that wants to buy in that stock. Who 'tis, though,
I can't guess. It ain't your Cabot, Bancroft and Cabot
crowd, Mr. Bangs. That's plain enough, too."

Galusha tried to look innocently interested.

"Oh—ah—yes," he said. "Is it?"

"Sartin 'tis. *They* wouldn't need to be sendin' anybody
to buy my shares, would they? They've bought 'em already.
The whole thing is queer. Look here! Why should anybody be chasin' *me* for those shares? Why don't they get
a list of stockholders from the books? Those transfer books
ought to show that I've sold, hadn't they? They would, too,
if any transfer had been made. There ain't been any made,
that's all the answer I can think of. I signed those certificates of mine in blank, transferred 'em in blank on the
back. And somebody—whoever 'twas bought 'em—ain't
turned 'em in for new ones in their own name, but have
left 'em just the way they got 'em. That's why Raish and

his crowd think I've still got my stock. Now ain't that funny, Mr. Bangs? Ain't that strange?"

It was not at all funny to Galusha. Nor strange. The light keeper tugged at his beard and his shaggy brows drew together. "I don't know's I did right to let go of that stock of mine, after all," he said, slowly. "Don't know as I did, no."

Galusha asked him why.

"Because I don't know as I did, that's all. If I'd hung on I might have got more for it. Looks to me as if Raish's crowd, whoever they are, are mighty anxious to buy. And the Denboro Trust Company folks might bid against 'em if 'twas necessary. They've got too much of that stock to let themselves be froze out. Humph! . . . Humph! I ain't sure as I did right."

"But—but you did get a profit, Captain Hallett. The profit you—ah—expected."

"Humph! I got *a* profit, but how do I know 'twas the profit Julia meant? I ought to have gone and asked her afore I sold, that's what I ought to have done, I cal'late."

He frowned heavily and added, in a tone of gloomy doubt: "I presume likely I've been neglectin' things—things like that, lately, and that's why punishments are laid onto me. I suppose likely that's it."

Galusha, of course, did not understand, but as the captain seemed to expect him to make some remark, he said: "Oh—ah—dear me! Indeed? Ah—punishments?"

"Yes. I don't know what else they are. When your own flesh and blood——" He stopped in the middle of his sentence, sighed, and added: "Well, never mind. But I need counsel, Mr. Bangs, counsel."

Again Galusha scarcely knew what to say.

"Why—ah—Captain Hallett," he stammered, "I doubt if my advice would be worth much, really, but such as it is I assure you it——"

Captain Jethro interrupted.

"Counsel from this earth won't help me any, Mr. Bangs,"

he declared. "It's higher counsel that I need. Um-hm, higher."

He walked away without saying more. Galusha wondered what had set him off upon that tack. That afternoon, while in the village, he met Nelson Howard and the latter furnished an explanation. It seemed that the young man had been to see Captain Jethro, had dared to call at the light with the deliberate intention of seeing and interviewing him on the subject of his daughter. The interview had not been long, nor as stormy as Nelson anticipated; but neither had it been satisfactory.

"It's those confounded 'spirits' that are rocking the boat," declared Nelson. "The old man practically said just that. He seems to have gotten over some of his bitterness against me—perhaps it is, as you say, Mr. Bangs, because I have a better position now and good prospects. Perhaps it is that, I don't know. But he still won't consider my marrying Lulie. He seems to realize that we could marry and that he couldn't stop us, but I think he realizes, too, that neither Lulie nor I would think of doing it against his will. 'But why, Cap'n Hallett?' I kept saying. '*Why?* What is the reason you are so down on me?' And all I could get out of him was the old stuff about 'revelations' and 'word from above' and all that. We didn't get much of anywhere. Oh, pshaw! Wouldn't it make you tired? Say, Mr. Bangs, the last time you and I talked you said you were going to 'consider' those Marietta Hoag spirits. I don't know what you meant, but if you could consider some sense into them and into Cap'n Jeth's stubborn old head, I wish you would."

Galusha smiled and said he would try. "I don't exactly know what I meant, myself, by considering them," he admitted. "However, I—ah—doubtless meant something and I'll try and—ah—consider what it was. It seems to me that I had a vague thought—not an idea, exactly, but—— Well, perhaps it will come back. I have had a number of—ah—distractions of late. They have caused me to forget the spirits. I'm very sorry, really. I must try now and reconsider the considering. Dear me, how involved I am getting!

Never mind, we are going to win yet. Oh, I am sure of it."

The distractions to which he referred were, of course, the recent and mysterious machinations of Raish Pulcifer. And he was to be again distracted that very afternoon. For as, after parting with Howard, he was walking slowly along the main road, pondering deeply upon the problem presented by the love affair of his two young friends and its spirit complications, he was awakened from his reverie by a series of sharp clicks close at his ear. He started, looked up and about, and saw that he was directly opposite the business office of the great Horatio. He heard the clicks again and realized that they were caused by the tapping of the windowpane by a ring upon a masculine finger. The ring appeared to be—but was nŏt—a mammoth pigeon-blood ruby and it ornamented, or set off, the hand of Mr. Pulcifer himself.

Galusha stared uncomprehendingly at the hand and ring. Then the hand beckoned frantically. Mr. Bangs raised his eyes and saw, through the dingy pane, the face of the owner of the hand. The lower portion of the face was in eager motion. "Come in," Mr. Pulcifer was whispering. "Come on in!"

Galusha wonderingly entered the office. He had no desire for conversation with its proprietor, but he was curious to know what the latter wanted.

"Ah—good-afternoon, Mr. Pulcifer," he said.

Raish did not answer immediately. His first move was to cross to the door by which his visitor had entered, close and lock it. His next was to lower the window shade a trifle. Then he turned and smiled—nay, beamed upon that visitor.

"Set down, set down, Perfessor," he urged, with great cordiality. "Well, well, well! It's good to see you again, be hanged if it ain't now! How's things down to the bluffs? Joggin' along, joggin' along in the same old rut, the way the feller with the wheelbarrer went to market? Eh? Haw, haw, haw! Have a cigar, Perfessor?"

Galusha declined the cigar. He would also have declined

the invitation to sit, but Mr. Pulcifer would not hear of it. He all but forced his caller into a chair.

"Set down," he insisted. "Just as cheap settin' as standin' and consider'ble lighter on shoe leather, as the feller said. Haw, haw! Hey? Yes, indeed. Er—— Have a cigar?"

But Galusha was still resolute as far as the cigar was concerned. Raish lighted one himself and puffed briskly. To a keen observer he might have appeared a trifle nervous. Galusha was not a particularly keen observer and, moreover, he was nervous himself. If there had been no other reason, close proximity to a Raish Pulcifer cigar was, to a sensitive person, sufficient cause for nervousness.

Mr. Pulcifer continued to talk and talk and talk, of the weather, of the profits of the summer season just past, of all sorts of trivialities. Mr. Bangs' nervousness increased. He fidgeted in his chair.

"Really," he stammered, "I—I fear I must be going. You will excuse me, I hope, but—ah—I must, really."

Pulcifer held up a protesting hand. It was that holding the cigar and he waved it slowly back and forth. One of Galusha's experiences had been to be a passenger aboard a tramp steamer loaded with hides when fire broke out on board. The hides had smoked tremendously and smelled even more so. As the dealer in real estate slowly waved his cigar back and forth, Galusha suddenly remembered this experience. The mental picture was quite vivid.

"Wait, Perfessor," commanded Horatio. "Throttle her down. Put her into low just a minute. Say, Perfessor," he lowered his voice and leaned forward in his chair: "Say, Perfessor," he repeated, "do you want to make some money?"

Galusha gazed at him uncomprehendingly.

"Why—ah—— Dear me!" he faltered. "I—that is— well, really, I fear I do not fully grasp your—ah—meaning, Mr. Pulcifer."

Raish seemed to find this amusing. He laughed aloud. "No reason why you should yet awhile, Perfessor," he declared. "I'll try to get it across to you in a minute, though.

What I asked was if you wanted to make money. Do, don't you?"

"Why—why, I don't know. Really, I——"

"Go 'way, boy!" derisively. "Go 'way! Don't tell me you don't want money. Everybody wants it. You and me ain't John D.'s yet, by a consider'ble sight. Hey? Haw, haw! Anyhow *I* ain't, and I'll say this for you, Perfessor, if you are, you don't look it. Haw, haw!"

He laughed again. Galusha glanced despairingly at the locked door. Mr. Pulcifer leaned forward and gesticulated with the cigar just before his visitor's nose. The visitor leaned backward.

"If—if you don't mind," he said, desperately, "I really wish you wouldn't."

"What?"

"Put that thing—that cigar quite so near. If you don't mind."

Raish withdrew the cigar and looked at it and his companion.

"Oh, yes, yes; I see!" he said, after a moment. "You object to tobacco, then?"

Galusha drew a relieved breath. "Why—ah—no," he said, slowly, "not to—ah—tobacco." Then he added, hastily: "But, really, Mr. Pulcifer, I must be going."

Pulcifer pushed him back into the chair again. His tone became brisk and businesslike. "Hold on, Perfessor," he said. "You say you want to make money?"

Galusha had not said so, but it seemed scarcely worth while to deny the assertion. And Raish waited for no denial. "You want to make money," he repeated. "All right, so do I. And I've got a scheme that'll help us both to make a little. Now listen. But before I tell you, you've got to give me your word to keep it dark; see?"

Galusha promised and Raish proceeded to explain his scheme. Briefly it amounted to this: Galusha Bangs, being a close acquaintance of Martha Phipps and Jethro Hallett, was to use that acquaintanceship to induce them to sell their shares in the Development Company. For such an effort, if successful, on the part of Mr. Bangs, he, Horatio Pulcifer, was prepared to pay a commission of fifty dollars, twenty-five when he received Martha's shares and twenty-five when Jethro's were delivered.

"There," he said, in conclusion, "is a chance I'm offerin' you, as a friend, to clean up fifty good, hard, round dollars. What do you say, old man?"

The "old man"—Galusha winced slightly at the appellation—did not seem to know what to say. His facial expression might have indicated any or all of a variety of feelings. At last, he stammered a question. Why did Mr. Pulcifer wish to obtain the Development stock? This question Raish would not answer.

"Never mind," he said. "I do, that's all. And I've got the money to do it with. I'll pay cash for their stock and I'll pay you cash when you or they hand it over. That's business, ain't it?"

"But—but, dear me, Mr. Pulcifer, why do you ask *me* to do this? Why——"

"Ain't I told you? You're a friend of mine and I'm givin' you the chance because I think you need the money. That's a reason, ain't it?"

"Why—yes. It is—ah—a reason. But why don't you buy the stock yourself?"

For an instant Raish's smoothness deserted him. His temper flared.

"Because the cussed fools won't sell it to me," he snapped. "That is, they ain't said they'd sell yet. Perhaps they're prejudiced against me, I don't know. Maybe they will sell to you; you and they seem to be thicker'n thieves. Er—that is, of course, you understand I don't mean—— Oh, well, you know what I mean, Perfessor. Now what do you say?"

Galusha rose and picked up his hat from the floor.

"I'm afraid I must say no," he said, quietly, but with a firmness which even Raish Pulcifer's calloused understanding could not miss. "I could not think of accepting, really."

"But, say, Perfessor——"

"No, Mr. Pulcifer. I could not."

"But why not? If—— Well, I tell you, maybe I might make it sixty dollars instead of fifty for you."

"No. I couldn't, Mr. Pulcifer. . . . If you will kindly unlock the door?"

Pulcifer swore. "Well, you must be richer'n you look, that's all I've got to say," he snarled. He kicked the waste-basket across the room and growled: "I'll get the stuff away from 'em yet, just the same. What the fools are hangin' on for is more'n I can see. Martha Phipps was down on her knees beggin' me to buy only a little spell ago. Old Jeth, of course, thinks his 'spirits' are backin' *him* up. Crazy old loon! Spirits! In this day and time! God sakes! Humph! I wish to thunder I could deal with the spirits direct; might be able to do business with *them*. Perfessor, now come, think it over. There ain't anything crooked about it. . . . Why, what is it, Perfessor?" eagerly. "Changed your mind, have you?"

Galusha's expression had changed, certainly. He looked queerly at Mr. Pulcifer, queerly and for an appreciable interval of time. There was an odd flash in his eye and the suspicion of a smile at the corner of his lips. But he was grave enough when he spoke.

"Mr. Pulcifer," he said, "I appreciate your kindness in —ah—considering me in this matter. I—it is impossible for me to accept your offer, of course, but—but——"

"Now, hold on, Perfessor. You think that offer over."

"No, I cannot accept. But it has occurred to me that perhaps . . . perhaps . . . Mr. Pulcifer, do you know Miss Hoag?"

"Hey? Marietta Hoag? *Know* her? Yes, I know her; know her too well for my own good. Why?"

"Have you any—ah—influence with her? That is, would she be likely to listen to a suggestion from you?"

"Listen! *She?* Confound her, I've got a note of hers for seventy-five dollars and it's two months overdue. She'd *better* listen! Say, what are you drivin' at, Perfessor?"

Galusha deposited his hat upon the floor again, and sat

down in the chair he had just vacated.   Now it was he who, regardless of the cigar, leaned forward.

"Mr. Pulcifer," he said, "an idea occurred to me while you were speaking just now.   I don't know that it will be of any—ah—value to you.   But you are quite welcome to it, really.   This is the idea——"

CHAPTER XVIII

I F Ras Beebe or Miss Blount or some others of the group of East Wellmouthians who guessed Galusha Bangs to be "a little teched in the head," had seen that gentleman walking toward home after his interview with Mr. Pulcifer in the latter's office—if they had seen him on his way to Gould's Bluffs that day, they would have ceased guessing and professed certain knowledge. Galusha meandered slowly along the lane, head bent, hands clasped behind him, stumbling over tussocks and stepping with unexpected emphasis into ruts and holes. Sometimes his face wore a disturbed expression, almost a frightened one; at other times he smiled and his eyes twinkled like those of a mischievous boy. Once he laughed aloud, and, hearing himself, looked guiltily around to see if any one else had heard him. Then the frightened expression returned once more. If Primmie Cash had been privileged to watch him she might have said, as she had on a former occasion, that he looked "as if he was havin' a good time all up one side of him and a bad one all down t'other."

As a matter of fact, this estimate would not have been so far wrong. Galusha was divided between pleasurable anticipation and fear. There was adventure ahead, adventure which promised excitement, a probable benefit to some individuals and a grievous shock to others, and surprise to all. But for him there was involved a certain amount of risk. However, so he decided before he reached the Phipps' gate, he had started across the desert and it was too late to turn back. Whether he brought his caravan over safely or the Bedouins got him was on the knees of the gods. And the fortunes of little Galusha Bangs had been, ere this, on the knees of many gods, hawk-headed and horned and crescent-crowned, strange gods in strange places. It was quite useless to worry now, he decided, and he would calmly wait and see. At the best, the outcome would be good, delightful. At the worst, except for him—well, except for him it could not be much worse than it now was. For him, of course—he must not think about that.

He endeavored to assume an air of light-hearted, care-free innocence and sometimes overdid it a bit. Primmie, the eagle-eyed, remarked to her mistress: "Well, all's I can say is that I never see such a change in a body as there is in Mr. Bangs. He used to be so—so quiet, you know, all the time, and he is yet most of it. When I used to come along and find him all humped over thinkin', and I'd ask him what he was thinkin' about, he'd kind of jump and wake up and say, 'Eh? Oh, nothin', nothin,' Primmie, really. Er—quite so—yes.' And then he'd go to sleep again, as you might say. But he don't do so now; my savin' soul, no! This mornin' when I says, 'What you thinkin' about, Mr. Bangs?' he says, 'Nothin', nothin', Primmie,' same as usual; but then he says, *'Don't* look at me like that, Primmie. I wasn't thinkin' of anything, I assure you. Please don't *do* it.' And then he commenced to sing, sing out loud. I never heard him do it afore and I don't know's I exactly hanker to have him do it again, 'cause 'twas pretty unhealthy singin', if you ask *me*. But what——"

"Oh, now run along, run along, Primmie, for mercy's sakes! I never heard any one use so many words and get so little good out of 'em in my life. Let Mr. Bangs alone."

"*I* ain't doin' nothin' to him. Lord of Isrul, no! But, Miss Martha, what started him to singin' all to once? If 'twas somebody else but him and I didn't know the cherry rum was all gone, I——"

"What? What's that? How did you know the cherry rum was all gone?"

Primmie blinked and swallowed hard. "Why—er—why

—er—Miss Martha," she stammered, "I—I just happened to find it out—er—sort of by accident. Zach—Zacheus Bloomer, I mean—over to the lighthouse, you know——"

"There, there! Know? Of course I know Zach Bloomer, I should think I might. Don't be any sillier than the Lord made you, Primmie. It isn't necessary."

"Well—well, you see, Miss Martha, Zach he was over here one time a spell ago and—and—— Well, we got to—to kind of arguin' with one another—er—er—arguin', you know."

"Yes, I know. I ought to. Go on."

"Yes'm. And Zach he got to—to bettin', as you might say. And we got talkin' about—er—cherry rum, seems so. It's kind of funny that we done it, now I come to think of it, but we did. Seems to me 'twas Zach started it."

"Um. . . . I see. Go on."

"Well, we argued and argued and finally he up and bet me there wasn't a drink of cherry rum in this house. Bet me five cents, he did, and I took him up. And then I went and got the bottle out of the soup tureen in the closet and fetched it and showed it to him. 'There!' says I. 'There's your drink, Zach Bloomer,' says I. 'Now hand over my five cents.' 'Hold on, Posy,' he says, 'hold on. I said a drink. There ain't a drink in that bottle.' 'Go 'long,' says I, 'the bottle's half full.' But he stuck it out there wasn't a drink in it and afore he'd pay me my bet he had to prove it to himself. Even then, after he'd swallowed the whole of it, he vowed and declared there wasn't a real drink. But he had to hand over the five cents. . . . And—and that's how I know," concluded Primmie, "that there ain't any cherry rum in the house, Miss Martha."

Miss Phipps' remarks on the subject of the wily Mr. Bloomer and the rum drove the thoughts of Mr. Bangs' odd behavior from the mind of her maid. But the consciousness of conspiracy was always present with Galusha, try as he might to forget it. And he was constantly being reminded—of it. Down at the post office at mail time he would feel his coat-tail pulled and looking up would see the face of Mr. Pulcifer solemnly gazing over his head at the rows of letter boxes. Apparently Raish was quite unconscious of the little man's presence, but there would come another tug at the coat-tail and a barely perceptible jerk of the Pulcifer head toward the door.

Feeling remarkably like a fool, Galusha would follow to the front steps of the post office. There Raish would suddenly and, in a tone of joyful surprise, quite as if they had not met for years, seize his hand, pump it up and down and ask concerning his health, the health of the Gould's Bluffs colony and the "news down yonder." Then, gazing blandly up the road at nothing in particular, he would add, speaking in a whisper and from the corner of his mouth: "Comin' along, Perfessor. She's a-comin' along. Keep your ear out for signals. . . . What say? Why, no, I don't think it does look as much like rain as it did, Mr. Bangs."

One evening Galusha, entering the Phipps' sitting room, found Lulie there. She and Martha were in earnest conversation and the girl was plainly much agitated. He was hurriedly withdrawing, but Miss Phipps called him back.

"Come in, Mr. Bangs," she said. "I think Lulie would like to talk to you. She said she would."

"Yes. Yes, I would, Mr. Bangs," put in Lulie, herself. "Could you spare just a minute or two?"

Galusha cheerfully avowed that he had so many spare minutes that he did not know what to do with them.

"If time were money, as they say it is," he added, "I should be a—ah—sort of mint, shouldn't I?" Then he smiled and added: "Why, no, not exactly that, either. A mint is where they make money and I certainly do not make time. But I have just as much time as if I did. Yes—ah—quite so. As our philosophizing friend Zacheus is so fond of saying, I have 'all the time there is.' And if time *is* money—why—ah. . . . Eh? Dear me, possibly you ladies know what I am talking about; *I* don't."

They both burst out laughing and he smiled and stroked his chin. Martha looked him over.

"What makes you so nervous, Mr. Bangs?" she asked.

He started and colored. He was a trifle nervous, having a shrewd suspicion as to what Miss Hallett wished to talk with him about. She promptly confirmed the suspicion.

"Mr. Bangs," she said, "I am in such trouble. It's about father, as usual. I'm afraid he is at it again."

"Eh? I beg pardon? Oh, yes, certainly."

Martha shook her head. "He hasn't the slightest idea what you mean, Lulie," she declared. "That's why he says 'Oh, yes, certainly.' She means, Mr. Bangs, that Cap'n Jethro is beginnin' to break out with another attack of Marietta Hoag's spirits, and we've been tryin' to think of a way to stop him. We haven't yet. Perhaps you can. Can you?"

Lulie went on to explain. Her father had been more gloomy and thoughtful for the last week or two. She had noticed it and so had Zach. He talked with her less and less as the days passed, lapsed into silences at meals, and on nights when he was supposed to be off duty and asleep she often heard him walking about his room. If she asked him, as, of course, she often did, what was the matter, if he was not feeling well or if there was anything troubling him, he only growled a negative or ordered her not to bother him.

"And when, last Wednesday at supper," she went on, "Zach said something about the engine for the foghorn not working just as it should, father's answer showed us both what was in his mind. I had guessed it before and Zach says he had, but then we knew."

"Tell Mr. Bangs what he said," urged Martha.

"He didn't say so very much, Mr. Bangs, but it was the way he said it. He glowered at poor Zach, who hadn't said or done anything wrong, and pulled his beard as he always does. Then he said: 'There's no wonder the engine's out of kilter. There's no wonder about that. The wonder is that anything's right aboard here. We've been trying to steer without a compass. We've got so we think we don't need a pilot or a chart, but are so everlasting smart we can cruise anywhere on our own hook.' 'Why, father,' said I, 'what do you mean?' He glared at me then. 'Mean?' he asked. 'I mean we've had guidance offered to us, offered to us over and over again, and we've passed it by on the other side.'"

She paused. Galusha looked puzzled.

"Ah—um, yes," he observed. "On the other side? Yes—ah—quite so."

"Oh, that was just his way of speaking, Mr. Bangs. I tried to change the subject. I asked him if he didn't think we should report the engine trouble to the inspector when he came next month. It was a mistake, my saying that. He got up from his chair. 'I'm going to report,' he said. 'I'm going to make my report aloft and ask for guidance. The foghorn ain't the only thing that's runnin' wild. My own flesh and blood defies me."

Martha interrupted. "You hear that, Mr. Bangs?" she said. "And we were all hopin' *that* snarl was straightenin' itself out."

Galusha looked very uneasy. "Dear me," he said. "Really, now. Oh, dear!"

"Well," continued Lulie, "that was enough, of course. And the next day, last Thursday, Zacheus said Ras Beebe told him that Ophelia—that's his sister, you know—told him that Abel Harding told her that his wife said that Marietta Hoag told *her*—I *hope* I've got all the 'hims' and 'hers' straight—that Cap'n Jeth Haliett was going to have another séance down at the light pretty soon. Marietta said that father felt he needed help from 'over the river'. . . . What is it, Mr. Bangs?"

"Oh, nothing, nothing. For a moment I did not get the —ah—allusion, the 'over the river,' you know. I comprehend now, the—ah—Styx; yes."

But now Martha looked puzzled.

"Sticks!" she repeated. "Lulie didn't say anything about sticks. Neither did Cap'n Jethro. Spirits he was talkin' about."

"Yes, I know. Certainly, quite so. The shades beyond the Styx."

"*Shades? Sticks!* For mercy's sakes, Mr. Bangs——!"

Lulie laughed aloud. "He means the River Styx, Martha," she explained. "Don't you know? The river of the dead, that the ancients believed in, where Charon rowed the ferry."

And now Martha laughed. "My goodness gracious me!" she cried. "Yes, yes, of course. I've read about it, but it was a long while ago. Mr. Bangs, I'm dreadfully ignorant, I realize it about once every ten minutes when I'm with you. Perhaps I've got a little excuse this time. I've been figurin' I must buy new curtains for the dinin' room. I was thinkin' about it all this forenoon. And when *you* began to talk about shades and sticks, I—— Mercy me! I am funny, I declare!"

She laughed again and Lulie and Galusha joined her. They were still laughing when the dining room door opened. Mr. Bloomer's substantial if not elegant form appeared.

"Ain't buttin' in, be I?" inquired Zach. "I knew you was over here, Lulie, so I stopped to tell you the news. It's all settled."

"Settled?" Lulie and Martha repeated the word together. Zach nodded, portentously.

"Um-hm," he declared. "Settled 's the word. The whistle's piped to quarters. All hands, alow and aloft, are ordered to report on board the good ship *Gould's Bluffs Lighthouse*, Cap'n Jethro Hallet commandin', on Friday next, the —er—I-forget-what of this month, at seven bells in the——"

"Zach! Zach!" broke in Lulie. "Stop it! What are you talking about?"

"Talkin' about what I'm tryin' to tell you," said Zacheus, who seemed, for him, a good deal disturbed. "All able believers, fo'mast hands, and roustabouts and all full-rated ghosts, spooks, sperits and Chinee controls are ordered to get together in the parlor next Saturday night and turn loose and raise—whatever 'tis they raise. Signed, Marietta Hoag, Admiral, and Cap'n Jethro Hallett, Skipper. There, by Godfreys! Now if you don't know 'tain't my fault, is it? Yes, sir, there's goin' to be another one of them fool sea-ants, or whatever 'tis they call 'em, over to the house next Friday night. And I think it's a darn shame, if you want to know what *I* think. And just as you and me, Lulie, was hopin' the old man was gettin' so he'd forgot Marietta and all her crew. A healthy note, by Godfreys, ain't it now!"

"A healthy note," or words to that effect, was exactly what it was; Martha and Lulie were in thorough accord with Zach as to that. Galusha did not say very much. He rubbed his chin a good deal and when, after Bloomer had departed, Lulie came close to breaking down and crying, he still was silent, although nervous and evidently much disturbed. Lulie bravely conquered her emotion.

"Please don't mind me," she begged. "It's awfully silly of me, I know. But, you see, Nelson and I had really begun to think that perhaps father had broken away from—from all that. For a time he was—oh, different. Nelson told you that he bowed to him once and I told you how—— But what is the use? Here he goes again. And now goodness knows what dreadful ideas that Hoag woman will put into his head. Nelson and I had hoped that perhaps—perhaps we might be married in six months or a year. Now—— Oh, it is *so* discouraging!"

Martha soothed her, told her not to be discouraged, that no doubt this spirit outbreak would be only a mild one, that she was sure Captain Jeth would "come around all right" in time, and grasped at any other straws of comfort she found afloat. Galusha stood awkwardly by, his face expressing concern, but his tongue silent. When Lulie declared she must go home, he insisted upon walking to the light with her.

"But you don't need to, Mr. Bangs," she declared. "It is a pleasant night and such a little way. And you know I am used to running about alone. Why, what on earth do you think would be likely to hurt me, down here in this lonesomeness?"

Nevertheless, he insisted. But, although she chatted during their short walk, it was not until they reached the light keeper's gate that he spoke. Then he laid a hand on her arm.

"Ah—ah—Miss Lulie——" he began, but she stopped him.

"I thought we had settled long ago," she said, "that I wasn't to be 'Miss' Lulie. Now you are beginning again."

"Yes—yes. I beg your pardon, of course. Well, Miss—— Oh, dear me, *how* ridiculous I am! Well, Lulie, I should like to tell you a story. May I?"

It seemed a queer place and an odd time to tell stories, but she said of course he might.

"It wasn't a very long story," he went on, "but it is a true one. I happened to think of it just now while we were talking, you and I and—ah—Miss Martha. It is about me. On one of my expeditions in Egypt, Miss Lu—— Oh, good gracious!—— On one of my Egyptian expeditions, Lulie, I was in search of a certain tomb, or group of tombs. It was on this expedition, by the way, that we found the very remarkable statue of Amenemhait; Amenemhait III, you know."

Lulie smiled. "I *don't* know," she said, "but it doesn't matter."

"Eh? Oh, no, not at all, not in the least. He was a Pharaoh of the first Theban period. But that doesn't matter either; and he hasn't anything to do with this story. We had learned of the existence of this group of tombs, or that they had existed at one time, and of their approximate location, from an inscription dug up by myself at——"

The door of the light keeper's cottage swung open with a bang. A voice roared across the night.

"Lulie!" shouted Captain Jethro. "Lulie!"

The Bangs' story broke off in the middle. Its narrator and his young companion turned startled faces toward the sound.

"Lulie!" bellowed Captain Jeth, again. "Lulie!"

Lulie answered. "Why, yes, father," she said. "I am right here, at the gate. Why are you shouting so? What is the matter?"

The captain seemed much surprised. He raised a hand to shield his eyes from the lamplight in the room behind him.

"Hey?" he queried. "Where be you? You ain't right there at the gate, are you?"

"Why, yes, of course I am."

"Humph! . . ." Then, with renewed suspicion, "Who's that with you?"

"Mr. Bangs. I ran over to Martha's for a minute or two, and he walked home with me."

"Good-evening, Captain Hallett," hailed Galusha. Captain Jethro pulled his beard.

"Humph!" he grunted. "Humph! Mr. Bangs, eh? . . . Humph! I thought—— Cal'late I must have fell asleep on the sofy and been dreamin'. . . . Humph! . . . Lulie, you better come in now, it's chilly out here. Mr. Bangs can come, too, I suppose likely—if he wants to."

It was not the most cordial of invitations and Galusha did not accept it.

"I must get back to the house, Captain," he said. "It *is* chilly, as you say. No doubt he is right, Lulie. You mustn't stay. Good-night."

"But, Mr. Bangs, you haven't finished your story."

"Eh? Dear me, so I haven't. Well——"

"Lulie!" Captain Jethro's voice was fretful. "Lulie, you come along in now. I want you."

Lulie shook her head resignedly. "Yes, father," she replied, "I'm coming this minute. You see?" she whispered. "He is getting back all the impatience and—and strangeness that he had last fall. It is that dreadful spirit business. Oh, dear!"

Galusha softly patted her shoulder. "I won't finish my story," he said, in a low tone. "It isn't necessary, because I can tell you the—ah—moral, so to speak, and that will do as well. We found those tombs at last by doing a thing which, we were all sure, was the worst thing we could possibly do. It turned out to be that 'worst thing' which saved us. And—and I wish you would think that over, Lulie," he added, earnestly. "It looked to be the very worst thing and —and it turned out to be the best. . . . Ah—good-night."

But she detained him. "I don't understand, Mr. Bangs,"

she said. "What do you mean? You said you were going to tell me the moral of your story. That isn't a moral, is it?"

"Eh? No—ah—no. I suppose it isn't. But—but you think it over, to please me, you know. A—a something which looked to be the worst that could happen was the miracle that gave us our tombs. Perhaps the—perhaps what you dread most may give you yours. Not your tomb; dear me, no! I hope not. But may be the means of—of saving the situation. There, there, I must go. Good-night."

"Wait, wait, Mr. Bangs. . . . Oh, yes, father, I'm coming now. . . . Mr. Bangs, what *do* you mean? What I dread the most? What I dread—I think I dread that silly séance next Saturday night more than anything else. Mr. Bangs, you don't mean——"

"Now, now, now, Lulie. I mustn't say a word more. I—I have said too much, I know. Just think over the—ah—moral, that's all. Think it over—but don't mention it to any one else, please. Good-night. Good-night, Captain Hallett."

He hurried away. Lulie stared after him, wonderingly; then she turned and walked slowly and thoughtfully to the door. Her father regarded her with a troubled expression.

"I dreamed," he said, slowly, "that Julia come to me and said somethin' about you. I don't seem to recollect just what 'twas she said. But 'twas somethin' about you—somethin' about me lookin' out for you. . . . Seem's if," he added, doubtfully, "as if she said you'd look out for me, but that's just foolishness and wouldn't mean nothin'. It couldn't be, that couldn't. . . . Humph! Well, come on in."

The remainder of that week the séance to be held in the light keeper's cottage on Saturday evening was much talked about. The devout, including the Beebes, the Hardings and the Blounts. were quite excited about it. The scoffers derided and waxed sarcastic. Of these scoffers the most outspoken was Horatio Pulcifer. He declared that the whole fool business made him tired. Old Cap'n Jeth Hallett must be getting cracked as one of them antique plates. He wasn't sure that the selectmen hadn't ought to stop the thing, a lot of ninnies sitting in a round circle holding hands and pretending to get spirit messages. Huh! Just let 'em get a message that proved something, that meant something to somebody, and he'd believe, too, he'd be glad to believe. But he was from Missouri and they'd got to show him. With much more to the same effect.

In private, and in the ear of Galusha Bangs, he made a significant remark.

"Go?" he repeated. "Me go to that séance thing? Not so you'd notice it, Perfessor. I'm what they call a wise bird. I get up early, a consider'ble spell before breakfast. Um-hm, a consider'ble spell. Saturday night I'm goin' to be a long ways from Gould's Bluffs lighthouse, you bet on that."

Galusha expressed surprise and gave reasons for that emotion. Raish winked and nodded.

"Yes, I know," he said, "but I'm goin' to have what they call an alibi. You ain't been to court much, I presume likely, Perfessor, so you may not be on to what alibi is. When Bill Alworthy was hauled up for sellin' without a license we had an alibi for him. He proved he was fourteen mile away from where he sold the stuff—I mean from where they said he sold it—and it was that what got him off. Well, on Saturday night I'm goin' to have an alibi. I'm goin' to be settin' in at a little penny-ante in Elmer Rogers' back room over to the Centre. An alibi's a nice thing to have in the house, Perfessor. Hey? Haw, haw, haw! Yes, sir-ee! In case there's any talk they won't be able to pin much on your Uncle Raish, not much they won't."

He nudged the Bangs' ribs and walked off, chuckling. Galusha, too, smiled as he watched him go. Both he and Mr. Pulcifer seemed to find amusement in the situation. Yet and Galusha realized it, there was also for him that element of risk

On Thursday Captain Jethro stopped at the Phipps' home to invite its inmates to the Saturday evening meeting. His invitation was not precisely whole-hearted, but the reason he gave for offering it caused its acceptance.

"Lulie seems to want you and Mr. Bangs," he said, "so come along if you feel like it. I know you're one of the don't-believers, Martha, and I guess likely Bangs is, but never mind. The door's open if you want to come. Maybe you'll hear somethin' that'll lead you to the light; let's hope so. Anyhow, Lulie wants you."

It will be noticed that Primmie's name was not mentioned in the invitation, but that did not prevent her acceptance. That evening, after the supper dishes were washed, Miss Phipps heard agonized wails coming from the kitchen and, going there, found her maid seated in a chair, swaying back and forth, and, as Zach Bloomer once described a similar performance, "tootin' her everlastin' soul into the harmonica."

"I'm practicin' up for Saturday night," she informed her mistress, cheerfully. "I've been tryin' to think up some other hymn tunes and I've thought of one, but I can't remember what 'tis, the whole of it, I mean. You know, Miss Martha, the one about:

'Oh, what a sight 'twill be
    When the somethin'-or-other host we see,
As numberless as the sands on the seashore.'

What kind of a host is it, Miss Martha? All I can think of is 'rancid' and I'm plaguy sure 'tain't *that*."

Martha burst out laughing. "It is 'ransomed,' Primmie," she said. "But if you're figurin' on playin' that thing over at the séance, I'm afraid you'll be disappointed. Cap'n Jethro has had the old melodeon repaired, I believe. And, so far as I've heard, you haven't been asked to come, have you?"

Primmie became a statue of despair.

"Oh, Miss Martha," she pleaded, *"can't* I go? Can't I please go? You're goin' and so's Mr. Bangs, and—and I do like 'em so, those spirit meetin's. They scare me 'most to death and I just love 'em. *Please* can't I go, Miss Martha?"

Martha took pity on her. "Well, all right, Primmie," she said. "Go, if you want to. I don't believe Jethro will care. And," with a shrug, "I don't know as another idiot, more or less, added to the rest of us, will make much difference."

Saturday, the eventful day, or the day of the eventful evening, was fine and clear. At noon an unexpected event, the first of several, occurred; Zacheus, bringing the mail from the post office, brought a large and heavy letter addressed to Galusha Bangs, Esq., and stamped in the upper left-hand corner with the name of the National Institute of Washington. Galusha opened it in his room alone. It was the "plan," the long-ago announced and long-expected plan in all its details. An expedition was to be fitted out, more completely and more elaborately than any yet equipped by the Institute, and was to go to the Nile basin for extended and careful research lasting two years at least. And he was offered the command of that expedition, to direct its labors and to be its scientific head. Whatever it accomplished, he would have accomplished; the rewards—the understanding gratitude of his fellow archæologists the world over would be his, and his alone.

He sat there in his room and read and reread the letter. The terms in which the offer had been made were gratifying in the extreme. The confidence in his ability and scientific knowledge were expressed without stint. But, and more than this, between the lines he could read the affection of his associates there at the Institute and their pride in him. His own affection and pride were touched. A letter like this and an offer and opportunity like these were wonderful. The pride he felt was a very humble pride. He was unworthy of such trust, but he was proud to know they believed him worthy.

He sat there, the many sheets of the letter between his fingers, looking out through the window at the brown, wind-swept hollows and little hills and the cold gray-green sea beyond. He saw none of these. What he did see was the long stretch of ridged sand, heaving to the horizon, the brilliant blue of the African sky, the line of camels trudging on, on. He saw the dahabeah slowly making its way up the winding river, the flat banks on either side, the palm trees in silhouetted clusters against the sunset, the shattered cornice of the ruins he was to explore just coming into view. He saw and heard the shrieking, chattering laborers digging, half naked, amid the scattered blocks of sculptured stone and, before and beneath them, the upper edge of the doorway which they were uncovering, the door behind which he was to find—who knew what treasures.

"Mr. Bangs," called Martha from the foot of the stairs, "dinner's ready."

Galusha was far away, somewhere beyond the Libyan desert, but he heard the summons.

"Eh?" he exclaimed. "Oh, yes, yes, Miss Martha, I am coming."

As he descended the stairs, it occurred to him that the voices calling him to dinner across the sands or beneath the palms would be quite different from this one, they would be masculine and strange and without the pleasant, cheerful cordiality to which he had become accustomed. Martha Phipps called one to a meal as if she really enjoyed having him there. There was a welcome in her tones, a homelike quality, a . . . yes, indeed, very much so.

At table he was unusually quiet. Martha asked him why he looked at her so queerly.

"Eh? Do I?" he exclaimed. "Oh, I'm so sorry! I wasn't aware. I beg your pardon. I hope you're not offended."

She laughed. "Mercy me," she said, "I'm not offended so easily. And if your absent-mindedness could make me take offense, Mr. Bangs, we should have quarreled long ago. But I should like to know what you were thinkin' about. You sat there and stared at me and your face was as solemn as—as Luce's when it is gettin' past his dinner time. You looked as if you had lost your best friend."

He did not smile even then. Nor did he make any reply worth noting. As a matter of fact, he was awakening to the realization that if he accepted the call to Egypt—and accept he must, of course—he would in solemn truth lose his best friend. Or, if not lose her exactly, go away and leave her for so long that it amounted to a loss. He must leave this dining room, with its plants and old pictures and quaint homeliness, leave the little Phipps' cottage, leave its owner. . . . The dazzling visions of sands and sphinxes, of palms and pyramids, suddenly lost their dazzle. The excitement caused by the reading of the letter dulled and deadened. The conviction which had come upon him so often of late returned with redoubled vigor, the conviction that he had been happy where he was and would never be as happy anywhere else. Egypt, even beloved Egypt with all the new and wonderful opportunities it now offered him, did not appeal. The thought was alarming. When he did not want to go to Egypt there must be something the matter with him, something serious. What was it?

After dinner he told her of the offer which had been made him.

"Perhaps you would like to see the letter," he said. "It is a very kind one. Dear me, yes. Much kinder than I deserve."

She read the long letter through, read the details of the great plan from end to end. When the reading was finished she sat silent, the letter in her lap, and she did not look at him.

"They are very kind to me, aren't they?" he said, gravely. "Very kind and generous. The thought of it quite—ah—overwhelms me, really. Of course, I know what they say concerning my—ah—the value of my service is quite ridiculous, overstated and—and all that, but they do that thinking to please me, I suppose. I . . . Why—why, Miss Martha, you—you're not——"

She smiled, a rather misty smile. "No," she said, "I'm not. But I think I shall if you keep on talkin' in that way."

"But—but, Miss Martha, I'm so sorry. I assure you I did not mean to hurt your feelings. If I have said anything to distress you I'm *very* sorry. Dear me, dear me! What did I say? I——"

She motioned him to silence. "Hush, hush!" she begged. "You didn't say anything, of course, except what you always say—that what you have done doesn't amount to anything and that you aren't of any consequence and—all that. You always say it, and you believe it, too. When I read this letter, Mr. Bangs, and found that *they* know what you really are, that they had found you out just as—as some of your other friends have, it—it——"

She paused. Galusha turned red. "I—I——" he stammered. "Oh, you mustn't talk so, Miss Martha. It's all nonsense, you know. Really it is."

She shook her head and smiled once more.

"All right," she argued. "Then we'll call it nonsense; but it's pretty glorious nonsense, seems to me. I do congratulate you, Mr. Bangs. And I congratulate the Institute folks a great deal more. Now tell me some more about it, please. Where is this place they want you to go to?"

That afternoon Galusha spent in wandering about the countryside. He went as far from home as the old graveyard in South Wellmouth. He took a long walk and it should have been a pleasant one, but somehow it was not, particularly. All he could think of was the two facts—one, that he had been offered a wonderful opportunity, for which he should be eagerly and hugely grateful; two, that he was not grateful at all, but resentful and rebellious. And what on earth was the matter with him?

Martha was setting the supper table when he came in. He went to his room and when he came down supper was almost ready. Primmie was in the kitchen, busy with the cooking.

"We're having an early supper, Mr. Bangs," said Martha. "That everlastin' séance begins about half past seven, so Cap'n Jethro took pains to tell me, and he'll be crosser'n a hen out in a rainstorm if we're not on time."

Galusha looked surprised. He had forgotten the séance altogether. Yes, he had quite forgotten it. And, up to that noon, he had thought of very little else the entire week. What *was* the matter with him?

"Lulie is goin' to send Zach over to tell us when they're ready to set sail for Ghost Harbor," went on Martha. "That will save us watchin' the clock. What say?"

But he had not said anything and ᴖhe went on arranging the dishes. After an interval she asked a question.

"How soon—that is, when will you have to leave us—leave here, Mr. Bangs?" she asked. She was not looking at him when she asked it.

Galusha sighed. "In about two weeks, I—ah—suppose," he said.

"Oh!"

"Ah—yes."

There was another silent interval. Then Martha turned her head to listen.

"Wasn't that an automobile I heard then?" she asked. "Yes, it is. It can't be the Spiritualist crowd comin' so soon. No, it is stoppin' here, at our gate. Is it Doctor Powers, I wonder?"

She went to the window, pulled aside the shade and looked out.

"It is a big car," she said. "It isn't the doctor, that's sure. There's a man gettin' out, a big man in a fur coat. Who on earth——?"

Steps sounded without upon the walk, then there was a knock upon the side door, that of the dining room. Martha opened the door. A man's voice, a brisk, businesslike voice, asked a question.

"Why, yes," replied Miss Phipps, "he lives here. He's right here now. Won't you step in?"

The man who had asked the question accepted the invitation and entered the dining room. He was a big, broad-shouldered man in a raccoon motor coat. He took off a cap which matched the coat and looked about the room. Then he saw Galusha.

"Why, hello, Loosh!" he said.

Galusha knew him, had recognized the voice before he saw its owner. His mouth opened, shut, and opened again. He was quite pale.

"Ah—ah—why, Cousin Gussie!" he stammered.

For the man in the fur coat standing there in Martha Phipps' dining room was the senior partner of Cabot, Bancroft and Cabot.

CHAPTER XIX

FOR perhaps thirty seconds after the exchange of greetings, the trio in the Phipps' dining room stood where they were, practically without moving. Mr. Cabot, of course, was smiling broadly, Miss Phipps was gazing in blank astonishment from one to the other of the two men, and Galusha Bangs was staring at his relative as Robinson Crusoe stared at the famous footprint, "like one thunderstruck."

It was Cabot who broke up the tableau. His smile became a hearty laugh.

"What's the matter, Loosh?" he demanded. "Great Scott, old man, I expected to surprise you, but I didn't expect to give you a paralytic stroke. How are you?"

He walked over and held out his hand. Galusha took it, but he looked as if he was quite unaware of doing so. "Cousin Gussie!" he repeated, faintly. Then he added his favorite exclamation. "Dear me!"

Even Martha, who by this time was used to his eccentricities, thought his conduct strange.

"Why, Mr. Bangs," she cried, "are you sick? What is it?"

Galusha blinked, put a hand to his forehead, knocked off his spectacles, picked them up again and, in doing so, appeared to pick up a little of his normal self.

"Why, Cousin Gussie," he observed, for the third time; adding, "I—I am surprised."

His cousin's laugh made the little room echo.

"Good, Loosh!" he exclaimed. "I guessed as much; you

325

looked it. Well, it is all right; I'm here in the flesh. Aren't you glad to see me?"

Galusha stammered that he was very glad to see him—yes, indeed—ah—quite so—very, of course.

"Ah—ah—won't you sit down?" he asked.

Martha could stand it no longer. "Why, mercy's sakes, Mr. Bangs," she exclaimed, "of course he'll sit down! And he'd probably take off his coat, if you asked him."

This pointed hint had an immediate effect. Her lodger sprang forward.

"Oh, dear me!" he cried. "I'm so sorry. Of course, of course. I *beg* your pardon, Cousin Gussie."

He hindered a little more than he helped with the removal of the coat and then stood, with the garment in his arms, peering over the heap of fur like a spectacled prairie-dog peeping out of a hole.

"Ah—sit down, sit down, please," he begged. "I—ah—please do."

Again Martha interrupted. "Here, let me take that coat, Mr. Bangs," she said, and took it forthwith. Galusha, coming to himself still more, remembered the conventionalities.

"Oh, Miss Phipps," he cried, "may I introduce my—ah—cousin, Mr. Cabot. Mr. Cabot, this is the lady who has taken charge of me, so to speak."

Both Martha and Cabot burst out laughing.

"That sounds as if I had arrested him, doesn't it?" observed the former. "But it is all right, Mr. Cabot; I've only taken him to board."

"I understand. Well, unless he has changed a lot since I used to know him, he needs some one to take charge of him. And it agrees with him, too. Why, Loosh, I thought you were an invalid; you look like a football player. Oh, pardon me, Miss Phipps, but don't trouble to take that coat away. I can stay only a little while. My chauffeur is waiting outside and I must get on to the hotel or I'll be late for dinner."

Martha, who was on her way to the hall and the coat

rack, turned. "Hotel?" she repeated. "What hotel, Mr. Cabot?"

"Why, the Something-or-other House over in the next town. The Robbins House, is it? Something like that."

"Robbins House? There isn't any. Oh, do you mean Roger's Hotel at the Centre?"

"Why, yes, that is it. I was told there was a hotel here, but they forgot to tell me it was open only in the summer. What sort of place is this Roger's Hotel?"

Martha looked at him and then at Galusha.

"Altogether too bad for any relation of Mr. Bangs's to go to," she declared. "At least, to eat supper. You and Mr. Bangs will excuse me, won't you? I'll be right back."

She hung the fur coat upon the rack and hastened back through the dining room and out into the kitchen. Cabot took a chair and turned toward Galusha.

"She is a capable woman," he observed, with a jerk of his head toward the kitchen door. "She has certainly taken good care of you. You look better than when I saw you last and that was—— Good Lord, how long ago was it?"

Galusha replied that it was a good many years ago and then switched the subject to that which was causing painful agitation in his bosom at the moment, namely, the reason for his cousin's appearance in East Wellmouth.

Cousin Gussie laughed. "I came to see you, Loosh," he declared. "Family ties, and all that. I thought I would run down and get you to picnic on the beach with me. How is the bathing just now?"

The chill October wind rattled the sash and furnished answer sufficient. Galusha smiled a sad sort of acknowledgment of the joke. He did not feel like smiling. The sensation of sitting on a powder barrel had returned to him, except that now there was no head to the barrel and the air was full of sparks.

"I—I did not expect you," he faltered, for the sake of saying something. Cabot laughed again.

"Of course you didn't," he said. "Well, to tell you the truth, I didn't come purposely to see you, old man. There has been a little business matter down here which hasn't gone as I wanted it to, and I decided, pretty much on the spur of the moment, to motor down and see what was the matter. The friend for whom I was trying to handle the thing—it is only a little matter—was coming with me, but this morning I got a wire that he was detained and couldn't make it. So, as it was a glorious day and my doctor keeps telling me to forget business occasionally, I started alone. I didn't leave town until nearly eleven, had some motor trouble, and didn't reach here until almost five. Then I found the fellow I came to see had gone somewhere, nobody knew where, and the hotel was closed for the season. I inquired about you, was given your address at the post office, and hunted you up. That's the story."

Galusha's smile was less forced this time. He nodded reflectively.

"That explains it," he said, slowly. "Yes, quite so. Of course, that explains it."

"Explains what?"

"Why—ah—it explains why you came here, you know."

"Well, I hope it does. That was the idea. If it doesn't I don't know what will."

Miss Phipps entered briskly from the kitchen. She proceeded to set another place at the supper table.

"Mr. Bangs," she said, "hadn't you better take Mr. Cabot up to your room? Probably he'd like to clean up after ridin' so far. Better go right away, because supper is nearly ready. Mr. Cabot, it is Saturday night and you'll get a Saturday night supper, beans and brown bread. I hope you won't mind."

Galusha's relative was somewhat taken aback.

"Why, Miss Phipps," he protested, "of course I can't think of dining here. It is extremely kind of you, but really I——"

Martha calmly interrupted. "It isn't kind at all," she said. "And it isn't dinner, it is supper. If you don't stay I shall think it is because you don't like baked beans. I may as well tell you," she added, "that you will get beans and nothin' else over at Elmer Roger's. They won't be as good as these, that's all. That isn't pride," she continued, with a twinkle in her eye. "Anybody's beans are better than Elmer's, they couldn't help bein'."

The visitor still hesitated. "Well, really, Miss Phipps," he said, "I—— Well, I should like to stay. I should, indeed. But, you see, my chauffeur is outside waiting to take me over to the Roger's House."

Martha smiled. "Oh, no, he isn't," she said. "He is havin' his supper in the kitchen now. Run along, Mr. Bangs, and you and your cousin hurry down as soon as you can."

On the way upstairs Cabot asked a question.

"She is a 'reg'lar' woman, as the boys say," he observed. "I like her. Does she always, so to speak, boss people like that?"

Galusha nodded, cheerfully. "When she thinks they need it," he replied.

"Humph! I understand now what you meant by saying she had taken charge of you. Does she boss you?"

Another cheerful nod. "I *always* need it," answered Galusha.

Martha, of course, presided at the supper table. Primmie did not sit down with the rest. She ate in the kitchen with the Cabot chauffeur. But she entered the dining room from time to time to bring in hot brown bread or beans or cookies, or to change the plates, and each time she did so she stared at Cousin Gussie with awe in her gaze. Evidently the knowledge that the head of Cabot, Bancroft and Cabot was sitting there before her had impressed her hugely. It was from Cabot, Bancroft and Cabot, so Primmie remembered, that Mr. Bangs had procured the mammoth pile of bank notes which she had seen upon her mistress's center table. She had never actually been told where those notes came from, but she had guessed. And now the proprietor of the "money factory"—for that is very nearly what it was in her imagination—was there, sitting at the Phipps' dining table, eating the baked beans that she herself had helped prepare. No wonder that Primmie was awe-stricken, no wonder that she tripped over the mat corner and just escaped showering the distinguished guest with a platterful of those very beans.

Mr. Cabot seemed to enjoy his supper hugely. He was jolly, talkative, and very entertaining. He described his camp sojourn in Nevada and, according to him, life in a mountain sanitarium, under the care of a doctor and two husky male nurses, was a gorgeous joke. Martha, who, to tell the truth, had at first secretly shown a little of Primmie's awe, was soon completely at ease. Even Galusha laughed, though not as often. It was hard for him to forget the powder barrel sensation. Each time his cousin opened his mouth to speak, he dreaded to hear reference to a dangerous subject or to be asked a question which would set fire to the fuse.

The clock struck seven. Martha glanced at it and suddenly uttered an exclamation.

"My goodness gracious!" she exclaimed. "I declare, Mr. Bangs, you and I have forgotten all about that blessed séance. And half past seven was the time for it to begin. Good gracious me!"

Galusha started. "Dear me, dear me!" he cried. "So it was. I had completely forgotten it, really I had."

He put his hand to his forehead.

"I shall have to go to it," declared Martha. "Lulie begged me to come and the cap'n won't like it if I stay away. But I don't see that you need to, Mr. Bangs. You and your cousin can stay right here and talk and be comfortable. He is goin' to stay overnight. Oh, yes, you are, Mr. Cabot. I wouldn't let a stray cat go to Elmer Roger's hotel if I could help it, to say nothin' of Mr. Bangs' cousin. The spare room's all ready and Primmie is up there now, airin' it. She took your bag up with her; I had your chauffeur bring it in from the car."

Her guest stared at her for a moment, laughed and shook his head.

"Well, really, Miss Phipps," he said, "I don't know what

to say to you. You rather take me off my feet. It is very kind of you and, of course, I am very much obliged; but, of course, too, I couldn't think of staying."

"Now, please, Mr. Cabot! It isn't the least little bit of trouble, and that's honest. Mr. Bangs, you tell him to stay."

Galusha, thus appealed to, tried to say something, but succeeded only in looking distressed.

"We *want* him to stay, don't we, Mr. Bangs?" urged Martha.

"Why—why, certainly. Oh, yes, indeed. Ah—yes," faltered Galusha. If there was one thing which he distinctly did not want, it was just that. And there was no doubt that Cabot was wavering.

"But, you see, Miss Phipps," said Cousin Gussie, "it will be quite impossible. My chauffeur——"

"Yes, I know. I'm awfully sorry I haven't got a room for him. I wish I had. But he can go to Elmer's. He wouldn't mind so much—at least I hope he wouldn't—and there's a garage for the car over there. I spoke to him about it and he's only waitin' for you to say the word, Mr. Cabot."

The visitor protested a bit more and then yielded.

"Frankly, Miss Phipps," he said, "I have been wanting to stay ever since I entered your door. This house takes me back to my boyhood, when I used to visit my great-uncle Hiram down at Ostable. You remember him, Galusha, Uncle Hiram's dining room had the same wholesome, homey atmosphere that yours has, Miss Phipps. And I honestly believe I haven't enjoyed a meal since those old days as I have enjoyed this supper of yours."

Martha colored with pleasure. Galusha, forgetting his powder barrel, beamed in sympathy.

"But there is just one more thing," continued Cousin Gussie. "You and Bangs were going out somewhere, were expected at some—er—social affair, weren't you?"

Miss Phipps and her lodger exchanged looks. Both appeared embarrassed.

"Well—well, you see," faltered the former. Then, after

a moment's reflection, she added, "Well, I'll tell you, Mr. Cabot."

She did tell him, briefly, of Captain Hallett's spirit obsession, of her friendship and sympathy for Lulie. She said nothing, of course, concerning the latter's love story.

"So," she said, in conclusion, "although I haven't the least bit of belief in Marietta Hoag or any of her séances, I am sorry for Cap'n Jethro and I am very fond of Lulie. She is worried, I know, and she has asked me to be there to-night. You and Mr. Bangs will excuse me, everything considered, won't you?"

But Galusha had something to say. "Miss Martha," he said, "I am afraid I must go, too. I promised Mr.—ah—um —I mean I promised Lulie I would be there. And this is going to be a very important séance."

Martha turned to him.

"It is?" she asked. "Important—how? What do you mean?"

Her lodger looked as if he had said more than he intended. Also as if he did not know what to say next. But Cabot saved him the trouble.

"I wonder if I might attend this—er—function?" he suggested. "It is in the nature of a public affair, isn't it? And," with a twinkle of the eye, "it sounds as if it might be interesting."

Galusha and Miss Phipps regarded him gravely. Both seemed a little troubled. It was Martha who answered.

"There isn't any real reason why you shouldn't go, if you want to, Mr. Cabot," she said. "There is only one thing— only one reason why I didn't say yes right away. I guess Mr. Bangs knows that reason and feels the same as I do about it. Don't you, Mr. Bangs?"

Galusha nodded.

"You see," went on Miss Phipps, "Cap'n Hallett is kind of—well, queer in some ways, but he has been, in his day, a good deal of a man. And his daughter is a lovely girl and I think the world of her. I wouldn't want to hurt their

feelings. If they should see you laugh—well, you understand——"

Cousin Gussie nodded.

"Don't say any more, Miss Phipps," he replied. "It is
quite all right. I'll stay in your home here and be perfectly
happy."

"But you didn't wait for me to finish. I was goin' to say
that if you should laugh you must manage not to let any one
hear you; especially Cap'n Jeth. Lulie has lots of common
sense; she wouldn't mind except for the effect on her father,
and she realizes how funny it is. But her father doesn't
and—and he is pretty close to the breakin' point sometimes.
So save up your laughs until we get back, please."

"You seem to take it for granted that I shall feel like
laughing. Perhaps I sha'n't. I only suggested my attending
this affair because I thought it would be a novelty to me."

"Yes, yes, of course. Well, it will be a novelty, I guess
likely, and a pretty novel novelty, too. But there's one thing
more, Mr. Cabot, that I want you to promise me. Don't
you dare take that crowd at that séance as a fair sample of
Wellmouth folks, because they're not."

"Why, Miss Phipps——"

"Because they're not. Every town and every neighborhood, city or country, has its freaks and every freak within
five miles will be over in that lighthouse parlor to-night.
Just take 'em for freaks, that's all, but *don't* take 'em for
samples of our people down here." She paused, and then
added, with an apologetic laugh, "I guess you think I am
pretty peppery on the subject. Well, I get that way at times,
particularly just after the summer is over and the city crowd
has been here lookin' for 'characters.' If you could see
some of the specimens who come over from the hotel, see the
way they dress and act and speak! 'Oh,' one creature said
to me; 'oh, Miss Phipps,' she gushed, 'I am just dyin' to
meet some of your dear, funny, odd, quaint characters.
Where can I find them?' 'Well,' said I, 'I think I should
try the Inn, if I were you. There are funnier characters
there than anywhere else I know.' Of course, I knew she

was at the Inn herself, but that didn't make it any the less true. . . . There! I've preached my sermon. Now, Mr. Cabot, we'll go into the sittin' room and let Primmie clear off the table. Zach Bloomer—he's the assistant light keeper—is comin' to tell us when it's time to go to the séance."

In the sitting room they talked of various things. Galusha, listening to his cousin's stories and jokes, had almost forgotten his powder barrel. And then, all at once, a spark fell, flashed, and the danger became imminent.

Said the banker, addressing Martha and referring to her lodger: "What does this cousin of mine find to do down here, Miss Phipps? How does he manage to spend so much money?"

"Money?" repeated Martha. "He—spend money? Why, I didn't know that he did, Mr. Cabot. He is very prompt in paying his board. Perhaps I charge him too much. Is that what you mean?"

"I guess not. He hasn't paid you thirteen thousand dollars for board, has he?"

"Thirteen thousand dollars! Well, I guess not—scarcely. What are you talkin' about, Mr. Cabot? What is the joke?"

"I don't know. That's one of the things which, now that I am down here, I should like to find out. Somehow or other, since he has been on the Cape, he has managed to get rid of over thirteen thousand dollars. He *says* he has given it to some of his mummy-hunting friends, but I am rather suspicious. He hasn't been organizing a clam trust, has he, Miss Phipps?"

Plainly, Martha did not know what to make of this speech. It was a joke, of course, but just where the point of the joke was located she was not sure. To her, thirteen thousand dollars was an enormous sum. The idea that her lodger, gentle, retiring little Galusha Bangs, possessed a half of that fortune was a joke in itself. But . . . And then she saw Galusha's face and the expression upon it.

"Why—why, Mr. Bangs!" she exclaimed.

Cabot turned and he, too, saw the expression. He burst out laughing.

"See!" he cried. "Doesn't he look guilty? It *is* a clam trust, Miss Phipps. By Jove, Loosh, you are discovered! Galusha Bangs, the Clam King! Ha, ha, ha! Look at him, Miss Phipps! Look at him! Did you ever see a plainer case of conscious guilt? Ha, ha!"

He was enjoying himself hugely. And really Galusha was a humorous spectacle. He was very red in the face, he was trembling, and he appeared to be struggling for words and finding none.

"I—I insist," he stammered. "I—I mean I protest. It is ridiculous—ah—ah—absurd! I—I——"

His cousin broke in upon him. "Ha, ha!" he cried. "The secret is out. And you gave me to understand the mummy-hunters had it. Oh, Galusha!"

Galusha made another attempt.

"I—I told you——" he faltered. "I—I told you——"

"You told me it had gone to Egypt. But I was suspicious, old man. Why, Miss Phipps, isn't it glorious? Look at him!"

Martha was looking. Her face wore a puzzled expression.

"Isn't it glorious?" repeated Cousin Gussie.

She shrugged. "I suppose it is," she said. "Maybe it would be more so if I knew what it was all about. And Mr. Bangs doesn't look as if he found much glory in it."

"Of course he doesn't. Serves him right, the rascal. You see, Miss Phipps, I am supposed to take care of his money for him, and, while I was away in the mountains, my secretary sent him a check for over fourteen thousand dollars, sent it to him by mistake. *I* never should have done it, of course. I know him of old, where money is concerned. Well, almost immediately after receiving the check, up he comes to our Boston office and——"

"Cousin Gussie! I—I protest! I——"

"Up he comes, Miss Phipps, and draws five thousand of the fourteen thousand in cash, in money, and takes it away with him. Then——"

"Cousin Gussie! Mr. Cabot!"

The tone in which Galusha spoke was so different from

his usual one, and the fact of his addressing his relative as "Mr. Cabot" so astonishing, that the latter was obliged to stop even in the full tide of his enjoyment of the joke. He turned, to find Galusha leaning forward, one hand upon the center table, and the other extending a forefinger in his direction. The finger shook a little, but its owner's countenance was set like a rock. And now it was not crimson, but white.

"Mr. Cabot," said Galusha, "I must insist that you say no more on this matter. My personal business is—ah—presumably my own. I—I must insist. Insist—ah—absolutely; yes."

His cousin looked at him and he returned the look. Cabot's hesitation was but momentary. His astonishment was vast, but he accepted the situation gracefully. He laughed no more.

"I beg your pardon, Galusha," he said. "I'm sorry. I had no thought of offending you, old man. I—well, perhaps I am inclined to joke too freely. But, really, I didn't suppose—I never knew you to be——"

He paused. Galusha's expression did not change; he said nothing.

"I am very sorry," went on the banker. "It was only thoughtlessness on my part. You'll forgive me, Loosh, I hope."

Galusha bowed, but he did not smile. A little of the color came back to his cheeks.

"Ah—ah—— Yes, certainly," he stammered. "Certainly, quite so."

He sat down in his chair again, but he did not look in Miss Phipps' direction. He seemed to know that she was regarding him with a fixed and startled intentness.

"Five thousand dollars!" she said, in a low tone. Neither of the men appeared to hear her. Cabot, too, sat down. And it was he who, plainly seeking for a subject to relieve the tension, spoke next.

"I was telling my cousin," he said, addressing Martha, "that I came down here to attend to a little matter of business. The business wasn't my own exactly, but it was a commission from a friend and client of mine and he left it in my charge. He and I supposed we had an agent here in your town, Miss Phipps, who was attending to it for us, but of late he hasn't been very successful. I received a letter from Williams—from my friend; he is in the South—asking me to see if I couldn't hurry matters up a bit. So I motored down. But this agent of ours was not in. Probably you know him. His name is Pulcifer."

Martha and Galusha started simultaneously.

"Pulcifer?" queried Martha. "Raish Pulcifer, do you mean?"

"It doesn't seem to me that his Christian name is——What did you say, Miss Phipps?"

"I said 'Raish'; that's what every one down here calls the man I mean. His real name, of course, is Horatio."

"Horatio? That sounds more like it. I didn't hire him—Williams did that—and I have never met him, although he and Thomas, my secretary, have had some correspondence. Wait a moment, I have his name here."

He took from his pocket a memorandum book and turned over the leaves.

"Yes," he said, "that's it. Horatio Pulcifer. Here is his card. 'Horatio Pulcifer, Dealer in Real Estate of All Kinds; Cranberry Bog Property Bought and Sold; Mortgages Arranged For; Fire, Life and Accident Insurance; Money Loaned; Claims Adjusted; Real or Household Goods Auctioned Off or Sold Private; etc., etc.' Humph! Comprehensive person, isn't he? Is this the fellow you know, Miss Phipps?"

Martha nodded. "Yes," she said, "I know him."

Cabot glanced at her. "I see," he observed. "Well, what sort of a character is he? Would you trust him?"

She hesitated. "Why—why," she replied, "I suppose I should, if—if——"

"If he was not too far away, or around the corner, or anything like that? I understand."

Martha was a bit disturbed. "You mustn't put words in my mouth, Mr. Cabot," she said. "I didn't say Raish Pulcifer was dishonest."

"No, that is true. And I beg your pardon for asking embarrassing questions. I have seen some of the fellow's letters and usually a letter is a fairly good indication of character—or lack of it. I have had my surmises concerning the ubiquitous Horatio for some time."

Martha seemed to be thinking.

"I understood you to say he was your agent for somethin' down here, Mr. Cabot," she said. "Sellin' somethin', was he? That kind of an agent?"

"No. As a matter of fact, he was supposed to be buying something, but he hasn't made much progress. He started out well, but of late he seems to have found trouble. I am rather surprised because we—that is, Williams—pay him a liberal commission. I judge he doesn't hate a dollar and that kind of man usually goes after it hammer and tongs. You see—— But there, I presume I should not go into particulars, not yet."

"No, no, Mr. Cabot. Of course not, of course not."

"No." Cabot had been turning over the leaves of the memorandum book while speaking. "And yet," he went on, "there are one or two names here concerning which you might be able to help us. Pulcifer writes that two of the largest stockholders. . . . Humph! . . . Eh? Why, by Jove, this is remarkable! You are Miss Martha Phipps, aren't you?"

"Yes."

"Was your father, by any chance, James H. Phipps?"

"Yes."

"Well, I declare! This *is* remarkable. . . . And—why, you have been speaking of a Captain—er—Jethro Somebody? Is he—— He isn't Jethro Hallett, is he?"

"Why, yes. I told you his name. He is the light keeper here at Gould's Bluffs and we are all goin' over to his house in a few minutes, for the séance, you know."

"Well, well, well! And here I have been sitting and talking with one of the very persons whom I came down here hoping to see."

"To see? You came down here hopin' to see *me?* Mr. Cabot, is this another joke?"

"Not a bit of it. If it is, the joke is on me for not identifying you with the Martha Phipps that Pulcifer writes he can't do business with. Miss Phipps, you own something we want to buy."

"I? Somethin' you want to buy?"

"Yes. Williams wants to buy it and I am interested with him. Miss Phipps, you own two hundred and fifty shares of the stock of the Wellmouth Development Company, don't you?"

He must have been surprised at the effect of this question. Martha stared at him. Then, without speaking, she turned and looked past him at Galusha Bangs. She looked so long and so steadily that Cabot also turned and looked. What he saw caused him to utter an exclamation.

"For heaven's sakes, Loosh!" he exclaimed.

His cousin, as white as the proverbial sheet, which means much whiter than some sheets, Elmer Rogers', for example, was slowly rising from his chair. One hand was pressed against his forehead and he looked as if he were dazed, stunned, suffering from a stroke. As a matter of fact, he was suffering from all three. The spark had at last reached the powder and the barrel was in the very act of disintegrating.

"Galusha," demanded Cousin Gussie, "are you sick? What is it?"

Galusha did not answer. Before the alarmed banker could repeat his question there came a knock at the door.

"Miss Martha," called Primmie, in tremulous excitement. "Miss Martha, Zach he's come and he says the séance is just a-goin' to begin and Cap'n Jeth says to hurry right straight over. Zach says the old man is as tittered up and nervous as ever he see him and 'twon't do to keep him waitin' a minute. My savin' soul, no! Zach says for all hands to heave right straight ahead and come."

CHAPTER XX

IN the melodramas, the sort which most people laugh at as "old-fashioned" and enjoy thoroughly, there is usually a scene in which the hero, or the heroine, or both, are about to be drowned in the sinking ship or roasted in the loft of the burning building, or butchered by the attacking savages, or executed by the villain and his agents. The audience enjoys some delightful thrills while watching this situation —whichever it may be—develop, but is spared any acute anxiety, knowing from experience that just at the last moment the rescuing boat, or the heroic firemen, or the troops, or a reprieve from the Governor, will arrive and save the leading man or woman and the play from a premature end and for another act.

It does not happen as often in real life, at least one cannot count upon it with the certainty of the theater. But when Miss Primrose Cash knocked upon the door of the Phipps' sitting room and delivered her call to the séance, she was as opportune and nick-of-timey as was ever a dramatic Governor's messenger. Certainly that summons of hers was to Galusha Bangs a reprieve which saved him from instant destruction.

Cousin Gussie, who had been on the point of repeating his demand to know if his relative was ill, turned instead to look toward the door. Martha, whose gaze had been fixed upon her lodger with an intentness which indicated at least the dawning of a suspicion, turned to look in the same direction. Galusha, left poised upon the very apex of the explosion, awaited the moment when the fragments, of which he was one, should begin to fall.

But they did not fall—then. Primmie gave them no opportunity to do so.

"Miss Martha," she cried, "Miss Martha, do you hear me? Zach—he says——"

Her mistress answered. "Yes, yes, Primmie," she said, "I hear you." Then, turning again toward the banker and his relative, she said, "Mr. Cabot, I—did I understand you to say——?"

"Miss Martha!" The voice outside the door was more insistent than ever. "Miss Martha, Zach he says we've all hands got to come right straight off, 'cause if we don't there'll be hell to pay. . . . My savin' soul, I never meant to say that, Miss Martha! Zach, he said it, but I never meant to. I—I—— Oh, my Lord of Isrul! I—I—oh, Miss Martha!"

Further wails of the frightened and repentant one were lost in an ecstatic shout of laughter from Mr. Cabot. Martha slowly shook her head.

"Well," she observed, dryly, "I guess likely we'd better go, hadn't we? If it is as bad as all that I should say we had, sure and certain. Primmie Cash, I'm ashamed of you. Mr. Cabot, we'll finish our talk when we come back. What under the sun you can possibly mean I declare I don't understand. . . . But, there, it will keep. Come, Mr. Bangs."

She led the way from the sitting room. Cabot followed her and, staggering slightly and with a hand still pressed to his forehead, Galusha followed them. He was saved for the time, he realized that, but for such a very short time. For an hour or two he was to hang in the air and then would come the inevitable crash. When they returned home, after the séance was over, Martha would question Cousin Gussie, Cousin Gussie would answer, then he would be questioned and—and the end would come. Martha would know him for what he was. As they emerged from the Phipps' door into the damp chill and blackness of that October evening, Galusha Bangs looked hopelessly up and down and for the first time in months yearned for Egypt, to be in Egypt, in Abyssinia, in the middle of the great Sahara—anywhere except where he was and where he was fated to be.

The windows of the light keeper's cottage were ablaze as they drew near. Overhead the great stream of radiance from the lantern in the tower shot far out. There was almost no wind, and the grumble of the surf at the foot of the bluff was a steady bass monotone.

Zacheus, who had waited to walk over with them, was in a fault-finding state of mind. It developed that he could not attend the meeting in the parlor; his superior had ordered that he "tend light."

"The old man says I hadn't no business comin' to the other sea-ants thing," said Zach. "Says him and me ain't both supposed never to leave the light alone. I cal'late he's right, but that don't make it any better. There's a whole lot of things that's right that hadn't ought to be. I presume likely it's right enough for you to play that mouth organ of yours, Posy. They ain't passed no law against it yet. But——"

"Oh, be still, Zach Bloomer! You're always talkin' about my playin' the mouth organ. I notice you can't play anything, no, nor sing neither."

"You're right, Pansy Blossom. But the difference between you and me is that I know I can't. . . . Hey? Why, yes, Martha, I shouldn't be a bit surprised if the fog came in any time. If it does that means I've got to tend foghorn as well as light. Godfreys!"

Before they opened the side door of the Hallett home, the buzz of voices in the parlor was distinctly audible. Lulie heard the door open and met them in the dining room. She was looking anxious and disturbed. Martha drew her aside and questioned her concerning her father. Lulie glanced toward the parlor door and then whispered:

"I don't know, Martha. Father seems queer to-night, awfully queer. I can't make him out."

"Queer? In what way? He is always nervous and worked up before these silly affairs, isn't he?"

"Yes, but I don't mean that, exactly. He has been that way for over a week. But for the last two days he has been

—well, different. He seems to be troubled and—and suspicious."

"Suspicious? Suspicious of what?"

"I don't know. Of every one."

"Humph! Well, if he would only begin to get suspicious of Marietta and her spirit chasers I should feel like givin' three cheers. But I suppose those are exactly the ones he isn't suspicious of."

Lulie again glanced toward the parlor door.

"I am not so sure," she said. "It seemed to me that he wasn't as cordial to them as usual when they came to-night. He keeps looking at Marietta and pulling his beard and scowling, the way he does when he is puzzled and troubled. I'm not sure, but I think something came in the mail yesterday noon and another something again to-day which may be the cause of his acting so strangely. I don't know what they were, he wouldn't answer when I asked him, but I saw him reading a good deal yesterday afternoon. And then he came into the kitchen where I was, took the lid off the cookstove and put a bundle of printed pages on the fire. I asked him what he was doing and he snapped at me that he was burning the words of Satan or something of that sort."

"And couldn't you save enough of the—er—Old Scratch's words to find out what the old boy was talkin' about?"

"No. There was a hot fire. But to-day, when the second package came, I caught a glimpse of the printing on the wrapper. It was from The Psychical Research Society; I think that was it. There is such a society, isn't there?"

"I believe so. I . . . Ssh! Careful, here he is."

Captain Jethro strode across the parlor threshold. He glared beneath his heavy eyebrows at the couple.

"Lulie," he growled, "don't you know you're keepin' the meetin' waitin'? You are, whether you know it or not. Martha Phipps, come in and set down. Come on, lively now!"

Martha smiled.

"Cap'n Jeth," she said, "you remind me of father callin' in the cat. You must think you're aboard your old schooner givin' orders. All right, I'll obey 'em. Ay, ay, sir! Come, Lulie."

They entered the parlor, whither Galusha, Mr. Cabot and Primmie had preceded them and were already seated. The group in the room was made up about as on the occasion of the former séance, but it was a trifle larger. The tales of the excitement on the evening when the light keeper threatened to locate and destroy the "small, dark outsider" had spread and had attracted a few additional and hopeful souls. Mr. Obed Taylor, driver of the Trumet bake-cart. and a devout believer, had been drawn from his home village; Miss Tamson Black, her New Hampshire visit over, was seated in the front row; Erastus Beebe accompanied his sister Ophelia. The Hardings, Abel and Sarah B., were present and accounted for, and so, too, was Mrs. Hannah Peters.

Galusha Bangs, seated between Miss Cash and the immensely interested Cousin Gussie, gazed dully about the circle. He saw little except a blur of faces; his thoughts were elsewhere, busy in dreadful anticipation of the scene he knew he must endure when he and his cousin and Miss Phipps returned to the house of the latter. He did not dare look in her direction, fearing to see once more upon her face the expression of suspicion which he had already seen dawning there—suspicion of him, Galusha Bangs. He sighed, and the sigh was so near a groan that his relative was startled.

"What's the matter, Galusha?" he whispered. "Brace up, old man! you look as if you were seeing spooks already. Not sick—faint, or anything like that?"

Galusha blushed. "Eh?" he queried. "Oh—oh, no, no. Quite so, really. Eh? Ah—yes."

Cabot chuckled. "That's a comprehensive answer, at any rate," he observed. "Come now, be my Who's-Who. For example, what is the name of the female under the hat like a—a steamer basket?"

Galusha looked. "That is Miss Hoag, the—ah—medium," he said.

"Oh, I see. Did the spirits build that hat for her?"

Miss Hoag's headgear was intrinsically the same she had worn at the former séance, although the arrangement of the fruit, flowers, sprays and other accessories was a trifle different. The red cherries, for example, no longer bobbed at the peak of the roof; they now hung jauntily from the rear eaves, so to speak. The purple grapes had also moved and peeped coyly from a thicket of moth-eaten rosebuds. The wearer of this revamped millinery triumph seemed a bit nervous, even anxious, so it seemed to Martha Phipps, who, like Cabot and Galusha, was looking at her. Marietta kept hitching in her seat, pulling at her gown, and glancing from time to time at the gloomy countenance of Captain Jethro, who, Miss Phipps also noticed, was regarding her steadily and slowly pulling at his beard. This regard seemed to add to Miss Hoag's uneasiness.

The majority of those present were staring at the senior partner of Cabot, Bancroft and Cabot. The object of the attention could not help becoming aware of it.

"What are they all looking at me for?" he demanded, under his breath.

Galusha did not hear the question, but Primmie did, and answered it.

"They don't know who you be," she whispered.

"What of it? I don't know who they are, either."

Miss Cash sniffed. "Humph!" she declared, "you wouldn't know much worth knowin' if you did—the heft of 'em. . . . Oh, my savin' soul, it's a-goin' to begin! Where's my mouth organ?"

But, to her huge disappointment, her services as mouth organist were not to be requisitioned this time. Captain Hallett, taking charge of the gathering, made an announcement.

"The melodeon's been fixed," he said, "and Miss Black's kind enough to say she'll play it for us. Take your places, all hands. Come on, now, look alive! Tut, tut, tut! Abe

Hardin', for heaven's sakes, can't you pick up your moorin's, or what does ail you? Come to anchor! Set down!"

Mr. Harding was, apparently, having trouble in sitting down. He made several nervous and hurried attempts, but none was successful. His wife begged, in one of her stage whispers, to be informed if he'd been "struck deef." "Don't you hear the cap'n talkin' to you?" she demanded.

"Course I hear him," retorted her husband, testily, and in the same comprehensively audible whisper. "No, I ain't been struck deef—nor dumb neither."

"Humph! You couldn't be struck any dumber than you are. You was born dumb. Set *down!* Everybody's lookin' at you. I never was so mortified in my life."

The harassed Abel made one more attempt. He battled savagely with his chair.

"I *can't* set down," he said. "This everlastin' chair won't set even. I snum I believe it ain't got but three laigs. There! Now let's see."

He seated himself heavily and with emphasis. Mr. Jim Fletcher, whose place was next him, uttered an agonized "Ow!"

"No wonder 'twon't set even, Abe," he snorted. "You've got the other laig up onto my foot. Yus, and it's drove half down through it by this time. Get *up!* Whew!"

A ripple of merriment ran around the circle. Every one laughed or ventured to smile, every one except the Hardings and Captain Hallett and, of course, Galusha Bangs. The latter's thoughts were not in the light keeper's parlor. Cousin Gussie leaned over and whispered in his ear:

"Loosh," whispered Mr. Cabot, chokingly, "if the rest of this stunt is as good as the beginning I'll forgive you for handing that fourteen thousand to the mummy-hunters. I wouldn't have missed it for more than that."

Captain Jethro, beating the table, drove his guests to order as of old he had driven his crews. Having obtained silence and expressed, in a few stinging words, his opinion of those who laughed, he proceeded with his arrangements.

"Tamson," he commanded, addressing Miss Black, "go and

set there by the organ. Come, Marietta, you know where your place is, don't you? Set right where you did last time. And don't let's have any more mockery!" he thundered, addressing the company in general. "If I thought for a minute there was any mockery or make-believe in these meetin's, I—I——" He paused, his chest heaving, and then added, impatiently, but in a milder tone, "Well, go on, go on! What are we waitin' for? Douse those lights, somebody."

Miss Hoag—who had been glancing at the light keeper's face and behaving in the same oddly nervous, almost apprehensive manner which Martha had noticed when she entered the parlor—took her seat in the official chair and closed her eyes. Mr. Beebe turned down the lamps. The ancient melodeon, recently prescribed for and operated upon by the repairer from Hyannis, but still rheumatic and asthmatic, burst forth in an unhealthy rendition of a Moody and Sankey hymn. The séance for which Galusha Bangs had laid plans and to which he had looked forward hopefully if a little fearfully—that séance was under way. And now, such was the stunning effect of the most recent blow dealt him by Fate, he, Galusha, was scarcely aware of the fact.

The melodeon pumped on and on. The rustlings and shiftings in the circle subsided and the expectant and shivery hush which Primmie feared and adored succeeded it. Miss Black wailed away at the Moody and Sankey selection. Miss Hoag's breathing became puffy. She uttered her first preliminary groan. Cousin Gussie, being an unsophisticated stranger, was startled, as Mr. Bangs had been at the former séance, but Primmie's whisper reassured him.

"It's all right," whispered Primmie. "She ain't sick nor nothin'. She's just a-slippin' off."

The banker did not understand.

"Slipping off?" he repeated. "Off what?"

"Off into sperit land. In a minute you'll hear her control talkin' Chinee talk. . . . There! My savin' soul! hear it? . . . Ain't it awful!"

"Little Cherry Blossom" had evidently been waiting at

the transmitter. The husky croak which had so amazed Galusha was again heard.

"How do? How do, everybodee?" hailed Little Cherry Blossom. "I gladee see-ee you. Yes, indeedee."

Cabot made mental note of the fact that the Blossom spoke her spirit pidgin-English with a marked Down-East accent. Before he had time to notice more, the control announced that she had a message. The circle stirred in anticipation. Primmie wiggled in fearful ecstasy.

"Listen!" commanded Little Cherry Blossom. "Everybodee harkee. Spirit comee heree. He say-ee——"

"Ow-ooo-ooo—ooo—OOO!!"

As prophesied by Mr. Zacheus Bloomer, the fog had come in and Zacheus, faithful to his duties as associate guardian of that section of the coast, had turned loose the great foghorn.

The roar was terrific. The windows rattled and the whole building seemed to shake. The effect upon the group in the parlor, leaning forward in awed expectation to catch the message from beyond, was upsetting, literally and figuratively. Miss Tamson Black, perched upon the slippery cushion of a rickety and unstable music stool, slid to the floor with a most unspiritual thump and a shrill squeal. Primmie clutched her next-door neighbor—it chanced to be Mr. Augustus Cabot—by the middle of the waistcoat, and hers was no light clutch. Mr. Abel Harding shouted several words at the top of his lungs; afterward there was some dispute as to just what the exact words were, but none whatever as to their lack of propriety. Almost every one jumped or screamed or exclaimed. Only Captain Jeth Hallett, who had heard that horn many, many times, was quite unmoved. Even his daughter was startled.

But perhaps the most surprising effect of the mammoth "toot" was that which it produced in the spirit world. It seemed to blow Little Cherry Blossom completely back to her own sphere, for it was a voice neither Chinese nor ethereal which, coming from Miss Hoag's lips, shrieked wildly: "Oh, my good land of love! Wh—what's that?"

It was only after considerable pounding of the table and repeated orders for silence that Captain Jethro succeeded in obtaining it. Then he explained concerning the foghorn.

"It'll blow every minute from now on, I presume likely," he growled, "but I don't see as that need to make any difference about our goin' on with this meetin'. That is, unless Marietta minds. Think 'twill bother you about gettin' back into the trance state, Marietta?"

Erastus Beebe had turned up one of the lamps and it happened to be the one just above Miss Hoag's head. By its light Martha Phipps could see the medium's face, and it seemed to her—although, as she admitted afterward, perhaps because of subsequent happenings she only imagined that it seemed so—it seemed to her that Marietta was torn between an intense desire to give up mediumizing for that evening and a feeling that she must go on.

"She looked to me," said Martha, "as if she was afraid to go on, but more afraid to stop."

However, go on she did. She told the light keeper that she guessed she could get back if Tamson would play a little spell more. Miss Black agreed to do so, provided she might have a chair instead of a music stool.

"I wouldn't risk settin' on that plaguy, slippery haircloth thing again for no mortal soul," declared the irate Tamson, meaning, doubtless, to include immortals. A chair was provided, again the lights were dimmed, and the séance resumed, punctuated now at minute intervals by the shattering bellows of the great foghorn.

In a few minutes the messages began to arrive. They were of similar vague import to those of the previous séance and, couched in Little Cherry Blossom's weird gibberish, were vaguer still. Occasionally a spirit seeking identification went away unrecognized, but not often. For the most part the identifying details supplied were so general that they were almost certain to fit a departed relative or friend of some one present. And, as is usual under such circumstances, the would-be recognizer was so pathetically eager to recognize. Even Galusha, dully inert as he was

just then, again felt his indignation stirred by the shabby
mockery of it all.

Obed Taylor received a message from his brother Daniel
who had died in infancy. Daniel declared himself very
happy. So, too, did Ophelia Beebe's great-aunt Samona,
who had "passed over" some time in the 'fifties. Aunt
Samona was joyful—oh, so joyful. Miss Black's name was
called.

"Tamson!" croaked Little Cherry Blossom. "Some one
heree wantee Tamson."

Miss Black uttered an exclamation of startled surprise.
"Good gracious me!" she cried. "Who is it?"

"Namee seem likee—likee Flora—Flora—somethin'," announced the control. The circle rustled in anticipation while
Tamson ransacked her memory.

"Flora?" she repeated. "Flora?"

"Yes—yes. Flora—ah—ah—somethin'. Somethin'—
soundee likee somethin' you ring."

"Somethin' I *ring*. Why, all a body rings is a bell. Hey?
My heavens above, you don't mean Florabel? That ain't
the name, is it—Florabel?"

"Yes—yes—yes—yes." Little Cherry Blossom was eagerly
certain that that was the name.

"Mercy on us! Florabel? You don't mean you've got a
message from my niece Florabel Tidditt, do you?"

"Yes—yes—yes—oh, yes!" The control was just as certain that niece Florabel was on the wire.

"I don't believe a word of it."

This unusual manner of receiving a message shocked the
devout. A murmur of protest arose.

"Now, now, now, Tamson," remonstrated Miss Beebe.
"You mustn't talk so. Course you believe it if the control
says so."

"I don't neither. Florabel Tidditt ain't dead. She's as
well as I be. I had a letter from her yesterday."

There was considerable agitation for a few minutes.
Then it developed that the Florabel seeking to communicate
was not Miss Tidditt, but another, a relative so long gone

that Tamson had forgotten she ever existed. At length she was brought to the point of admitting that it seemed as if she had heard of a cousin of her grandmother's named Florabel or Annabel or something. The message was not very coherent nor particularly interesting, so the incident ended.

A short time later came the sensation which was to make the evening memorable in East Wellmouth's spiritualistic circles. Little Cherry Blossom called the name which many had expected and some, Lulie Hallett and Martha Phipps in particular, dreaded to hear.

"Jethro!" croaked the Blossom. "Jethro!"

Captain Hallett had been very quiet, particularly since the Florabel message was tangled in transit. Martha could see his shaggy head in silhouette against the dim light of the lamp and had noticed that that head scarcely moved. The light keeper seemed to be watching the medium very intently. Now he spoke.

"Yes?" he said, as if awakened from sleep. "Yes, here I am. What is it?"

"Jethro," cried the control once more. "Jethro, somebodee come speakee to you. . . . Julia! Julia!"

Captain Jethro rose from his chair. The loved name had as always an instant effect. His heavy voice shook as he answered.

"Yes, yes, Julia," he cried. "Here I am, Julia, waitin'—waitin'."

It was pathetic, pitiful. One listener in that circle felt, in spite of his own misery, a pang of remorse and a little dread. After all, perhaps it would have been better to——

"Julia," cried the light keeper. "Speak to me. I'm waitin'."

The foghorn boomed just here, but even after the sound had subdued Little Cherry Blossom seemed to find it difficult to proceed. She—or the medium—choked, swallowed, and then said:

"Julia got message. Yes, indeedee. Important message, she sayee, for Jethro. Jethro must do what she sayee."

The captain's big head nodded vigorously. Martha could see it move, a tousled shadow against the light.

"Yes, yes, Julia, of course," he said. "I always do what you say. You know I do. Go on."

"Father!" It was Lulie's voice, raised in anxious protest. "Father, please."

Her father sharply ordered her to be quiet.

"Go on, Julia," he persisted. "Tell me what you want me to do."

Again Little Cherry Blossom seemed to have difficulty in articulating. There was a quaver in her voice when she did speak.

"Julia say," she faltered; "Julia sayee 'Jethro, you sell R.P.'"

This was unexpected. It was not at all the message the group of listeners, with one exception, had anticipated. There was no hint of Nelson Howard here. They did not know what to make of it. Nor, it was evident, did Jethro Hallett.

"What?" he demanded. "What, Julia? I don't understand."

Little Cherry Blossom cleared her—or the medium's—throat and falteringly went on.

"Julia sayee 'Jethro, you sell R. P. what you got. Sellee him what you got, what he want buyee. You know. You sellee R. P. the stock.'"

But still it was clear that Captain Jeth did not understand.

"Sell R. P.?" he repeated. "R. P. Who's R. P.? And what . . . Eh? Do you mean——"

He paused. When he next spoke his tone was quite different. There was a deeper note in it, almost a note of menace.

"R. P.?" he said again. "Does 'R. P.' mean—is that supposed to stand for Horatio Pulcifer? Eh? Does 'R. P.' mean Raish Pulcifer?"

The control did not reply instantly. The light keeper pressed his question.

"Does it?" he demanded.

"Yes . . . yes," stammered the Blossom. "Yes, Julia say sellee Raish what he wantee buy."

"Wantee *buy?* What have I got he wants to buy?"

"Julia she sayee you know. She say 'De—De—Develop stock. That's it. Yes, Develop stock. She sayee you sell Raish Develop stock. She sayee she wantee you to. You do right then."

The foghorn howled once more. Captain Jethro was standing erect beside his chair. When, at last, he did speak, his tone was still more tense and threatening. Even the shallowest mind in that room—and, as Miss Phipps had said, practically every "crank" within ten miles was present— even the shallowest realized that something was impending, something ominous.

"Do you mean to say," demanded Jethro Hallett, speaking very slowly, "that Julia's, my wife's, spirit is tellin' me to sell my four hundred shares of Wellmouth Development stock to Raish Pulcifer? Do you mean that *she* says that?"

Little Cherry Blossom croaked twice, but the second croak was a feeble "Yes."

"*She* says that? Julia, my dead wife, tells me to do that?"

"Yes. Yes—yes—yes. She say you sell Raish four hundred Develop stock and you be so gladee. She be gladee, too. She——"

"*STOP!*"

The light keeper's shout rang through the room. "Stop!" he shouted again. "You—you *liar!*"

The word shot from beneath his teeth and, judging by the effect, might have hit almost every individual in the room. There was absolute silence for just the briefest instant; then a chorus of faint screams, exclamations, startled and indignant protests. Above them all Primmie's call upon her Lord of Isral sounded plainly. Captain Jethro paid no heed.

"You liar!" he roared again. "Out of my house, you swindler! You damned cheat!"

This blast, delivered with the full force of the old skipper's quarter-deck voice, had the effect of completely upsetting the already tense nerves of the majority in the circle. Two or three of the women began to cry. Chairs were over- turned. There was a babel of cries and confusion. The light keeper stilled it.

"Be still, all hands!" he shouted. "Turn up them lamps! Turn 'em up!"

Mr. Cabot, although himself somewhat startled and dis- turbed by the unexpected turn of events, was at least as cool as any one. He reached over the prostrate heap at his feet— it was Ophelia Beebe hysterically repeating: "He's gone crazy! He's gone loony! *Oh,* my soul! *Oh,* my land! *What'll* I do?" and the like—and turned up one of the lamps. Obed Taylor did the same with the other.

The sudden illumination revealed Captain Jethro, his face pale, his eyes flashing fire, holding the dumpy Miss Hoag fast in her chair with one hand and with the other brandished above her head like the hammer of Thor. The audience, for the most part, were in various attitudes, indicating alarm and a desire to escape. Mrs. Harding had a strangle hold on her husband's neck and was slowly but inevitably chok- ing him to death; Mrs. Peters, as well as Miss Beebe, was on the floor; and Primmie Cash was bobbing up and down, flapping her hands and opening her mouth like a mechanical figure in a shop window. Lulie and Martha Phipps, pale and frightened, were trying to force their way to the captain's side. Galusha Bangs alone remained seated.

The light keeper again commanded silence.

"Look at her!" he cried, pointing his free hand at the cowering figure of the medium. *"Look* at her! The lyin' cheat!"

Marietta was, in a way, worth looking at. She had shrunk as far down in the chair as the captain's grip would permit, her usually red face was now as white as the full moon, which it resembled in some other ways, and she was, evidently, as Primmie said afterwards, "scart to death and some left over."

Lulie called.

"Father, father," she pleaded. "Please—oh—please!"

Her father paid no attention. It was to Miss Hoag that he continued his attentions.

"You miserable, swindlin' make-believe!" he growled, his voice shaking with emotion. "You—you come here and—and pretend—— Oh, by the Almighty, if you was a man, if you wasn't the—the poor, pitiful fool that you be, I'd—I'd——"

His daughter had reached his side. "Father," she begged. "Father, for my sake——"

"Be still! Be still, girl! . . . Marietta Hoag, you answer me. Who put you up to tellin' me to sell that stock to Pulcifer? Who did it? Answer me!"

Marietta tried, but she could do little but gurgle. She gurgled, however, in her natural tones, or a frightened imitation of them. Little Cherry Blossom had, apparently, fluttered to the Chinese spiritland.

"I—I—— Oh, my good land!" she wailed.

"Answer!"

"Father—father!" cried Lulie. "Don't talk so! Don't act so!"

"Act so! Be still! Let me alone, Martha Phipps! This woman here is a cheat. She's a liar! How do I *know?* *Don't* ask such fool questions. I know because—because she says my wife—Julia—my wife—tells me to sell my four hundred shares of Wellmouth Development stock——"

"Yes, of course. But, perhaps——"

"There ain't any perhaps. You, woman," addressing the cowering medium, "didn't you say that?"

"Yes—oh, yes, Cap'n Jeth, I said it. *Please* don't!"

"And you pretended my dead wife's spirit said it, didn't you?"

"Yes. Yes, she did. Oh—oh——"

"She did not! Listen, all of you!" with scornful disgust. "Listen! That four hundred shares of Development stock this—this critter here says Julia knows I've got and wants me to sell to Raish Pulcifer I *sold* two months ago. Yes, by the everlastin'. I sold 'em! And—eh? Yes, there he is. I sold 'em to that Bangs man there. He knows it. He'll tell

you I did. . . . And now this swindler, this cheat, she—
she—— Who put you up to it? Who did? Was it Pulcifer?"

Marietta began to sob. "Ye-es, yes," she faltered. "He—
he said he——"

"I thought so. And you pretended 'twas my—my Julia,
my wife. . . . Oh, my God! And you've been pretendin' all
the time. 'Twas all cheatin' and lies, wasn't it? She—she
never come to you. She never told you nothin'. Ain't it
so?"

Poor, publicity-loving, sensation-loving Marietta's nerve
was completely gone. She sobbed wildly.

"Oh—oh, I guess so. I—I guess likely 'twas," she wailed.
"I—I don't know. I only——"

Captain Jethro took his hand from her shoulder. He
staggered a little.

"Get out of my house!" he ordered. "Out of my house—
all of you. You're all liars and cheats together. . . . Oh,
Julia! Oh, my Lord above!"

He collapsed in a chair and put his hands to his head.
Lulie, the tears streaming down her face, tried to comfort
him. Martha, also weeping, essayed to help. Cabot, walking over to where his cousin was standing, laid a hand on his
arm. Galusha, pale and wan, looking as if the world had
slipped from under him and he was left hanging in cold
space, turned a haggard face in his direction.

"Well, Loosh," said Cousin Gussie, dryly, "I think you
and I had better go home, hadn't we? This has been an interesting evening, an—ah—illuminating evening. You appear to be the only person who can add to the illumination,
and—well, don't you think it is time you did?"

CHAPTER XXI

GALUSHA did not answer. He regarded his relative vacantly, opened his mouth, closed it, sighed and turned toward the dining room. By this time most of the congregation were already in the yard and, as Cabot and his companion emerged into the dripping blackness of out-of-doors, from various parts of that blackness came the clatter of tongues and the sound of fervent ejaculations and expressions of amazement.

"Well! *Well!* Don't talk to *me!* If this don't beat all ever *I* see! . . ." "I should say it did! I was just sayin' to Sarah B., s' I, 'My soul and body,' s' I, 'if this ain't——' " . . . "And what do you s'pose made him——" "And when they turned up them lights and I see him standin' there jammin' her down into that chair and wavin' that big fist of his over top her head, thinks I, 'Good-*night!* He's goin' to hammer her right down through into the cellar, don't know's he ain't!' "

These were a few fragments which Cousin Gussie caught as they pushed their way to the gate. In one spot where a beam of light from the window faintly illuminated the wet, he glimpsed a flowered and fruited hat picturesquely draped over its wearer's ear while from beneath its lopsided elegance a tearful voice was heard hysterically demanding to be taken home. "Take me home, 'Phelia. I—I—I . . . Oh, take me home! I—I—I've forgot my rubbers and—and I feel's if my hair was comin' off—down, I mean—but—oh, I don't *care*, take me *home!*"

357

Galusha, apparently, heard and saw nothing of this. He blundered straight on to the gate and thence along the road to the Phipps' cottage. It seemed to Cabot that he found it by instinct, for the fog was so thick that even the lighted windows could not be seen further than a few yards. But he did find it and, at last, the two men stood together in the little sitting room. Then Cousin Gussie once more laid a hand on his relative's arm.

"Well, Galusha," he said, again, "what about it?"

Galusha heaved another sigh. "Yes—ah—yes," he answered. "Yes—ah—quite so."

"Humph! What is quite so? I want to know about that stock of the Wellmouth Development Company."

"Yes. . . . Yes, certainly, I know."

"That Captain—um—What's-his-name, the picturesque old lunatic with the whiskers—Hallett, I mean—made a statement that was, to say the least, surprising. I presume he was crazy. That was the most weird collection of insanity that I ever saw or heard. Ha, ha! Oh, dear! . . . Well, never mind. But what did old Hallett mean by saying he had sold *you* his four hundred shares of that stock?"

Galusha closed his eyes. He smiled sadly.

"He meant that he had—ah—sold them to me," he answered.

"Loosh!"

"Yes."

"Loosh, are you crazy, too?"

"Very likely. I often think I may be. Yes, I bought the —ah—stock."

"You bought the—— *You?* Loosh, sit down."

Mr. Bangs shook his head. "No, Cousin Gussie," he said. "If you don't mind I—I won't sit down. I shall go to my room soon. I bought Captain Hallett's stock. I bought Miss Phipps', too."

It was Cabot himself who sat down. He stared, slowly shook his head, and then uttered a fervent, "Whew!"

Galusha nodded. "Yes," he observed. "Ah—yes."

"Loosh, do you know what you are saying? Do you mean

that you actually bought Hallett's four hundred shares and this woman's——?"

"Miss Phipps is her name. Miss Martha Phipps."

"Yes, yes, of course. And you bought . . . Eh? By Jove! Is *that* what you did with that thirteen thousand dollars?"

Again Galusha nodded. "Yes," he said.

Cousin Gussie whistled again. "But why did you do it, Loosh?" he asked, after a moment. "For heaven's sake, *why?*"

Galusha did not answer immediately. Then he said, slowly: "If—if you don't mind, Cousin Gussie, I think I should tell *her* that first. That is, I mean she should—ah—be here when I do tell it. . . . I—I think I will change my mind and sit down and wait until she comes. . . . Perhaps you will wait, too—if you don't mind. . . . And, please—please don't think me rude if I do not—ah—talk. I do not feel—ah—conversational. Dear me, no."

He sat down. Cabot stared at him, crossed his knees, and continued to stare. Occasionally he shook his head, as if the riddle were proving too much for him. Galusha did not move. Neither man spoke. The old clock ticked off the minutes.

Primmie came home first. "Miss Martha said to tell you she would be over in a few minutes," she announced. "Cap'n Jeth, he's a-comin' 'round all right, so Miss Martha and Zach and them think. But, my savin' soul, how he does hang onto Lulie! Keeps a-sayin' she's all he's got that's true and honest and—and all that sort of talk. Give me the crawlin' creeps to hear him. And after that séance thing, too! When that everlastin' foghorn bust loose the first time, I cal'lated——"

Galusha interrupted. "Primmie," he suggested, gravely, "would you—will you be—ah—kind enough to go into the kitchen?"

"Hey? Go into the kitchen? Course I will. What do you want in the kitchen, Mr. Bangs?"

He regarded her solemnly. "I should like to have you

there, if you don't mind," he observed. "This gentleman and I are—we would prefer to be alone. I'm very sorry, but you must excuse me this time and—ah—go."

"Go? You want me to go out and—and not stay here?"

"Yes. Yes—ah—quite so, Primmie. Ah—good-night."

Primmie departed, slamming the door and muttering indignation. Galusha sighed once more. Then he relapsed into silence.

Twenty minutes later Martha herself came in. They heard her enter the dining room, then Primmie's voice in resentful explanation. When Miss Phipps did come into the sitting room, she was smiling slightly.

"Primmie's heart is broken," she observed. "Oh, don't worry, it isn't a very serious break. She hasn't had so much to talk about for goodness knows when and yet nobody wants to listen to her. I told her to tell Luce about it, but that didn't seem to soothe her much. Luce is Lucy Larcom, Mr. Cabot," she explained. "He is our cat."

Cousin Gussie, already a much bewildered man, looked even more bewildered, but Martha did not observe his condition. She turned to his companion.

"Mr. Bangs," she said, "it's all right. Or goin' to be all right, I'm sure. Cap'n Jeth is takin' the whole thing a good deal better than I was afraid there at first. He is dreadfully shaken, poor man, and he seems to feel as if the last plank had foundered from beneath him, as father used to say; but, if it doesn't have any worse effect than that, I shall declare the whole business a mercy and a miracle. If it has the effect of curin' him of the Marietta Hoag kind of spiritualism—and it really looks like a cure—then it will be worth all the scare it gave us. At first all he would say was that everything was a fraud and a cheat, that his faith had been taken away, there was nothin' left—nothin'. But Lulie, bless her heart, was a brave girl and a dear one. She said, 'I am left, father. You've got me, you know.' And he turned to her and clung to her as if she was his only real sheet anchor. As, of course, she is, and would have been always if he hadn't gone adrift after Little Cherry Blossom and such rubbish. Mr. Bangs, I——"

She paused. She looked first at Galusha and then at the Boston banker. Her tone changed.

"Why, what is it?" she asked, quickly. "What is the matter? . . . Mr. Bangs——"

Galusha had risen when she entered. He was pale, but resolute.

"Miss Phipps," he began, "I—I have been waiting to—to say something to you. I—ah—yes, to say something. Yes, Miss Phipps."

It was the first time he had addressed her as "Miss Phipps" for many months. He had, ever since she granted him permission and urged him to drop formality, addressed her as Miss Martha and seemed to take pride in that permission and to consider it an honor. Now the very fact of his returning to the old manner was, although she did not yet realize it, an indication that he considered his right to her friendship forfeited.

"Miss Phipps," he began once more, "I—I wish to make a confession, a humiliating confession. I shall not ask you to forgive me. I realize that what I have done is quite beyond pardon."

He stopped again; the road was a hard one to travel. Martha gazed at him, aghast and uncomprehending. Cabot, understanding but little more, shrugged his shoulders.

"For heaven's sake, old man," he exclaimed, "don't speak like that! You haven't committed murder, have you?"

Galusha did not answer nor heed him. It was to Martha Phipps he spoke and at her that he looked, as a guilty man in the prisoners' dock might regard the judge about to pronounce his death sentence.

"Miss Phipps," he began, for the third time, "I have deceived you. I—I have lied to you, not only once but—ah—ah—a great many times. I am quite unworthy of your respect—ah, quite."

Martha's face expressed many things, absolute amazement predominant.

"Why—why, Mr. Bangs!" she gasped. "What——"

"Pardon me," went on Galusha. "I was about to explain. I—I will try to make the explanation brief. It is—ah—very painful to me to make and will be, I fear, as painful for you to hear. Miss Phipps, when I told you—or gave you to understand—that my cousin here, or his firm, Cabot, Bancroft and Cabot, bought that—ah—Development stock of yours, I deceived you; I told you a falsehood. They did not buy it. . . . I bought it, myself."

He blurted out the last sentence, after a short but apparent mental struggle. Martha's chest heaved, but she said no word. The criminal continued:

"I will not attempt at this time to tell you how I was—ah—forced into buying it," he said; "further than to say that I—I had very foolishly led you to count upon my cousin's buying it and—and felt a certain responsibility and —a desire not to disappoint you. I—of course, I should have told you the truth, but I did not. I bought the stock myself."

Again he paused and still Martha was silent. Cousin Gussie seemed about to speak and then to change his mind.

"Perhaps," went on Galusha, with a pitiful attempt at a smile, "you might have forgiven me that, although it is doubtful, for you had expressly forbidden my lending you money or—or assisting you in any way, which I was—please believe this—very eager to do. But, after having bought it, I, as I say, deceived you, falsified, prevaricated—excuse me—lied to you, over and over. . . . Oh, dear me!" he added, in a sudden burst, "I assure you it is unbelievable how many falsehoods seemed to be necessary. I lied continually, I did, indeed.

"Well, that is all," he said. "That is all, I believe. . . . I—I am very sorry. . . . After your extreme kindness to me, it was—— I . . . I think perhaps, if you will excuse me, I will go to my room. I am—ah—somewhat agitated. Good-night."

He was turning away, but Cabot called to him.

"Here, wait a minute, Loosh," he cried. "There is one

thing more you haven't told us. Why on earth did you buy Hallett's four hundred shares?"

Galusha put his hand to his forehead.

"Oh, yes, yes," he said. "Yes, of course. That was very simple. I was—ah—as one may say, coerced by my guilty conscience. Captain Hallett had learned—I don't know precisely how, but it is quite immaterial—that Miss Phipps had, through me and to you, Cousin Gussie, as he supposed, sold her shares. He wished me to sell his. I said I could not. Then he said he should go to your office in Boston and see you, or your firm, and sell them himself. I could not allow that, of course. He would have discovered that I had never been there to sell anything at all and—and might have guessed what had actually happened. So I was obliged to buy his stock also and—and pretend that you had bought it. I lied to him, too, of course. I—I think I have lied to every one. . . . I believe that is really all. Good-night."

"One more thing, Loosh. What did you do with the certificates, Hallett's and Miss Phipps'? You got them, I suppose."

"Eh? Yes, oh, yes, I got them. I don't know where they are."

"*What?* Don't know where they *are?*"

"No. I took them to your office, Cousin Gussie. I enclosed them in a large envelope and took them there. I gave them to a person named—ah—Taylor, I think that was the name."

"Taylor? There is no Taylor in our office."

"It was not Taylor. It may have been Carpenter, although that doesn't seem exactly right, either. It was the name of some one—ah—a person who does something to you, you know, like a tailor or a carpenter or a—a butcher—or——"

"Barbour! Was it Barbour?"

"Yes, that was it—Barbour. I gave Mr. Barbour the envelope. I don't know what he did with it; I told him I preferred not to know. . . . Please excuse me. Good-night."

He turned abruptly and walked from the room. They

heard him ascending the stairs. For a moment the pair he had left looked at each other in silence. Then Cabot burst into a shout of laughter. He rocked back and forth in his chair and laughed until Martha, who was not laughing, began to think he might laugh forever.

"Oh, by Jove, this is funny!" he exclaimed, as soon as he could speak. "This is the funniest thing I ever heard of. Excuse the hysterics, Miss Phipps, but it certainly is. For the past month Williams and I, through this fellow Pulcifer down here, have been working heaven and earth to get the six hundred and fifty shares of that stock we supposed you and Hallett owned. And all the time it was locked up in my own safe there in Boston! And to think that old Loosh, of all persons, should have put this over on us. Ho, ho, ho! Isn't it rich!"

He roared and rocked for another interval. Still Martha did not speak, nor even smile. She was not looking at him, but at the braided rug beneath her feet, and he could not see the expression of her face.

"I may as well explain now," he went on, when this particular laugh was over, "that my friend Williams is one of the leading hotel men of this country. He owns two very big hotels in Florida and one in the Tennessee mountains. He has for some time been looking for a site on which to build another here on the northern coast. He was down this way a while ago and, quite by accident, he discovered this shore property which, he found out later, was owned by the Wellmouth Development Company. It was ideal, according to his estimate—view, harbor, water privileges, still water and surf bathing, climate—everything. He came to me and we discussed buying it. Then we discovered that this Development Company owned it. Fifty thousand dollars, the concern's capitalization, was too much to pay. A trust company over here in your next town had twelve hundred shares, but we found out that they knew the value of the property and, if they learned what we were up to, would hold for a fancy price. So, through this chap Pulcifer—we bought *his* five hundred shares—we began buying up the thirteen hundred which would give us a controlling interest and force the other crowd to do what we wanted. We picked up the small holdings easily enough, but we couldn't get yours or Hallett's. And for a very good reason, too. Ho, ho, ho! And old Loosh, of all people! Ho, ho!"

Still Miss Phipps did not laugh, nor did she look at him.

"By the way," he observed, "I presume my—er—relative paid you a fair price for the stock, Miss Phipps?"

"He paid me twenty dollars a share," she said, quietly.

"Did he, indeed! Well, that is more than we've paid any one else, except Pulcifer. We allowed him a commission—a margin—on all he succeeded in buying. . . . Humph! . . . And I suppose Galusha paid old Hallett par, too. But why he should do such a thing is—well, it is beyond me."

She answered, but still she did not look at him.

"He told you," she said. "He knew I needed money. I was foolish enough to let him guess—yes, I told him that I had a hard time to get along. He was interested and he tried to cheer me up by tellin' me he thought you might buy that stock of mine. He couldn't have been more interested if it had been somethin' of his own. No, not nearly so much; he and his own interests are the last thing he thinks about, I guess. And then he kept cheerin' me up and pretendin' to be more and more sure you would buy and—and when he found you wouldn't he—but there, he told us the truth. *I* understand why he did it, Mr. Cabot."

The banker shook his head. "Well, I suppose I do, too, in a way," he said. "It is because he is Galusha Bangs. Nobody else on earth would think of doing such a thing."

"No, nobody else would. But thirteen thousand dollars, Mr. Cabot! Why, that's dreadful! It's awful! He must have used every cent he owns, and I didn't suppose he owned any, scarcely. Oh, Mr. Cabot, I must pay him back; I must pay him right away. *Do* you want to buy that stock he bought? Will you buy it of him, so he can have his money again?"

She was looking at him now and her voice was shaking with anxiety. Cabot laughed once more.

"Delighted, Miss Phipps," he assured her. "That is what I have been trying to do for a month or more. But don't worry about old Galusha's going broke. He—why, what is it?"

"Oh, nothin'. I was thinkin' about what he did and—and——"

"Yes, I know. Isn't it amazing? I have known him all my life, but I'm never sure how he will fly off the handle next. Of course, I realize you must think him a perfect jackass, an idiot——"

"What! Think him *what?*"

"An idiot, an imbecile. Nine people out of ten, those who don't know him well, do consider him just that. Yet he isn't. In some respects he is a mighty clever man. In his own line, in this musty-dusty museum business of his, this Egyptology he is so cracked about, he is really very close to the top. Geographic societies all over the world have given him medals; he is—why, if he wished to he could write a string of letters after his name a yard long. I believe—hang it, it sounds absurd, but I believe he has been—er—knighted or something like it, in one heathenish little kingdom. And in Washington there, at the Institute, they swear by him."

She nodded. "They have just made him a wonderful offer to be the head of another expedition," she said.

"So? Well, I am not surprised. But in most respects, outside of his mummy-chasing, he is an absolute ass. Money? Why, he would give away every cent if it occurred to him to do so. *He* wouldn't know nor care. And what might become of him afterward he wouldn't care, either. If it wasn't that I watch him and try to keep his money out of his hands, I don't know what would happen. Kind? Yes, of course. And generous; good Lord! But when it comes to matters of sentiment like—well, like this stock business for example, he is, as I say, an ass, that's all. . . . I am telling you this, Miss Phipps, because I wouldn't wish you to consider old Loosh altogether a fool, but only——"

He was sitting there, his knee in his hands, gazing blandly at the ceiling and, in judicial fashion, summing up his rela-

tive's failings and virtues, when he was interrupted. And
the interruption was a startling one. Martha Phipps sprang
to her feet and faced him, her cheeks crimson and her eyes
flashing.

"Oh, how dare you!" she cried, with fiery indignation.
"How *can* you? You sit there and talk about him and—and
call him names in that—that condescendin' way as if he was
dirt under our feet and yet—and yet he's as far above us as
the sky is. Oh, how can you! Don't you see how good he
is? Don't you *see* how he's sufferin' now, poor soul, and
why? You say he doesn't care for money; of course he
doesn't. If it had cost fifty thousand and he had it, I
suppose he'd have used it just the same if he thought it
would help—help some friend of his out of trouble. But
what is tearin' him to pieces is the idea that he has, as he
calls it, cheated *me*. That he has lied to Jethro and to me
and hasn't been the same straight, honest—*gentleman* he always is. That's all. *He* doesn't give himself credit for
takin' his own money to help other folks with. *You* would,
I would, but *he* doesn't. He talks as if he'd robbed us, or
—or killed somebody or somethin'. He is the best—yes, I
think he is the best and finest soul that ever breathed. And
you sit there and—swing your foot and—and patronize—
and call him a fool. A *fool!* . . . I—I mustn't talk any
more or—or I'll say somethin' I'll wish I hadn't. . . . Good-
night, Mr. Cabot."

She had held her handkerchief tightly crumpled in her
hand during this outburst. Now she dabbed hastily with it
at either eye, turned and hastened into the dining room,
closing the door behind her.

A minute later Primmie came into the room, bearing a
lighted lamp.

"I cal'late now I can dast come in here, can't I?" she observed, with dignity. "Anyhow, I hope so, 'cause Miss Martha sent me. She said I was to show you where your bedroom was, Mr. Cabot."

The Boston banker, who had scarcely recovered from the
blast launched at his head by his hostess, rose, still blinking

in a dazed fashion, and followed the lamp-bearer up the steep and narrow stairs. She opened a door.

"Here you be," she said, tartly. "And I hope you'll sleep 'cause I'm precious sure *I* sha'n't. All I'll see from now till mornin' is Cap'n Jeth gettin' ready to lam that Marietta Hoag one over the top of the head. My Lord of Isrul! Don't talk to *me!*"

Cabot regarded her with interest. "What is *your* name?" he inquired.

"Primrose Cash."

"Eh? Primrose?"

"Um-hm. Name of a flower, 'tis. Some folks don't like it, but I do."

"Primrose!" The visitor slowly shook his head. "Well —er—Primrose," he asked, "is there any other asylum in this vicinity?"

"Hey? *Asylum?* What——"

"Never mind. I wondered, that's all. Good-night."

He took the lamp from her hand and went into his room. The amazed Primmie heard from behind the door of that room a mighty roar of laughter, laughter loud and long continued. Martha, in her room, heard it and stirred indignantly. Galusha, in his room, heard it and moaned.

He wondered how, in all the world, there was any one who, on this night of misery, could laugh.

CHAPTER XXII

THERE were two people in that house who ate a real breakfast the following morning. One was Primmie and the other was Augustus Cabot. It took much, very much, to counteract Miss Cash's attraction toward food, and as for the Boston banker, the combination of Cape Cod air and Martha Phipps' cooking had sharpened his appetite until, as he told his hostess, he was thoroughly ashamed, but tremendously contented.

Martha smiled a faint recognition of the joke. Galusha, sitting opposite her, did not smile; he was plainly quite unaware that there was humor anywhere. The little archæologist looked, so Primmie told Zach later on, "like one of them wax string beans, thin and drawed-out and yeller." He kept his gaze fixed on his plate and, beyond wishing her an uncertain good-morning, not once did he look at or venture to address Martha Phipps.

While they were at table Lulie came in. Considering all that she had undergone, the young lady was wonderfully radiant. Her eyes sparkled, there was color in her cheeks, and Mr. Cabot, who, in his time, had accounted himself a judge, immediately rated her as a remarkably pretty girl. Her first move, after greeting the company, was to go straight to Galusha and take his hand.

"Mr. Bangs," she cried, "how can I thank you? How can Nelson and I ever, ever thank you?"

Galusha's embarrassment managed to pump a little color into his wan cheeks. "I—I—ah—dear me, it was nothing,' he stammered. "I—I am—ah—yes, quite so. Please don't mention it."

369

"But I shall mention it. Indeed, I shall. Why, Martha, do you realize who was really responsible for father's being so suspicious of Marietta Hoag last evening? It was Mr. Bangs here, and no one else. Do you remember I told you that father had been receiving printed things, booklets and circulars, in the mails for the past few days, and that he had been reading them and they seemed to agitate him very much? Do you remember that?"

Martha said of course she remembered it.

"Yes. Well, those circulars and books came from the Psychical Research Society—the people who look up real spirit things and expose the other kind, the fraud kind, you know. Those told all about lots of cases of cheats like Marietta, and father read them, and he confessed to me this morning that they disturbed his faith in her a lot and he was suspicious when the séance began. Don't you know he hinted something about it?"

"Yes, yes, Lulie, I remember. But what did Mr. Bangs have to do with those circulars and things?"

"He sent them. Or he had them sent, I am sure. They came from Washington and who else could have done it? Who else would have had them sent-—from there—to father —and just at the right time? You did have them sent, didn't you, Mr. Bangs?"

Of course, the others now looked at Galusha and also, of course, this had the effect of increasing his embarrassment.

"Why—why, yes," he admitted, "I suppose I am responsible. You see, I—well—ah—I have friends at the Washington branch of the Society and I dropped a line requesting that some—ah—literature be sent to Captain Hallett. But it was nothing, really. Dear me, no. How is your father this morning, Lulie?"

Lulie's face expressed her happiness. "Oh, he is ever and ever so much better," she declared. "Last night I was so afraid that the shock and the dreadful disappointment and all might have a very bad effect upon him, but it hasn't. He is weak this morning and tired, of course, but his brain is perfectly clear and he talks as calmly as you or I. Yes, a good deal more calmly than I am talking just now, for I am very much excited."

She laughed a little. Then, with a blush which caused the Boston connoisseur to reëndorse his own estimate of her looks, added: "I just must tell you this, Martha, you and Mr. Bangs, for I know you will be almost as much delighted as I am—of course, I put in the 'almost.' This morning, a little while ago, I ventured to mention Nelson's name to father and to hint that perhaps now that he knew Marietta's 'medium' nonsense to be all a fraud, he would believe as I did that the things she said about Nelson were frauds, too. I said it in fear and trembling, and for some time he didn't answer. Then he called me to him and said he guessed I was probably right. 'You seem to have been right most of the time, Lulie,' he said, 'and I've been clear off the course.' Then he said something about his getting old and about ready for the scrap heap, but at the end he said: 'You ask that young Howard to cruise around here and see me some one of these days. I want to talk to him.' There!" triumphantly. "Isn't that splendid? Isn't that something for him to say?"

Martha beamed delightedly. "For your father to say it's more than somethin', it's a whole big lot," she declared. "Well, well, well! Cap'n Jeth invitin' Nelson to come and see him and talk with him! Mercy me! 'Wonders 'll never cease, fish fly and birds swim,' as my own father used to say," she added, with a laugh. "Mr. Cabot, excuse me for talkin' about somethin' you don't understand, but, you see, Lulie is—— Well, Primmie, what is it?"

Primmie's face expressed great excitement as she pushed it around the edge of the kitchen door. "My savin' soul!" was her salutation. "Who do you suppose is comin' right up our walk this very minute? Raish Pulcifer, that's who! And—and I bet you he's heard about last night's doin's, Miss Martha."

A little of Miss Cash's excitement was communicated to the others by her announcement. To every one except Mr. Bangs, of course. Galusha, after his acknowledgment of

Lulie's thanks, had relapsed into his absent-minded apathy. Martha looked at Lulie.

"Humph!" she said, after a moment. "Well, let him come, as far as I'm concerned. I never was afraid of Raish Pulcifer yet and I'm not now. Lulie, if you don't want to meet him, you might go into the sitting room."

Lulie hesitated. "Well, perhaps I will," she said. "Father has told me a little about—— Well, I imagine Raish will be disagreeable and I don't feel like going through more disagreeableness just now. I'll wait in here till he goes, Martha."

"Perhaps you'd like to go, too, Mr. Cabot," suggested Martha. Cabot shrugged. "Not unless you wish me to," he replied. "I've never met this agent of ours and I wouldn't mind seeing what he looks like. Williams hired him, so he doesn't know me from Adam."

For the first time that morning Miss Phipps addressed her boarder directly. "How about you, Mr. Bangs?" she asked.

Galusha did not appear to hear the question, and before it was repeated a knock, loud, portentous, threatening, sounded upon the door.

"Let him in, Primmie," commanded Miss Phipps.

Mr. Pulcifer entered. His bearing was as ominous as his knock. He nodded to Martha, glanced inquiringly at Cabot, and then turned his gaze upon Galusha Bangs.

"Well, Raish," said Martha, cheerfully, "you're an early bird this mornin'. How do you do?"

The great Horatio's only acknowledgment of the greeting was a nod. He did not even remove his cap. He was looking at the little man in the chair at the foot of the table and he seemed quite oblivious of any one else. And Galusha, for that matter, seemed quite as oblivious of him.

The Pulcifer mouth opened and the Pulcifer finger pointed. "Say," commanded Raish. "Say—you!" And as this seemed to have little or no effect upon the individual toward whom the finger pointed, he added: "Say, you—er—— What's-your-name—Bangs."

Galusha, who had been absently playing with his napkin, twisting it into folds and then untwisting it, looked up.

"Eh?" he queried. "Oh, yes—yes, of course. How do you do, Mr. Pulcifer?"

This placidity seemed to shut off Raish's breath for the moment, but it returned in full supply.

"How do I *do!*" he repeated. "Well, I ain't what you'd call fust-rate, I'd say. I'm pretty darn sick, if anybody should ask you. I've had enough to make me sick. Say, look here, Bangs! What kind of a game is this you've been puttin' over on me—hey? . . . Hey?"

"Game? . . . I—ah—pardon me, I don't know that I quite understand, Mr. Pulcifer."

"Don't you? Well, I don't understand neither. But I cal'late to pretty quick. What did Jeth Hallett mean last night by sayin' that he'd sold his four hundred Development a couple of months ago? What did he mean by it?"

Martha Phipps was about to speak. Cabot, too, leaned forward. But Galusha raised a protesting hand.

"Please," he said. "Mr. Pulcifer has a perfect right to ask. I have—ah—been expecting him to do so. Well, Mr. Pulcifer, I presume Captain Hallet meant that he had—ah—sold the stock."

"He did? I want to know! And what did he mean by sayin' he'd sold it to *you?*"

Again Miss Phipps and Cousin Gussie seemed about to take a hand and again Galusha silenced them.

"If you please," he begged. "It is quite all right, really. . . . I suppose, Mr. Pulcifer, he meant that he had done just that. He did. I—ah—bought his stock."

"You did! *You* did? Say, what kind of a—— Say, am I crazy or are you?"

"Oh, I am. Dear me, yes, Mr. Pulcifer. At all events, I purchased the stock from Captain Hallett. I bought Miss Phipps' shares at the same time."

It took more than a trifle to "stump" Raish Pulcifer. He was accustomed to boast that it did. But he had never been nearer to being stumped than at that moment.

"You—bought——" He puffed the words as a locomotive puffs smoke when leaving a station.

"Yes," said Galusha, calmly, "I bought both his and hers."

"You did! . . . You did! . . . Well, by cripes! But—but why?"

"Because, I—ah—— For reasons of my own, Mr. Pulcifer. Please pardon me if I do not go into that. I do not wish to appear rude, but the reasons are quite personal, really."

"Personal! . . . Well, I'll be dummed if this ain't the nerviest piece of brass cheek ever I—— Say, look here, Bangs! Why didn't you tell me you'd bought them shares? What did you—— Why, you must have had 'em all the time I was offerin' you commissions for buyin' 'em. Hey? *Did* you have 'em then?"

"Why—ah—yes, I did."

"And you never said nothin', but just let me talk! And—and how about this séance thing? You was the one put me up to making Marietta pretend to get messages from Jeth's wife tellin' him to sell his stock to me. *You* done it. I'd never thought of it if you hadn't put the notion in my head. And—and all the time—— Oh, by *cripes!*"

Again his agitation brought on a fit of incoherence. And he was not the only astonished person about that table. Galusha, however, was quite calm. He continued to fold and unfold his napkin.

"It may be," he said, slowly, "that I owe you an opology, Mr. Pulcifer. I did deceive you, or, at least, I did not undeceive you." He paused, sighed, and then added, with a twisted smile, "I seem to have been a—ah—universal deceiver, as one might say. However, that is not material just now. I had what seemed to me good reasons for wishing Captain Hallett to learn that Miss Hoag was not a genuine —ah—psychic. It occurred to me that a mention of his late wife's wish to have him sell something he did not possess might accomplish that result. I misled you, of course, and I apologize, Mr. Pulcifer. I am sorry, but it seemed necessary to do so. Yes, quite."

He ceased speaking. Martha drew a long breath. Mr. Cabot looked very much puzzled. Raish slowly shook his head. "Well!" he began; tried again, but only succeeded in repeating the word. Then he blurted out his next question.

"Who'd you buy them shares for?"

"Eh? For?"

"Yes, for. Who did you buy Cap'n Jeth's and Martha's stock for? Who got you to buy it? 'Twasn't the Trust Company crowd, was it?"

"The Trust Company? I beg pardon? Oh, I see—I see. Dear me, no. I bought the stock myself, quite on my own responsibility, Mr. Pulcifer."

Raish could not believe it. "You bought it yourself!" he repeated. "No, no, you don't get me. I mean whose money paid for it?"

"Why, my own."

Still it was plain that Horatio did not believe. As a matter of fact, the conviction that Galusha Bangs was poverty-stricken was so thoroughly implanted in the Pulcifer mind that not even a succession of earthquakes like the recent disclosures could shake it loose. But Raish did not press the point, for at that moment a new thought came to him. His expression changed and his tone changed with it.

"Say, Bangs," demanded he, eagerly, "do you mean you've still got that six hundred and fifty Development? Mean you ain't turned 'em over yet to anybody else?"

"Eh? Why, no, Mr. Pulcifer, I haven't—ah—turned them over to any one else."

"Good! Fust-rate! Fine and dandy! You and me can trade yet. You're all right, Perfessor, you are. You've kind of put one acrost on me, but don't make the mistake of thinkin' I'm holdin' that against you. No, sir-ee! When a feller's smart enough to keep even with your Uncle Raish in a deal then I know he gets up early—yes, sir, early, and that's when I get up myself. Hey, Perfessor? Haw, haw! Now, I tell you: Let's you and me go down to my office or somewheres where we can talk business. Maybe I might want to buy that stock yet, you can't tell. Hey? Haw, haw!"

He was exuding geniality now. But just here Mr. Augustus Cabot spoke. Judging by his face, he had enjoyed the passage at arms between his cousin and his business agent hugely. Now he entered the lists.

"That's all right, Pulcifer," he said. "You needn't trouble. I'll look out for that stock, myself."

Horatio turned and stared. He had scarcely noticed the visitor before, now he looked him over from head to foot.

"Hey? What's that?" he demanded. Cabot repeated his statement. Raish snorted.

"You'll look after the stock!" he repeated. *"You* will? Who are you?"

Cousin Gussie tossed a card across the table. "Cabot is my name," he said.

Galusha suddenly remembered.

"Oh, dear me!" he exclaimed. "I—I forgot. Please forgive me. Cousin Gussie, this is Mr. Pulcifer. Mr. Pulcifer, this gentleman is my—ah—Cousin Gu—I mean my cousin, Mr. Cabot, from Boston."

But Mr. Pulcifer did not hear. He was staring at the names of the individual and of the firm upon the card and icy fingers were playing tunes up and down his vertebrae. For the second time that morning he could not speak. Cabot laughed.

"It's all right, Pulcifer," he said, reassuringly. "You won't have to worry about the Development matter any longer. I'll handle the rest of it. Oh, you did your best. I'm not blaming you. I'll see that you get a fair return, even if you couldn't quite deliver. But you must keep still about the whole thing, of course."

Raish breathed heavily. Slowly the icy fingers ceased trifling with his spine and that backbone began to develop—quoting Miss Phipps' description—at least one new joint to every foot. He suppled visibly. He expressed himself with feeling. He begged the honor of shaking hands with the great man from Boston. Then he shook hands with Galusha and Miss Phipps. If Primmie had been present doubtless he would have shaken hands with her. When Cabot sug-

gested that the interview had best terminate, he agreed with
unction and oozed, rather than walked, through that doorway. Watching from the window, they saw him stop when
he reached the road, draw a long breath, take a cigar from
his pocket, light it, hitch his cap a trifle to one side, and
stride away, a moving picture of still unshaken and serene
self-confidence.

Cabot laughed delightedly. "That fellow is a joy forever,"
he declared. "He's one of the seven wonders of the world."

Martha sniffed. "Then the world better keep a sharp
watch on the other six," was her comment. "I wouldn't
trust Raish Pulcifer alone with Bunker Hill monument—not
if 'twas a dark night and he had a wheelbarrow."

Lulie came rushing from the sitting room. She had heard
all the Pulcifer-Bangs' dialogue and her one desire was to
thank Galusha. But Galusha was not present. While Martha and Mr. Cabot were at the window watching the departure of Raish, the little man had left the room.

"But I must see him," cried Lulie. "Oh, Martha, just
think! He is responsible for *everything*. Not only for
sending father the Psychical Society books, but for planning
all that happened at the séance. You heard what Raish
said. He said that Mr. Bangs put him up to bribing Marietta
to pretend getting the message ordering father to sell his
stock. Why, if that is true—and, of course, it must be—and
if—if Nelson and I should—if it *should* end right for us—
why, Martha, he will be the one who made it possible. Oh,
do you believe he did plan it, as Raish said?"

Martha nodded and turned away. "He seems to have
spent most of his time plannin' for other folks," she said.

"He didn't come through the sitting room," said Lulie,
"so he must be in the kitchen with Primmie. I'm going to
find him."

But she did not find him. Primmie said that Mr. Bangs
had come out into the kitchen, taken his hat and coat, and
left the house by the back door. Looking from that door,
they saw his diminutive figure, already a good distance off,
moving across the fields.

"He's on his way to the graveyard," declared Primmie. Cabot was startled.

"On his way to the graveyard!" he repeated. "Why, he looked remarkably well to me. What do you mean?"

Lulie laughingly explained. A few minutes later, declaring that she must leave her father alone no longer, she hurried away. Martha watched her go.

"She scarcely knows there is ground under her feet," she observed. "A light heart makes easy ballast, so my father used to say."

Cabot expressed his intention of starting for the city shortly after noon.

"Now that I know where those missing shares are, I can go with an easy conscience," he said. "I came 'way down here to get them and the faster I came the farther off they were. Ha, ha! It's a great joke. I've had a wonderful time, Miss Phipps. Well, I must see Galusha and get him to sell that stock to me. I don't anticipate much difficulty. The old boy didn't even know nor care where Barbour had put it."

Martha seemed to hesitate a moment. Then she said: "Mr. Cabot, I wonder if you could spare a few minutes. I want to talk with you about the money I owe—the money he *gave* me—for that stock, and a little about—about your cousin himself. Last night when you spoke of him I was—well, I was excited and upset and I didn't treat you very well, I'm afraid. I'm sorry, but perhaps you'll excuse me, considerin' all that had happened. Now I want to ask you one or two questions. There are some things I don't—I can't quite understand."

CHAPTER XXIII

AN hour or so later Galusha, sitting, forlorn and miserable, upon the flat, damp and cold top of an ancient tomb in the old Baptist burying ground, was startled to feel a touch upon his shoulder. He jumped, turned and saw his cousin smiling down at him.

"Well, Loosh," hailed the banker, "at your old tricks, aren't you? In the cemetery and perfectly happy, I suppose. No 'Hark from the tombs, a doleful sound' in years, eh? . . . Hum! You don't look very happy this time, though." Then, with a comprehensive glance at the surroundings, he shrugged and added, "Heavens, no wonder!"

The picture was a dismal one on that particular day. The sky was overcast and gray, with a distinct threat of rain. The sea was gray and cold and cheerless. The fields were bare and bleak and across them moved a damp, chill, penetrating breeze. From horizon to horizon not a breathing creature, except themselves, was visible. And in the immediate foreground were the tumbled, crumbling memorials of the dead.

"Heavens, what a place!" repeated Cabot. "It's enough to give anybody the mulligrubs. Why in the world do you come over here and—and go to roost by yourself? Do you actually *like* it?"

Galusha sighed. "Sometimes I like it," he said. Then, sliding over on the tomb top, he added, "Won't you—ah—sit down, Cousin Gussie?"

His relative shook his head. "No, I'll be hanged if I do!" he declared; "not on that thing. Come over and sit on the fence. I want to talk to you."

He led the way to a section of the rail fence which, although rickety, was still standing. He seated himself upon the upper rail and Galusha clambered up and perched beside him. The banker's first question was concerning the six hundred and fifty shares of Development stock.

"I know you gave the Phipps woman par for hers," he said. "You told me so and so did she. Did you pay old Whiskers—Hallett, I mean—the same price?"

Galusha shook his head. "I—ah—was obliged to pay him a little more," he said. "His—ah—wife insisted upon it."

"His wife? I thought his wife was dead."

"Yes—ah—she is. Yes, indeed, quite so."

When this matter was satisfactorily explained Cousin Gussie asked if Galusha would be willing to sell his recently purchased shares at the price paid. Of course Galusha would.

"I should be very glad to make you a present of them, Cousin Gussie," he said, listlessly. "I do not care for them, really."

"I don't doubt that, but you won't do anything of the kind. As a matter of fact, your buying those shares and taking them out of the market was a mighty good thing for us. That Trust Company crowd was getting anxious, so the Phipps woman says. By the way, I will send her a check at once for her shares and she will hand it over to you. She was very much disturbed because you had—as she called it —given her that five thousand dollars."

Galusha nodded sadly. "Of course," he said. "It was a —a very dreadful thing to do. Oh, dear!"

His relative, who was watching him intently, smiled. "She and I have had a long talk," he continued. "She couldn't understand about you, how you could have so much money to—er—waste in that way. I gathered she feared you might have impoverished yourself, or pledged the family jewels, or something. And she plainly will not be easy one moment until she has paid you. She is a very extraordinary woman, Loosh."

His companion did not answer. His gaze was fixed upon

a winged death's head on a battered slate gravestone near at hand. The death's head was grinning cheerfully, but Galusha was not.

"I say she is remarkable, that Phipps woman," repeated Cousin Gussie. The little man stirred uneasily upon the fence rail.

"Her—ah—name is Martha—Martha Phipps—ah—*Miss* Martha Phipps," he suggested, with a slight accent upon the "Miss." The banker's smile broadened.

"Apologies, Galusha," he said, "to her—and to you." He turned and gazed steadily down at his relative's bowed head.

"Loosh," he said.

"Eh?" Galusha looked up. "Eh? Did you speak?" he asked.

"I did. No, don't look at that gravestone, look at me. Say, Loosh, why did you do it?"

"Eh? . . . I beg pardon. . . . Why did I . . . You mean why did I—ah—buy the stock—and—and——"

"Of course. Why did you? Oh, I know she was hard up and feared she couldn't keep her home and all that; she has told me her story. And she is a good woman and you were sorry for her. But, my boy, to take five thousand dollars— even for *you* to take five thousand cold, hard, legal tender dollars and toss them away for something which, so far as you knew, was not worth five cents—that argues a little more than sympathy, doesn't it? And when you add eight thousand more of those dollars to the original five, then—— Why did you do it, Loosh?"

Galusha's gaze fell. He looked solemnly at the battered cherub upon the gravestone and the cherub's grin was broad.

"I bought Captain Hallett's stock," he explained, "because I did not wish Miss Mar—Miss Phipps to know that I had lied—and all the rest."

"Yes, yes, so you said. But why did you lie, Loosh? Why didn't you tell her that you couldn't sell her stock for her? She would have been disappointed, of course, but she would have understood; she is a sensible woman."

Galusha, apparently, was considering the matter. It was a perceptible interval before he answered.

"I don't know, Cousin Gussie," he confessed, after the interval was over. "Really, I don't know. I think I felt, as I told you last night, as if I had encouraged her to believe I should surely sell her shares and—and that, therefore, I would be responsible for her disappointment. And I—well, really, I simply could not face the thought of that disappointment and all it would mean to her. I could not, indeed, no. I suppose you consider it quite extraordinary, my feeling that so acutely. Dear me, I suppose most people would. But I felt it. And I should do the same thing again, I know I should."

"For her, you mean?"

"Yes—yes, of course, for her."

"Humph! Say, Loosh, may I ask you a purely personal question? Will you promise not to be offended if I do?"

"Eh? Why, of course, Cousin Gussie. Of course. Dear me, ask anything you like."

"All right. Loosh, are you in love with Miss Phipps?"

Galusha started so violently as to throw him off his balance upon the fence rail. He slid forward until his feet touched the ground. His coat-tails, however, caught upon a projecting knot and the garment remained aloft, a crumpled bundle, between his shoulder blades and the back of his neck. He was not aware of it. His face expressed only one emotion, great astonishment. And as his cousin watched, that expression slowly changed to bewilderment and dawning doubt.

"Well, how about it?" queried Cabot. "Are you in love with her, Loosh?"

Galusha's mouth opened. "Why—good gracious!" he gasped. "Dear me—ah—— Why—why, I don't know."

The banker had expected almost any sort of reply, except that.

"You don't *know!*" he repeated.

"No, I—I don't. I—I never thought of such a thing."

Cousin Gussie slowly shook his head.

"Loosh," he declared, "you are superb; do you realize it? So you don't know whether you are in love with her or not. Well, put it this way: Would you like to marry her, have her for your wife, live with her for the rest of your days?"

Galusha considered this astounding proposition, but only for the briefest possible moment. His gentle, dreamy, wistful countenance seemed almost to light up from within. His answer was given in one breath and as if entirely without conscious volition.

"Oh, very much," he said, in a low tone. "Oh, yes, very much."

The Boston banker had been on the point of laughing when he asked the question. But he did not laugh. He whistled instead. Then he smiled, but it was not a smile of ridicule.

Jumping from the fence rail, he laid a hand on his relative's shoulder.

"Well, by Jove!" he exclaimed. "Forgive me, old man, will you? I had no idea you were taking it so seriously. I . . . Well, by Jove!"

Galusha did not speak. The same queer ecstatic brightness was upon his face and he was looking now, not at the grinning cherub, but at the distant horizon line of gray-green ocean and slate-gray sky. Cabot's grip on his shoulder tightened.

"So you really want to marry her," he said. . . . "Humph! . . . Well, I'll be hanged! Loosh, you—you—well, you certainly can surprise a fellow when you really make a business of it."

The brightness was fading from Galusha's face. He sighed, removed his spectacles, and seemed to descend from the clouds. He sighed again, and then smiled his faint smile.

"Dear me," he said, "how ridiculous it was, wasn't it? You like a joke, don't you, Cousin Gussie?"

"Was it a joke, Loosh? You didn't look nor speak like a joker."

"Eh? Oh, yes, it was a joke, of course. Is it likely that a woman like that would marry *me*?"

Again he astonished his relative into turning and staring at him. "Marry you?" he cried. *"She* marry *you?* For heaven's sake, you don't imagine there is any doubt that she would marry you if you asked her to, do you?"

"Why, of course. Why should she?"

"Why *should* she? Why shouldn't she jump at the chance, you mean!"

"Oh—oh, no, I don't. No, indeed. You are joking again, Cousin Gussie, of course you are. Women don't like me; they laugh at me, they always have, you know. I don't blame them. Very often I laugh at myself. I am eccentric. I'm 'queer'; that is what every one says I am—queer. I don't seem to think just as other people do, or—or to be able to dress as they do—or—ah—oh, dear, everything. It used to trouble me a good deal when I was young. I used to try, you know—ah—try very hard not to be queer. I hated being queer. But it wasn't any use, so at last I gave up trying. My kind of queerness is something one can't get over, apparently; it's a sort of incurable disease. Dear me, yes, quite incurable."

He had moved forward and his coat-tails had fallen into their normal position, so the "queerness" of his outward appearance was modified; but, as he stood there, with his puzzled, wistful expression, slowly and impersonally picking himself to pieces, so to speak, Cabot felt an overwhelming rush of pity for him, pity and a sort of indignant impatience.

"Oh, shut up, Galusha!" he snapped. "Don't be so confoundedly absurd. You are one of the cleverest men in the world in your line. You are distinguished. You are brilliant. If you were as queer as Dick's hatband—whatever that is—it would make no difference; you have a right to be. And when you tell me that a woman—yes, almost any woman, to say nothing of one lost down here in these sand-hills—wouldn't marry you in a minute, you're worse than queer—you're crazy, absolutely crazy."

"But—but Cousin Gussie, you forget. If there were no other reasons, you forget what I have done. She could never believe in me again. No, nor forgive me."

"Oh, *don't!* You disturb my digestion. Do you suppose there is a woman on earth who wouldn't forgive a man who gave up thirteen thousand dollars just to help her out of a difficulty? Gave it up, as you did, without a whimper or even a whisper? And whose one worry has been that she might find out the truth about his weird generosity? Oh, Loosh, Loosh, you *are* crazy."

Galusha made no attempt to deny the charge of insanity. He was thinking rapidly now and his face expressed his thought.

"Do you—do you really think she might forgive me?" he asked, breathlessly.

"Think! Why, she and I had a long talk just before I came over here. She thinks you are the best and most wonderful man on earth and all she feared was that you had taken your last cent, or even borrowed the money, to come to her rescue. When I told her you were worth a quarter of a million, she felt better, but it didn't lessen her gratitude. Forgive you! Oh, good Lord!"

Galusha had heard only the first part of this speech. The ecstatic expression was returning. He drew a long breath.

"I—I wonder if she really would consider such a thing?" he murmured.

"Consider what? Marriage? Well, I should say she wouldn't take much time for consideration. She'll jump at it, I tell you. You are the one to consider, old man. You are rich, and famous. Yes, and, although I have never pinned quite as much faith to the 'family' idea as most of our people do, still we have a sort of tradition to keep up, you know. Now this—er—Miss Phipps is all right, no doubt; her people were good people, doubtless, but—well, some of our feminine second and third cousins will make remarks, Galusha. They surely will."

Galusha did not even trouble to answer this speech. His cousin continued.

"But that is your business, of course," he said. "And I honestly believe that in a good many ways she would make the ideal wife for you. She is not bad looking, in a wholesome sort of way, she is competent and very practical, has no end of common sense, and in all money matters she would make the sort of manager you need. She . . . Say, look here, have you heard one word of all I have been saying for the last three minutes?"

"Eh? . . . Oh, yes, indeed. Of course, quite so."

"I know better; you haven't."

"Yes—yes. That is, I mean no. . . . Pardon me, Cousin Gussie, I fear I was not paying attention. . . . I shall ask her. Yes, if—if you are *quite* sure she has forgiven me, I shall ask her."

He started toward the cemetery gate as if he intended asking her at the first possible moment. His cousin followed him, his expression indicating a mixture of misgiving and amusement. Suddenly he laughed aloud. Galusha heard him and turned. His slight figure stiffened perceptibly.

"I beg pardon," he said, after a moment. "Doubtless it is—ah—very amusing, but I confess I do not quite see the joke."

Cabot laughed again.

"Is it—ah—so funny?" inquired Galusha. "It does not seem so to me."

The banker took him by the arm. "No offense, old chap," he said. "Funny? Of course it's funny. It's wildly funny. Do you know what I was just thinking? I was thinking of Aunt Clarissa. What do you suppose she would have said to this?"

He shouted at the thought. Galusha joined him to the extent of a smile. "She would have said it was just what she expected of me," he observed. "Quite so—yes."

They walked on in silence for some time. Then Galusha stopped short.

"I have just thought of something," he said. "It—it *may* have some influence. She has often said she wished she might see Egypt. We could go together, couldn't we?"

Cousin Gussie roared again. "Of course you could," he declared. "And I only wish I could go along. Loosh, you are more than superb. You are magnificent."

He telephoned for his car and chauffeur and, soon after dinner, said good-by to his hostess and his cousin and prepared to start for Boston. The Sunday dinner was a bountiful one, well cooked, and he did justice to it. Galusha, however, ate very little. He seemed to be not quite certain whether he was at the table or somewhere in the clouds.

The chauffeur discovered that he had scarcely oil and gasoline sufficient for his hundred-mile trip and decided to drive to Trumet to obtain more. Cabot, who felt the need of exercise after his hearty meal, took a walk along the bluff edge as far as the point from which he could inspect the property owned by the Development Company.

He was gone almost an hour. On his return he met Galusha walking slowly along the lane. The little man was without his overcoat, his hands were clasped behind him and, although his eyes were open, he seemed to see nothing, for he stumbled and staggered, sometimes in the road and sometimes in the dead weeds and briars beside it. He did not see his cousin, either, until the latter spoke. Then he looked up and nodded recognition.

"Oh!" he observed. "Yes, of course. Ah—— How do you do?"

Cabot was looking him straight in the face.

"Loosh," he asked, sharply. "What is it? What is the matter?"

Galusha passed his hand across his forehead.

"Oh, nothing, nothing," he answered.

"Nonsense! You look as if—— Well, you can't tell me nothing is wrong. *Isn't* there something wrong?"

The saddest smile in all creation passed across Galusha's face. "Why—why, yes," he said. "I suppose everything is wrong. I should have expected it to be, of course. I—I did, but—ah—for a little while I was—ah—foolish and—and hoped. It is quite all right, Cousin Gussie, absolutely so. She said it was—ah—impossible. Of course it is. She is quite right. Oh, quite."

Cabot caught his meaning. "Do you mean to say," he

demanded, "that you asked that—that Phipps woman to marry you and she *refused?*"

"Eh? Oh, yes, she refused. I told you she would not think of such a thing. That is exactly what she said; it was impossible, she could not think of it."

"Well, confound her impudence! . . . Oh, all right, Galusha, all right. I beg your pardon—and hers. But, really——"

Galusha stopped him. "Cousin Gussie," he said, "if you don't mind I think I won't talk about it any more. You will excuse me, won't you? I shall be all right, quite all right—after I—ah—after a time, you know."

"Where are you going now?"

"Eh? Oh, I don't know. Just somewhere, that's all. Good-by, Cousin Gussie."

He turned and walked on again, his hands clasped behind his back and his head bent. Cabot watched him for several minutes, then, entirely upon impulse and without stopping to consider, he began what was, as he said afterwards, either the craziest or the most inspired performance of his life. He walked straight to the Phipps' gate and up the walk to the Phipps' door. His chauffeur called to him that the car was ready, but he did not answer.

Primmie opened the door in answer to his knock. Yes, Miss Martha was in the sitting room, she said. "But, my savin' soul, what are you doin' back here, Mr. Cabot? Has the automobile blowed up?"

He did not satisfy her curiosity. Instead, he knocked on the door of the sitting room and, when Miss Phipps called to him to come in, he obeyed, closing the door behind him. She was sitting by the window and her sewing was in her lap. Yet he was almost certain she had not been sewing. Her face was very grave and, although he could not see distinctly, for the afternoon was cloudy and the room rather dark, it seemed to him that there was a peculiar look about her eyes. She, like her maid, was surprised to see him again.

"Why, Mr. Cabot," she cried, rising, "what is it? Has something happened?"

He plunged headfirst into the business that had brought him there. It was the sort of business which, if approached with cool deliberation, was extremely likely never to be transacted.

"Miss Phipps," he said, "I came back here on an impulse. I have something I want to say to you. In a way it isn't my affair at all and you will probably consider my mentioning it a piece of brazen interference. But—well, there is a chance that my interfering now may prevent a very serious mistake —a grave mistake for two people—so I am going to take the risk. Miss Phipps, I just met my cousin and he gave me to understand that you had refused his offer of marriage."

He paused, momentarily, but she did not speak. Her expression said a good many things, however, and he hurried on in order to have his say before she could have hers.

"I came here on my own responsibility," he explained. "Please don't think that he has the slightest idea I am here. He is, as you know, the mildest person on earth, but I'm not at all sure he wouldn't shoot me if he knew what I came to say to you. Miss Phipps, if you possibly can do so I earnestly hope you will reconsider your answer to Galusha Bangs. He is very fond of you, he would make you a kind, generous husband, and, honestly, I think you are just the sort of wife he needs."

She spoke then, not as if she had meant to, but more as if the words were involuntarily forced from her by shock.

"You—you think I am the sort of wife he needs?" she gasped. *"I?"*

"Yes, you. Precisely the sort."

"For—for *him. You* think so?"

"Yes. Now, of course, if you do not—er—care for him, if you could not think of him as a husband—oh, hang it, I don't know how to put it, but you know what I mean. If you don't *want* to marry him then that is your business altogether and you are right in saying no. But if you *should* care for him and refused him because you may have thought there was any—er—unsuitability—er—unfitness—oh. the devil, I don't know what to call it—if you thought there was too large an element of that in the match, then I beg of you to reconsider, that's all. He needs you."

"Needs me? Needs *me?* . . . Oh—oh, you must be crazy!"

"Not a bit of it. He needs you. You have all the qualities, common sense, practicability, everything he hasn't got. It is for his sake I'm asking this, Miss Phipps. I truly believe you have the making or marring of his future in your hands—now. That is why I hope you will—well, change your mind. . . . There! I have said it. Thank you for listening. Good-day."

He turned to the door. She spoke once more. "Oh, you *must* be jokin'!" she cried. "How *can* you say such things? His people—his family——"

"Family? Oh . . . well, I'll tell you the truth about that. When he was young he had altogether too much family. Now he hasn't any, really—except myself, and I have expressed my opinion. Good-by, Miss Phipps."

He went out. Martha slowly went back to her rocking-chair and sat down. A moment later she heard the roar of the engine as the Cabot car got under way. The sound died away in the distance. Martha rose and went up the stairs to her own room. There she sat down once more and thought —and thought.

Some time later she heard her lodger's footstep—how instantly she recognized it—in the hall and then in his bedroom. He was in that room but a short time, then she heard him go down the stairs again. Perhaps ten minutes afterward Primmie knocked. She wished permission to go down to the village.

"I just thought maybe I'd go down to the meetin'house," explained Primmie. "They're goin' to have a Sunday school concert this afternoon at four o'clock. Zach he said he was cal'latin' to go. And besides, Mr. Bangs he give me this letter to leave to the telegraph office, Miss Martha."

"The telegraph office isn't open on Sundays, Primmie."

"No'm, I know 'tain't. But Ras Beebe he takes care of

all the telegraphs there is and telephones 'em over to Denboro, where the telegraph place *is* open Sundays."

"Oh, all right, Primmie, you may go. Is Mr. Bangs in?"

"No'm, he ain't. He's gone out somewheres. To walk, I cal'late. Last I see of him he was moonin' along over towards the lighthouse way."

Primmie departed and Martha, alone in the gathering dimness of the afternoon, resumed her thinking. It was an endless round, that thinking of hers—but, of course, it could end in but one way. Even to wish such things was wicked. For his sake, that was what Mr. Cabot had said. Ah, yes, but it was for his sake that she must remain firm.

A big drop of rain splashed, and exploded like a miniature watery bombshell, against the windowpane. Martha looked up. Then she became aware of a faint tinkling in the room below. The telephone bell was ringing.

She hurried downstairs and put the receiver to her ear. It was Mr. Beebe speaking and he wished to ask something concerning a message which had been left in his care by Primmie Cash.

"It's signed by that Mr. Galushy Bangs of yours," explained Erastus. "I've got to 'phone it to the telegraph office and there's a word in it I can't make out. Maybe you could help me, Martha, long's Bangs isn't there. 'Tain't nothin' private, I don't cal'late. I'll read it to you if you want I should."

He began to read without waiting for permission. The message was addressed to the Board of Directors of the National Institute at Washington, D. C., and began like this:

"Deeply regret necessity of refusing your generous and flattering offer to lead——"

It was just here that Mr. Beebe's ability to decipher the Bangs' handwriting broke down.

"I can't make out the next word, Martha," he said. "It begins with an E, but the rest of it ain't nothin' but a string of kinks. It's all head and no tail, that word is."

"What does it look like?"

"Hey? Looks like a whiplash or an eel, more'n anything else. It might be 'epizootic' or—or—'eclipsin'' —or—— The word after it ain't very plain neither, but I kind of think that it's 'expedition.' "

" 'Expedition'? Is the word you can't make out 'Egyptian'?"

"Hey? . . . 'Egyptian?' Well, I snum, I guess 'tis! 'Egyptian.' . . . Humph! I never thought of that. I——"

"Read me the whole of that telegram, Erastus. Read it."

Mr. Beebe read it. "Deeply regret necessity of refusing your generous and flattering offer to lead Egyptian expedition. Do not feel equal to the work. Decision final. Will write.—Galusha Bangs."

Martha's hand shook as it held the receiver to her ear. He had refused the greatest honor of his life. He had declined to carry out the wonderful "plan" concerning which he and she had so often speculated. . . . And she knew why he had refused.

"Erastus! Ras!" she called. "Hello, Ras! Hold that telegram. Don't send it yet. Do you hear?"

Mr. Beebe's voice expressed his surprise. "Why, yes, Martha," he said, "I hear. But I don't know. You see, Mr. Bangs, he sent a note along with the telegram sayin' he wanted it rushed."

"Never mind. You hold it until you hear from me again—or from him. Yes, I'll take all the responsibility. Erastus Beebe, don't you send that telegram."

She hung up the receiver and hurried to the outer door. Galusha was nowhere in sight. Then she remembered that Primmie had said he had gone toward the lighthouse. She threw a knitted scarf over her shoulders, seized an umbrella from the rack—for the walk showed broad splashes where drops of rain had fallen—and started in search of him. She had no definite plan. She was acting as entirely upon impulse as Cabot had acted in seeking their recent interview; but of one thing she was determined—he should not wreck his career if she, in any way, could prevent it.

She reached the gate of the government property, but she did not open it. She was certain he would not be in the light keeper's cottage; she seemed to have an intuition as to where he was, and, turning, followed the path along the edge of the bluff. She followed it for perhaps three hundred yards, then she saw him. He was sitting upon a knoll, his hands clasped about his knees. The early dusk of the gloomy afternoon was rapidly closing in, the raindrops were falling more thickly, but he did not seem to realize these facts, or, if he did, to care. He sat there, a huddled little bundle of misery, and her heart went out to him.

He did not hear her approach. She came and stood beside him.

"Mr. Bangs," she said.

Then he looked up, saw her, and scrambled to his feet.

"Why—why, Miss Martha!" he exclaimed. "I did not see you—ah—hear you, I mean. What is it? Is anything wrong?"

She nodded. She found it very hard to speak and, when she did do so, her voice was shaky.

"Yes," she said, "there is. Somethin' very wrong. Why did you telegraph the Institute folks that you wouldn't accept their offer? . . . Oh, I found it out. Ras Beebe couldn't get one word in your message and he read it to me over the 'phone. But that doesn't matter. That doesn't count. Why did you refuse, Mr. Bangs?"

He put his hand to his forehead. "I—I am sorry if it troubled you," he said. "I didn't mean for you to know it—ah—yet. I refused because—well, because I did not care to accept. The—the whole thing did not appeal to me, somehow. I have lost interest in it—ah—quite. Dear me, yes—quite."

"Lost interest! In Egypt? In such a wonderful chance as this gives you? Oh, you can't! You mustn't!"

He sighed and then smiled. "It does seem queer, doesn't it?" he admitted. "Yet it is quite true. I have lost interest. I don't seem to care even for Egypt. Now that is very odd."

"But—but if you refuse this what *will* you do?"

He smiled again. "I don't know," he said. "I don't seem to care. But it is quite all right, Miss Martha. Really it is. I—I wouldn't have you think—— Oh, dear, no!"

"But what *will* you do? Tell me."

"I don't know. No doubt I shall do something. One has to do that, I suppose. It is only that——" Then, as a new thought came to him, he turned to her in alarm. "Oh, of course," he cried, hastily, "I sha'n't remain here. Please don't think I intend imposing upon you longer. I shall go—ah—at once—to-morrow—ah—almost immediately. You have been extremely kind and long-suffering already and—and——"

She interrupted. "Don't!" she said, hurriedly. "Don't! Mr. Bangs, have you truly made up your mind not to go to Egypt with that expedition? Won't you *please* do it, if I beg you to?"

He slowly shook his head.

"It is like you," he said, "to take such an interest, but, if—if you don't mind, I had rather not. I can't. Really, I—ah —can't. It—— Well, the thought of it—ah—repels me. Please don't ask me, Miss Martha, because—I can't."

She hesitated. Then she said, "Would you go if I went with you?"

He had been looking, not at her, but at the sea. Now he slowly turned.

"Why—why——" he stammered. "Why, Miss—— Oh, dear me, you don't—you can't mean——"

She shook her head. "I suppose I mean anything," she said, "anything that will stop you from throwin' away your life work."

He was very pale and his eyes were fixed upon her face. "Do you mean——" he began, "do you mean you could—you would marry me?"

She shook her head again. "I think I must be crazy," she said, desperately. "I think we all must be, your cousin as well as the rest of us. He came to me a little while ago and asked me to—to say yes to you. *He* did! He, of all people! The—the very one that I—I——"

"Yes, yes, yes, of course." Galusha was trembling with eagerness. "Yes, of course. Cousin Gussie is an extraordinarily able man. He approves of it highly. He told me so."

She scarcely heard him. "Oh, don't you see," she went on, "why it would be wicked for me to think of such a thing? You are a great man, a famous man; you have been everywhere and seen everything; I haven't had any real education, any that counts besides yours; I haven't been anywhere; I am just a country old maid. Oh, you would be ashamed of me in a month. . . . No, no, no, I mustn't. I won't."

"But, Miss Martha——"

"No. Oh, no !"

She turned away. Galusha had what was, for him, an amazing and unprecedented inspiration.

"Very well," he declared. "I shall go to—to the devil, I think. Yes, I will. I shall give away my money, all of it, and go to the devil."

It was absurd enough, but the absurdity of it did not strike either of them then.

"Oh, *won't* you go to Egypt?" she begged. Won't you, *please?*"

He was firm. "No," he declared. "Not unless you go with me. Ah—ah—Miss Martha, will you?"

She hesitated, wrung her hands—and surrendered. "Oh, I suppose I shall have to," she said.

He did not dare believe it.

"But—but I don't want you to have to," he cried. "You mustn't marry me for—for Egypt, Miss Martha. Of course, it is too much to ask; no doubt it is quite impossible, but you—you mustn't marry me unless you really—ah—want to."

And then a very astonishing thing happened. Martha turned to him, and tears were in her eyes.

"Oh," she cried, breathlessly, "do you suppose there is a

woman in this world who wouldn't want to marry a man lik
you?"

After a while they discovered that it was raining. As
matter of fact, it had been raining for some time and wa
now raining hard, but as Galusha said, it didn't make a bi
of difference, really. They put up the umbrella, which unt:
now had been quite forgotten, and walked home along th
wet path, between the dripping weeds and bushes. It wa
almost dark and, as they passed the lighthouse, the grea
beacon blazed from the tower.

Galusha was babbling like a brook, endlessly but joyfu:
"Miss Martha——" he began. Then he laughed aloud, :
laugh of sheer happiness. "It—it just occurred to me," h
exclaimed. "How extraordinary I didn't think of it before
I sha'n't have to call you Miss Martha now, shall I? It :
very wonderful, isn't it? Dear me, yes! Very wonderful!

Martha laughed, too. "I'm afraid other people are goin
to think it is very ridiculous," she said. "And perhaps it is
Two middle-aged, settled folks like us startin' up all at onc
and gettin' married. I know I should laugh if it was any
body else."

But Galusha stoutly maintained there was nothing ridicu
lous about it. It was wonderful, that was all.

"Besides," he declared, "we are not old; we are just be
ginning to be young, you and I. Personally, I feel as if :
could jump over a bush and annihilate a—ah—June bug, a
Luce did that night when we went out to see the moon."

Luce himself was at the door waiting to be let in. H
regarded the pair with the air of condescending boredom
which the feline race assumes when confronted with the
idiosyncrasies of poor humanity. Possibly he was reflecting
that, at least, he knew enough to go in when it rained
Martha opened the door, but Galusha paused for a momen
on the threshold.

"Do you know," he said, "that, except—ah—occasionally
in wet weather, it scarcely ever rains in Egypt?"

CHAPTER XXIV

(A letter from Mrs. Galusha Bangs to Miss Lulie Hallett.)

Shepheard's Hotel, Cairo, Egypt, February tenth.

MY DEAR LULIE:

Well, as you can see by this hotel letter paper, here we are, actually here. Of course we are only a little way toward where we are going, but this is Egypt, and I am beginning to believe it. Of course, I can't yet quite believe it is really truly me that is doing these wonderful things and seeing these wonderful places. About every other morning still I wake up and think what a splendid dream I have had and wonder if it isn't time for me to call Primmie and see about getting breakfast. And then it comes to me that it isn't a dream at all and that I don't have to get up unless I want to, that I don't have to do anything unless I want to, and that everything a sensible person could possibly want to do I *can* do, and have a free conscience besides, which is considerable. I don't mean that I lay a-bed much later than I used to. I never could abide not getting up at a regular time, and so half past seven generally finds me ready to go down to breakfast. But, oh, it is a tremendous satisfaction to think that I could sleep later if I ever should want to. Although, of course, I can't conceive of my ever wanting to.

Well, I mustn't fill this whole letter with nonsense about the time I get up in the morning. There is so much to write about that I don't know where to begin. I do wish you could see this place, Lulie. I wish you could be here now looking out of my room window at the crowds in the street. I could fill a half dozen pages telling you about the clothes the people wear, although I must say that I have seen some whose clothes could be all told about in one sentence, and not a very long sentence at that. But you see all kinds of clothes, uniforms, and everyday things such as we wear, and robes and fezzes and turbans and I don't know what. You know what a fez is, of course. It's shaped like a brown-bread tin and they wear it little end up with a tassel hanging down. And turbans! To me, when I used to see pictures of people wearing turbans, they were just pictures, that's all. It didn't seem as if any one actually tied up the top of their head in a white sheet and went parading around looking like a stick with a snowball stuck on the end of it. But they do, and most of them look as dignified as can be, in spite of the snowball. And I have seen camels, quantities of them, and donkeys, and, oh, yes, about a million dogs, not one of them worth anything and perfectly contented to be that way. And dirt! Oh, Lulie, I didn't believe there was as much dirt in all creation as there is in just one of the back streets over here. Galusha asked me the other day if I didn't wish I could go into one of the houses and see how the people lived; he meant the poor people. I told him no, not if he ever expected me to get anywhere else. If the inside of one of those houses was like the outside, I was sure and certain that I should send for a case of soap and a hundred barrels of hot water and stay there scrubbing the rest of my life. And, oh, yes, I have seen the Pyramids.

Of course, you want to know how I got along on the long voyage over. I wrote you a few lines from Gibraltar telling you a little about that. I wasn't seasick a single bit. I think it must be in our blood, this being able to keep well and happy on salt water. Our family has always been to sea, as far back as my great-great-grandfather, at least, and I suppose that explains why, as soon as I stepped aboard the steamer, I felt as if I was where I belonged. And Galusha, of course, has traveled so much that he is a good sailor, too. So, no matter whether it was calm or blowy, he and I walked decks or sat in the lee somewhere and talked of all that had happened and of what was going to happen. And, Lulie, I realized over and over, as I have been realizing ever since I agreed to marry him, what a wonderful man he is and what a happy and grateful woman I ought to be—and am.

ou may be sure of that. Every day I make a little vow to
myself that I will do my best not to make him ashamed of
me. Of course, no matter what I did he would think it all
ight, but I mean to prevent other people from being ashamed
or him. That is, if I can, but I have so much to learn.

You should see how he is treated over here, by the very
inest people, I mean. It seems to me that every scientist or
explorer or professor of this or that from China to London
has been running after him, all those that happen to be in
this part of the world, I mean. And always he is just the
same quiet, soft-spoken, gentle person he was at the Cape,
but it is plain to see that when it comes to matters about his
particular profession, my husband is known and respected
everywhere. Perhaps you will think, Lulie, that I am
showing off a little when I write "my husband" like that.
Well, I shouldn't wonder if I was. Nobody could help being
proud of him.

I had a trial the other evening. That is, it seemed as if
it would be the greatest trial that ever I had to face and my,
how I dreaded it. Sir Ernest Brindlecombe, an English
scientist, and, so Galusha says, a very great man, indeed, is
here with his wife, and they have known Galusha for years.
So nothing would do but we must come to their house to dinner. He is in the English government service and they
have a wonderful home, more like a palace than a house—
that is, what I have always supposed a palace must be like.
I felt as if I *couldn't* go, but Galusha had accepted already,
so what was there to do?

Of course, you are wondering what I wore. Well, as I
wrote you from Washington, I had bought a lot of new
things. The wife of Professor Lounsbury, at the Institute,
helped me pick them out, and oh, what should I have done
without her! Galusha, of course, would have rigged me up
like the Queen of Sheba, if he had had his way. I tried going
shopping with him at first, but I had to give it up. Every
pretty dress he saw, no matter if it was about as fitting for
my age and weight as a pink lace cap would be for a cow,
he wanted to buy it right off. If the price was high enough,
that seemed to be the only thing that counted in his mind.
I may as well say right here, Lulie, that I have learned by
this time, when he and I do go shopping together, to carry

the pocketbook myself. In that way we can manage to brin
home something, even if it is only enough to buy a postag
stamp.

But I am wandering, as usual. You want to know abou
the dinner at the Brindlecombes'. Well, thanks to Mr
Lounsbury's help and judgment, I had two dresses to pic
from, two that seemed right for such a grand affair as I wa
afraid this was going to be. And I picked out a black sil
trimmed——

. . . . . .

(Two pages of Mrs. Bangs' letter are omitted here)

There is more of it at the top and bottom than there wa
to a whole lot of evening gowns I have seen, on the steame
and in Washington, but I can't help that. I guess I am ol
fashioned and countrified, but it does seem to me that th
place to wear a bathing suit is in the water, especially for
person of my age. However, it is a real sensible and rich
looking dress, even if it is simple, and I think you woul
like it. At any rate, I put it on and Galusha got into hi
dress suit, after I had helped him find the vest, and stoppe
him from putting one gold stud and two pearl ones in hi
shirt. *He* didn't notice, bless him, he was thinking o
everything but what he was doing at the minute, as he al
ways is.

So, both in our best bibs and tuckers, and all taut an
ready for the sea, as father would have said, we were drive
over to the Brindlecombe house, or palace, whichever you
call it. Mr. Brindlecombe—or Sir Ernest I suppose he shoul
be called, although *I* never remembered to do it, but calle
him Mr. Brindlecombe the whole evening—was a fleshy
bald-headed man, who looked the veriest little bit like Mr.
Dearborn, the Congregational minister at Denboro, and was
as pleasant and jolly as could be. His wife was a white-
haired little lady, dressed plainly—the expensive kind of
plainness, you know—and with a diamond pin that was about
as wonderful as anything I ever saw. And I kept thinking to
myself: "Oh, what *shall* I say to you? What on *earth* shall
we talk about?" and not getting any answer from myself,
either.

But I needn't have worried. She was just as sweet and
gentle and every-day as any one could be, and pretty soon

came out that we both loved flowers. That was enough, of
ourse, and so while Mr. Sir Ernest and Galusha were moon-
g along together about "dynasties" and "papyri" and
sphinxes" and "Ptolemies" and "hieroglyphics" and mum-
ies and mercy knows what, his wife and I were having a
vely time growing roses and dahlias and lilies. She told
e a new way to keep geranium roots alive for months after
king them up. She learned it from her gardener and if
ver I get a chance I am going to try it. Well, Lulie, instead
f having a dreadful time I enjoyed every minute of it, and
esterday Mrs. Brindlecombe—Lady Brindlecombe, I sup-
ose she really is—came and took me to drive. We shopped
nd had a glorious afternoon. I presume likely I said
Mercy me" and "Goodness gracious" as often as I usually
o and that they sounded funny to her. But she said "My
ord" and "Fancy" and they sounded just as funny to me.
.nd it didn't make a bit of difference.

There was one thing that came from our dinner at the
rindlecombes' which I must tell you, because it is so very
ke this blessed husband of mine. I happened to speak of
Irs. Brindlecombe's pin, the wonderful one I just wrote
bout. The very next day Galusha came trotting in, bub-
ling over with mischief and mystery like the boy he is in
 many things, and handed me a jeweler's box. When I
pened it there was a platinum brooch with a diamond in it
s big—honestly, Lulie, I believe it was as big as my thumb-
ail, or two thirds as big, anyway. This husband of mine
ad, so he told me, made up his mind that nobody's wife
hould own a more wonderful pin than *his* wife owned.
Because," he said, "nobody else has such a wonderful wife,
ou know. Dear me, no. No, indeed."

Well, I almost cried at first, and then I set about think-
ng how I could get him to change the pin and do it without
urting his feelings. As for wearing it—why, Lulie, I would
ave looked like the evening train just coming up to the
epot platform. That diamond flashed like the Gould's Bluffs
ght. The sight of it would have made Zach Bloomer feel
t home. And when I found out what it cost! My soul and
ody! Well, I used all the brains I had and strained them
little, I'm afraid, but at last I made him understand that
erhaps something a tiny bit smaller would look, when I

wore it in the front of my dress, a little less like a bonfir
on a hill and we went back to the jewelry store together
The upshot of it was that I have a brooch—lots smaller, o
course—and a ring, either of which is far, far too grand fo
a plain woman like me, and which I shall wear only on th
very stateliest of state occasions and *never,* I think, both a
the same time, and I saved Galusha a good many dollar
besides.

So, you see, Lulie, that he is the same impractical, absent
minded, dear little man he was down there in East Well
mouth, even though he is such a famous scientist and dis
coverer. I think I got the best salve for my conscience fron
knowing that, otherwise I should always feel that I neve
should have let him marry me. In most respects I am no
a bit the wife he should have, but I hope I am of some us
in his practical affairs and that at last I can keep him fron
being imposed upon. I try. For instance, on the steamer hi
cap blew overboard. I wish you could have seen the ca
the ship's steward sold him. The thing he bought at Ra
Beebe's store was stylish and subdued compared to it. An
I wish you could have seen that steward when I got throug
talking to him. Every day smooth-talking scamps, who knov
him by reputation, come with schemes for getting him t
invest in something, or with pitiful tales about being Ameri
cans stranded far away from home. I take care of thes
sharks and they don't bite me, not often. I told one shabby
red-nosed rascal yesterday that, so far as he was concerned
no doubt it was tough to be stranded with no way of gettin
to the States, as he called them; but that I hadn't heard ye
how the States felt about it. So I help Galusha with mone
matters and see that he dresses as he should and eats wha
and when he should, and try, with Professor King, his chie
assistant with the expedition, to keep his mind from worr
about little things. He seems very happy and I certainl
mean to keep him so, if I can.

We talk about you and Nelson and Captain Jethro ever
day. The news in your last letter, the one we found at Gib
raltar, was perfectly splendid. So you are to be married in
June. And Galusha and I can't come to your wedding; tha
is a shame. By the time we get back you will be so long
settled in the cottage at the radio station that it won't seen

ew at all to you. But it will be very new to us and we shall
ust love to see it and the new furniture and your presents
nd everything. We both think your father's way of taking
t perfectly splendid. I am glad he still won't have a word
o say to Marietta Hoag or her crowd of simpletons. Ga-
usha says to tell your father that he must not feel in the
east obliged to him for his help in exposing Marietta as a
heat. He says it was very good fun, really, and didn't
mount to much, anyway. You and I know it did, of course,
ut he always talks that way about anything he does. And
our thanks and Captain Jethro's pleased him very much.

Primmie writes that . . .

.   .   .   .   .   .

(A page omitted. See Primmie's letter.)

Please keep an eye on her and see that she doesn't set fire
o the house or feed the corn to the cat and the liver to the
ens, or some such foolishness. And don't let her talk you
eaf, dumb and blind.

There! this letter is so long that I think it will have to go
n a trunk, by express or freight or something. One week
nore and we start for upper Egypt, by water, up the Nile,
t first, then on by automobiles. Yes, little American auto-
nobiles. Galusha says we shall use camels very little, for
vhich I say "Hurrah, hurrah!" I can*not* see myself navi-
ating a camel—not for long, and it *is* such a high perch
o fall from. Our love to you and Nelson and to your
ather. And oh, so very much to yourself. And we *do*
vish we might come to your wedding. We shall be there in
pirit—and that doesn't mean Marietta's kind of spirits,
ither.

> Your affectionate friend,
> MARTHA BANGS.

A letter from Miss Primrose Cash to Mrs. Galusha Bangs.)

> East Wellmouth, Massachusetts,
> United States of America. January seventh.

DEAR MRS. MARTHA:

I take my pen in hand to write that I am first rate and
ne and dandy and hope you and Mr. Galusha are the same,
lthough I am **homesick** for the sight of you and hope you

ain't. I mean homesick. By this time I calculate you mu
be somewheres over in Egypt or Greek or China or lar
knows where. I am sending this letter to the address yo
give me and if you don't get it before you get there you w
then, I hope and trust. And I hope, too, you had a goo
voyage and was not washed overboard or seasick like Ca
tain Ephraim Small's son, Frankie D., who had it happen
him up on the fish banks, you remember. I mean the wasl
ing overboard happened to him for, of course, I don't kno
whether he was seasick or not, though I presume likely, fo
I always am, no matter if it's carm as a milpond, but an
how they never found his body, poor soul. I presume likel
you want to hear the news from around here at East Wel
mouth. Well, there ain't none, but I will try and tell a
there is that I can think of. The hens are well and Lue
Larkum is fine and dandy and appytite, my savin' soul.
tell him he will eat me out of house and home, though
realize it ain't neither of them mine, but yours, Mrs. Marth
Captain Jethro is doing fine. For a spell after the sean
where your husband made a fool out of Maryetter Hoa
and Raish Pulcifer to thank the Lord, he was reel kind o
feeble and Lulie and me and Zach was worried. But he
swell now and all hands is talking about his making up wit
Nelse Howard and agreeing for him and Lulie to get mar
ried and live over to the Radyo stashun pretty soon I pre
sume likely, for the weding is to be held in June so Zac
says. At first go off, Captain Jeth he calculated maybe h
would heave up, I mean his job tending light, and go liv
along with them, but after he got feeling better he said h
wouldent but would stick to the ship and keep on the cours
long as he could stay aflote. That's what Zach says he sai
and I tell you I am mity glad, because if I was Lulie an
Nelse I wouldent want anybody even if it was my ow
father coming to live along with me and bossing things, be
cause Captain Jeth couldent no more stop bossing than h
could stop pulling his whiskers and he won't never stop tha
long as he ain't parulised. So he will live here along wit
Zach and them two will tend light and Lulie can come ove
and see her pa every little spell and they can telyfone bac
and forth between times. And she and Nelse have been u
to Boston to pick out fernichure and ain't they enjoying i

y lord of isryel. Lulie is about as loony over getting mar-
ed as ever I see anybody unless it was you and Mr. Bangs,
rs. Martha. I seen Raish Pulcifer down street yesterday
d he said give you his love when I wrote. I told him I
essed likely you could get along without any special love
his and he said never mind I could keep it myself then.
told him I could get along without it a considerable sight
ttern I could with it. He is as sassy and fresh as ever
d more so to on account of Mr. Cabot paying him so
ch money for his stock. And the new hotel is going to
bilt over on the land by the Crick and all hands says
s going to be the best in the state. Raish has got a whole
w rigout of clothes and goes struting around as if every-
ing was due to his smartness. Zach says Raish Pulcifer
running for the job of first mate to the Allmighty but he
n't hardly calculate he will be elected. Maryetter Hoag
going to heave up speritulism so Tamson Black told me
e heard and going to help in a millunary store over to Onset
xt summer. Maybe it's so and maybe it ain't, because
mson is such an awful liar you can't depend on nothing
e says. Zach says if an eel tried to follow one of Tam-
n's yarns he would get his backboan in such a snarl it
uld choak him to death. And Zach says he calculates
aryetter will take little Cherry Blossom in silent partener.
ch comes over to see me sometimes nights after supper
d we set in the kitchen and talk and talk about you and
r. Galusha mostly, but about Lulie and Nelse and Captain
th, too, and about everybody else we happen to run afoul
or that comes handy. Zach is real good company, al-
ugh he does call me Posy and Pink and Geranyum and
ar land knows what and keeps his talk agoing so nobody
se can't scarcely get a word in between breaths. He says
l you that he will keep a weather eye on me and see that
didn't get the lockjor nor swallow my mouthorgan nor
thing. I tell him nobody could get lockjor where he was
account of watching how he keeps his own jor agoing.
e means well but he is kind of ignorant Zach is. Speaking
weather reminds me that the northeast gale we had last
ek blowed the trellis off the back part of the house and
ped the gutter off the starboard side of the barn. I had
n Fletcher put it on again and he charged me three dollars,

the old skin. I ain't paid him yet and he can whisle fo
his money till he whisles one dollar off the bill anyhov
There, Mrs. Martha, I have got to stop. Luce is aroun
screeching and carrying on for his dinner till you woul
think he hadent had anything for a month instead of onl
since breakfast. I will write again pretty soon. Lots c
love to you and Mr. Bangs and do tell me when you go t
ride on a camel. That would be some sight, I will say, an
Zach he says so, too, but he bets you can do it if you set ou
to and so do I. Anyhow, you can if Mr. Galusha skipper
the cruise because that man can do anything. And to thin
that I used to calculate he had the dropsy or was a under
taker or a plain fool or something. Well, you can't neve
tell by a person's looks, can you, Mrs. Martha. Zach say
so, too.

Yours truly,

PRIMROSE CASH.

P.S.   Have you seen Mr. Bangs dig up any mummies yet
How he can do it and keep out of jale, my saving soul,
don't know. To say nothing of maybe catching whateve
it was they died of.

P.S.   Won't you please try and see if you can't have :
tintype took when you ride the camel and send me one?

(Extracts from a letter from Mr. Galusha Bangs to Mr
Augustus Cabot.)

. . . And so, as you see, Cousin Gussie, we are getting o
well with the work of preparation and shall be ready to leave
soon.   Our excavating this season will be but preliminary
of course, owing to our late start.   I am enjoying it all im
mensely and it is wonderfully exhilarating and inspiring to
be back once more in the field. But my greatest inspiration i
my wife. She is a remarkable woman. A most extraordinary woman, I assure you. How in the world I manage
to exist without her companionship and guidance and amazingly practical help all these years I cannot imagine.   And
did not really exist, of course, I merely blundered along
She is—well, I really despair of telling you how wonderfu

he is. And when I think how much of my present happiness
owe to you, Cousin Gussie, I . . .

. . . .

But the greatest miracle, the miraculousness—I don't know
here is such a word, but there should be—of which sets me
vondering continually, is that she should have been willing
o marry an odd, inconsequential sort of stick like me. And
find myself saying over and over: *"What* have I ever done
o deserve it? . . ."

Mr. Cabot was reading the letter from which these ex-
racts were made to a relative, a Miss Deborah Cabot, known
o him and the family as "Third Cousin Deborah." At this
oint in the reading he looked up and laughed.

"By Jove!" he exclaimed. "Isn't that characteristic?
sn't that like him? Well, I told him once that he was mag-
ificent. And he is, not as I meant it then, but literally."

Third Cousin Deborah sniffed through her thin nostrils.

"Well, perhaps," she admitted, "but such a performance as
his marriage of his is a little too much. *I* can't understand
im, Augustus. I confess he is quite beyond *me."*

Cabot smiled. "In many things—and possibly the things
hat count most, after all, Deborah," he observed, "I have
ome to the conclusion that old Galusha is far beyond the
iajority of us."

THE END